The NOTABLE BRAIN OF
MAXIMILIAN PONDER

J.W. Ironmonger was born and grew up in East Africa. He has a doctorate in zoology, and was once an expert on freshwater leeches. He is the author of *The Good Zoo Guide*, was part of a world record team for speed reading Shakespeare, and once drove across the Sahara in a £100 banger. He lives in rural Shropshire with his wife, Sue, and has two grown-up children. *The Notable Brain of Maximilian Ponder* is his first novel.

The

NOTABLE BRAIN
OF MAXIMILIAN
PONDER

J.W. IRONMONGER

PHOENIX

A PHOENIX PAPERBACK

First published in Great Britain in 2012
by Weidenfeld & Nicolson
This paperback edition published in 2013
by Phoenix,
an imprint of Orion Books Ltd,
Orion House, 5 Upper St Martin's Lane,
London WC2H 9EA

An Hachette UK Company

1 3 5 7 9 10 8 6 4 2

A CIP catalogue record for this book
is available from the British Library

ISBN 978-1-7802-2083-3

Typeset by Input Data Services Ltd,
Bridgwater, Somerset

Printed in Great Britain by Clays Ltd, St Ives plc

The Orion Publishing Group's policy is to use papers that
are natural, renewable and recyclable products and
made from wood grown in sustainable forests. The logging
and manufacturing processes are expected to conform to
the environmental regulations of the country of origin.

www.orionbooks.co.uk

For Sue

1

MAX

Maximilian Ponder is lying face up, dead, on the dining table in his own front room. This is something you really should know, right from the start.

Max would also have wanted you to know that this is an Henri II-style, French, walnut, extending dining table, standing on solid turned legs with fretwork decor to the middle, and also a fine ebony and sandalwood inlay. It was designed by the French furniture-maker Nicolas Rastin, and probably dates from around 1900. It was almost certainly made in a workshop in Paris under Rastin's supervision. There. Max was very keen on that sort of detail.

Lifting Max onto the table, I had to be careful not to scratch the polished surface. Max would not have appreciated being the cause of a scratch. I made sure that I removed his shoes and his ostrich-leather belt with metal studs (provenance unknown to me), and then I hefted him aboard like a package. Max is not a heavy man, but I'm not as fit as I once was. There will be a lot of blood over the next hour, so I've folded a couple of white bath-towels, wrapped them around a bread board, and placed them beneath his head. The blood won't do the Rastin table much good I don't suppose, but I shall mop up as best as I can. Then again, who knows? Maybe blood *is* good for polished walnut tables. But that is the point, you see. I really don't have the right experience for any of this. Very little experience of death or decapitation, and no experience at all of French polishing.

Max isn't my first dead body, you understand; but he is the first that I've had to lift up onto a table. I could have left him on the floor, but that would have seemed disrespectful. Also, the blood would certainly have been bad for the carpet. But really that wasn't the main reason. There is a lot still to be done, and it wouldn't do to have Max lying on the floor in his own vomit. It would perhaps have been easier to leave him on the settee in the drawing room, and I did consider this; but in the end I went for the Rastin table. This is the table in his library, the room where Max lived out thirty years of his life. It's the table where he and I sat for countless meals, hidden from the world behind heavy brocaded curtains, so it feels appropriate, somehow, to lay him here. Besides, I'm going to need a good, hard surface.

I haven't called out the police yet. There are things to do first. Eventually, of course, they shall have to come. Other people too. Pathologists perhaps. Journalists even. Max would have liked that. They will want to know how it happened and I shall have to tell them the whole story. Recent events will be easy; I can say this event happened at this time, and that event happened then, and I was in such-and-such a place while Max was in some other place. If they need it, I could put together a detailed dossier for them.

But I dare say they won't believe me. Not at first. Maybe not ever. I haven't had many dealings with the police, but whenever I do meet a policeman I feel guilty, no matter how clean my conscience. I shall probably behave like a guilty killer and that won't help.

Of course when I do tell them the story, I shall have to tell them the *whole* story. I will need to explain about The Catalogue, and I can just imagine their faces. Will they even *begin* to understand? Will I be able to make it clear before they lose interest? Probably I should begin with the day that Max swallowed the fifty-pence piece. It was a turning point after all. Or maybe that would be going back too far. Then again, I could argue that that was the day when the whole thing started, because it was then that I offered Max my reluctant consent to participate in his great project. I have often blamed that on the fifty-pence piece.

Or we could go back further – to the day when we buried Libby the dog. I don't look forward to telling the police about that day. It might be easier to go back even further, to the day when Max swallowed the sixpence. That was the day when I discovered I could see into the future. Or I thought I could. Which is what mattered.

In a sense, as Max would say, there is no beginning. Only the Big Bang and the great coincidence of natural laws that led to an ever-expanding universe, with cooling planets and atmospheres and primordial soup and the perplexing imperative of natural selection that led ultimately to you and me and to Max Ponder lying dead on the walnut extending Rastin table. That is the story, Max would say, as if detail never bothered him. But of course it did bother him. It obsessed him. This is why he would want you to know the provenance of the walnut extending dining table. He would want you to know that he died wearing a Dege & Skinner charcoal-grey, single-breasted suit with a faint stripe, twenty-eight-inch inside leg and thirty-four-inch waist. The suit is one of half a dozen replicas, made by Dege & Skinner, of a suit they once made for Max's father, who first bought it from their fitting rooms in Savile Row sometime between 1965 and 1970. It doesn't look particularly unfashionable today, although it is slightly worn at the knees and elbows. It was Max's favourite suit.

He would be offended if I failed to mention the Breitling watch that he bought in Rome in April 1973, which has kept near-perfect time since the day of purchase. Not that Max would have known if it had *not* kept perfect time. This watch set the time of his universe for the past three decades and he never checked it against any other piece – how could he? The grandfather clock in the hall has always been notoriously slow, and Max reset that every day or so, but he always used the Breitling as the master. Once or twice I checked it against my own watch, but it always seemed close enough to the real time, so I never reset it. It is a classic Breitling Chronomat, hand-wound, with a mechanical two-register chronograph. It has a silver-and-black dial with two subsidiary dials for recording continuous seconds, and an outer sliding-rule rotating bezel for the calculation of air speeds and so on. I know all of this because I have seen where Max recorded it in The Catalogue, volume CCXI. There are other clocks in the house, of course, but apart from the grandfather clock, none has been wound for three decades and each sits silently frozen somewhere back in 1975. I will probably leave them like this. Somehow it wouldn't seem right to reawaken them from their slumbers – to refill the silence of this house with the tick of forgotten clocks.

Max would also want me to point out the monogrammed Cartier cufflinks he is wearing, in yellow fourteen-carat gold with chain-link connection. And his black brogues, which I have now removed, size eight and a half, made by Audley Shoemakers of Duke of York Square in Chelsea. And the fact that Max would have wanted you to know all this detail, you understand, would not be a reflection of his vanity. Max was certainly arrogant and indisputably vain, but rarely to the point of ostentation. It would be because Max operated at this level of detail.

His work, I suppose, is complete. Death makes it complete. Max had no one he could ask to complete his great catalogue. It could only ever be the product of a single brain. Now it surrounds him, on three walls, floor to ceiling, on shelves that span the room like a medieval library; 358 volumes of autobiographical ramblings bound in Morocco leather, eleven hundred or so blue appendix volumes, and almost 11,000 day logs in fourteen grey lever-arch files. There are 1,600 books and folders in all. It will be his memorial and his mausoleum. I doubt if any great library or institution would wish to house the thing so, god knows, it will probably stay here. Maybe I will have to convert the place into some precocious museum or auction the whole thing to someone as eccentric, as driven, as he. Maybe.

I assume, of course, that he left The Catalogue to me. His last will and testament, if it exists, was one document he never shared.

Death makes you reflect, doesn't it? Particularly when the deceased is lying only feet away on a walnut table, face up, in a charcoal-grey suit with a faint stripe, waiting for his head to be removed from his body. Max's tie had been pulled loose, and it stank of vomit, so I have taken the liberty of removing it and replacing it with my own. It will only be temporary. In a short while I will have to untie it again. My tie is a humble nylon confection of blue hexagons from Marks & Spencer, but it goes well enough with his pale-blue shirt. Max's tie was silk, with a bold red stripe on a dark-blue field. I am afraid I don't know the provenance, although it will, of course, be itemised somewhere in The Catalogue. It was almost certainly one of the captain's ties. The captain, by the way, was Max's father. Max's *late* father. I suppose I'm going to have to tell *that* story to the police as well, although parts of it must still be on their records; but I doubt if there are any policemen around who still remember it.

It occurs to me that when the police do eventually arrive, I could avoid telling them *any* of the story. Instead I could suggest that they read The Catalogue for themselves! Max Ponder's very own *magnum opus*. Would that be cruel? It would be like giving them *A la Recherche du Temps Perdu* in the original French and telling them that the key to their investigation was buried somewhere within the seven inscrutable volumes of Proust. And of course it *is* all there in The Catalogue if you choose to look for it, although what there is of an index is not particularly helpful, and Max never used a computer or even a typewriter so everything he wrote was in his slanty, loopy handwriting, in his Indian ink, 1.3mm, narrow, italic, precise, consistent, longhand. Even after thirty years, you could compare the handwriting from volume I with that of volume CCCLIX and I would defy you to tell the difference or to identify in correct chronology, sample pages taken from say, years one, six, eleven, seventeen, twenty-two and thirty. There was almost a pathology to his handwriting: invariable, homogeneous capitals, a sans-serif palace script of flowing lines, flighty punctuation, hyphenated word breaks at line ends, unnecessarily long crosses on his 't's and italic flecks over his 'i's. I'm not even sure how easy it will be for an outsider to read it. As for me, I'm so familiar with Max's hand that I can pick up a volume and read without correction.

We don't encounter handwriting much any more, do we? Except for our own notes and scribbles, we rarely have to decipher the calligraphy of others. Postcards, of course, can still confuse. Christmas cards can be a mystery. Everything else comes to us neatly typed or texted, spell-checked, emailed, or laser-printed. But Max, in his methodical, meticulous way, was no longer a creature of this world. He started volume I with his first Sheaffer Visulated reservoir pen with fourteen-carat gold nib in 1975, before personal computers and bubble-jet printing, and we bought his paper ready-ruled in foolscap size from Hawksley and Nether of Knightsbridge, and he had his volumes bound in red Morocco and embossed in twelve-carat gold-leaf twenty-eight-point Roman type by Ernest Cabwhill & Sons of Fulham Road SW4. The late Ernest Cabwhill was Max's great-uncle. How could he, Max, convert from this timeless process? Should I have brought him a typewriter? Should I have introduced him to dot-matrix printers and the Commodore-Pet computer in

1981? Should he have bewildered students of posterity with a procession of print technologies from fading dot-matrix documents with rip-clean edges to fancy laser-printed A4 80gsm, with a variety of fonts and typefaces: yesterday Arial, today Times New Roman, tomorrow Verdana, justified, bold, italic, easy to read, timeless, soulless, and a million miles removed from the close connection he wanted to convey from brain to pen to paper?

2

THE BEGINNING

Today is Monday 27 June 2005. This is the day that Max died. But this isn't where the story begins of course. Today is the day of the Final Act. Today is the day when the story ends.

The end of a story is easy to define, isn't it? It is when we all live happily ever after; or else, perhaps, it's the day when we haul the bodies off the stage and 'the rest is silence'.

The beginning is so much harder. So here is one place where it might have all begun. I'm going to go right back. Not as far as the Big Bang – you may be pleased to hear – but at least as far as the story goes, and as far as my memory will allow. The boy in this part of the story is me. Was me. I was eight years old. I wish that I could comfortably write about this boy in the third person now, because that is how I see him, so young and so small and so different from the ponderous, bewhiskered, greying bulk that is me today. He is a far and distant creature, this boy, removed in time and space, ignorant of the flotsam and persiflage of the world. He has never used a mobile phone or watched an episode of *ER* or thrown soil into the mouth of a grave. He doesn't understand continental drift or currency speculation or compassion fatigue. He has never heard The Beatles. On this day, when it all starts, the boy is standing at the top of his garden watching a woman cutting sugar cane in the field.

That should be how the story begins. A boy, an African valley, and a woman cutting cane.

It was as the boy was watching that a very strange thing happened. Or rather, it *seemed* as if a very strange thing happened. Sometimes the two things can be the same. And the way it happened, exactly, was this.

*

It was a still day, and the sun was high. The boy had taken off his hat to swat away the flies. Down the red murrum driveway and across the track stood the rows of sugar cane, motionless in the steady, steamy heat. The woman was bowed at the back, like a tree bent by the wind, and she swung a metal panga, sharp and swift, so that the blade struck the very base of each cane, *thwack, thwack, thwack*. The woman was known to the boy – to me. Her name was Mrs Mukuti. She was the wife of the farmer, the mother of Ebrahim and Alfred and Monday and little Mbewa. She wore a long, soiled apron and a bright-yellow headscarf and she carried little Mbewa swathed and watchful on her back.

I watched Mrs Mukuti as she cut with metronomic precision, *thwack, thwack, thwack*, and as each blow struck, a cane would drop, and so practised was her swing that the canes fell in rows waiting to be rolled into bundles. I had watched this scene before, in this field, in other fields, but for the first time, I noticed a phenomenon that struck me as peculiar. The sound of the thwack did not come, as I expected, at the very point when the panga struck the cane. Instead it came as Mrs Mukuti's arm swung back, and just before it began the next blow. Watching from my vantage point on the hillside, at the moment of impact, there was only silence. But then, as Mrs Mukuti's arm recovered for the next swing, there was a sound. A *thwack*.

We know, of course. We scientific people, we understand that the speed of sound in hot and heavy air is a sluggish thing. We have seen it too, in the puff of smoke from a starting pistol with the bang struggling on behind. But the boy was eight, and he'd never seen or heard such a thing before. Strike – pause – *thwack*, strike – pause – *thwack*. And then it came to him – to me – in one of those revelations that come only to the specially blessed. I was seeing into the *future*! Just a short, short time into the future admittedly, but the future all the same. The thought stuck me to the spot, and the small, undeveloped part of my mind that dealt with logic began to kick in to examine the theory. Could it be true that I – Adam Last, had seen the blow delivered *before* it had actually happened?

We want to tell young Adam how wrong he is, we twenty-first-century people with our ways to measure all things, smug with our instruments and textbooks and theories. But Adam is beyond our reach. He is in 1962 on a hillside in Africa, a little white boy, barefoot and freckled and crew-cut, and he has just discovered that he can see things before they even happen. One day he will forget the blinding insight that came to him from a woman in a field of cane. One day he will accept the laws of nature as codified and named and proscribed by the men in universities that he has never seen or even heard of. He will understand that the speed of light is very, very, much faster than the speed of sound. He will come to appreciate that everything we see and hear is, to some extent, in the past. But today he is a seer, a prophet. Today he can glimpse into the future, just a tiny way. And that makes him special.

THE CATALOGUE OF A
HUMAN BRAIN

Now, where are my manners? This needs to be Max's story, and I can, it occurs to me, at least get Max to introduce himself. I have in my hands the first bound volume of his catalogue which includes, obligingly, an introduction of a sort. The gold-embossed title on the front cover reads, in twenty-eight-point Roman type:

```
M.Z.Q.K.J.C.PONDER
THE CATALOGUE OF A HUMAN BRAIN
VOLUME I
THE JUSTIFICATION
JULY 1975
```

Open it up and flip through the flyleaves to page one. Welcome to the writing of Max Ponder. Dive on in.

```
I am Maximilian Zygmer Quentin Kavadis John
Cabwhill Ponder. My name includes every
letter of the Roman alphabet with the
exception of the letter F. My father, it
seems, took exception to F. In case you think
my name is a little out of the ordinary,
I should point out that my father was Captain
Maximilian Rybault Fonsekker John Cabwhill
Ponder. He had an F but no V, Q, Z or G, so
that gives me the edge I think. My father's
sister was christened Zinnia Delicious
Meretricious Expeditious Meriel Cabwhill
Ponder, and my uncle, Aunt Zinnia's twin, was
plain Martin Ponder, a name whose roots can
```

be traced back to a christening concession my
grandfather, the captain's father, made to
our grandmother and which he always regretted.
Uncle Martin regretted it too. I once
discovered some juvenilia of his in which he
had signed his name, falsely, as Martin
Krepotkin Xerxes McGungler Al'khazam Ponder,
which proves my point. There are few things
so valuable in life as a memorable name. It
could be a given name or your family name,
but the combination must be memorable and, if
possible, unique. Ask Salvador Dali or
Immanuel Kant or Niccolo Machiavelli if they
would rather have been christened John or
Brian or Robert. Ask Winston Churchill if he
might have preferred Nigel. Ask Napoleon
Bonaparte if, perhaps, he should have favoured
Pierre. Ask William Shakespeare, who might
(if he were able to reply) ask, 'what is in
a name?' and point out, considerately, that
a rose by any other name would smell as sweet.
Fine, Will, I would riposte, so long as your
only concern is the way you smell. A narcissus
by any other name would smell just as sweet,
and it could be easier to spell, but would it
conjure up images of vanity and self-delusion,
of the beautiful, conceited youth admiring
his own reflection, deceived even unto his
death by the nymph Echo? Probably not.
Delphiniums would smell as sweet but they'd
be much less pretentious. Names are more than
just labels; they come laden with layers of
meanings and associations. Advertisers
struggle endlessly, and invest massively, to
formulate exactly the right name for a new
product, a name that will help to identify a
briefly enduring brand, yet we name our
children on a whim and condemn them to carry

that name for a lifetime. Lying entwined in bed at night, drifting into sleep we might ask each other, 'Do you like the name Barry?' 'No, too casual. What about Nigel?' 'No, too effeminate.' 'How about Brian?' 'How about Martin?' and we end up with the name that offends us least on that particular night, based upon the Barry that we met at the office and the Nigel who works at the off-licence and the Martin who presents snooker on late-night television.

It doesn't have to turn out badly, of course. Parents can, from time to time, agree on great names. Imagine this, back in 1934 in Tupelo, Mississippi: a couple lying entwined in bed murmuring, 'Elvis? How do you think that sounds? Elvis Presley? Elvis Aaron Presley?' Or then again, in New York sometime in the 1850s, a pair of Dutch immigrants eager to give their son a positive brand decide, one dark, passionate night, upon Theodore. It would go well with their surname Roosevelt and they could always shorten it to Teddy.

But enough about names.

This is part one of day one of volume one of what will soon become the most audacious thesis ever submitted for the degree of Philosophae Doctor at the University of Cambridge. My aspiration – my intention even – is to spend the next three years isolated, absolutely and completely, from all external influence, and to spend that time diligently recording and cataloguing the entire contents of my brain. As far as I know, this has never been done, so as a contribution to the philosophical knowledge of humankind it will be unique.

Every human brain is unique, so this catalogue will never be a generic document. One day, perhaps a hundred years from now, we might decode the whole DNA of a single human just as we have already done with the Tobacco Mosaic Virus. I can't help with that because my understanding of biochemistry is too feeble. What I want to accomplish is a similar exercise but instead of listing the base pairs of the DNA molecule, I will list the discrete atoms of human memory from the first twenty-one years of a human life. It is a daunting challenge. How do I untangle it all?

Did you know that if all the world were to be rendered invisible with the single exception of nematode worms, then you would still be able to find your way around and recognise people and places? Apparently we are all covered by a film of these tiny thread worms, although now I come to recount this startling fact I'm suddenly uneasy. Maybe it isn't true after all. I'm not quite sure how this whole invisibility thing could work. After all, if you can't see the nematodes now, then how would you suddenly spot them once the world was invisible? Also, if you were invisible, like H.G. Wells' *Invisible Man*, then how would your retina work? Light would pass straight through it. You'd be blind. And actually, if all the world were rendered invisible, then we'd all be blind, in which case the world might as well be visible, nematodes or not.

The only nematode that I can be confident of actually having seen was a ten-inch-long pinkish-brown specimen of *Ascaris lumbricoides*, a parasitic roundworm that infects the human gut. It was about the width

of my little finger and maybe three times as
long, and it lay safely pickled in a white
enamel tray of formalin, waiting for students
to dissect it as part of a zoology practical
examination at Cambridge where I was a
volunteer invigilator. Around one quarter of
the world's population has at least one of
these in their small intestines. This is what
I learned that day. The female parasite lays
about two million eggs a day which all emerge
in human shit and develop into larvae without
the inconvenience of having to find any
intermediate host. Thereafter they sit around
in the soil waiting for fruit to fall, at
which point they take up a new position on
the surface of the fruit and simply wait to
be eaten. It doesn't have to be fruit. You
can pick up Ascaris infection from grass and
dirty hands. No wonder I am now so obsessive
about cleanliness. I know about things like
Ascaris lumbricoides. These are the kinds of
things I think about.

That introductory section is just so typical of Max – at least in the
early volumes. Later, the tone changes, but only slightly. The books
become more formal. He drops the stream of consciousness that
made the early volumes so charming and readable and descends,
much of the time, into the inevitable lists.

How quaint, by the way, that Max imagined it would take us a
hundred years to decode the human genome. I suppose we all did
back in 1975. In reality, it was done and dusted before Max's fiftieth
birthday. It might have been rewarding to have been able to tell
him, but that would never have been possible. Max closed himself
off from the outside world to compile his catalogue, and great
events such as this simply passed him by.

Anyway, there in the introduction to volume I is Max as I knew
him – lofty, playful, capricious, arrogant. He was wholly aware of
these aspects of his character, and even flaunted them. Look how

he starts by extolling his ridiculous, protracted name. Like a vainglorious Malvolio, he struts his name before us, right in the opening page of what he knows will be a substantive document, his life's work no less, and then before we know where we are, he is toying with us, introducing Immanuel Kant and Narcissus and Elvis Presley. What is all that about? A few pages ago I wrote that Max was rarely ostentatiously vain. And yet here he is, boasting on the page, playing a deliberate game of confusion and misdirection. One moment Elvis, and then suddenly with no warning, nematodes. Nematodes! How did he get from Elvis to nematodes? More significantly, why did he choose to do this in chapter one of his *opus*? It may have been to illustrate the whimsical nature of his thought process, the impulsive and fickle way his mind would flit and flutter and settle on unlikely topics. After all, he would do this in conversation too. We could be discussing anything – say, the nature of time, in one of those strange, conflicted conversations we held – and suddenly he would slap his knee and laugh. 'Carousels!' he might exclaim, 'Do you remember them? I once went on a carousel in Slough and I swear to god it must have been rattling round at fifteen miles an hour – now I know that doesn't *sound* fast, but that used to be my average cycling speed – quite something when you're coming downhill on a pushbike. That's how I reckoned up the speed of this carousel. I reckoned I could just about keep up with it pedalling flat out. What do you imagine the centripetal force would be on a hobby horse at fifteen miles an hour? I'm damned if I can remember the formula. It'll be in the book somewhere. Slough! god! I went to a dance in Slough once. Hideous. I ended up dancing with a dreadful girl called Wiggins. Emeline, I think. Or was it Harriet? Her father was a curate at the parish church in Windsor. Fifteen miles an hour. By god. Nearly threw me off. The carousel that is. Not the girl. Mind you, she probably threw me off too only I was probably too pissed to remember. Funny old thing the brain, eh? Funny thing.'

4

SIXPENCE

Let's go back to 1962 and the young Adam Last. We've been drifting away from the point and we need to get the beginning of this story nailed. You'll remember we were watching Mrs Mukuti and the field of sugar cane. Well, down the valley and over the dry ditch lay a field of long, yellow grass that grew past the waist height of an eight-year-old. The boy, Adam Last, took the well-worn, single-track Kikuyu path at an effortless run. I had followed this path before a hundred times, as it wound across the valley from my home to Marcel's home. Marcel was my friend. Barefoot I ran, careless of injury, of sharp stones, of hidden roots, careless even of venomous snakes; careless as only an eight-year-old boy who has just discovered he can see into the future can be. Snakes could not harm me now. I could *see* that fleeting second into the future where a snake might be lying on the path, and then, if I saw one, I could check my step, side-step away, or jump.

Here in this field, on this very Kikuyu path, less than a year before, a man had stepped on a puff-adder which lay sunbathing, camouflaged against the dirt. The man was a distant cousin of Mrs Mukuti, and there was much wailing in the valley when his body was carried up Westfield Drive on the shoulders of a keening crowd. I had watched them, standing in my garden in about the same place as I stood months later, when I realised I could see into the future. The puff-adder itself had been beaten to death and was held aloft on a stick, fat and broken like the severed arm of a baby. My mother, hearing the commotion, came out into the garden to find out what was going on. Seeing the bloated body of the man who had suffered the snake bite, she gave a gasp of horror and ushered me indoors, no doubt to protect me from the trauma of seeing a dead man. I was seven years old then and I had been much more interested in seeing the snake.

There were few bridges in this part of Kikuyuland, but at one point a black iron water-pipe crossed the Kirichwa river, about ten feet above the water. The Kikuyu people would walk over the pipe as if it were simply a continuation of the path – which, in a sense, it was. On this day, the day when I had seen into the future, I ran along the water pipe with barely a glance, then climbed the steep pathway up the valley-side. Some days had passed since I last saw Marcel and I needed to tell him about the woman with the panga and the way that I could see into the future.

The Dupont house dominated the valley. I could see a boy standing by the gate. He was the right age, the right height, the right build, the right Caucasian stock to be Marcel; but I knew instantly that he was *not*. And that was strange, for this was Marcel's house, and there were no other boys of Marcel's age in the close.

The boy was standing very still. He turned his head slowly as I ran up the lane, and fixed his eyes on me. But he didn't move towards me, and he didn't move away. Immediately, I dropped from a run to a walk, then to a standstill at a point far enough away to have to call out to him but not close enough to make it seem like a conversation.

'Where's Marcel?' I shouted, casually.

The boy didn't answer immediately. He looked at me for a moment as if curious, then replied, 'I don't know anyone called Marcel.'

I moved a little closer and we observed each other. The new boy was standing at the entrance of Marcel's driveway. If I wanted to go up to the house and knock on the door then I needed to go past him. That wouldn't necessarily have been difficult, but the boy was standing in place like a guard, bang in the middle of the drive, and there is an unspoken protocol when you are eight that forbids you to just saunter past. A little closer and I could see that he was just a shade smaller than me. That was good. Already that set up a hierarchy. Age and size are crucial when you're eight. I would not, could not, talk to, say, a nine-year-old. Not unless we had established what our relationship was, who was more senior, who spoke first. This boy was slighter than me, his complexion was paler, he seemed younger. All this gave me courage. I moved closer still.

'Marcel lives here,' I said, airily. 'This is his house.'

'Not any more,' said the new boy. 'We live here now.'

'Liar!'

'Am not!'

Impasse. I looked around for some proof. Mr Dupont's Ford Zephyr in the driveway, its doors always flung open to keep the interior from roasting in the sun – that would have been the kind of evidence I needed. But it wasn't there. Instead there was a Land Rover and a grey Vauxhall Velox. I looked around for other evidence. Marcel's bicycle on the lawn – missing. Mrs Dupont's old black perambulator on the verandah – also missing. And, come to think of it, where were the spaniels that normally ran out to greet me? Was there nothing left to prove that this was, in truth, Marcel Dupont's home and this pasty-faced boy was an interloper? I shot a glance up to the black pepper tree.

'There,' I said, almost triumphantly, 'Marcel's tree-house.'

The boy turned slowly, almost reluctantly, to follow my gaze. You could barely see the tree-house underneath the rich canopy of leaves and it was clear that the boy was seeing it for the first time. His expression changed to a look of wonder.

'Golly!' he said slowly. '*Goll*-eee.'

As we climbed up into the tree, I showed him where all the best steps were. A bent nail, a hole in the bark, a notch in the branch. The boy was at once cautious of ascending, and driven by curiosity to explore the tree-house at the top. Once there, we sat side by side with our bare legs swinging over the edge and looked out over the Kirichwa Kubwa valley, over the low christ-thorn hedge, past the dense prickly pear patch, over where the yellow grass fields began.

'What's your name?' I asked him eventually.

'Max,' he said. 'What's yours?'

'Adam.'

My friend Marcel, it seemed, had really gone. Overnight, and unexpectedly, he had departed from my life. His family had packed up and headed off back to Paris without so much as a goodbye; at least not to me. That was the way it was sometimes. Parents would make their plans but they wouldn't share them with the children.

We were too young to understand. It would upset us to know. We would worry about missing our friends, about losing our possessions. We would fret about what might happen to the dogs. Homes in this part of town were generally owned or leased by companies or government agencies who brought expatriate Europeans out on short-term contracts. When the job was done, the family would fly home. It could all happen within the space of a week. Or perhaps there was a family crisis back home. Bad news had been delivered by the telegram boy on his heavy black bike. A grandparent was ill. Someone had died. Something other had happened. I had seen it all transpire before, to the friends and business colleagues of my parents, but never to my closest friend. It felt to me like a bereavement.

Down across the valley, I could see Mrs Mukuti, still in the field of cane, her panga still swinging, just a small, distant figure. I strained my ears for the thwack, but none came. Seeing her reminded me why I had set off for Marcel's house in the first place.

'I can see into the future,' I said to Max.

Max looked at me. 'No you can't.'

'I can.'

He made a face. 'How?'

I explained about Mrs Mukuti and the panga and the thwack. I pointed out the distant figure. 'I see things just before they happen,' I told him.

Max seemed to consider this hypothesis. 'How far in the future?'

'Just a couple of seconds,' I told him. 'Like this.' I clicked my fingers twice. An exaggeration, of course, of the time delay that I had observed, but maybe this boy Max wasn't possessed of sufficient imagination to grasp the implications of even the shortest glimpse into the future. 'It means I won't tread on snakes,' I told him, to emphasise the great import of this discovery.

'Snakes!' he said in alarm. 'Goll-eee!'

Marcel would have understood, of course. He would have shared every bit of my excitement. He would have run with me back across the valley, back over the pipe bridge, back up to my garden, and there we would have stood and replayed the phenomenon with Mrs Mukuti as the unwitting agent of our discovery. Then, in all likelihood, we would have gone looking for snakes in order to prove the practical applications of the miracle we had unearthed.

Max, on the other hand, demonstrated no such willingness to accept my story. After thinking about it, he put his hand into his pocket and drew out a closed fist.

'OK then,' he said, 'tell me what I've got in my hand.'

This gambit confused me. 'I can't see through hands,' I snapped. 'I can see the *future*.' I decided, in that moment, that Max was stupid.

Max looked at me and blinked. 'This *is* the future,' he said, ''cos in ten seconds I'm going to open my hand and show you what I'm holding. So I'll count in my head and when I get to ten I'll open my hand. If you can really see into the future, then you'll just shout out what it is before I get to ten.'

I reflected on this proposition and saw that it was not, after all, quite so ridiculous. 'OK.'

'Right,' said Max, 'One, two ...' he fell silent.

I tried to focus on his hand, staring impossibly into the future.

'Hah!' Max sprung open his fist. 'I told you.' He held a small, unfamiliar silver coin in his palm.

'What is it?' I picked up the coin. It was similar in size and colour to the Kenyan fifty-cent piece, but was sufficiently different to present me with an excuse.

'It's a sixpence, you fool!' Max snatched it back. 'Haven't you seen a sixpence before?'

'No. We don't have sixpences here,' I pouted. 'I didn't have time to see it properly.'

Max's eyes twinkled. 'OK. One more test. I'm going to toss this sixpence in the air and before it comes down you have to shout where it's going to land.'

I looked around the floor of the tree-house. There didn't seem to be too many options. 'What do you mean?'

'I mean, is it going to land in the tree-house, or is it going to fall down there?' he indicated the ground beneath. 'Or is it going to land somewhere else?'

It seemed pretty straightforward. I nodded assent.

'Shout it out – OK?' Max said.

'OK.'

He positioned the sixpence on his thumb, and as he paused he caught my eye and I saw the faintest flicker of mischief. It was going to be a trick. But what?

The coin sprang up from his thumb, spinning vigorously. I tried with desperation to see into the future but no images came, so I saw that I was going to have to gamble.

'In the tree-house!' I shouted.

But I was wrong. For just as the spinning coin passed his face, Max flipped back his head and opened his mouth, and the sixpence disappeared. He gave a gulp and I stared at him in amazement. 'You swallowed it?' I asked.

He opened his mouth and thrust out his tongue. The little silver coin had gone.

5

ALL ABOUT THE RAIN

So is this the real start of Max Ponder's story? I can imagine recounting this beginning to the policemen and policewomen of the Buckinghamshire Constabulary and I can picture the impatience on their faces. Is the incident with the sixpence such a significant moment? Does it really have any bearing on the death and dismemberment of a middle-aged man in a country house in England four decades later? If I were a policeman I should probably want to wrap up this case without delving into prehistory. I daresay they will be far more interested in the events of the past few hours than they will ever be in a party trick played in a tree-house several thousand miles away and a long, long time ago. So why do I feel the need to start unravelling Max's story here? Is it, perhaps, just a significant story from *my* life, one in which Max Ponder also played a role? Maybe this is just an Adam Last perspective, some personal self-aggrandisement from a bit-part player. Maybe I don't belong in Max's story at all. After all, it wasn't me who spent thirty years behind heavy brocaded curtains scrawling out the contents of my brain. Maybe I *am* just a footnote.

But that isn't the way I feel, not right now. It was me, Adam Last, who had to heft Max Ponder's body, still warm and pliable, onto the Rastin walnut extending table. It will be me, the same Adam Last, who will have to carefully cut through the skin of Max's neck. That makes me more than just a footnote. I will be the one who will have to slice through his trachea, through his carotid vein and artery, through the dozen or more different muscles of the neck: the levator scapulae, the sternothyoideus, the sternocleidomastoid muscle, a tangled network of sinewy, fresh, pink meat. You see how I've been doing my homework for this. It will be me, gloved and aproned, who will have to force the knife between two of his vertebrae, severing cartilage and muscle and spinal cord. Me who will disengage head and body.

And yes, it will be me too, who will have to sit in a windowless room with a bare table and two hard chairs answering aggressive questions from policemen who are bound to be more than a little suspicious about my involvement with Max's death. 'Tell us where his head is,' they will demand. And I will refuse. It won't look good. Instead I will start by telling them the story of a boy who swallowed a sixpence. Still. That is the way it must be.

I remember a day in June 1972, a third of a century ago. A summer's day, but one of dreadful rain. Max and I were at a Melanie concert outdoors at the Crystal Palace Bowl in London, enduring what seemed like an oceanic deluge from an unforgiving sky. We were seventeen going on eighteen. One hour of rain was enough to wet us. Two hours soaked us through. After three hours, we were at one with the water, insensible to the unremitting downpour. Max stood through the whole thing, transfixed like an oak, obstinately ignoring the rivulets of water that flowed down his unwashed hair, over his forehead, his eyes, his lips.

'Max, do you want to go?' I shouted to him at one point, referencing the line of wet hippies who had already lost the battle of wills against the rain and were heading out of the arena. Afterwards, when we had stayed for every encore, and Joe Cocker had stormed onto the stage for the final act, we both turned away and trudged through mud towards the station.

As was usual with Max, we couldn't walk straight to the exit. Instead, we had to retrace our steps exactly, and since we had entered at the back and swung all the way around the huge audience looking for a good place close to the stage, we had to walk back by the same circuitous route. It was a course that would imply several unnecessary minutes in the rain, but I knew better than to argue with this curious pantomime. As we slogged far enough away from the banks of loudspeakers to make conversation bearable, Max said something that I immediately brushed off as an idle pledge.

'I shall never see another concert,' he said.

'Why not?' I asked.

He shrugged. 'I just won't.'

'You will.'

'No. No. This was too extreme.'

I knew Max, but perhaps I should have known him better. I believed he meant what he said, but I thought it was his way of expressing his emotion after two hours of Melanie and five hours of rain. I thought this was his *review*.

On the train, bedraggled, standing in a corridor, Max tried to explain. 'I want to be able to replay every moment,' he said, 'I want to be able to shut my eyes and be there again.'

'Yeah, I know what you mean.' But I didn't, of course. Not really.

'I wanna have some real total recall, like a memory tape of the whole experience,' he went on. 'I wanna be able to see that little smile she did when she played 'Ruby Tuesday', hear the music just the way it was, all those people singing, that strong vein of dope smoke from the hippies behind us, I wanna feel the rain ...'

'Couldn't you edit out the rain?' I asked, trying to inject some lightness.

Max shot me a scornful look. 'It was *all about* the rain,' he said. He shut up then and hugged his little tin.

6

VOLUMES

On the shelves of Max's library at The Pile, there are 358 red
volumes, each splendidly bound in Moroccan leather by the august
firm of Earnest Cabwhill & Sons Bookbinders. Each volume is
about two inches thick, and because Max used foolscap paper from
the start, which is thirteen and a half inches high, the volumes stand
around fourteen inches on the shelves. Altogether, they take up
around sixty linear feet or so of shelf space. Max wrote on one side
of the paper only, and as the ink dried on each page he would flip
the sheet over and place it, perfectly aligned, in a wooden box file,
where the pages would gradually accrue. On the last day of the
month, he would tie the volume with white string and leave it on
the table in the hall.

The table, by the way, is an elegant console table made by
Thomas Chippendale the younger, who was, according to Max, the
eldest of Chippendale's eleven children. It has a cross-banded top
over a carved frieze, and is made in yew from a design by
Chippendale himself. I'm including this detail, you understand, only
because Max would have wanted me to. Details are the essence of
Max's story. My own tendency would be to overlook all of these
particulars, but I do want you to have a sense of Max's world as
he saw it, and I know that whenever he stopped by the table with
a manuscript, his mind would flit to Thomas Chippendale the
younger, and he would perform a mental checklist, ticking off the
points that he could remember.

The manuscript, then, would be left for me to collect and deliver
to Cabwhills. A bookbinder at Cabwhills would sew the pages using
an oversewing technique where the loose pages are clamped, holes
are punched, and lockstitches used to bind the pages together. Then
they would apply the leather binding, and emboss the cover

and the spine. The process would take around three weeks, so, conveniently, I would collect the finished, bound volume when I called to deliver the manuscript for the succeeding month. We would always make this exchange in person. Max never had sufficient confidence in the postal service to entrust them with his work.

Each volume would consist, typically, of 300 sheets of paper or thereabouts, which sounds like a great deal, but of course amounted to just ten sheets a day. The pages were (and still are) unnumbered, so Cabwhills would rely on me to deliver the document collated in the correct order.

The volumes in Max's library are sorted chronologically by month with volume I, the book we opened earlier, at the very left-hand end of the top-left shelf. They then proceed from left to right in true library order as if this were the British Library or the Library of Congress. There are six tiers of shelves on the north wall of the library and they are almost full. The red Morocco-bound volumes are Max's narrative of his 360 months spent in seclusion. Volume 359 will be waiting at Cabwhill's for me to collect. The final volume, what there is of it, still needs binding.

Those are the red volumes. But we are not done. Now let us turn our attention to the blue volumes. These are the appendices. They were never sent away for binding because they started life as ready-bound notebooks, each with 120 narrow-feint-ruled pages. Max bought these notebooks himself in June 1975, the month before he started his project. He bought them from a stationer in Reading who imported them from Hong Kong: a dozen boxloads, each containing one hundred notebooks. They are A4 in size which means that they stand around a foot high on the shelves. There are eleven thousand of these, so while each is only around half an inch thick, they occupy much the same shelf space as the narrative volumes. Each blue notebook has a number written in Indian-ink on the spine. As you might by now expect from Max, the numbers are in roman numerals from appendix I to appendix MC. He numbered them and positioned them on the shelves while I was still up at Keele finishing my final exams, in the week before his twenty-first birthday. They are sorted, like the narrative volumes, in numerical order, and they occupy shelves on the west and the east walls.

We are still not done, for then there are the day logs. Max would scribble down the details of each day onto loose-leaf A4 feint-ruled sheets with two punchholes. These constituted his log of incidents and events that, despite the monotony of his lifestyle, nonetheless accumulated new and inconvenient memories. The day logs include details of the meals he ate, any conversations he had with me, incidents such as a leaking pipe, or a heavy thunderstorm or a blown light bulb, anything that threatened to upset the ordered tranquillity of his life in The Pile. There are 141 grey Punchline A4 lever-arch files of day logs, marching along the shelves like the case records in a coroner's office. The files are numbered on the spines according to the days that they record. So the first file reads 1–108, and the second reads 109–194, and the last reads 10,905– with the final date, of course, incomplete. Max's last complete day log was numbered 10,940. He died on day 10,951. That would be today.

The main volumes, the red ones, constitute Max's autobiography and the monologue of his life. The blue appendices, in contrast, were his *lists*. Appendices I–V attempt to summarise the contents of the other 10,995 blue appendix notebooks. Appendixes VI–X do a similar job but they itemise the main contents of the red volumes. These are not, of course, a proper index. They form a kind of cross-reference, a set of contents pages, if you like.

Page 1 of appendix I is probably the very first page that Max wrote as part of the project. It starts like this:

```
Father: Appendix XI
Mother: Appendix XII
Uncles: Appendix XIII
Aunts: Appendix XIV
```

And so it goes on. It is a lengthy list. Family and friends fill up a full ninety volumes. He anticipates thirteen appendix volumes of history – appendices CI (Ancient Rome) to CXIII (American History); appendices on philosophy stretch from CXIV (Ancient Philosophy) to CXXV (Eastern Philosophy), including volumes on metaphysics, aesthetics, cosmology, the mind and a whole lot more. There are volumes on celebrities, artists, thinkers, politicians and sportsmen; on recipes, card games, cars, and religions; there are volumes on countries (Kenya is appendix CLVIII, America is CLIX); there are volumes on the Bible, and astronomy, and paintings and architecture, on proverbs and metaphors, poetry and novels.

Yet, despite this optimistic start, Max must have known, even then, what a wholly inadequate list it would prove to be. If he had *really* felt confident in July 1975 that this initial list would suffice, then he should have started out with around 300 blue notebooks. But, as we have seen, he had already been to the stationers in Reading and had bought four times that number, then spent several hours unpacking, numbering, and positioning them neatly on the library shelves. He knew, *of course he knew*, that one notebook alone would never cover novels, or idioms, or animals, in the way that his initial index had foreseen. He had hoped, I know, that all the arcane details of everyday life would find their way into the red volumes, but it very soon became clear that there was no room for all this detail in the narrative pages.

There is a problem, you see, for anyone who decides to catalogue every single memory that resides in a human brain; that problem derives from the myriad things that we all know, and that we all expect each other to know, but that we would never, ever, contemplate recording. Let's give just a few examples as they might apply to Max. They would include things like the conversation he had in a bookshop with the man who was looking for Herodotus, or the interior design of the saloon bar of the Royal Oak public house in Marlow, or the layout of the shelves in the Safeway store in Henley, the half-forgotten lyrics of The Beatles songs, the landmarks on the road between Richmond and London, the taste of African pilsner beers, the smells of African townships, the noise of the traffic in Rome, the feel of crisp, clean cotton sheets, the jokes inside Christmas crackers, the items on the menu at the New Bengal restaurant in Cambridge, the presents he got for his tenth birthday, the way that steam comes out of the road in New York City, the surprisingly confident way that a three-legged dog runs, the different shapes that girls come in, patterns that you can draw with a spirograph, the varieties of different urinals, the London underground map, how to crack Brazil nuts, the sculptures of Henry Moore, the view from the Eiffel Tower, the nightmares of childhood, the cures for a tickly cough, the way to pronounce Cholmondeley, the parrot sketch from Monty Python, the carvings made by the Akamba people, the physical contortions of every pornographic image he had ever seen, the little hairs on a flowering cactus, things that Tony Blackburn said on his Radio 1 show, how to put up an ironing board, the songs of blackbirds, acceptable patterns for ties, how to do double-entry bookkeeping, how canal locks work, the pattern of stars in the constellation of Orion, the different cuts of meat you can get from a cow, how to tune a twelve-string guitar, the way that Americans pronounce aluminium, the story of Robin Hood and Little John, common names you might give to a dog, the telephone number of the flat in Dorset Square, the rules of contract bridge, the meanings of acronyms like BOAC and NATO and BBC, the Scottish accent, how to convert miles into kilometres, the different flavours of Italian ice cream ...

I think you get the point.

Nonetheless, Max's list on day one established the pattern for the first appendices, and the rest was just added on. Not all of the blue appendix volumes are full, but many are, and their contents continue into overflow volumes, often several times over.

Max wrote on both sides of every page of the appendices using the same Sheaffer Visulated reservoir pen with fourteen-carat gold nib that he used for the narrative volumes. To maintain consistency, I bought him three dozen identical pens at huge expense and he kept them all in his top drawer, picking one to use at random. He drew his diagrams using a pale-yellow Berol 2B pencil, helping himself to one from a large boxful of ready-sharpened pencils and re-sharpening them when he needed to, using a beautiful brass, desk-mounted Royal Sovereign pencil-sharpener that once belonged to the captain.

Once he had drawn his pencil sketches, he would ink them in using a Rotring technical drawing pen with a 0.3mm nib. He started in 1975 with around six Rotring pens and a dozen nibs, and over the years I have been called upon to provide him with countless more. He would soak the used nibs overnight in lukewarm water and Fairy Liquid, and in the morning he would rinse them several times and leave them to dry on the draining board in the kitchen. Max wasn't a skilled artist, but soft pencil and Rotring pen can turn the most amateur sketch into a drawing with at least some professional sheen. He would occasionally cross-hatch or stipple his drawings to improve their appearance, although he would argue that the drawings were not intended to be artistic, they were simply there to help record the details of his memory. So he would draw maps of towns, plans of houses, diagrams to show the layout of furniture in a room or the relative positions of stick-people in a conversation. There are plenty of things he wouldn't attempt – he never had a go at faces or anatomy; he rarely did a plan-view of buildings, and he only undertook landscapes where there was a feature that he would feel confident in drawing. But flick through any volume at random – in particular the appendices – and you will see hundreds of Max's sketches.

He didn't use his informal writing style quite so often in the appendices, and he tried, not always successfully, to itemise and number things; so, for example, I appear in all the appendices as [AL] for Adam Last, and most encounters with me are assigned a sequential number. Max has his own recollection of our first meeting at the end of the drive in March 1963, and here it is catalogued as [AL: 1321] because it is the 1321st memory he has recorded that includes me. This is despite the fact that this memory describes our first-ever encounter; it is not the *order* in which events occurred that earn the number, it is the order in which they are recorded. By the time he got to writing about our first meeting, we had already run through 1,320 items, mainly conversations with me that he had set down.

Unlike the main red Morocco-bound narrative volumes, the appendices, of course, weren't dated. They were essentially living lists that Max could add to at any time, whenever a thought struck. If, for example, he suddenly came across the memory of a bull-mastiff dog, he could pull down appendix CCLXXII from the shelf and add the bull-mastiff to his list of dog breeds. Max usually knew where to find just about anything in The Catalogue. If I were to ask him, for example, 'where do I find greyhounds?' he would reply without even looking up. 'Look in Dogs CCLXXII bottom shelf on the left. Or did you want that day we went to Swindon Dog Track? That's December '92 I think. About halfway through. Fourth shelf down on the left.'

Very often the same nuggets of information appear both in the autobiographical narrative and in the lists, but Max was never concerned that he was documenting the same memory twice. 'It is easier than jumping up and down all the time to check if it is already written somewhere,' he argued. And although he was probably right, jumping up and down to check other volumes was nonetheless something that happened a great deal. When Max was at his desk, he was always surrounded by open notebooks and volumes, checking and cross-checking. There were always gaps on the shelves, and volumes would pile up around his chair. It was one of my unspoken duties each time I visited Max in the library, to quietly return the books to the shelves, each one in its place.

7

EASTLANDS

I haven't thought about those days in Africa for so long now that they seem like little more than a flickering black-and-white film in which people walked strangely and spoke in a language that no longer exists. Once, a few years ago, I tried to talk to Max about False Memory Syndrome; only I couldn't use that specific expression to describe it because I was worried that this might be a syndrome that wasn't identified and named until *after* Max began work on The Catalogue, and the rules were very strict about that sort of thing. Instead I asked him if he thought that we could be persuaded to believe that we had memories we never really had. I'm not sure that the conversation took us very far.

It all seems to come back to those distant days in Kenya, and I don't know any more if my own memories are real, or imagined. Still, let us accept my memories for the time being. I need to explain about that time, and what it was like in the 1960s. You need to understand this if you really want to understand Max. Kenya was the place that shaped him, that made him what he was. That is what Max himself would have argued. Max, you see, was a disciple of the philosopher John Locke. For Max the early memories of childhood are the ones that shape our lives. He would explain, if ever you should have asked him, that the experiences of Kenya were imprinted on his *tabula rasa* – on the blank slate of his childhood psyche.

To Max at eight years old, Africa must have seemed a very foreign place, a hot, dry land of dust and flies and mosquitoes and biting ants and the fear of snakes. To me, of course, it was home. I was born there, at the Queen Elizabeth Hospital which is just a few miles from Nairobi city centre. Today I think it is called the Kenyatta Hospital. If you took me to Nairobi, I do believe I could drive you there. The map of the city is still indelibly written in my brain. Of course it would be a thirty-year-old map, and that could be a problem. If I were Max, recording this for posterity, then I would draw you that map in 2B pencil and Rotring pen, starting perhaps with the winding roadway from Embakazi Airport down to Uhuru Highway, and then developing into a street map of the city centre, with a trail of spidery roads leading out. One road would lead to Wilson Airport and Nairobi National Park and the township of Karen. Another road would lead towards Adam's Arcade, Dagoretti Corner and onwards towards the Rift Valley and Naivasha. A third would take you down Argwins Khodek Road, past Kilimani Junior School which I once attended, dipping down into the valley, then turning right into the lanes that lead to the dusty suburb of Eastlands where Max and I first met. Other roads would lead out to Westlands, and to Thika. If I close my eyes I can travel them.

Here is part of Max's description in volume CX:

VOLUME CX
AUGUST 1984

Kimathi was our house-servant. [See appendix CCXLIII KIM01]. Look how I use that term, 'house-servant'. Even here in The Catalogue I can't bring myself to use the term we all used quite unselfconsciously then – 'Houseboy'. I wonder why not? It must indicate some residual guilt. Every European home had a houseboy, or two. The houseboy would occupy the 'Boy's Quarters' and no European home in Nairobi was built without such quarters discreetly placed behind it. Thinking back now, I can't help feeling appalled by the breathtaking imperialism of the idea, of the patronising language we used to express it, and of the astonishing casual racism that it surely represented. But at the time none of this *post hoc* guilt existed. For me as a child, the Boy's Quarters was the most exciting and romantic part of any house in Nairobi, and this is where on the long afternoons and evenings of childhood, we would gravitate and spend so much of our time.

Boy's Quarters rarely constituted more than two or three dark rooms set around a cement yard. [See appendix CCXLIII] (*Here Max obligingly includes four ink sketches.*) Perhaps the originators of the design felt that they were somehow mimicking the layout of Kikuyu huts and a native village. Cooking was always done outside on a charcoal stove, washing at a standpipe, and the toilet was no more than a grim hole, often in a hut some way from the rooms. Here, in the Boy's Quarters, the Houseboy would live with his extended family and his animals – some chickens perhaps, often a goat. Kimathi had a wife, Elizabeth, and four children [appendix CCXLIII].

Generally the package would also include a small patch of land that the family would cultivate. The rooms were barely furnished – a mattress on the floor, perhaps a chair. Most of the living was done out of doors. Which is one of the things that Adam and I enjoyed. We would join Kimathi and his family sitting on their verandah, or Ebrahim and his family at the quarters behind Adam's house, and we would prattle away in Swahili. They would share their posho with us and we would warm our hands over the glowing stove, and wash our plates with mud, and piddle in their toilet hole.

It was a strange, ambivalent, way to grow up – an experience shared, I am sure, by every white child in colonial Africa who grew up comfortable in both cultures, fluent in both languages, flitting back and forth unquestioningly between the dark, squalid rooms of the Boy's Quarters and the brightly lit, lavishly furnished homes of the colonisers.

If I seem to be passing judgement upon this equivocal lifestyle, then it is the peculiar judgement of hindsight. Neither Adam nor I had any concept of racism. Certainly, as white children, we were spared the humbling effects. But like every colonial child, I am sure, the thought torments me. God knows, I've discussed this often enough with friends at Eton and Cambridge. Some of my Cambridge friends have a censorious view of me simply because I was a part of this divided social order, as if somehow being a child in this imperial regime at this time in history makes me complicit. It might have been more acceptable, in their eyes, if I had somehow become a progressive, intent on overthrowing the status quo. But could I? I was just a kid. Did I really grow up as part of an exploitative, racist, culture? And if I did, should it reflect upon me? Did I willingly and knowingly subjugate and exploit? Pendulum-like, my own judgement has matured, developed and revised with the passage of time.

Adam frets about this as if we were somehow collaborators in a historical crime, quislings perhaps, like the Vichy officials in France who went along with the Nazi occupiers because it was in their interests to do so. But was there really a crime? There was injustice, to be sure, but then our whole planet is a turmoil of injustice. I have walked across the border between San Diego and Tijuana [appendix CLIX] and seen how an imaginary line in the sand has become a military frontier separating wealthy Californians from the indigent of Mexico. There, the affluent liberals of West Coast USA don't even have the blessing of an ocean divide to keep them from coming face to face with impoverished children. Yet they seem to manage to square their liberal, Christian views on neighbourly love with a casual disregard for poverty on their doorstep. So does distance matter? We Ponders, I think, were no less collaborators in the poverty of Africa, living cheek by jowl with the poor in Kenya, than we were when we were living half a world away in Buckinghamshire and quietly ignoring the privations of people in the so-called 'third world'.

You may think it a comfortable post-rationalisation, aimed at appeasing my own conscience, but here is what I think today (tomorrow maybe my views will pendulum again): we were all creatures of our time, black and white alike. We all grew up with received ideas, and we all had to struggle to change them. The white people we knew were, with few exceptions, kind and well-intentioned. At least, they seemed to be. Very few were rich - not by European or American standards. I exclude my own family from this category of course. The Ponders were rich beyond avarice, but even O and The captain were happy to embrace a lifestyle that fell well below their real means. For the rest of the expatriate community, there was no fabulous wealth, no extravagance, just a genial work ethic and an expectation that with just a little saving they could afford that refrigerator, that motor mower, that holiday in Malindi. They were very rich by African standards, but there was a sort of tacit understanding that this gulf was a historic one. I think it was also assumed and expected that the gulf would narrow. I wonder whether it ever has - or if it ever will?

Most of the white Kenyans were an overspill of the civil service, or else they were into construction or farming or they were building embryonic industries. They genuinely believed they were helping to create a new country, somehow sculpting a new Western country out of the African bush. Their horizons were high, but their ideals terribly British - had they been able to, they would have recreated Surrey right there, with the added benefit of perpetual summer. British institutions prevailed. Milkmen, clattering before dawn, delivered bottles to the doorstep. Carol-singers caroused at Christmas. Bonfires were set alight on November 5th. Radios were tuned to the BBC. Cars drove on the left side of the road. There were golf clubs and race courses and policemen with truncheons, flower beds and nicely trimmed lawns. But it wasn't Surrey. It was Africa. And so the carefully laid out estates, and lanes with proper British names such as 'Westfield Drive' and 'Convent Gardens' and 'Glendower Road' all sweltered under the blazing equatorial sun, grew red from the hot dust of the dry season, or wallowed in the swirling mud of the monsoon. Lizards scuttled along walls and under eaves. Predatory mosquitoes buzzed invisibly in the dark. Huge, unfamiliar flowers bloomed from luxuriant tongues of green.

Lavender blossom from the high jacarandas
blew like cherry petals up the street, and
gardens were kept green by the incessant thuss
thuss thuss of sprinklers.

Does any of this help to explain Max Ponder's state of mind? I can't resist the feeling that somehow it does. I shall probably show this section to the police psychologists. It will help to establish the background. Max, I will explain, was never great at adapting to new situations, and the older he became, the harder it was for him to adjust. I may be fumbling for a point here, but bear with me just a little. You see, when Max as an impressionable child became part of imperial and post-colonial Kenya, he was drawn into a mind-set that I know he found difficult to shed, despite the protestations he makes so persuasively in the passage we have just shared. Englishmen were still *Englishmen* then, and the Ponders were as English as they come. This was a time and a place that suited the Ponders to such a degree that you could almost imagine the Almighty crafting the unique circumstances of geography and sociology to meet the peculiar eccentric and very English nature of the Ponder family. Here they could be wealthy without ostentation. Here they could bask in their natural hegemony, but in a wholly English way, and all this with the bountiful benefits of a tropical clime and the unlimited resources to enjoy it to the full.

Of course, by the time Max closed himself away in The Pile with his catalogue, it was 1975 and the tide had turned for the die-cast Englishman so familiar to us from the worlds of Evelyn Waugh or P. G. Wodehouse. Yet this was the very world that Max knew and grew up in. Max knew it all too well to simply let it slide away. That's what makes me so sure this background played a part in his destiny. The era of Harold Wilson and collective pay-bargaining and eye-watering taxes and the onward march of European socialism sat uncomfortably on the shoulders of a young man who had sailed effortlessly through a cosseted childhood in the colonies, and an education at Eton and Cambridge. Max, I feel, would have thrived as a colonial governor, perhaps with a plumed hat, sipping iced gins on a terrace and complaining about the heat. He would, as a young adult, have fitted very comfortably, if he had been allowed through a time-slip back into the world of 1960s Kenya. I see this more clearly now than I ever did. It was a time when proud tradition still sat vestigial among those of British blood, and nowhere was this truer than among Captain and Mrs Ponder and their Nairobi set. A collar and tie should be worn to church, but not a regimental tie; no, a regimental tie would be worn to one's club; dinner should be served just-so, with the silverware laid out in such and such an order, and a chap should always stand if a woman enters the room, and we should *all* stand for 'God Save the Queen' and the 'Hallelujah Chorus', and we should clap politely at cricket when a chap is out; ladies who smoke should use a long, silver cigarette-holder, and men should pomade their hair and part it sharply on the left; cigars should be lit directly after dinner and the port should always be passed around to the fellow on your left, shoes should always be left outside the bedroom door at night for unseen hands to collect and shine them, and generally the faults of the world should be laid in conversation at the feet of the Americans (too arrogant), the Africans (too lazy), or the French (too French). Finally, and this is an important one, camaraderie should always be edged with just the right measure of racial arrogance, the total conviction that anything English is altogether right, and anything else is somehow a departure from the proper way of doing things.

You may, I am sure, prefer to believe that all these things belonged to an age long before the enlightened days of the 1960s. But this was not Belgravia, this was Africa, and here the deep traditions of Englishness would evaporate more slowly than back home. Here, after all, there were no working-class Britons to threaten the way of life. There were only poor Kenyans, and a spattering of middle-class British, and just a few of European blood who, frankly, didn't count for much. However much Max might bleat about the great sense of goodwill among expatriate Britons, and however much he might try, in volume CX, to position the Ponders among those middle-class Europeans who staffed the civil service and the police force and who worked the farms, this wasn't the whole truth. The Ponders were an outrageously rich family, and this, more than anything, established their position in the strict collective hierarchy. Max could choose to ignore this fact, could overlook the fact that the Ponders and the Lasts could never really mix socially, but the truth remains: there was a divide, and it was a particularly English divide in which social position depended upon which school you attended, which clubs you frequented, who you were seen with, and the accent you spoke with. Families who, in the Home Counties may have been somewhere below the aristocratic pecking order, could, in the empire, aspire to something approaching minor royalty. The Ponders might be seen at the governor's ball, or be photographed meeting Jomo Kenyatta. VIP visitors would come to Kenya and somehow they would all end up together at the top table at the garden party, the VIPs and the Ponders and the Delameres and the rest of Nairobi's social elite. The Ponders were effortless masters at cultivating the exact level of upper-class eccentricity that would make them interesting but not objectionable in the circles in which they moved. They were masters, you might say, in the proper way of doing things.

Still, it wasn't Surrey, and the proper way of doing things was in constant conflict with the climate and the fact that this was a bustling, multi-racial frontier town, a pioneer city, a railhead on the massive railway from Mombasa to Lake Victoria. Nairobi was to Max – and to me – the best, most exciting, colourful, vibrant city that ever was. The streets bustled with Indian traders and African markets, with American tourists festooned with cameras, and Akamba craftsmen selling hand-carved souvenirs, with expatriate families, and middle-class Kenyans in suits and ties, and half-naked Masai – tourists too to their capital city, clad in blankets and armed with spears.

In 1962 Max and I were both too young to understand the turbulent contradictions of this young society, but we had a sense of its magic. We knew that we were lucky to be children in among this richness, to share in the natural abundance and splendour of this country.

Did this influence the delicate psyche of eight-year-old Max? Did his arrival in Kenya come at a tender time in his mental development? Did it scrawl a deep impression on his *tabula rasa*? Max certainly believed that it did. I'm sure that a psychoanalyst could outline the impact that it might have had, uprooting Max from the green, rolling pastures of the Home Counties, from a land of grey skies and red buses and pillar boxes to this hot, dusty city of thorn trees and snakes and barefoot children. But if all that were true, then I never saw it at the time. I saw only a boy who was not Marcel. A boy with a pensive manner, a slow, curious look, a deliberate way of doing things. A boy with the nerve and sense of the dramatic to swallow a sixpence just to make a point.

8

HERACLITUS

How do you know what you know? I ask this because it was an obsession of Max's. Take a look at any extract from Max's catalogue, pulled pretty much at random. He might be writing about the universe, or the poetry of Robert Browning, or the way to make a Samurai sword; but how do any of us know this stuff? 'Your brain is not a computer,' Max would often say. 'Theoretically, you could dissect a computer and lay out its inner workings on a slab. You could analyse the data content of every discrete bit and byte on every reel of tape and every punch-card, unravelling them as a stream of zeros and ones and ones and zeros; and given a knowledge of mathematics and machine code and ASCII or whatever other dark mysterious arts you might need, you could reassemble it all into a meaningful catalogue of everything that the computer holds in its memory banks.' Max's understanding of computers was fairly primitive. 'Maybe one day,' he would add, 'we shall be able to do this with a human brain.'

I would listen to these polemics with as little comment as I could manage.

'Imagine a brain slopped out into a mortuary tray, wrinkled and yellow and wet, glistening with blood and neural fluids,' Max would say. 'Is it the brain of a genius or a fool? Can you tell? Could the owner of this brain speak five languages? Could he identify fine French wines? Could he carry out complex mental arithmetic? We don't know. In the end your brain is nothing more than a dead piece of meat, like an ox tongue or a pig's liver sitting in a butcher's fridge. This brain could decline Latin verbs? So what? It can't decline them now. Einstein's brain is still around somewhere, pickled in a bottle on a lab shelf. Maybe somewhere in that lump of meat lie the secrets of the universe. Here's a scalpel and a magnifying lens – can you find them? Can you discover $E=MC^2$?'

To which, of course, no answer was expected. Max was the master of the rhetorical question.

'You know a strange thing?' Max asked me once as we sat together in his library watching pine logs crackle and pop on the fire. 'Who was it that said you can never step into the same stream twice?'

I didn't answer him of course. To answer would have been to drive him to instant anger. I knew his rules well enough by this point. This must have been some time around 1995 – twenty years into the project.

'It was that Greek, wasn't it?' he said, 'Heraclitus. No man ever steps in the same river twice, for it's not the same river and he's not the same man. What was that poem about Heraclitus? Do you remember it? It has one of the most hauntingly memorable verses.' He started to recite.

They told me Heraclitus, they told me you were dead.
They brought me bitter news to hear and bitter tears to shed.
I wept as I remembered how often you and I
Had tired the sun with talking and sent him down the sky.

'I've never heard that poem,' I said, as I so often did when Max was in full flow.

'Well I guarantee you'll remember that first verse,' he said. 'I'll recite it again, and then you'll remember it for ever.'

'I'm not so sure,' I said. 'I don't have a great head for poetry.'

'You will for this one,' he said, and he gave me the verse again. It echoed in my mind. I've just written it here from memory so, damn him, he was right.

'There is a second verse,' said Max, as I rehearsed the words. 'The second verse is not so easy to recall.'

And now that thou art lying, my dear old Carian guest,
A handful of grey ashes, long, long ago at rest,
Still are thy pleasant voices, thy nightingales, awake;
For Death, he taketh all away, but them he cannot take.

(And just so that you know, I've had to look the second verse up. Max, of course, recorded it – in appendix CCXLIII.)

The room was silent.

'Who wrote the poem?' I asked.

'It reminds me of you and me,' said Max, avoiding my question. 'We tire the sun with talking, and send it down the sky.'

'No we don't,' I said. 'Your curtains are always closed.'

'You know what I mean.'

'I suppose.'

'Anyway; Heraclitus. That was who said you can never step into the same stream twice. But more than that, no two people can ever step into the same stream.'

'I suppose not.'

'No two people can ever see the same play, or watch the same sunset, or hear the same song. Not only are your eyes and ears different, and your perspective, but the filter of your brain – all the knowledge of your past – is different.'

'Where are you going with this, Max?'

'I don't like you saying that. "Where are you going with this?" It sounds like a modern idiom.'

'Of course it isn't modern. People have been saying that since before you or I were born.'

Max fell silent and scribbled a note in his day log. I knew he was recording this 'new idiom' so that he could excise it from his catalogue – this uncomfortably polluting expression from the 1990s that now had a place in his brain but didn't belong. After a moment he looked up. 'Imagine I were to go to a football match with Alf Ramsey,' he said, picking up the conversation exactly where he had left it.

'And ...'

'And we sat side by side. We wouldn't see the same match. He'd see thousands of things that would be invisible to me because I wouldn't know what I was supposed to be looking for.'

'Your point is?'

'No point at all. Just an observation. A very curious observation, don't you think?'

'If you say so.'

*

I'm bringing up these memories of Max because they may help to explain his state of mind. Courts are very particular, so I've heard, about establishing 'state of mind'. I have no experience of this sort of thing. I've never been in a court, and I don't understand psychology. But even I can see that sometimes a human mind can develop a dangerous way of thinking, and this needs to be taken into account.

Of course, if I knew about Max's state of mind, if I understood where his life was leading, then am I wholly blameless? Should I have done something? Should I have called in the police? Should I have alerted them to the fact that a psychotic recluse was in danger of taking his own life – or even of getting someone *else* to take his life for him? Perhaps I should. There are certainly times, dark times, when I believe so myself. I could have called in Social Services years ago. I could have gone along to the NHS and had Max sectioned under the Mental Health Act. Perhaps under a sub-section that accommodates individuals with obsessive personalities who are driven to catalogue their own brain. I imagine a transit van full of psychoanalysts screeching up the driveway, and a corps of black-sweatered charge-hands breaking through the door to carry Max in a straitjacket, muzzled and struggling, out to a Black Maria. But how could I have done that to my friend? Could I have stood on the gravel driveway as he was manhandled into the back of the van, screaming soundlessly into his gag as needles were plunged into his veins? It would have been a horrible echo of the time when the police scooped him up in March 1974, having accused him of killing the captain. I will have to tell you that story too, but for now, I should just explain that I may have been complicit by my inaction on that occasion. Could I really have done it again? What if he had caught my eye? Could I have handled the guilt?

I know, of course, that the reality would have been somewhat different. It might not have been a cadre of brutal paramilitary psychologists, but an amiable analyst with a slow manner and a pipe, driving up to The Pile in a Morris 1000 convertible. He might have set up a station outside Max's library and coaxed Max out into the light with reasoned argument. They might have discussed Wittgenstein and Max might have introduced the subject of Heraclitus. He might have shown him The Catalogue and maybe the amiable old analyst would have recognised the value of it. He might have negotiated a contract with an academic publishing house, arranged for an honorary doctorate from a reputable university, helped to set up lecture tours for Max to Ivy League Universities in America ...

But what is the point of all this musing anyhow? I never did call an analyst. No Black Maria showed up. No amiable analyst. No lecture tour. What did happen was much more mundane. Or maybe it was more dramatic. Right now, I'm too close to see it all properly. Perspective will come later. Right now, I have a knife to wield.

9

DISEMBODIED HEADS

The old Dupont house, where Max and his family lived, was a mile from a parade of shops known as Eastlands Arcade. There was a small grocery store, and a butcher, and a shop that sold hardware, and a little shop that sold newspapers and stationery, imported magazines and books. It was an easy walk. At least, it was usually an easy walk, although getting there with Max was rarely straightforward. The first time I went there with him we were dispatched under the watchful eye of Ayah Mboya, who had been recruited by O, Max's mother, to 'watch Max'. The mile-long walk was considered sufficiently hazardous that he had to have an escort. I was scornful of this arrangement, and deliberately walked on the opposite side of the lane, kicking my feet in the dust. Ayah Mboya seemed equally contemptuous. She dawdled behind, keeping Max in sight, but giving him sufficient space so that it might appear that they were not really together. As we sidled along to the arcade, a disconnected triangle of walkers, Max would stop to examine anything new. And, to begin with, almost everything was new.

'What's that?' he would demand.

'What's what?'

'That. That plant?'

I would examine the plant from a safe distance on the other side of the road. Ayah Mboya would affect complete disinterest, trying to make it look as if she did not belong to this party at all.

'It's a plant,' I would reply.

'What kind of plant?'

'Dunno.'

'*Goll-ee.*' Then Max would examine the plant as if concerned that it might conceal some hidden threat. Finally, satisfied, we would resume the walk.

'I wish you knew its name,' he would say, as if he were already compiling a mental inventory of African flora and fauna. But within a few yards there would be another new thing.

Animals were even more arresting than plants. I had long ago stopped noticing the lizards that flitted in and out of the undergrowth, but every one seemed to catch Max's attention. Butterflies were clearly a phenomenon he'd never witnessed before – at least not on such a scale and in such colours. And ever since I'd told him to look out for snakes, he'd scanned the paths mechanically as if one might be lurking at every step. Safari-ant trails made his eyes widen as though he'd witnessed some magic trick, and termite trails up the trunks of trees, sublimely constructed from mud, would make him gape. Locusts, and fat, black beetles, and ant bear holes – all these things and more would interrupt our journey.

Why did I befriend this strange boy, this pale, quizzical character with his thousand questions about the mundane features of the world? There were other children in the area that I might equally well have recruited in search of a best friend. There was Karl Drury. He was practically a neighbour. I could walk to his house without having to negotiate the pipe bridge. Or else there was Huey Lowe. But he was a bit too young, and Huey had loud, older brothers who hung around too much and threw stones at birds. Eileen Latimer was a girl. And Wolfie Knauer spoke very broken English. So maybe I *was* looking for a soulmate, someone I could hang around with, the way I'd hung around with Marcel. But it wasn't a lot of fun being Max's friend. Not as much fun as it had been with Marcel. At times, in fact, it was sheer hard work. And today, so many years later, I wonder if it was ever fun at all.

'Let's walk a different way home,' I suggested after we'd done all we wanted to do at the arcade. This was on our first visit, before I knew better.

Max looked startled.

'I know a shortcut,' I told him. I called to Ayah Mboya and pointed down the Kirichwa Valley. She nodded mutely.

'We can cut down the path there, then up the back behind your house, and over the fence. It comes out right by your Boy's Quarters.'

Max seemed to be transfixed to the spot. He shook his head violently. 'No,' he said.

'It's a shortcut,' I repeated.

'No.' He was emphatic.

'Why not?'

Max's eyes looked wild for a moment, as if he were casting around for support. 'We have to go back the *same* way.'

'No we don't. This is a shortcut.'

'No.'

'Yes it is. Look.' I pointed. 'You can see the roof of your house from here. There's a path. I've done it millions of times.'

But Max was not to be swayed. He stood shaking his head, and after a while Ayah Mboya came to his rescue. We walked back down Westfield Drive, the way we had come, in our established triangle. When we reached his lane I took off over the valley, down the Kikuyu path and over the pipe bridge, towards my home, and left him standing three yards ahead of his ayah, watching as I disappeared into the long grass.

But soon I was back. Another day. Another hot African day. I was drawn to this boy who had swallowed the sixpence. I found him standing at the end of his drive, in the middle of the gateway, just as I had on that first day when I'd come calling for Marcel. He stood swinging a long stick, drawing a semi-circle in the soft murrum dust at his feet. And another day. Standing at the bottom of the black pepper tree, looking up at the tree-house. Or on the swing seat with a book. Or sitting in the Boy's Quarters talking with Mrs Kimathi. Or on his haunches, mesmerised by a column of ants.

There was a trick I used to do with ants that Ebrahim had taught to Marcel and me. I tried to teach it to Max. You pick up a big safari-ant, taking care to pinch it hard behind the head so that it cannot swing around and bite you, and then you goad it into nipping the hem of your shorts. As it clasps its mandibles onto the cotton, you nip off its head with your thumbnail and finger, leaving the head forever fixed, like a miniature trophy, on your shorts. With patience you can garland your shorts with ant heads. Max was fascinated by the game. Several times he snatched at an ant too hard, only to crush it to death before it could take the trophy bite. And several times he was bitten. Safari-ants have a powerful bite for their size, and they spray the bite with formic acid. It isn't as bad as a wasp sting, but you soon learn not to invite it. However, Max had persistence. On my next visit he sported the best shroud of ant heads around each leg I'd seen. He showed them to me proudly.

It is a long time since I thought of that circle of disembodied heads. They will be recorded somewhere in The Catalogue, of course. There are probably a dozen pages or more that recount the natural history of the safari-ant, at least as far as Max could recall it. There will be ink drawings, descriptions of the ant trails, anecdotes about being bitten by ants, about coming across ants in unexpected places, about ants in the larder, not to mention an account of the shorts and the garland of disembodied heads. And that is what Max himself is about to become. A severed head, his mandibles forever clamped shut. I wonder if he ever thought about those ants when he made plans for his own dismemberment. Did he imagine that each ant head might conceivably have contained a tiny spark of consciousness, an awareness of its own mortality? Did they feel those fingernails pinching through the ant equivalents of the levator scapulae, the sternothyoideus, and the sternocleidomastoid muscles? Did they make an involuntary attempt to disengage themselves from the useless mouthful of cotton that they'd been tricked into biting, with such fatal consequences?

Probably not. But that wouldn't have stopped Max from speculating. Speculating was something he did well.

10

BOOKS

VOLUME XX
FEBRUARY 1977

Welcome to volume twenty. I've been a little
scared about even starting this. It's going
to be a biggie. How big? I'm not too sure.
This will be strange. It will be difficult.
I am about to kick off my memory-catalogue of
books. I have several appendix notebooks
prepared [CXLIX, CL and CLI to begin with],
but I am rather expecting these to overspill.
   And how should I do it? I've been struggling
with this.
   Imagine if I were to recall a book that
I had once read. Let's pick one at random.
Why don't we start with *Lord of the Flies*?
That would be pretty typical. OK, it isn't
enough for The Catalogue just to say I once
read *Lord of the Flies*. Actually, I read it
twice, but that is beside the point. The
challenge is, how much of it do I really
remember? How much can I regurgitate,
reconstitute, recreate from that fragile
ephemera we call human memory – a frail enough
thing as I have been discovering these past
twenty months. And here's the thing, which
I suspect is going to hurt any novelist
reading this catalogue: in the end you
remember very little indeed.

So how do we do this? I could try to rewrite *Lord of the Flies*, but that would be a work of imagination, not a work of memory. I could say something like this: (1) This novel is by William Golding, British novelist, and a Cornishman if I remember rightly. I'm going to guess he wrote it some time in the 1950s, but I can't really be too sure. (2) I read it in a paperback edition with a picture of a wild pig on the cover. Actually it was more like the silhouette of a pig – yellow against a black background. (3) It is around 200–300 pages long – maybe 100,000 words. (4) It starts with a group of boys on a tropical island. As the plot unravels, we learn that they have been stranded there after a plane crash. There are no adults. The main character is called Ralph, another is called Piggy, and a third is called Jack. (5) This is essentially an allegorical novel, exploring the nature of humanity and the strands that bind our fragile civilisation, and as such it belongs with that strain of English fiction that could also be said to include *Gulliver's Travels*, *1984*, and *Brave New World*.

And now what? I struggle to remember a single additional name. I can describe the great themes of the novel, the gradual peeling away of the layers of civilisation from this group of boys to reveal a primitive core of barbarism and cruelty. I could pick out some of the highlights in the story, showing how a very English group of schoolboys become war-painted, spear-waving savages. But this approach risks becoming a review, not a recollection. Can I remember the opening line? No, I cannot. It was probably something like: 'Ralph scrambled down onto the sand and looked at the plume of smoke rising from the distant rocks.' But equally it may have been: 'Day broke over the island to reveal a miserable group of boys standing wet and listless on the edge of the sand.' You see, I remember the gist of the whole thing, but none of the actual detail, and not one single line. Well, perhaps just one line. There is a scene that sticks in my memory in which the hapless Piggy is thrown from a cliff by a falling rock, levered malevolently by a member of the rival tribe – it may have been Jack, or perhaps one of Jack's minions. Piggy falls to his death in the foaming water below. And the line I remember? It is this: 'His head opened, and stuff came out.' Not the most edifying line, but clearly a memorable one. Another boy – perhaps his name was Steven or maybe Simon? Yes, I think it was Simon – did he have his throat cut? I seem to remember his body floating out to sea. There was a seashell, a conch, which became a symbol of authority. Piggy's glasses were appropriated to make fire. There were wild scenes involving the capture and slaughter of a pig. And Piggy, I recall, suffered from asthma. The other boys would tease him about it. But how, how, how, am I to catalogue these fragments of a story into discrete particles of memory? It is a horrible dilemma because, damn it, if you were to ask me in conversation if I knew *Lord of the Flies*, I would certainly tell you that I remember it well. It's a book I love. If I were to pick it up now and reread it, then every chapter would seem familiar, and I would recognise whole passages; I would even be able to tell you what was coming next. But away from the book, relying solely

on the accessible data in my brain, I am
stumped. My pathetic memory has archived the
whole book beyond any recollection.

Books. Of the many, many, things I owe to
the captain, one of the most lasting has been
my love of books. I don't think I ever told
him this. It is only now, relating all this,
that it occurs to me that such a fundamental
feature of my life owes almost everything to
him, despite the fact that he, himself, was
not a great reader.

It seems to have started when we uprooted
from Marlow and settled in Nairobi. I had
owned books before, of course, but I remember
very few of them. They would have been *Janet
and John* and *The Little Red Hen* and *Chicken
Little*. They were insignificant. But when we
moved to Eastlands things must have changed.
I was growing up. Maybe I was just ready for
books at that age, or maybe it was the shock
of Africa.

Then one day the captain came home and
announced that he'd discovered an interesting
second-hand book shop in Nairobi. Did I want
to visit? We went together, the two of us –
a little conspiracy. And in the most
disreputable corner of Bazaar Street, we came
upon the shop. It was owned by a Sikh who sat
be-turbanned and immobile in a dark corner
while his customers browsed the books. Hardly
any light seemed to penetrate the murky
interior, but in the gloom the shelves that
ran from floor to ceiling in the network of
tiny rooms were deep with books – random
books, some with luxurious red leather spines
and gold-embossed titles, some tatty
paperbacks, torn and faded. 'Pick whatever
you want,' the captain said. And I did. I came

away with a whole box of books. This was our first visit, but dozens more followed over the years, and every time we came to explore the treasure trove, we would stagger home with a cardboard box stuffed to the brim with books of every kind. And as the years passed, so the selection developed. From *Beano* annuals and *Grimm's* fairy tales, my collection matured to encompass *Tales of the Arabian Nights*, *Moby Dick*, *Robinson Crusoe*, *Treasure Island*, *Gulliver's Travels*, and *Black Beauty*. There were adventure annuals, and volume after volume of *Biggles*. There were encyclopaedias, atlases, gazetteers, and compilations of *Knowledge* magazine, the story of Everest, and everything I could find by Jim Corbett including at least two copies of *Man Eaters of Kumaon*. There were tales of Sherlock Holmes, and there was H.G. Wells and Jules Verne, and stories about time-machines and men on the moon. I had books that were too young for me and books that were too old for me. I had books that were written for boys and books that were written for girls. No matter. I read them all. I had *Emil and the Detectives* and I had *Heidi*. I had *The Count of Monte Cristo* and I had *Pollyanna*. There were faded pulp magazines with monsters on the cover, and picture books, and everything Enid Blyton ever wrote, from stories about kids in trees to Mr Meddle and the Famous Five. Every one I read and, as often as not, re-read. There were the Greek myths – the fall of Troy and the Iliad and the Argosy. There were volumes of poetry. There were stories of ancient Rome.

My home library grew to rival the bookshop itself. The captain built me shelves, and every few months he would have to extend them. Adam would come to visit and we'd spend all day in the dusky shade, buried in books, while outside the sun bore down.

My books grew organically up the walls of my room. I graduated from Just William to Billy Bunter, then to Jennings and Derbyshire, and then on to *Tom Brown's School Days*. And of course there were volumes of Edgar Rice Burroughs' 'Tarzan' books that told tales of an Africa I couldn't recognise, and H. Rider Haggard's immortal stories of Alan Quartermain, lavishly illustrated. Everywhere books. I'm covering a decade or so here, but in time the collection verged on the magnificent. One shelf held a load of *National Geographic* magazines. Most of the pictures were in black and white, but I would read them faithfully and store them in date order. I had about five bibles because it seemed important then to have every possible translation. I had virtually everything Gerald Durrell ever wrote. I had curious old copies of Ripley's *Believe it or Not*; half a dozen Dickens novels, well-thumbed paperbacks by Ian Fleming, P. G. Wodehouse, Robert Heinlein and George Orwell. Classics and trash shared shelves, sat together, equally revered. When I discovered Asimov around the age of eleven or twelve, it meant more shelves.

The books became more than just something to read; they became esoteric possessions, present on the wall because I liked the look and the feel and the smell of them. Never mind that many were too childish or too trite. I saw a value in books and hoarded them like a jealous monarch. If one went missing,

I would spot it in a flash. I assumed ownership
of the captain's collection of Jungle Doctor
books. 'You may as well keep them in here
with all of mine,' I told him. I salted away
O's Agatha Christies.

In time the bookstore had very few new books
to feed my hunger for words. In time too, as
I began to bring new books home from school
in England in my teens, I had enough science
fiction to outnumber the classics. But I'm
getting ahead of myself. The whole enterprise
started in the days before television invaded
our world. Books were the great escape.
I wonder how many books I read late into the
night – and after lights-out, with a dim
yellow torch under the covers.

The old bookstore must have survived on
books abandoned by expatriates packing to go
back home to England. As departing families
anxiously weighed their tea-chests of
belongings, the books must have seemed surplus
to requirements. As I was later to discover
to my lasting regret, books – especially
faded, second-hand ones – were a heavy and
expensive commodity to transport the
thousands of miles back to Britain. And so
they would end up at the bookstore in Bazaar
Street. I always knew when a new consignment
had arrived. I would recognise every new spine
on the shelves, take it down and show it to
the captain. 'What do you think, Cap'n?'
I would ask. 'OK, if you want it,' he would
say.

Eventually I would discover the hard way
that everything comes around. When I was
sixteen and at school in England, and my
family was packing to come home for the very
last time, all my precious books would end up

back at the bookstore. It was like a bereavement. I received the news with a sense of numbness and shock. 'Where are my books?' I asked, as we unpacked the consignment of crates back at The Pile.

'We sold them,' Aunt Zinnia replied.

Sold them!

And so, as a student, humbled by undergraduate penury, I would scour second-hand bookshops and Christmas bazaars for books. In a sense, perhaps, I was trying to recreate that thrill that I had in my boyhood, discovering all those dark, mysterious spines, all those stories, all that magic.

Indigence made me more discerning. At twenty, books lined the walls of my bedroom in much the same way as they had when I was twelve; but the collection I rebuilt lacked the magic of my childhood library. It was more worthy, perhaps, but was it as magical? I had F. Scott Fitzgerald and Evelyn Waugh and plenty of Dickens. I had *Portnoy's Complaint* and *The Virgin Soldiers* and *The Carpetbaggers, Catch 22, Moby Dick, Lord of the Flies* and *The Lord of the Rings*. I had Proust and Sartre, and I had volumes of philosophy and poetry and textbooks on history and science and ideas.

But I never again possessed a single *Biggles* novel, or a *Beano* annual. I managed to accumulate more than a dozen Asimovs, but I can't remember the last time I read one. I did end up with a shelf full of 1950s *National Geographics*, but I hardly ever took them down.

11

RIGOR MORTIS

Bad news. Rigor mortis has set in. I find myself quite unprepared for this. I'd always intended to get the job done straight away, but then I got to thinking that a few short hours to compose myself wouldn't do any harm, and I spent the time pottering around, collecting my thoughts and generally trying to build up the courage to do the wretched deed. I'd somehow forgotten about rigor mortis. Does it always happen like this? I went in to see Max, and took with me the knives and a saw, and found him as stiff as the Rastin table.

I have no experience; that's my difficulty here. You can read all you like about the muscles of the neck, but nowhere does it tell you to get cracking right away because within a hour or so your levator scapulae, your sternothyoideus, your sternocleidomastoid will be as rigid as a plaster cast. The only experience I've had with rigor mortis was with Captain Ponder and the wretched dog, Libby. I didn't really want to tell that story yet, although I suppose I must, but it does mean jumping forward in the narrative. Max always used to jump around in his narratives, so I could make this *intentional* – a blurring of the conventional linear form. Max would approve. Although I have no doubt that the ladies and gentlemen of the Buckinghamshire constabulary will lose patience if I take this approach with them.

There is another reason, of course, why I would have to raise the story of Captain Ponder and Libby the dog sooner or later, and that relates to what happened immediately afterwards. Were it not for the incident with the captain and the dog, then, very probably, I should not be sitting in a heavily curtained room with the cold, unyielding cadaver of my once best friend. But then again, maybe I would. Who can ever tell? Our own memories are fallible enough, we can barely describe what was, so how can we hope to describe what *might have been*?

The first time I met Captain Ponder, he seemed to stand about seven feet tall with cold, grey eyes and a moustache that engulfed most of his head. Well, that's the way he looked to an eight-year-old. In reality, he was just a little taller than I am now, maybe six foot one or six foot two, but he had a military bearing that made him appear taller than he was. And ah, that moustache; at eight years old I was most taken with the moustache. It was a Dickensian feature, thick and bushy, and it spread across his face like a herbaceous border. You just don't see facial hair like that any more.

Hark at me! I sound like Max.

The captain, when I first met him, wore pomade on his greying hair, which shone like chrome. He had an aquiline nose with a prominent ridge, and he probably had flared nostrils, although the moustache would have hidden them. He may also have had a mouth, but the luxuriant moustache concealed all features from the tip of his nose to midway down his chin. He wore his hair in a severe short-back-and-sides as all men of his generation did, and there was a tidemark where his closely clipped sideburns suddenly sprouted gloriously into the moustache. Perhaps tidemark is the wrong word. It was more like a forest margin where the grasses suddenly metamorphose into a giant stand of trees. He bent at the waist when he talked to children, like a soldier at attention commanded to bend, or a penknife folded part of the way down. He was a construct; an assembly of vestigial military organs, built to resemble a soldier, given the rank of captain, and then abandoned to a world where captains no longer had a purpose.

You understand this is the present day *me* and my observations of the captain – Adam Last, fifty years old, and a cynic. If I were to meet Captain Ponder *now* for the very first time, I'd laugh at his assumed rank and authority, his ponderous military bearing and ridiculous moustache. But back then I wasn't a fifty-year-old cynic and *Guardian*-reader and opponent of war. I was terrified by him.

Captain Ponder cantilevered towards me. 'Name?' he enquired, his voice emerging from the undergrowth.

I probably gawped back at him. I may have stammered my name. The fact is that I am really no better at recalling the conversations of four decades ago than you are, or anyone else is, except perhaps for Max. But while Max struggles with his great catalogue for total authenticity of recollection, I can at least dispense with that pretence and aim for an approximation. So here goes:

'Adam,' I almost certainly would have stammered. 'Adam Last.'

The captain levered himself back up to vertical. 'Your father has a sense of humour then?'

'Yes, sir.' My father did *indeed* have a sense of humour, but I couldn't fathom the captain's logic. I'm still not sure if I can. No doubt he was contrasting 'Adam', the first man in creation, with 'Last', but I'm not sure that I would have seen any humour in that. Max thought it hilarious. He started to laugh, a squeaky annoying laugh, a 'hee hee hee hee hee' of a laugh. The captain was drawn into this and began to laugh too, more of a 'haugh haugh haugh', slapping young Max on the back as if the mirth of the moment was too much to bear. Goddamnit, I was eight! I laughed too, unsure quite why I was doing it but aware that I was supposed to. The awkward fact that I was, in some dark way, the object of the merriment did not entirely escape me. I wanted to flee the Ponder home, back across the valley to Westfield Close, never to return.

But you will know from your own childhood that your friends' parents are always a little alarming at first and I did warm to the captain eventually. Or, at least, I grew more familiar with him as the years passed, so that he became progressively less fearsome. Max writes about his father with such affection in The Catalogue that I'm almost ashamed to say that I don't really recognise the captain I knew. The captain that I remember was always a little remote. He always looked a bit out of place, as if trapped in a different time zone, like a Cossack hussar at a pop concert. I wouldn't have thought him capable of intimacy or affection. But Max would probably nod knowingly. 'No two people can ever watch the same football match,' he would surely remind me.

A year or two after the Ponders arrived in Eastlands, the captain shaved off his moustache. I never knew what prompted the exfoliation. One day he simply arrived at a parents' day at Kenton shorn of whiskers and I never saw him with facial hair again. Max, astonishingly, barely seemed to notice. When I spoke to him about it, he simply shrugged. 'Oh, has he?' he replied when I mentioned the missing moustache. 'I dare say he'll grow another one.'

It seems clear to me now, with the benefit of four decades of hindsight, that Max and the captain did have a strangely unique relationship. Max would interpret each of the captain's ponderous admonitions and announcements as statements of affection, laden with shared humour. He would laugh incessantly and annoyingly, impressed by every word that passed the great man's concealed lips. 'Tee hee hee,' Max's body would sway with merriment, and his face would explode with pure happiness. Then the captain would guffaw in his turn, and a self-reinforcing cycle of mutual amusement would strike up. I wasn't the first, I'm sure, to feel vaguely excluded by this. Even Max's mother, O, would smile wryly as the father–son charade swung into action. It was a relationship that didn't seem to change much as the years advanced. Max learned to tone down the irritating giggle; perhaps he began to recognise the looks of incomprehension on the faces of third parties, and so in time his reaction to the captain was contained to a broad grin and an occasional chuckle. The captain would still guffaw lightly after most of his pronouncements anyway, as if he found himself eternally amusing.

But again I find myself being uncharitable. From time to time, the captain could be genuinely amusing, although it took me some time to learn this. And I think that Max was able to recognise the dark lode of humour that probably lay at his core. Maybe everything the captain did, or said, was intentionally comic, but at such a deep level that no one save for Max and the captain could recognise it. Yes, he was a military anachronism, cast afloat into a world in which he no longer had a home, but in another world, at another time, he might have been a humorist or a philosopher.

If I were a psychologist, I'd probably believe that Max's relationship with his father was a key indicator of Max's own behaviour. Of course that's probably true of us all.

But I have a story to tell here, the story that I promised at the beginning of the chapter, the story that begins with the captain and the dog Libby and a case of rigor mortis. It is probably the key story in this whole tale, not because there was any special significance associated with the dog Libby, but because one event that day led to another which, in turn, led to another and so on, like a domino cascade.

This all happened when Max and I were nineteen. I'll fill in some of the key events of the missing years in due course, but this is one of the non-linear parts of the narrative and it needs to be told here. So, let me get my thoughts in order ...

It happened on a March weekend in 1974 when I travelled down from university to spend half-term at the Ponders' family home in Buckinghamshire. Max and I had gone our separate ways after Kenton, which was the prep school we had both attended in Nairobi. Max had gone on to Eton, and from there he'd lived up to the captain's vicarious ambitions by continuing on to Cambridge, Gonville and Caius, the captain's old college, to read philosophy. I'd ended up at a minor public school in Ramsgate, and from there I'd progressed undramatically to the University of Keele, a red-brick place close to nowhere in particular except perhaps the M6 motorway. During the years when Max was at Eton and I was in Ramsgate, we sustained our friendship through little more than occasional weekends, or half-terms, which we normally spent at the captain's draughty apartments in London. I would jump on the train from Ramsgate to Victoria with a single change of clothes stuffed into a gunny bag, and I would change out of my grey worsted school uniform in the cramped train toilet. From Victoria I would walk to the captain's apartment in Dorset Square; up Grosvenor Place alongside the unwelcoming walls of Buckingham Palace, through Hyde Park, and then north along Gloucester Place. Max, on the other hand, would be collected from Eton in a taxi and would arrive without even loosening his Eton tie.

Despite the longer journey, I would usually arrive first. I would lurk outside looking as if I didn't belong there, often sitting on the step.

Now that we were nineteen, you see, and Max had ended up at Cambridge and I'd settled at Keele, it seemed that our carefully preserved friendship might just peter out over the simple matter of motorway miles. Our lives were on different trajectories now. We had new circles of friends. Yet whenever Max wrote or called, there was always an urgency to his invitations; we *had* to meet up, we *had* to spend time together, there were always things he *had* to tell me.

So we'd arranged to link up for a half-term weekend at the place Max had always called 'The Pile'. It is, of course, the house I'm in now, Max's home, the place where Max lies dead, the home of The Catalogue. But this, as it happens, was the first time I'd seen it. Over the years I'd become used to the apartment in Dorset Square, and I'd even stayed overnight at O's echoing family home in Devon. But somehow I'd avoided the family seat, The Manor House at Medenfield, just upriver from Marlow.

It was twenty-one months after the Melanie concert at Crystal Palace Bowl. I'd come down in response to an invitation that had arrived through the post. Max said he *had* to see me. There were things I *had* to know. He enclosed a rail ticket and a timetable which showed the trains that I would need to take from Stoke-on-Trent to Crewe and from Crewe to Reading. So I complied.

We have no real sense of foreboding, do we? We follow the arrows and markings of our lives with no sense of a destination. And this is how it was for me, and how it became for Max and for the captain, and for all the others who were swept up in that weekend.

The captain met me at Reading Station. I struggled off the train with a lumpy rucksack hanging loosely from one shoulder, carrying my guitar, and wearing a Jim Morrison T-shirt, bell-bottom loons and a sheepskin coat that was my most prized possession. It was bright for a March day. The captain was sitting on a bench on the station platform, hidden behind a *Financial Times*, and I almost walked right past him. I was looking for Max, expecting Max to be there to meet me. Instead there was the captain. I shook his hand, ready for the strong handshake. It had been two years or more since we'd last set eyes on each other, and I was conscious that while I had changed, grown taller, had affected, long, unwashed hair and seventies sideburns, the captain was exactly the way I had always remembered him, erect and pomaded, and sadly still *sans* moustache.

'Isn't Max here?' I heard myself asking.

'Ah. Max is back at The Pile,' said the captain, 'a touch of his old problem, if you know what I mean.'

I didn't know what the captain meant, but I nodded anyway. But then again, perhaps I *did* know. I knew Max pretty well, and if he had an old problem then it must be one of the ones I already knew about.

The captain led me out of the station towards an ageing Volvo estate, daubed here and there with orange anti-rust paint, and I guessed correctly that this must be the Ponder family car. The back seats were folded down flat and among the assorted items of luggage and torn map books, lying prostrate on the frayed carpet, was a dead black Labrador. In the back of the family car.

This was a Ponder thing, and I need to explain. All these little things, you see, they help to explain the Ponder mind-set. The old car. The dead Labrador. They go with the ridiculous names, the flamboyant moustache, the rambling manor, the blind, old retainer I had yet to meet, the business interests in India and Kenya and who-knows-where that evaded all explanation. The rules that you and I live by – the mores and expectations and behaviours – never seemed to apply to the Ponders. I know, for example, I just *know*, that when the Ponders went to Africa in 1963, they didn't plan for months and set off in trepidation like I'm sure my family did. No, they would have packed up on a whim and caught the first BOAC Comet 4 or whatever it was back then, and probably quaffed champagne en route. Spontaneity was their forte. On one occasion I travelled up from Ramsgate to Dorset Square, only to discover that Max had been dispatched on a piece of family business to Simla in India. It was a last-minute thing and I hadn't been informed. I'd arrived and waited endlessly on the steps, until eventually the housekeeper, the chain-smoking Mrs Drabble, had emerged with a cigarette on her lip, a note of apology, and a letter of introduction to the Sloane Club in Chelsea where I was assured of a bedroom and a complimentary meal. Sending Max off to India like that was a typical Ponder thing. I suppose it isn't too hard to imagine, given the appropriate set of conditions and sense of urgency, another family impulsively chucking their teenager on a plane to Asia to sort out some family business. But somehow, with the Ponders, I had come to expect this sort of behaviour. Indeed, it happened with unerring frequency. Not necessarily India, but even as I rode the train to Reading, I had been wondering whether Max would, in fact, be there at the station to meet me.

And then there was the car, of course. Today it might be

fashionable to drive a banger when you could comfortably afford a Rolls. It might be seen as some sort of statement. You might even approve, imagining, perhaps, that the car represented a commitment to reducing the owner's carbon footprint, an opposition to planned obsolescence, a recognition that expensive cars are phallic extensions, no more capable of getting you from A to B any faster than any other, and in reality offering only marginally more comfort. But, in 1974, people didn't make statements like this with their cars. Nobody even thought about carbon footprints. Besides, the Ponders didn't go in for statements. If the Ponders chose to drive a battered old Volvo instead of a Rolls-Royce, it wasn't that they couldn't afford the Rolls. It was, well, it was just a Ponder thing. They hadn't quite got around to it. They were absurdly fond of the old car. It had been a gift from an old aunt who would be offended. Et cetera. Et cetera.

'Sorry about Libby,' barked the captain as he slung my rucksack into the back alongside the dead dog. 'Poor girl went doolally. Went off her legs and I've just taken her to the vet for the old j … jab.' He beckoned me to relinquish my guitar, but I indicated that I'd prefer to carry it with me.

'As you wish,' he said. 'Fifteen. Pretty good age for a lab. Bit sad, I'm afraid. Anyway, the vet offered to dispose of her but I said "No". Plenty of room to bury her back at The P … Pile.'

We climbed into our respective seats and he revved up the engine. The car sprang backwards and we were away.

'So. How've you been?'

'Fine, thank you, sir.'

'How's Keeble?'

'Keele, sir.'

'Ah yes, of course. Keele. Shropshire?'

'Staffordshire.'

'Yes.'

'It's fine, sir.'

'Good. Good.'

We drove for a while in silence.

'Good,' he added.

It should have been an awkward encounter, but somehow it wasn't. When you grow up seeing your friend's parents regularly, always having the same cross-examination – school and family, exams and achievements – you eventually feel relaxed in their company. They've seen you as a child; you don't have many secrets. You've seen them at their most casual moments, at picnics, sprawled over sofas, angry, sad, jubilant. The only barrier is that strange generation thing that limits conversation to a one-way litany of responses. To underline the effect, Aunt Zinnia was waiting at the front door so I didn't have much time to gawp at the place.

'Adam,' she cooed, 'how wonderful to see you.' She brushed my cheek in what may have been a kiss. 'How are you?'

'I'm fine, Miss Ponder.'

'How's Keele?'

'Fine.'

The first time I met Aunt Zinnia was at the old Dupont house in Convent Gardens about a year or so after Max and his parents arrived in Nairobi. Back then, Zinnia would have been thirty-something. She had recently divorced (I discovered this much later), and had flown out to Nairobi to see the captain, her brother, presumably in the hope that a change of scenery might ease the pain. She stayed, and she appeared to have been living with the Ponders ever since. When the family returned to England late in 1971, Zinnia had returned too, and she had taken up residence in The Pile. In the ten years I'd known her I had learned (from Max) of a passage of boyfriends, each as disreputable as the last. These relationships always seemed fairly casual. If I were asked for an amateur analysis here, I would say that Zinnia was probably done with serious relationships after the divorce. She didn't need a breadwinner. She needed company perhaps; but not that badly. She slid back into English society, resumed life as Miss Ponder, and that was how things stayed.

'Max is up in his room,' Aunt Zinnia said to me. 'A touch of the jitters. I'm sure Cap told you.'

'Yes.'

'He'll be right as rain soon. In fact, I'll call him down now.'

'OK.'

'I've made up one of the spare bedrooms. We'll get Tutton to unpack your things.'

'Really, there's no need to bother.'

'Don't be ridiculous, dear boy. You're practically family.' Aunt Zinnia took my arm and started up the front steps. 'Did Cap explain about poor Libby?'

'Yes.'

'Poor old girl. We're frightfully cut up about it you know. Still, we soldier on.'

'I'm sure she had a good life,' I said.

Aunt Zinnia stopped and gave me a sad smile. 'Yes,' she said. 'She did have a good life, I suppose. She was Dolly's dog. Have you met Dolly?'

'Yes.' Dolly was the ever-smoking Mrs Drabble who looked after Dorset Square. While the Ponders had been in Kenya she and Libby, it seemed, had had full run of the manor. On the Ponders' return, they'd dispatched Dolly back to London and kept the dog. Another Ponder thing.

An ancient man met us at the front door, shabbily dressed. He had the opaque spectacles and white stick of a blind man.

'Tutton will show you your room,' said Aunt Zinnia.

A while later I was left to my own devices to explore the house and grounds. Max still had not emerged from wherever it was that his 'jitters' had driven him, and I had no idea where to find him. Aunt Zinnia assured me once more that he 'would be down very shortly', and why didn't I explore the house? I felt like one of those impoverished weekend guests in a Jane Austen novel, a humble visitor in awe of the great home. And I was, I suppose, truly in awe. Max's routine dismissal of the place as 'The Pile' had left me expecting a gothic ruin. Instead I discovered a sprawling Georgian manor down half a mile of driveway; a grand red-brick building with castellated turrets at the end of each wing, rolling lawns and anarchic shrubberies that wound down to the river. Inside were sweeping staircases, polished balustrades, chandeliers, and bric-a-brac from every continent where the Ponder family had ever made a home: ornate Indian furniture, Bokhara rugs, African figurines and, of course, the Rastin dining table we met earlier, and the one where ... well, you know that bit.

It was while I was admiring the dining table that I was interrupted by the captain. He appeared behind me, almost making me jump.

'Adam, old chap, would you mind terribly giving me a hand with Libby? We ought to bury the old girl before she starts to stink out the place.'

'Oh. Absolutely, sir. Of course.'

We went into the garden and the captain hunted out an old wheelbarrow. 'This ought to do,' he said.

I wheeled the barrow to the car, and we hefted the dog into it. It was then that I made my first acquaintance with the phenomenon I am facing now: rigor mortis. Libby was perfectly stiff, her legs splayed out as if she were running.

'She's gone all stiff, sir,' I told the captain.

'So I see.'

In the barrow Libby did not fold neatly. She lay like an inverted statue, her legs in the air.

'There's a place we tend to use for this sort of thing down by the orchard,' said the captain. I followed him obediently and we stopped under a little copse of trees.

'Here I think,' he said. 'Mind you, we need to be careful we don't come across any other specimens down there. There could be a few.'

He produced a couple of spades and we started to dig. Half-term, I thought. I could be at Keele hanging out with my friends. Instead I was in a strange garden with a cranky old soldier burying a rigid dog.

We dug in silence, and even though it was only March, we were working up a sweat. The soil wasn't easy. There were rocks and tree roots, and there was a sticky heaviness to each spadeful.

'We're going to have to make the hole a lot wider,' I said, after the grave began to take shape.

'Nonsense,' said the captain. 'We should fit her in there okay.'

'Sir, she has rigor mortis. Her legs are sticking out. If we lay her on her back then the grave will need to be a lot deeper. If we lay her on her side she just won't fit. We'll have to make it wider.'

'I see.'

'Or we could wait until the rigor mortis subsides,' I said. 'I don't know how long that will take. Maybe not too long.'

The captain looked thoughtful. 'I'd rather not keep the family waiting though. Best to get these things over with, don't you think?'

'Then what shall we do?'

The captain gave a kind of a grimace. 'We're going to have to break her legs,' he said.

I was in no position to argue with his logic. The dog was dead after all. The captain leaned heavily on his spade and seemed to wobble. 'Help me d ... down,' he said, 'I'll do it.' He held out his hand and I saw that it was shaking.

I found myself possessed by a sense of the inevitable. I had never known this dog, so only I could do the deed.

'That's OK. I'll do it. You may want to look the other way, sir,' I said.

A glance passed between us.

'Thank you, Adam,' the captain replied, then he turned away.

From these small moments, our lives are made. I sensed in that instant a change in the long-established balance between the two of us. It was part of that process we all discover as we grow older, as we begin to assume responsibilities and duties that used to fall to our parents or elders. Captain Ponder was, and always would be to me, *the captain*, the stoic, austere, erect and once moustachioed man, capable of anything, frightened of no one. I was the eight-year-old who had stood before him and stammered my name on the verandah of a house in the suburbs of Nairobi, and suffered his humiliating laughter. But eleven years had passed. Somehow we had crested a brow in the journey of our lives and were confronted with a new, and much stranger, view than the one we had shared before. Here, on that March day in the grounds of The Pile, the captain turned away while I smashed down with my heavy spade onto the splayed legs of the Labrador.

It took a dozen or more blows, and then it was done. The captain never turned around; not once. I went to the shed and found an old dust-sheet, and brought it back to the scene. Then I leaned down by the shallow grave and wrapped the broken body of the dog until, as a parcel, she looked almost peaceful. Then I planted my spade in the heap of soil. Only then did I tell the captain that he could turn around.

We surveyed the job together.

'Adam ... you have a c ... c ... courageous sp ... spirit,' said the captain. The stammer was uncharacteristic, but I put it down to the stress of the situation.

'Thank you, sir.' I was breathing heavily from the exertion of the digging, and the events that had succeeded it. Looking down into the grave, I became worried that blood from the broken legs was starting to show through the dust-sheet. I took a spade-full of soil and covered the stains.

'Do you have a moment for a bit of a ch ... chat, Adam?' asked the captain. He was looking away from me again, as if he were talking to someone else.

'Sir?'

'I think I can trust you, Adam. I wasn't sure if I could ... but I think perhaps this ...' he indicated the grave with a shake of his head, 'Well ... perhaps I can.'

I wasn't sure how to reply – or even if I *should*.

'You're M ... Max's best friend, Adam. Always have been.'

'Yes, sir.'

'That's why I'm telling you this. I can't tell Max, you see.'

'Can't tell him what, sir?'

'Ah.' The captain turned to face me, then he looked away again. 'I'm fifty-one years old, Adam. Not a great age really. Probably seems a great age to you though.'

'No, sir. Not really.'

'Nonsense. Of course it does. You're only what? Eighteen?'

'Nineteen, sir.'

'Nineteen. Yes, of course. Of course,' the captain seemed to reflect on this. Then he drew a decisive breath. 'Fact of the matter is, Adam, I'm on my way out.'

'Way out, sir?'

'I'm dying. I have a brain tumour.'

'Oh.' I didn't know what to say. I was stunned, not so much by the revelation, as by the fact that the captain was making this revelation to *me*.

'I have an astrocytoma,' the captain continued. 'It isn't a small thing you see. Apparently it's a star-shaped thingummy with little tumour points that reach all around the brain. So there's no way they can take the damned thing out.'

'I understand,' I said. I must have blinked at him, because he turned away. 'How long have you known?'

'Oh, quite a few months I suppose.'

'And how ... how ...'

'How long do I have? Ha! Wouldn't it be nice to know, eh? All the chaps at the Marsden can tell me is that I'm doing jolly well to have got this far.'

'I see.'

'F ... Funny thing,' he said, 'but I can't f ... feel the blighted thing. I know it's there, of course. It makes me black out from time to time. Shouldn't be driving, strictly speaking. The doctor chappie told me not to drive, but damnit how am I supposed to get about?'

'Quite,' I said, thinking of the journey back from the station. Then, after a moment, I added, 'Max doesn't know?'

'No.'

'How about Aunt Zinnia?'

'Haven't got around to telling her yet.'

'So who *does* know?' I asked, 'Apart from the doctors.'

The captain fixed me with his gaze and I thought for the first time that his eyes seemed milky and his skin yellow.

'You do,' he said.

We stood and looked at each other, and time passed. On the river, a hundred feet away, a boatload of noisy revellers slooped by. If I had turned my head away for just a moment, I would have caught sight of them gliding past behind the curtain of the weeping willow. I could hear the clinking of glasses and hoots of laughter from young men, and for an instant I thought of *Three Men in a Boat*, who must have sailed this very stretch of river on their way to Hampton Court. And then, as quickly as it had sailed into earshot, the boat was gone.

'I'm not quite sure what you want, sir?'

The captain looked at me and seemed to blink in slow motion. 'I can't tell them, Adam.'

'Of course you can, sir. If you can tell me ...'

'It isn't the same, old chap. I do want to tell them, but I never seem to find the right moment. And when I do ... well, I end up saying something else altogether. And now, well, I just think it would be so much better if they didn't know.'

We stood together, looking down into the grave.

'It's the same thing my own father had,' he said, after a while. 'Mind you, we didn't know what it was until after he died. D ... didn't have fancy X-ray gizmos in those days.'

'I see.'

'He was only fifty. S ... so I guess I've outlived him.'

'Right.' I found myself unable to think of anything to say.

'All a bit sad at the end,' said the captain. 'The bally thing grows so fast it eats up the brain. The old chap simply went d ... d ... doolally.'

I hesitated. 'You mean ... you mean he lost his memory?'

'Oh god. His memory, his eyesight, his sense of balance, his knowledge of language, his control over his b ... bodily functions. God. It was awful, Adam. I can't tell you.'

'... and you think ... you think the same ...'

'... that the same is going to happen to me? Well I certainly hope not, old man. But there's no saying. It all depends where the tumour grows, you see. It picks off bits of the b ... brain like a sniper, so you only have to hope that it will take out the bit that controls your heartbeat before it takes out the bit that controls your b ... b ... bowels. Anyway.'

'Yes, sir.'

Today I'm not far off the age that the captain was then. If someone told me *now* what the captain told me on that day in March 1974, I like to think I should know what to think, how to react, what to say. I'd commiserate, to start off with. I would express my sense of shock. I would try to explore the prognosis a little. Could there be a cure if you were to travel to America perhaps? And then I would get practical. I would describe a course of action, and explain what I intended to do, to what effect, and in what order. But we are different people at nineteen. We navigate the rocks of life in a more casual way. We don't think about dying, not really. So, even in the presence of death, with the stiff and lifeless Libby at our feet, I still don't think I saw the dark reality that the captain was painting for me. Eventually it was the captain himself who had to point out the consequence that I had failed to grasp.

'You do understand what I'm saying, don't you?' he asked.

'Yes, sir. I think so, sir.'

'It's called "Turcot Syndrome Variant 4", Adam. It's a fam ... familial thing. You know what that means, don't you?'

'Yes, sir.'

'My father had it, Adam. My grandfather ... well, we don't really know. What we *do* know is that he died at forty-six. And actually, if you go back, it turns out that we Ponders are all pretty short-lived. My younger brother, Martin, died, you know?'

'Yes. I thought ... I mean ... Max told me that was a car crash.'

The captain gave a snort. 'Ah yes, it was. Of course it was. It *was* a car crash, Adam. At the age of forty-five.'

'I see.'

'Yes, Adam. But you still don't see what I'm *really* saying, do you?'

I had been looking away, but now I was forced to meet his eye. There was a pause, and then I got it.

'Max,' I whispered.

'Exactly.'

'And he doesn't know?'

The captain's voice seemed to drop. 'He doesn't suspect a thing, old chap. And that's the way I'd like to keep it. I don't want him to go through life with this thing hanging over him like some S ... ... Sword of Damocles.'

The implications began to swim into view.

'I should probably spell it out,' the captain said. 'Max has a fifty per cent chance, that's what the docs say.'

'Right.'

'He's not as tough as I am, Adam. If he has to watch me die the same way that I had to watch my father die, well then ...' He left the thought trailing. 'So that g ... gives us two options, doesn't it?'

'I'm not sure I ...'

'Option one, I find a quick way out. No one reveals anything. That's the doctor–patient thing, you understand.'

'You mean suicide?' I asked.

'Steady on. B ... bit of a strong word that, don't you think? Not really suicide to jump off a cliff if you're already falling. Bit of a rubbish metaphor, but you know what I mean.'

'Not exactly ...'

'B ... besides, I'm not the suicidal type, I'm afraid. That's the weakness of option one. No chance of b ... blessed relief from the old army revolver. There's always the hope of a sudden accident, of course – not too outrageous given the symptoms – but it's not really something we can plan for.'

'So, option two?'

'Ah. Well, this is where you come in, Adam. I need you to take Max away.'

'Away?'

'Exactly. Look, do you mind if we sit down?'

I shook my head and the captain lowered himself on to the grass. I sat uncomfortably next to him. We avoided dangling our legs into the grave.

'Where do you want me to take him?' I asked.

'Well I was thinking Australia. We have a small b ... business there. Property, you know. Mines and stuff. The trouble is, I just don't think Max would go there on his own. But if *you* go, Adam, well then he would too. I'd p ... put him in charge and you could be D ... D ... Director of International Operations, or some such. You'd only need to go for a year. The first news Max would get about ... well ... would be the end. I'd make sure of that.'

'Sir, I'm in my second year at university. So is Max.'

The captain seemed to reflect on this. 'Is that a d ... dreadful problem?'

'Well it is rather, sir. You can't just up and leave university halfway through your course.'

'Ah. That means you won't go?'

'Well, sir, no. Not really.'

'Hmm. In that case, we're on to option three.'

'I thought you said there were only two options?'

'Ah,' he said, and for an instant I may have seen a twinkle in his eye, and so perhaps have found something of that curious seam of humour that linked him so closely to Max. 'Well, there's a little lesson, eh? Never reveal all your options until you've explored your p ... preferred ones. As it happens, there is another option.' He paused. '*I* go to Australia.'

I could feel the damp from the grass working its way into my trousers.

'I think it's a bit wet here, sir.'

'I think you're right,' he said. 'We should be getting up.'

Neither of us moved.

'What about Aunt Zinnia?' I asked him.

'What about her?'

'Might she get it? The cancer?'

The captain bobbed his head a little. 'Apparently not,' he said. 'Seems like this thing just goes for the Ponder males. Thank god, I suppose.'

'Is there anyone else ...?'

'No.' He shook his head. 'Just me. And Max.'

'Do you want to call anyone else here?' I asked eventually, 'to see Libby ... laid in the ground?'

'Ah. Yes. Very good.' The captain stared up towards the house, appearing to welcome the change of subject. 'I suppose ... look, would you mind?'

'No. You go ahead. I'll wait here.'

The captain lifted himself cumbersomely and started off towards the house. He walked, I noticed for the first time, with a curious rolling gait, almost a limp. I stood up, conscious that I was playing a role in a family drama – a *Ponder* family drama.

A few moments later, Aunt Zinnia appeared with Max. The captain came rolling behind them, his walk still lopsided.

I greeted Max with a boyish hug. His face looked pale. 'Thanks for all this,' he said.

'No probs.' At that moment I actually felt grateful to be in the position I was in – to be the man with the spade, remote yet not removed from the whole ceremony.

Aunt Zinnia was crying.

Max thanked me for helping to dig the grave. His 'jitters', I now realised, were a reaction to the loss of the dog.

Then Aunt Zinnia disappeared and reappeared with some daffodils. She laid them carefully onto the parcel that was Libby's folded body and then we all stood awkwardly, looking down into the little grave.

Another noisy boat drifted by. We stood and waited for it to pass.

'Shall I fill it in now?' I asked.

'We should say a few words first,' said Aunt Zinnia. 'Cap, would you say something?'

'Of course,' said the captain dutifully. He straightened up to his usual erect bearing. 'G ... g ... good old Libby.' He was stuttering uncharacteristically again. 'You were a jolly g ... good old g ... girl. We're jolly well going to miss you.' He paused. This obviously wasn't enough. He cleared his throat. 'S ... somewhere I expect you'll still be chasing rabbits up there in heaven. Still be ch ... ch ... chewing an old slipper or two. You've been a jolly good companion. Bon voyage.'

'Bon voyage,' echoed the family.

'Now. Anyone for a shot of the hard stuff to toast the old girl?' said the captain.

'Dolly should really be here,' said Aunt Zinnia.

'My dear she'd have to come all the way from L ... London.'

'It's not that far though, is it? And Libby was her dog.'

'I know. But she hasn't seen her in years. Champagne, I think. M ... Max would you give Adam a hand filling in that soil?'

12

KENTON

I think we should make some effort here to go back to the linear narrative. This whole timeline is becoming far too fractured, and I can't think about that day in 1974 any longer. Not right now with Max lying dead on the dining table. Max often called me a cold fish, but I'm not so cold that I can simply sit in a room with my dead friend and reflect easily on all the bad things that brought us to this point.

I do know, of course, that the forensic psychologists will want to dwell on that day; especially on the events that followed the funeral of Libby the dog. The timing of it, just fifteen months before Max shut himself away in The Pile, makes it seem like a critical point. But it was never easy to understand Max's mind, even on a good day, and maybe his thoughts were already turning in that direction anyway. The captain was already dying. And I can't prove that the ghastly events of that day on their own drove Max into reclusion. Perhaps he had travelled most of that journey already, before the day of the fencing bout, the day that we buried the dog, the day that Captain Ponder was rushed into hospital.

So let me go back again to a much earlier time. I can only share with you properly those experiences that Max and I have in common, but there is plenty of material in these alone to build a good understanding of who Max was, and maybe, just maybe, why he did what he did.

So let's go back again to the 1960s. On Sunday 5 May 1962, Max and I started boarding school in Nairobi. This was only ten weeks after the day we'd first met, the day that Max swallowed the sixpence and I could see into the future.

The reality of leaving home and the prospect of a probable ten to twelve-year stretch as a boarder in unfriendly, institutional surroundings is a tough one, especially at eight years of age. Overdressed in military-grey cotton shirts and knee-length shorts, with ridiculous purple-and-grey ties and grey flannel hats, all the new boys assembled in the quad and paraded obediently to meet the headmaster. Unseen hands whisked away our heavy trunks of itemised clothing: four pairs of grey shorts (tick), one pair blue football shorts (tick), one dress hat (tick), one spare hat (tick), twelve pairs of knee-high socks (tick), two pairs of garters (garters!). Each item had a name-tag lovingly sewn into place. No sweets were allowed. No clothes apart from the uniform. Our instructions had been most precise. One cricket bat, one tin linseed oil, one fountain pen, notepaper, envelopes, stamps.

Among all the displaced, anachronistic institutions of colonial Africa, Kenton College Boy's Preparatory School deserves a special mention. Here, on the sun-baked highlands of the Dark Continent, the British had bequeathed a school in the model of Winchester or Harrow. The bleak granite building, built along the lines of a rococo mansion, concealed cool, parquet-floored corridors, austere classrooms, a grand dining hall, an assembly hall with rows of low benches, and dormitories laid out like hospital wards. Youthful teachers fresh from Oxford or Cambridge, new to the tropics and unattached, were visited upon us to teach us Latin, English grammar, French, scripture, and arithmetic. We were the young gentlemen of the fading empire. Pronunciation was important. Deportment. Respect for Authority. Obedience. Compliance. And Christian Virtues. This was more than a school; it was an academy of Britishness. Not one black or brown countenance disturbed the parade of anxious white faces beneath the ridiculous felt hats as we lined up for inspection (hair combed, parting perfectly straight, fingernails scrupulously clean and unbitten, garters tight, socks up).

Rules were absolute. Standards of behaviour precisely prescribed. We rose at six for physical education. Then a shower. Then breakfast. Then morning prayers. Then lessons. Then lunch. Then lessons. Then games. Then showers, dinner and evening prayers. Six days a week with a routine of services and bible study on a Sunday.

I might have expected Max to be a victim of the worst kind of homesickness at Kenton. He was always such a home-body, such a slave to the certain comforts of home that the displacement we endured at Kenton could easily have become too much for him. But there was a stubborn streak in Max which rescued him from the desolation that often engulfed the rest of us. Today I think psychologists would say he was in 'denial', but I'm not sure that this was wholly true. For most boys the first few terms at the school were an ordeal to be borne stoically, like rebellious captives quietly observing the rules of their captors, one eye always on escape. But, curiously, the strict regimen of life at Kenton seemed to suit Max. He was always most comfortable when he had a clearly identified routine, and few places rely so heavily on the careful timetabling of daily activities as a boarding school. Our lives were ordered by the striking of the school bell. From the bell that signalled the moment to awake, to the final bell that spelled lights-out, we metered our activities by its sound.

Recalling this now, with Max lying dead in the next room, I'm trying to make sense of this strange contradiction in Max's character. On the one hand he was the least conformist person I have ever known. Who, after all, conforms to society's rules by drawing the curtains on life for thirty years? Obedience only came naturally to Max when the rules seemed to fit his comfortable understanding of the way that the world should work. On the other hand, as long as the rules didn't contradict his sometimes tortured logic, he was happy to comply. And with a few exceptions, as we shall soon see, he rarely strayed beyond the rules.

The headmaster at Kenton was the Reverend Perks. He probably had a first initial, but I don't recall it. The boys called him Pinky. The implied affection in this nickname makes it singularly inappropriate. The Reverend Perks was not a man, in my recollection, who inspired affection in anybody. From a distance of four decades or more, I can now accurately describe him; he was a brutal, sadistic bastard. We may not have had the vocabulary to describe him thus at the time, but we had the sentiment. He was hated as much as any man can be hated by a school of 111 boys. Fat and bombastic, swathed in his black-and-purple clerical robes, he would berate us from the pulpit on Sundays in a thunderous voice, hijacking the sermon to condemn whatever dreadful failing in our behaviour had most recently come to his notice. Never one to practise the biblical forgiveness that he publicly espoused, he exercised his authority over us by diligent and frequent use of the cane. The headmaster's study occupied a central ground-floor location, with bay windows overlooking the staff lawns. A central feature of his study was a large, floral sofa, and it was over this that penitent boys were expected to bend in order to receive their punishment. The ceremony was always the same. A guilty boy would be admitted. He would stand stiffly to attention hoping that, at this eleventh hour, there might be a reprieve. There never was. The Reverend Perks would withdraw a fresh cane from a rack menacingly placed beside his desk and he would flex it. 'Tell me why you're being caned,' he would demand.

And pitifully we, the condemned, would bleat out the reason. We were talking after lights-out; we were running in the corridor; we were insolent to a teacher: the list of possible misdemeanours was only bounded by the imagination of the teachers and the sadism of the headmaster.

'Bend over,' he would command, and helplessly we would submit. Whack, whack, whack. The strokes would crack across our small behinds like rifle fire, and all around the school would hold its breath, the crack of the cane echoing along the corridors so that there was nowhere it could not be heard.

Whack whack whack.

The caned boy was not permitted to stand until instructed. Any boy who tried to stand up before the good reverend told him to do so earned an extra stroke. And every stroke, or so it seemed, was delivered with every ounce of force that the head could muster. To call a caning painful, however, would be to misunderstand the whole nature of the punishment. The punishment of caning lay in its cold ritual: the day or more that you had to wait, the inevitable punishment drawing closer; the half-hour outside the headmaster's study, standing erect and terrified against the wall; the humiliation of bending over to accept the beating; the fear and the domination. Of course it was painful too, although the pain, curiously, was never immediate. It began as a dull burning sensation that only reached the level of true pain when the victim left the headmaster's study. The strokes would frequently draw blood – more on some boys than others –

but always the backside would welt and bruise and the bruises would last for a month or more.

Perversely, therefore, the cane left its casualties with a badge of honour. At the first opportunity, in the dormitory, the changing room, or the baths – a crowd would crush around the beaten. A good four-stroke caning could leave a bottom proudly slashed with four clear lines. When two or more strokes hit the same spot, the bruising was more dramatic, but less aesthetic, and we all believed that Perks deliberately spaced the stripes for better effect. He was as anxious to view the results of his handiwork as anyone and would appear in the changing room to inspect the stripes. 'Let's see those stripes!' he would bark, and the victim would have to turn his naked behind to be inspected by the bully who had delivered the bruises.

So how did this affect Max? Well to understand this, you need to understand a boy named Taylor, and to understand a cycle of events that would alter the behaviour of Max Ponder for the rest of his life.

Taylor was the boy who, during our years at Kenton, must have been thrashed more than any other. He was a likeable lad, but incorrigible. He was the only boy we knew who held little fear of Perks, or of the cane, or of anything else for that matter. For Taylor, lights-out in the dormitory was the cue for misbehaviour. He would trampoline from bed to bed, insensitive to the occupants, whooping like a gibbon. He would shout insults after the matron only seconds after the lights had gone out. He would fill his mouth with water and spit it right across the dorm at boys in the opposite beds. He was a bully, but not a malevolent one; his bullying grew more from an ignorant insensitivity to the feelings of others than from a wilful desire to hurt or terrorise. Today he would probably be diagnosed as hyperactive. We might say that he had attention deficit disorder. Back then, we simply called it naughtiness. He was always ebullient and full of energy. If he was the only one behaving badly, he would goad others into joining, and if this failed he would threaten. Any day without a fight seemed to him like a missed opportunity. The chances of getting caught were always perilously high, but Taylor never seemed to care. In this respect, god, how we all admired him. Taylor's backside was like an impressionist painting in which layer upon layer of stripes criss-crossed and merged and faded. He acted as if caning was of no consequence. He would strut out of the headmaster's office and laugh, like Randall McMurphy in *One Flew Over the Cuckoo's Nest*, his disrespect for authority made greater by the inability of authority to cow him.

And so we come to Max. Because Max and Taylor, although never especially close, were to share a particular destiny. And it sprang in part from Taylor's cavalier attitude to the cane. In time, you see, his attitude began to infect others. The boys closest to Taylor, his cadre of admirers and hangers-on, started to act as if the cane meant nothing. They borrowed some of Taylor's swank. And then one night, when the lights went out, Taylor climbed up onto his bed and began to taunt us – we the placid majority in the dorm who routinely evaded caning by the simple expedient of obedience to the rules.

'You're a load of bloody cowards,' he spat at us. 'You're bloody sissies, frightened of the cane. Ooh ow. Frightened of the cane.'

'Don't say bloody,' came a fierce whisper from a bed nearby.

Taylor leaped from his bed to the next one where Trevor McIvor, the probable source of the whisper, lay feigning sleep.

'You're a sissy, McIvor,' he taunted. 'Sissy sissy sissy. Never been caned. Never been caned. Frightened of a little stick.'

These performances of Taylor's were nothing new, but they were dangerous. Noise attracted attention, and teachers prowled the corridors at night.

'Taylor, get back into bed,' I whispered loudly. 'You'll get us *all* caned.'

'Oooh! Get you all caned, will I? Taylor sprang from McIvor's bed and materialised on mine. At this point, the danger level for me rose sharply. Any teacher intervening now would send both of us down to the headmaster's study. There could be no mitigation for the boy whose bed had been invaded. As far as the rules were concerned, any incident that broke school rules involving two boys implied the guilt of both.

It was at that moment that every boy in the dorm heard the tell-tale sound of a door creaking open at the end of our corridor. Footsteps approached. Even Taylor's bravado didn't go so far as to invite deliberate arrest and punishment. He turned to spring back onto his bed. It should have been a matter of two bounds – from my bed to McIvor's, and from McIvor's bed to his own – but he found his way blocked. By Max.

Max Ponder was standing on McIvor's bed looking belligerent. He was holding the tin in which he kept his letters and most private personal possessions.

'I'm not scared of the stupid cane,' said Max. He began to beat the tin with a monotonous clank.

Taylor stopped for an instant, taken aback by this unexpected gambit.

'You've never had the cane,' he riposted. 'You don't know how much it hurts.'

'I don't care,' said Max defiantly.

We could hear the footfalls in the corridor. Taylor had been thrown off guard by Max's intervention but, after all, he was Taylor, the most fearless boy in the dorm. Anyone else would have sprinted back to his bed. But Taylor knew only one response.

'We're not scared of the stupid cane!' he shouted.

'We're not scared of the stupid cane!' chanted Max, beating out the rhythm on his tin.

'Ponder, what are you doing?' I whispered urgently.

'We're not scared of the stupid cane,' Max and Taylor sang in unison.

'You might not be but I jolly well am. Get off my bed!'

Thirty minutes later, standing in the corridor outside the head-master's study, waiting for the fateful punishment, I found myself between Max and Taylor. McIvor, another innocent, was there too.

'How many do you think we're going to get?' Max asked us.

I flinched. Talking in the corridor was a heinous offence. I gave him a deadly look: talk if you must, but don't implicate me.

But Max laughed out loud. 'Who cares if he catches us talking?' he said, suddenly sounding like Taylor. 'What can he do, cane us?'

We all saw his point. And in no time we were talking like young boys always will, as if the shadow of the cane had been wholly forgotten, because Max's logic – Taylor's logic – suddenly made sense. The only way to avoid punishment was to earn *maximum* punishment. Perks could not deliver more than six strokes. That was the law, as we understood it. At least, it was the custom. No boy had ever received more than six. We were all expecting four strokes – the usual for routine offences such as talking after lights-out – but so what if he gave us six? Could it really hurt that much more?

Within moments it was bedlam in the corridor. Max started up a chorus of 'we're not afraid of the stupid cane'. And then the Reverend Perks emerged, thunderous, still in his cassock from evening prayers with the senior boys, and we fell silent, our brief rebellion ended.

'How dare you make this noise outside my office!' he roared at us belligerently, and we cowered. 'How dare you!'

Taylor went in first and there was a long, agonising wait. The school fell silent. Down the corridors a cold quiet descended so that it was easy to imagine every boy in every bed holding his breath. The tell-tale sounds of a caning would be heard in every corner of the school. But first, a long wait. Taylor would be giving an account of himself. The headmaster would be flexing the cane.

Then, at last, the silence was broken by the crack of the cane, brutally loud. We gasped. There was a long wait until the second crack, and again until the third. Outside, in a pathetic little line like lambs, we were shaking with fear. Crack – four, CRACK – five – CRACK – six. We exhaled, waiting for the door to burst open and for Taylor to emerge, grinning as he always did. But the door didn't open. There was silence. Then CRACK again. Seven! We looked at each other in alarm. Had the headmaster lost count? CRACK – eight! Clearly not. CRACK – nine!

And then the door opened. I caught sight of Taylor being led forcibly by his shoulder out of the room. He turned his face away, but I alone saw what no one else in the school had ever seen. Taylor was crying.

In the end, they expelled Taylor for being a bad influence. From the school's perspective, he probably was. For Max, however, his influence was inspiring. I know this because I've read it in Max's catalogue. I shall point out the section to the detectives, and maybe they will start to understand that when Max chose to break the rules, he was inspired by a nine-year-old boy.

It wasn't the same for me. Taylor was a rebel, and by the time

I could identify with the cause, it was too late for rebellion. That's the way it goes. Max's subsequent insurgencies were much more considered than Taylor's ever were. Max, after that day, would pick his battles carefully; but pick them he would, and never again would he fear the consequences. We three came away with five strokes apiece. Clearly the Reverend Perks had identified Taylor as the ringleader, and had singled him out for a particularly sadistic thrashing. But there was general agreement that Max, McIvor and I had not escaped lightly either. Accounts of the caning reached us from all quarters of the school. Everyone, it seems, had heard the crack of the cane – had counted the nine strokes suffered by Taylor, had remarked at the firecracker volume of the strokes.

For several weeks we bore the stripes, red and raw at first, later blue and bruised, finally pink and fading. We all four showed our stripes proudly in the dorm the next morning, and then again in the school baths in the evening, and in time the soreness and tenderness were gone. To add to the discomfort of the caning, Perks had given McIvor, Max, and me four clear strokes on the buttocks and the fifth, cruelly, on the thighs where it would hurt even more, and where it would make sitting down particularly painful for days to come.

But this isn't how the story ends. This isn't the story of a caning. It is the story of a life-changing moment. For me, it was neither my first caning, nor my last; it was just another shameful, humiliating and painful encounter.

But for Max it was something different. For Max it was the beginning of a lifetime of rebellion. His was a cautious, measured rebellion, but it was rebellion nonetheless. From this moment on, for Max, obedience became optional, conformity a matter of personal choice, not regulation. Max had learned defiance that day, but he had also learned the lesson that the cane was intended to teach. He had learned pragmatic submission.

I went in for my punishment before Max, so I didn't see him emerge from the caning, but I did hear the strokes, and counted them as I lay in bed still trembling from the pain and the adrenalin. I saw Max slip back into the dorm and slide quietly into his bed. No one dared speak. But in the faint light from the window I saw Max's face and his eyes were dry.

Then, in a gesture that sent a shiver through us all, Max was back on his feet, and standing on his bed. In the dark and quiet of the dorm, he yelled out the full measure of his resolve, and the words that he shouted out were these: 'I'M NOT AFRAID OF THE SILLY OLD CANE! I'M NOT AFRAID OF THE SILLY OLD CANE! I'M NOT AFRAID OF THE SILLY OLD CANE!'

The shout echoed around the dorm and down the corridors and into the halls and into every corner of every room. And even after the shout had ended, we could still hear it, that shrill treble, that near scream, that mutinous, terrifying yell of freedom.

13

THE MEMORY CHAMBER

VOLUME XLIV
FEBRUARY 1979

I'm walking down a corridor; perhaps it's
more of a tunnel than a corridor. It is dimly
lit, and it seems to lead onwards into an
ever-darkening gloom. There are doors on both
sides, but no windows, and the walls are as
smooth as ceramic. The tunnel descends slowly
like a very shallow staircase, and the deeper
I travel, the farther back I go in time.
I look at the doors as I pass, and each one
seems vaguely transparent, as if it were made
of smoky glass. Behind the doors I can see
events from my past. Behind this door I can
see O holding my hand as we climb up the
gangplank to board the SS *Usoga* at Kisumu
Docks. She is wearing pale-green nail varnish
and her thumbnail is digging into my palm.
I see her from behind and from above, which
is not the perspective I ever had in life
yet, astonishingly, here she is, and here
I am, and together we climb the gangplank
and behind us trails Adam, and this is surely
exactly how it was. There are colours and
noises and smells and all of these things add
to the richness and the veracity of the
image.

Behind another door I can make out Callum

Anderson-Ffienes. He has me cornered in the junior locker at Eton and he's about to give me a black eye. Nothing I can do now will stop him. His arm is already swinging back and all I can do here is watch it happen.

Behind this door is Adam, fishing the bodies of dead men out of the Nile. The expression on his face makes it seem as if this is something he does most days.

Behind another door I can see Elenora in the gown she wore to the Savoy party in December 1973. We are getting ready to leave our suite to go downstairs and Elenora, as she adjusts my tie, gives me a look that tells me she would rather not go. She hates this kind of ostentatious event. We step out into the corridor and she mouths something to me. The words are, 'let's just stay up here and fuck each other senseless'. I can make every effort to will the feeble-minded youth that is me, standing there in his dinner jacket and silk bow-tie, to scoop her up and carry her back into the bedroom and tear the red gown off her body but, here in the memory chamber, I can only watch. I see the Max of my memory take Elenora's hand and pull her reluctantly towards the stairs.

This, then, is my Memory Chamber. This is where I come to revisit and rediscover my past. If I push open a door the reminiscences come to life. A light goes on, like the light in a refrigerator, and characters within the chamber begin to move. I occupy each room like a hidden cameraman, viewing each scene, not through my own eyes, but through the imaginary eyes of a third person who can pan around the scene unnoticed, can float above and look down upon events, or who can sink into any body to see the scene from that participant's eyes.

Reassembling memories is rather like the work of a fossil-hunter trying to reconstruct a Diplodocus from just a few fragments of bone. After all, fragments of memory are all we have. When you see the skeletons of great reptiles recreated in the Natural History Museum in Kensington, you can detect the flights of fancy that the palaeontologists have made, linking this scrap of bone to that one and these to this other one until, 'hey presto', a whole dinosaur has emerged. They can get away with this because other fossils in other museums have helped them fill in the gaps, and so it is with memory. When I remember Elenora at the Savoy, I cannot recall the colour of the wallpaper in the corridor, or the paintings that hung on the walls, or the furniture, or the chandeliers. All I have is a fragment, a glimpse of Elenora's face and her gown and those whispered words. But in the Memory Chamber I can try to assemble these with all that I know about hotel corridors in general, and of the Savoy in particular, the style of artwork that normally prevails, and now, from my position as the remote cameraman, I can look down on an altogether richer scene in which the wallpaper is deep red and the walls are hung with Restoration paintings in gilded frames. This is how we always do it.

Here is a later scene with Elenora. We are walking down Oxford Street the morning after the Savoy party. The Christmas decorations are up and the lights are twinkling. There are traders selling hot chestnuts and decorations and cheap gifts and wrapping paper. Christmas music is playing in the shops. There is a Salvation Army band beating out carols. There are black taxis and red buses and Christmas trees festooned with glitter and swarms of tourists in heavy coats and shoppers weighed down with gifts. Or are there? Because every one of these details comes courtesy of a hundred visits to Oxford Street around Christmas. In reality, I cannot recall a single face from the crowd that day with Elenora. If you were to subpoena me as a witness to identify one shopper from a line-up, then I could not. Neither, I suspect, could you. But what I can do, in my Memory Chamber, is to populate Oxford Street on that day with a general crowd of all the people and appurtenances of Christmas, so that when I replay my conversations with Elenora – even though those too are mere fragments – I can see the whole thing as if it were a film.

We went into Selfridges. The music playing was 'Merry Xmas Everybody' by Slade, but I only know that because they played it at the Savoy party the night before. I bought Elenora some perfume in a little pink bottle and the name of the perfume was . . .

And here is one of a host of details that my Memory Chamber cannot furnish. I could say that the perfume was 'Chanel No. 5', but it wasn't. It seems acceptable for my Memory Chamber to ornament a memory with general details drawn from experience, but it is unacceptable to supply a specific detail. So the Memory Chamber has rules. It can draw upon a library of stock-material to colour the scene, but it cannot add new particulars.

On the pavement on the north side of Oxford Street, I bought Elenora a woolly pom-pom

hat with a holly motif. She pulled it over
her ears and gave a comedy pout, then she
kissed me firmly on the lips. 'That was my
moment,' she said. I asked her, 'What moment?'
and she said, 'That was the moment when
I realised that you and I are going to live
together, have kids together, grow old
together and die together.' Then she linked
arms with me and we walked down the street
towards Oxford Circus.

14

LONDON

There was a day in May 1973, when Max and I and a dozen or so of his friends descended on the captain's apartment in Dorset Square for a hedonistic weekend. Our intention was to unwind with generous helpings of alcohol, marijuana, intellectual banter, and close proximity to individuals of the opposite gender. We were eighteen. Max had hosted these weekends once or twice a term since we'd been in the sixth form, and they generally followed much the same order of service. The captain was absent, as he invariably was, and only the watchful presence of Mrs Drabble kept our behaviour moderately in check. I brought my guitar, at Max's request, and we all sprawled in the front room making music, rolling reefers and eating toast.

I can no longer remember the roll call of everyone there. Some were regulars at the apartment, part of Max's circle, if he could ever have been said to *have* a circle. Some people drifted in and later disappeared. Of the ones that I can remember that May weekend, one couple made straight for the bedroom and spent the best part of the time shagging. There was an Iranian guy – an earnest communist called Mohammed Hussein Moussavi – who was reading philosophy at Cambridge with Max, and Mohammed's girlfriend, whose name I no longer remember, but who had curly blonde hair, and who kept taking tabs of acid and was generally off somewhere on a high of her own. There were a couple of long-haired guys with bushy sideburns from Caius; one played a mean harmonica and the other played bass guitar. There was Davy Morris, Max's friend from Eton, who wore goldfish-bowl glasses, and his Australian girlfriend who sang vocal harmonies. There was an Irish girl called Patty, with wide brown eyes and a surprised expression, who wore a sheepskin kaftan and had an infectious laugh. She was a friend of the Ponders, apparently. There was my friend Moira from Keele, who wasn't really my girlfriend but who was generally happy playing that role as long as I didn't get serious. And there was Elenora Twist, Max's girlfriend from Cambridge. There was also an Indian guy called Ravi who had something to do with the captain's business interests in New Delhi, and who just happened to be staying at the apartment that weekend as a guest of the family. He was a whole lot older than us, but he seemed so happy to be included in Max's party that we all relaxed and accepted him. Pretty soon he was just one of the crowd and, not long after, he bunked off with Patty, who never lost her expression of surprise.

What did we do that weekend? We hung out, that was what we did. A bunch of us took a taxi up to Highgate to visit Karl Marx's tomb and Mohammed laid some flowers. Later, some of the party went into town, hoping to see a show, but they ended up in a West End pub and came back bladdered. Max didn't go out at all. He rarely did. Instead, he stayed at the flat being mine host. I remember he was a little pale that weekend. He'd just come back from a trip to Rome – the trip during which he'd bought his Breitling watch – and he'd eaten some dodgy pasta, or maybe he had a cold. I played a little guitar with the guys from Caius and Moira sang when she could remember the lyrics and Davy Morris's Australian girlfriend sang harmony. Mrs Drabble cooked up a huge pan of scrambled eggs. Mohammed and his spaced-out blonde talked earnestly about Trotsky, and the couple in the bedroom fucked each other. Elenora smoked a lot of dope and wandered around the apartment with her tits out. It seemed pretty normal.

The sleeping arrangements for the weekend were fairly ad hoc. There were four bedrooms in the apartment but one, of course, was reserved for Mrs Drabble. The master bedroom was taken by the couple who spent the weekend in flagrante, and the other double was occupied by Max and Elenora. That left a room with two single beds that had been promised to Moira and me, except that Ravi had already made himself at home in that room and no one wanted to chuck him out. So there was one spare bed for anyone prepared to share the room with Ravi, and after some discussion that bed went to Patty, who by all accounts ended up wasting her single bed, spending most of

Saturday night tucked in with Ravi. The rest of us slept on sofas, or dangling over armchairs, or on the floor. Moira and I hadn't brought sleeping bags so we hunkered down on the hearth rug under a spare eiderdown.

By tradition, the Dorset Square weekends began on Friday night with some heavy drinking and rowdiness, and meandered through to Sunday evening with most of the time spent recovering from a hangover or tanking up for one. The nights went on late and the days began around lunchtime with breakfast for the early risers. By Sunday evening most of the crowd should have left and gone home. By tradition also, Sunday night was *our* time. Max and I would hang on for the extra night even though he'd be late back at Eton or late for a tutorial at Cambridge and I'd earn a reprimand for missing a night at school, or else miss a nine o'clock lecture at Keele. Anyway. We used the time to catch up. We used the time to waste away hours at the Bear and Staff pub, just around the corner from the apartment, and there we would drink beer and talk about girls and exhibit our laddish humour.

This Sunday, however, there were four of us: Max and Elenora and me and Ravi. It wasn't the same. We did some half-hearted cleaning up, then we slumped. It was 27 May 1973. Max and I had been at university for two and a half-terms and we were still trying to keep our friendship going despite five years' separation at different schools in different counties, despite the fact that we no longer shared the same interests, the same friends, the same tastes in music.

Elenora made a herbal tea that probably contained hashish, then we sat and contemplated. Max had a way of sitting cross-legged like a guru. He was doing that and talking about philosophers.

'Do you know what I like about Descartes?' Max asked the world. 'First of all, he has a great adjective based on his name.'

'All philosophers do,' Ravi objected.

'Yes, they do. Platonic is a good one, isn't it? Then there are all the "ians" – Aristotelian, Freudian, Jungian. But Descartes gets "Cartesian". How did that happen?'

'Surely they don't *all* get adjectives?' I asked.

'Sure they do. It's a perk of the job.'

'What about Wittgenstein?'

'Who was a fellow of Trinity College. Did you know that? Wittgensteinian.'

'Quite a mouthful.'

'He also worked in the path lab at Newcastle's Royal Victoria Hospital in 1942 on wages of four pounds a week. He probably wouldn't have appreciated Wittgensteinian as an adjective though. He held that words were no more than ambiguous symbols.'

'I see. And the other thing about Descartes?'

'Ah yes. George Bernard Shaw, by the way – not strictly a philosopher, but his adjective is "Shavian". How did he get that?'

'I've no idea.'

'Maybe Shawian was too unpronounceable.'

'Probably.'

'When I become a famous philosopher, I want something more individual than "Ponderian".'

'You could always have "Ponderous",' said Ravi.

'Fuck off,' said Max.

'Ponderosan,' I suggested.

'You can fuck off too, Last. I want *Ponderic*.'

'You were saying something about Descartes?'

'Ah yes. Well he kind of founded rationalism.'

'And that's the other interesting thing about him?'

'Yes.'

Ravi lowered himself into one of the armchairs. 'He also invented graphs.'

'Graphs?'

'Yes indeed. He was the founder of the principle of Cartesian coordinates. Named after him, you see. He invented the idea one day while lying in bed, watching a fly on his ceiling. He thought, 'Aha – I can plot the position of the fly if I know how far down one wall he is – the x axis – and how far up the other wall – the y axis. And hey presto, he had invented graphs.'

'That was the other interesting thing about Descartes,' said Max. 'He got his inspiration from flies.'

'And from sitting in an oven,' said Ravi. 'When he wasn't watching flies he would sit in an oven and think.'

During all of this, Elenora was browsing the books on the captain's shelves, affecting ignorance of the conversation. She drew out a volume and held it up. 'Here's a game,' she announced. She came and sat alongside me on the sofa.

'I don't like games,' protested Max.

'Then it isn't a game. It's a piece of research.' She opened the book on her knee. '*The International Film Guide* by Peter Gowland,' she read. 'Published 1972.'

'That isn't a game,' said Max, 'it's a film guide.'

'I know it's a film guide, stupid,' said Elenora. 'I'm going to use it to calculate how many films you've seen in your life.'

'What? You mean my *whole* life?'

'Your *whole* life. OK, this is how it works. This guide lists 4,500 films. Now, we'll start by assuming that every film you've ever seen is listed in here.'

'Well, that's a crap assumption for a start,' declared Max.

'No it isn't. This is a comprehensive guide to all English language films that have been on public release since god knows when. So, I'm going to read you a random sample of one hundred titles and you need to tell me if you've seen each film or not. Then, at the end, we multiply the number you've seen by forty-five and that is the number of films you've seen in your life.'

'I don't get it,' I said, too slow at maths, 'why multiply by forty-five?'

'Because there are four and a half thousand films in the book,' explained Ravi, 'And we are taking a sample of one hundred. One forty-fifth.'

'I see.'

'It wouldn't work for me,' said Ravi, 'I've seen mainly Indian films and they won't be listed.'

'No,' said Elenora, 'you're right. You could go though all four thousand odd films and count the ones you've seen. Or you can take a smaller sample and multiply up.'

Max was suddenly transfixed. 'I like the sound of this,' he said enthusiastically. 'Let's do it.'

That was all the encouragement Elenora needed. She started to open random pages, shutting her eyes, and stabbing the page with a finger, then reading out the film titles. With each one, Max became more animated.

'*The Great Escape*?'

'YES, of course! Who hasn't? Steve McQueen and the motorbike.'

'That's one out of one. *Barney and the Motorbike*? Hey – another motorbike!'

'Never heard of it.'

'It's a 1936 film by Dominic Rodea.'

'Never heard of him either.'

'*The Maltese Falcon*?'

'Heard of it, but never seen it,' said Max. 'Humphrey Bogart and that other guy.'

'Alan Ladd?'

'That's the guy. And Lauren Bacall, of course. It's a Philip Marlowe novel. *The Maltese Falcon* is some kind of statuette. Amazing how much stuff you absorb culturally about a film you've never *seen*. Does that count though?'

'No. One out of three,' said Elenora.

'Even though I can practically tell you everything about it?' asked Max. 'I bet it had Peter Lorre in it too.'

'It didn't. *The Long Weekend*?'

'No. I know it won an Oscar though.'

'*The Great Waldo Pepper*?'

'No.'

'*North by North West*?'

'Are you kidding? I've seen every film Hitchcock ever made.'

In Nairobi, when Max and I first met, in the days before TV invaded our world, the best access we had to films was the drive-in cinema on the Thika Road. In fact, the drive-in was *way* better than TV. My parents weren't particularly cinema folk – there was, after all, a hint of the irreligious about Hollywood that would have offended my mother – but the captain and O were cineastes. We would bundle into their Vauxhall Velox and set off in the evenings to the drive-in, stopping to collect a raft of our friends along the way. We saw some great films back then: epics like *Ben Hur* and *Spartacus* and *El Cid*, *The Magnificent Seven*, *Lawrence of Arabia*, and *Around the World in Eighty Days*. We saw comedies like *Those Magnificent Men in their Flying Machines*. We saw westerns long forgotten, and war films, and romances. There was always a B feature. And we nearly always went in convoy with the Ponders' friends in their trucks and sedans.

Drive-ins are a great way to watch movies. You wait until dark and then congregate in a riot of cars in a huge parking lot in front of a massive screen, and a crackly speaker is thrust through your window, and there you can sit safely scoffing popcorn and engaging in noisy ribaldry without offending other viewers. The captain and O would generously take the back seat and we boys would crush in along the front seat to watch mesmerised through the windscreen. Smoke would curl up from the captain's pipe and O's Russian cigarettes, but it didn't bother us. Vendors would knock on the windows selling hotdogs and cashew nuts and slices of pineapple and barbecued corncobs. Teenagers in the cars alongside would wrap limbs around each other and the windows would steam up. It was a joyous, magical occasion, and a great way to discover film. The projector beam would light up at the back of the lot to a chorus of approving hoots, and someone would adjust the volume on the speakers and then we'd be away, lost in another world.

And so it was that Max and I discovered cinema together. We discovered Johnny Weissmuller's *Tarzan*, and John Wayne's slow-talking cowboy, and Errol Flynn's *Robin Hood*. The drive-in didn't just show new releases, it showed classics from the forties and fifties too, and Max and I didn't care what the feature was; the *event* was the visit to the drive-in.

So Elenora's survey of Max's cinema experience was broadly the same as mine, film for film, until we drifted apart in our teens and made new lives in England.

'*Performance*?' Elenora asked.

'Seen it,' I said.

'I haven't,' said Max.

And there you had it, a measure of our continental drift.

We grew bored long before we'd reached one hundred films, but Ravi did the maths for us anyway, even told us the ninety-five per cent probability range based upon sample size. I can't remember the outcome, but I do remember that Max and I had seen several hundred films apiece – and this in the days before videos or DVDs or Internet downloads. And I would probably have forgotten about this little survey of Elenora's, or just dismissed it as a game, except for the fact that Max had clearly drawn more from the experiment than Elenora had intended. When we'd finished up and written down the scores, Max leapt to his feet, inspired.

'You could use this,' he cried, 'for just about anything. You could use it to find out how many books you've ever read.'

'Only if you had a complete catalogue of books,' said Ravi, bemused by Max's enthusiasm.

'Of course,' said Max, 'but you could use it for how many countries you'd visited, for example.'

'But you wouldn't *need* to,' I said. 'Most people can list the countries they've visited on one hand.'

'OK – how many words do you know then? Hmm?' He strode to a shelf and pulled down a fat dictionary. 'I'll read out some words at random and you tell me if you know them.'

'Max I don't want to play this,' said Elenora, disturbed by the direction the conversation had taken.

'You would need to know how many words are in the dictionary to start off with,' said Ravi, 'or else you won't be able to do the calculation.'

'And what constitutes a "word" anyway?' asked Elenora. 'Is "fuck" a word? I bet it isn't in there.'

'It is,' said Max triumphantly, flicking through the pages.

'OK – what about "fucking", what about "fuckers", what about "fuckable" and "fuckwit"?'

'OK, OK!' Max threw down the dictionary. 'Not words then. But just about anything else that you could list. Philosphers. Poems. LPs. French irregular verbs. Cricketers. You could catalogue a whole brain this way, just by sampling. That's what I'll do for my philosophy project.'

Elenora shot me a glance and I looked up at Max. 'Good idea,' I said. 'Although, it isn't exactly philosophy, is it?'

'Not exactly philosophy? Of course it's philosophy. Philosophy means the love of knowledge, but how do we quantify knowledge? Well? That's what I'm going to do.'

'Right.'

'I'm going to pick a person – I'm going to pick you, Adam, because you're my mate and I know you won't mind – and I'm going to quantify the contents of your brain. I'm going to break it down into as many categories of things I can devise and I'm going to source master lists from the library, and then I'm going to give you samples, just like we did with the films. Ravi can do the maths. And at the end of it we'll know exactly how much you know. It'll be brilliant! I'll call it, "A Snapshot of a Human Brain".'

'Max, I don't know,' I protested, 'how long will this all take? I mean, I'm in Keele and you're in Cambridge and ...'

'We can do it by post,' continued Max, unabated. 'I could send you lists of, say, a thousand Spanish nouns and you simply tick the ones you recognise. Then I multiply it all up and conclude that you can understand forty-seven words of Spanish. And we could do the same for German. Russian. Latin. The list is endless.'

'Yes,' I said, 'it's the very endlessness of the list that worries me.'

'This could replace exams, you know.' Max suddenly sounded serious. 'Why set dull exam essays for students when you could sample their knowledge using a simple survey?'

'Because they could always lie,' said Ravi, amiably, 'and tick every one.'

'Good point. You'd need to mix in a number of dummy items. In fact, I'll do that with you, Adam. We have to be sure you don't lie to try to impress us with how much you know.'

'I wouldn't lie,' I said indignantly.

'Of course not,' said Max, then he suddenly slapped his forehead. 'How stupid of me. I don't need to use you, Adam, do I? You're right. It would be too hard to orchestrate between Cambridge and Keele, even with a reliable postal service. Besides, it would cost us a fortune in stamps.'

'You're not using me,' said Elenora, firmly.

'Don't worry, my little flower petal,' said Max, 'I won't need to use you either. I'll use *myself*!'

15

ONE CALENDAR MONTH

Here are some more of Max's musings from volume I. I like volume I. It is still full of optimism and flights of fancy. During that first month in The Pile when Max was developing his routine, and I was developing mine, it did seem as if we were embarking on a great voyage of scientific exploration. We knew the basic rules. Max would spend the days writing and recording his memories; I would protect him from all external influences. I had a real job, a day job, managing Ponder Estates. (I may need to explain that to the police too, in case they think I was just a freeloader in this whole affair). I had a real office – the small suite of rooms in the gate-house at The Pile that used to be Tutton's apartment – and this is where I worked. But my evenings and weekends and spare hours would be spent at The Pile. We knew exactly how long the whole enterprise would take – thirty-six months. That would be more than enough time for Max to disgorge every atom of memory from his brain onto the page. Thirty-six months didn't seem unreasonably long, given the huge scientific and philosophical import of the project. Elenora would visit regularly and provide Max with some physical comfort, and when the whole deed was done we would throw a huge party, invite Max's friends from Cambridge, Max and Elenora would announce their engagement, and I would continue as the manager of Ponder Estates with whatever life I might have managed to build for myself in the intervening three years.

It was all much more relaxed then. Max wanted seclusion so that his memory wouldn't be polluted by contemporary events. At the beginning he was easy enough about visitors, and would work in the library with the curtains open so that he could see the river and watch the pleasure boats go past. We even had a telephone in The Pile then. It seems hard to believe now.

I'm not sure quite how or when things started becoming less comfortable. It certainly wasn't in month one; although, now I come to think of it, right from the beginning Max was a little edgy about having too much going on around him. The turning point may have been in September 1975, month three, when I rather carelessly came into the library carrying a newspaper with a front-page report of a bombing at the London Hilton. I had intended to settle down and read the paper while Max worked.

Max caught sight of the newspaper and was livid. 'For god's sake, Adam, are you a complete imbecile? What the hell do you think you're doing bringing that in here?'

'You don't have to look at it,' I defended myself.

'How can I avoid looking at it? Look, if this project is to stand any chance of working then I have to be completely insulated from the outside world. Don't you see that?'

'Well yes, but …'

'I'm getting sick and tired of spending the whole day writing stuff in my day log when I should be working on The Catalogue. It's going to take me half an hour to write down what I've just read on the front page of that damn paper and to set down this conversation. So no "buts". No newspapers. And get that damn phone disconnected. It rang today for about twenty minutes and when I finally answered, it was someone from the office wanting my signature on some document, and *you're* supposed to be looking after that side of things.'

'OK, OK. I shall disconnect the phone.'

'Good.' Max stood up and walked over to the bay windows that looked out over the neat lawn with its croquet hoops and stone sundial, the gravel walks, and the trimmed shrubbery, down to the apple orchard where the bones of Libby the dog lay buried, and further to the great weeping willows that overhung the river bank, dangling their fingers of green into the water, and then the river itself, and beyond the river to the meadows and distant church spires of Buckinghamshire. A men's-eight rowing boat scudded rapidly past. It may have been the Oxford crew out training. Two oar-strokes and the boat was gone leaving just a wake behind and a disturbed swan who turned her neck to watch it pass. Max surveyed all this for the briefest of moments and then he pulled the curtains, shutting the room into semi-darkness.

'I don't want any external influences at all,' he said decisively.

I think that was the last time he ever looked out at that view in daylight.

VOLUME I
JULY 1975

I wonder how many different types of memory
there are? I can think of a few. If you were
to ask me now, 'what is the highest mountain
in the world?' I'd answer 'Everest' and I'd
give you that answer in a heartbeat. I would
barely have to think about it. It would be a
reflex answer. You could probably do the same.
That is real, instantly accessible memory,
an archive of cross-referenced facts and
figures like a mental encyclopaedia, available
to us any time we want it. It is, if you
like, in the top drawer of the mental cabinet.
Curiously, however, if you were to ask me,
'what is the highest mountain in Nepal?' then
it would take me fractionally longer to
answer. I guess that is because instead of
retrieving one file from the top drawer of the
cabinet - the file marked 'world's highest
mountain' - I'm now going down a decision
tree which says: (1) Ooh . . . is this a trick
question? (2) Do I know any mountains in
Nepal? (3) Isn't Everest in Nepal? (4) Of
course it is (5) Or is it in Tibet? (6) No -
I'm sure it *is* in Nepal. Actually, I think
it straddles the border. That must mean
Everest is still the answer (6) Everest. What
this tells me is that memory involves all
sorts of cross-wiring and quality control
before it bubbles up to the surface. In the
first case I'm accessing what my brain thinks

are solid facts and in the second I'm having
to check the facts against a rather more
nebulous piece of knowledge - the knowledge
that Everest is in Nepal - and that piece of
knowledge is in the third drawer down on the
left-hand side, over by the drinks cabinet.
Metaphorically speaking.

Actually, when we speak about memory, it
all tends to be metaphorical anyway. What
are we doing when we retrieve 'Everest' from
the drawer? And what about those nuggets of
data that are there somewhere in the miasma
of memory but don't seem to want to be found?
Who was that actor in that soap commercial -
you know - the one who was in that programme
about wildebeest castration? The one with the
face? What was his wretched name? It is on
the tip of my tongue. It'll come to me.

When I was trying to quantify my memory
from tabulated lists, such as the
International Film Guide, I soon came across
a problem. It was easy enough with *Duck Soup*.
Great Film. Seen it three times at least.
Groucho Marx is Rufus T. Firefly, the corrupt
president of a Ruritanean republic, and
Margaret Dumont is, as usual, the reluctant
love interest. The film has one of the best
comic scenes in cinema, that bit when Groucho
in his nightshirt meets his doppelganger on
the other side of (what used to be) a mirror.
But what about *Horse Feathers*? Have I seen it
or haven't I? I know that I've seen lots of
Marx Brothers' films - we used to catch them
at the drive-in on the Thika Road, O and the
captain and Adam and I. Hey ho. What times
those were. But still. Did we catch *Horse
Feathers*? It isn't the one with the train,
that's *Go West*. It isn't the one at the

opera. That's *Night at the Opera*. Obviously.
It isn't even the one at the horse races
because that one is - surprise - *Day at the
Races*. So do I mark it as a 'Not seen?'
Strictly speaking, I should. But here comes
the crunch. Supposing you were to have this
conversation with me, and supposing you
described a scene from *Horse Feathers*, and
supposing I immediately recognised it. What
then? And this isn't a theoretical problem
related to just one Marx Brothers' film. It is
a fundamental problem that straddles my whole
project and relates to a whole category of
memory that we don't like to think about;
that is, memory that you have but that you've
forgotten you have. This is the involuntary
memory that Proust wrote about. The file is in
the drawer but the label is missing. Pull
out the unlabelled file and aha! Of course.
You remember it *now*. But leave the file in
the drawer and you don't even know it is
there.

Spooky.

Let's think of another example. Ask me if
I know the Swahili word for 'friend'. Actually
I do know it - and of course if I *didn't,*
then I couldn't give you the example. But a
few months ago, someone asked me to say
something in Swahili, the way that people
sometimes do when you tell them you used to
live somewhere exotic. I said, 'but what do
you want me to say?' And she suggested, 'you
are my friend'. But, damn me, I didn't know
the word. I strained and I sweated. I lay
awake at night. I tried going through the
alphabet in search of a prompt. But no, the
word wasn't there. Once, in the distant past,
I had known it, and now I didn't. I became

convinced that if I ever heard the word again
it would seem quite unfamiliar. I'd look it
up in an English–Swahili dictionary and say,
'wapukiloni – well hey, I don't know if I ever
knew that.' Or maybe there was no such word
in Swahili. Maybe the concept of a 'friend'
couldn't be concentrated into a single word
and maybe they would say 'a person with whom
I like to spend my time'. But then, out of
the blue, I was on a bus in London and two
African guys sat in front of me, and lo-and-
behold they were chatting away in Swahili. My
radar tuned in, as it does, and then, like a
bloody great tsunami, this word emerged in
slow motion and came thundering through the
ether towards me, a suffocating deluge of a
word, a word that slapped me across the face
like a saltwater surge, and the word was –
'rafiki'. Now, I can honestly swear that you
could have strapped me naked to a wheel and
threatened to apply ten thousand volts to my
bollocks and you couldn't have coaxed that
three-syllable word out of my sluggard brain.
And yet it was there all along. Maybe a
hypnotist could have wheedled it out, but
I doubt it. I had archived it in a file
labelled, 'Never to be Needed Again'. And
there it had languished for years, a useless,
unnecessary memory, occupying space in the
memory bank but never used, like a shrunken
jumper that hangs forlornly at the back of
an attic wardrobe.

Now, here again is the thing. How much stuff
do we have locked up like that? The answer,
mercifully, is loads and loads and loads.
Positively gargantuan quantities of data. My
personal feeling now is that all the minutiae
of every single conscious day are in there

somewhere. All the conversations you have ever had; all the people you ever met; all the things you ever heard; every word you ever read. Maybe the information degrades very slowly over time, like snapshots fading in an album. But I bet it's all there. So sometimes you turn on the telly and you watch, only half concentrating and suddenly, this seems familiar, and guess what . . . it's a film you saw years ago. And now, all of a sudden, you remember what happens next.

Thank god we can't access all this stuff. Can you imagine what it would be like to remember everything in your top-drawer memory? A policemen would ask you where you were on Thursday 27 March ten years ago at 3.00 p.m. and you'd say 'standing on the corner of Church Street and the park waiting for a blue Volkswagen to pass so that I could cross the road.' Phew. Somewhere, there must be aliens who have brains like that.

Do you have a memory for jokes? I'll find myself sitting in a pub with a whole crowd of friends and after a few beers someone will tell a joke. And then another chap will tell a joke. And before long everyone has a joke they want to share. And of the jokes they tell, at least half are jokes where I already know what the punchline will be. More. Probably seventy-five per cent. And yet, here is that brain thing again – all this time I'm sitting there trying to think of a joke to tell and, god help me, I don't have a single joke in my brain. Not one lousy, unfunny joke. Except perhaps the one about the fellow who is queuing to see St Peter, you know the one, it takes ages to tell, and it isn't really funny anyway, and in the end

he was 'in this fridge', and I only know the
damn joke because it's the only one I ever
tell, and I can't tell it any more because
everybody knows it. So what does my brain do
with all the rest of the jokes I hear? Where
does it file them? Why doesn't my brain have
an archive called 'jokes' in which every
funny story I have ever heard is carefully
catalogued for fast retrieval should the need
arise?

Anyway, I decided that the original brain
measure based on the *International Film Guide*
was never going to work. It would measure the
stuff in the top drawer, and some of the
stuff in the archive and, in the end, what
was it a measurement of? It wouldn't be a
measure of my memory. It would only be a
measure of how often I've been to the cinema
because ultimately every film I've ever seen
is stored in my mind somewhere – and who
would be interested in how many times
Maximilian Ponder has been to the cinema?
Not even me. What interests me is how much
I really remember from all those hours spent
sitting in front of the screen. How much have
I retained? That is why I had to scrap the
film guide approach. What I needed wasn't a
sampling technique. I needed a way to measure
the things I really know. All the bits and
pieces that I haven't archived. All the Mount
Everests and the *Duck Soup*s and the Swahili
nouns. So, welcome to volume one. I aim to be
the first person ever to take a detailed
inventory of every fact and statistic and
atom and iota of memory in my poor, addled
brain.

And here is the twist. If I can't remember

a fact in one calendar month, then I'm going
to say it simply isn't there.

One calendar month. That should be time
enough to shuffle through the brain's cardex
system. I'm going to start each month with a
list of facts that I need to try to recover
from the central archive somewhere in my
medulla oblongata, or wherever it is in that
grey lump of goo that sits between my ears
and behind my eyes. Then any facts that
I can't recall in a month simply aren't there.

I don't know why I didn't think of it
before.

Some of the facts are going to be boring
lists. Lists of dog breeds with descriptions:
the Golden Retriever – a gun dog standing
about two feet high, with yellowish brown
fur, a pleasant temperament, a longish tail.
The Dachshund – a little dog with short legs,
short, black fur with some light brown around
the underside, maybe about six to eight
inches high, pointy face. The French Poodle
. . . Well, you get the idea.

There's going to have to be an autobiography
in here. That is going to take more than a
month. I plan to write a chapter of the
autobiography each month. And a big chunk of
each month will simply be a narrative. This
sort of thing.

Places will be a weird thing to record. You
know how some places, especially childhood
places, are so familiar, so engraved in the
memory that you seem to know every tree,
every paving stone, every sign. I could walk
down the lane from The Pile into Marlow and
every step would be so well known to me that
I could tell you if someone had rearranged
the ornaments in a window of any house along

the route, or repainted a gate, or bought a new car. I daresay there are places where you could do the same. Now, here's a thing: I feel as if I could do much the same for Eastlands in the mid-sixties, or for big chunks of Nairobi. That's the way memory works. If I were to be dropped back onto, say, Kenyatta Avenue in 1968, I know it would all be there in my brain somewhere. Yet when we revisit a place from our childhood, even a place that hasn't changed much such as a beach or a park, it isn't really the same as we remember, is it? Maybe memory mutates slowly like DNA. Perhaps every year, say, five per cent of the memory atoms simply flip; so a memory that says 'this wall is green' suddenly mutates to one that says 'this wall is brown', and another memory atom that says 'this house has a wooden gate' simply disappears. If this were true, it would mean that if you were to revisit a place after ten years, only fifty per cent of your memory would be accurate, and if you were to go back after twenty years, it would seem to have changed almost beyond recognition. Since I'm only twenty-one, perhaps this is something I could test once this project is over. When I complete the catalogue, in three years' time, I could start to revisit places I will have described in detail, and I shall be able to compare the way they are, in reality, with the way I have recorded them.

Then, how will I describe all the people I know? I can't just settle for a list of names: Mickey Migdoll, Peter Gerstrom, Eileen Kenny, Richard Nightingale – that's a meaningless list. No. I shall have to develop a pen portrait of each and every one. So,

let's try an easy one just to start with:
Wolfgang Koch [WOLFGANG 01]. I only ever met
him one time - one spring - so he is easy to
capture, and I don't remember much about him,
although I did get to see his dick.

He stayed with us at the Youth Hostel in
Fontainebleu, but we had met him in Paris
before that. It was in April 1970, when Adam
and I were fifteen. We were hitch-hiking
around Europe at the time. These were the
days when both our families were still in
Africa, while Max and I were at school in
England. We would spend Christmas and Summer
in Kenya with our families, but the spring
holiday was a time to go travelling. The plan
was to get to the French Alps to do some
skiing. That was the time we spent a night
in the prison cells in the Bois du Boulogne,
a dodgy quarter of Paris. And this came about
because it was Easter, and all of the cheap
hotels were full, and we couldn't get into
the *auberge de la jeunesse*, and it was
snowing, so we had tried to sleep on a Metro
platform. The gendarmes had hauled us off,
and chucked us into a cell with one other
occupant, and this other occupant was not
happy to be woken at one in the morning and
relieved of two of his three blankets on such
a cold night to help warm up two filthy English
hippies. Anyway, this was Wolfgang. By the
morning he had forgiven us. He was a German
student, about twenty years old, with wild,
black hair and a slight moustache, and only
a half-grasp of English. When the gendarmes
released us at about 6.00 a.m., they also
released Wolfgang and we stuck with him all
the way out of Paris on a bus to Fontainebleu.
He did a kind of twisted tour-guide commentary

for us, often lapsing into big chunks of
German that we didn't understand. '*Zis ist
der gevurisher gristenburker shop vith ze
gurdy vurdy vomen wiz ze big, bouncy titties
und de burgy burgy burgies.*'

'Yes, Wolfgang. Thank you for that
illuminating guidance.'

'*Und over zehr – zat is de futball stadze.*'

Now look what I'm doing. I'm <u>making stuff
up</u> that isn't strictly part of my memory.
I'm trying to illustrate the sort of things
Wolfgang was saying, but I'm having to do it
by invention and <u>that</u> is going to be firmly
against the rules from now on. If you chop
off my head and centrifuge the contents and
distil my memory molecules down, you'll never
find one that says '*burgy burgy burgies*'
because Wolfgang never actually said that.
Only that was what he was <u>like</u>. So how, in
god's name, am I going to deal with
conversation? How many conversations do you
really remember word for word?

And now, all of a sudden, here's another
problem. I do have a memory molecule that
says '*burgy burgy burgies*', and it is the
memory that I have just created by writing it
down here in volume I.

Damnit. This is going to be harder than
I thought.

Wolfgang wore a red-check shirt, the kind
a lumberjack might wear, and a grey, hooded
duffel coat. Adam and I had rucksacks, but he
had a little aluminium suitcase that looked
rather ridiculous. When we got to the hostel
at Fontainebleu, we pooled resources for
dinner, bought provisions from a boucherie,
and Wolfgang did the cooking. We stood in
the little communal galley kitchen at the

hostel and watched him fry up some German sausage, giving us his half-English commentary as he did.

There were two American girls in the lobby with oversized rucksacks. We had passed them as they struggled to dismount their baggage. Now they peered through into the kitchen and seemed to mistake Wolfgang for the resident chef.

'Are you guys like making the meal?' asked one.

'Yeuggh,' said the other when she saw the sausages.

'Could you just cook me an egg?' said the first, a little sourly.

Wolfgang shot me a mischievous expression.

'Me too,' said the second. 'Could you just do me an egg?'

Adam looked as if he was about to say something, but Wolfgang piped up, 'Sure, two eggs. How vould you like zem cooked?'

'Over easy,' said one.

'Sunny side up,' said the other.

'Vould you like some toast viz ze eggs?'

'Sure yeah. Brown please.'

'Do you have white? I'll have white if you have it.'

'Vould you like a glass of Coca-cola?'

'That would be good.'

'You sit down. I vill get one of ze vaiters to bring it.' He glanced at Adam and me. We were to be his vaiters. When we were alone, he cracked a couple of eggs into a pan.

'You're really going to make them their eggs?' I asked him.

'Sure.' He opened our precious cans of Coca-cola. Then he found two glasses and filled them.

'I'll take them through,' said Adam.

'Vun minute,' said Wolfgang, 'I am not done.' He reached down and undid the zip of his trousers, and then he pulled out his dick. I remember it was a distastefully large thing, fat, pale, uncircumcised, extravagantly pointed. He dangled it into one of the glasses of Coke, and then used it to give the second a stir. Then, tucking his wet dick away, he passed the glasses to Adam. 'Now you can take zem,' he said.

16

THE FENCING MATCH

Well, I've done it. In the end I used the rough-wood saw from the log shed. I didn't recognise a single muscle. I started by putting a canvas draw-string bag over Max's head, the one that I'd bought for this very task. Then I used two leather belts as tourniquets, making tight new holes for the buckles, took a very deep breath, and pulled both belts taut around Max's neck. I sawed hard between them, and I did it all without stopping for air. It was a whole lot worse than breaking the legs of a dead dog. Despite the tourniquets, lots of blood still went on the towels, quite a bit made it to the table, and some even ended up on the carpet, but what the heck? I'm not trying to conceal a crime here. I'm not going to try to hide the fact that I've just sawed off the head of my friend with a rough-wood saw. The whole point is that it *had* to be done. So much for the levator scapulae, the sternothyoideus, and the sternocleidomastoid. Under assault from a heavy saw they are nothing more than pink meat.

I feel a little sick, but proud of myself. It wasn't the surgically precise decapitation that I had planned, but the outcome was the same. I sealed Max's head, still covered by the drawstring bag, in a huge polythene freezer bag, placed it into a cool box, and packed it with ice from the freezer. Then I took it out to my car and put the box on the back seat, reflecting wryly that this was the first time Max had left The Pile in three decades.

I drove to a lock-up garage in Henley-on-Thames. It is a premises owned by Ponder Estates, part of the property portfolio that I manage, but it is not a property that you will easily find on any company paperwork. The licensed owner is a holding company in Mumbai, which itself is owned by a property management company in the Isle of Man, and that company is owned by Ponder Estates.

I daresay a diligent detective could follow the trail, but not without some complicated warrants and plenty of air miles.

I keep very little in the lock-up garage, except for a set of commercial freezing equipment, a back-up generator, and some batteries. The whole unit, you see, has been equipped for this purpose, and this alone.

I took Max's head out of the box, dropped it into a foil bag, and vacuum-sealed it. Then I lowered it carefully, using wooden tongs, into a flask of liquid nitrogen, which boiled violently on cue. Despite everything that Max believed, I knew that this would damage his brain more than it would preserve it. Nitrogen is liquid at around $-200°C$. This is so cold that it will freeze a five kilogram head and brain incredibly fast, and this will create needle-sharp crystals in every cell that will tear the brain apart. Any scientist who wants to thaw and examine Maximilian Ponder's notable brain will discover an organ as soft as French cheese or the flesh of a defrosted strawberry.

I'm back now, at The Pile. It's dusk. I've pulled open the curtains in the library, and the warm glow of a June sunset fills the room for the first time in thirty years.

Now that the unpleasant business of decapitation and cryogenics is complete, I have the courage to record more about that day in 1974 when we buried the dog. Let me pick the story up where I left off.

We left Libby in the ground, and made our way back up the garden to the house. I went to get washed. I was the one with the soil on his hands.

Later, we sat in the drawing room sipping champagne. Max perched on the edge of the captain's chair. His jitters had disappeared. Aunt Zinnia and the captain were strangely distant. Zinnia sat deep in an armchair, brooding.

Let me tell you some more about Aunt Zinnia. She does, after all, play a part in this story. Aunt Zinnia wore her dark hair like Joan Baez, in the style of an ageing hippy, parted in the middle, long, and badly brushed. She'd developed a pout since I'd last seen her, a belligerent pursing of the lips, and an insouciant expression that seemed to convey a sense of hurt. She was a few years younger than the captain, so she must have been forty-six or forty-seven or so, yet she dressed like a Woodstock teenager. She was wearing flared jeans that day, a cheesecloth shirt, and a cambric smock that was too large for her slight frame. She would forever be a solitary twin now, one half of a set, like a singular bookend. Uncle Martin, I had learned, lay in the graveyard at Marlow. He'd been dead a year. Max had told me about the crash, and I hadn't given it much thought until my conversation with the captain. A car crash is a car crash.

But maybe the police know more. I can't imagine it could be relevant unless they hope to establish some family pattern of suicide. And even then, as I say, it wouldn't be relevant. Max wasn't suicidal or depressed. He was driven.

Could I have said something then about the captain's condition, as we sat and quaffed champagne? Should I? I tried once or twice to catch the captain's eye, but he appeared to be avoiding me. Whatever he had said to me, down in the orchard, he seemed to believe that it was enough. I could have said, 'Max, your father has something to tell you,' and that, perhaps, would have goaded the truth out of the captain. I could have said, 'Max, *I* have something to tell you. Your father is dying. He has a hideous inherited disease that will slowly mash up his brain. In just a few decades, the same thing will probably happen to you.' Ridiculous. How could I have shattered this little Ponder montage with such devastating news? Besides, it had been a confidence, and I knew Max well enough to understand why the captain wanted to keep the truth from him.

Eventually, after we had downed a bottle of champagne, Max drifted over to where I sat toying with my empty glass.

'Do you want to come up?' he asked.

'OK.'

I got up, nodded politely to Aunt Zinnia and to the captain and followed Max upstairs to his room, which turned out to consist of half of the attic. I don't remember too much about the room as it was, and that may be because over the years I have become too familiar with the room as it is *now* – because now, today, this room is *my* room. I could say it is my apartment. I have a permanent bed here and some clothes. I don't live here, not really, but I have spent a lot of nights in this place over the thirty years that Max has been incarcerated in The Pile. So if I have to describe the room as it was *that* day, the day I first saw it, the day we buried the dog, the day of the fencing match, the day that I learned about the captain's astrocytoma, I would have to mix memory with imagination in a way that Max would never allow in The Catalogue. The room was, and still is, a long, L-shaped space that runs the whole length of the East Wing, an attic huge enough to hold a party in one sweep of the L while operating a bowling alley in the other. It was lit, and still is, by narrow skylight windows on either side. When it was Max's room it would have been filled with his junk, the paraphernalia of teenage years: records, posters, sports-kit, schoolbooks, unwashed clothes. I don't really know. I can no longer picture it. I have edited down this memory, and the memory of that day, to just those bits I want to remember – *need* perhaps to remember.

Max put a record on the turntable and sat gloomily on the bed. I cleared a space on an armchair. Santana emerged from the speakers. *Abraxas* perhaps; I can't be sure.

'Thanks for doing that,' he said to me after a while, 'with Libby.'

'It was nothing.'

'Thanks anyway.'

Should I have told him then about his father? There was a moment, just a moment, when I could have spoken without too much awkwardness. I could have said it kindly. I could have said, 'Max, there's something you ought to know about the captain.' He would have looked up sullenly, and I would have said, 'he has a brain tumour. It's killing him. That's why he's walking strangely. It's why he stutters sometimes. It's why he looks ill. He has black-outs. He shouldn't be driving. He's dying, Max. Dying.'

I could have said it, but I didn't. And I wonder if it would have made much difference if I had. The Ponder family weren't the type to change their behaviour just because of an obstacle like a brain tumour. Instead I chatted inanely about something else entirely. I asked Max about Cambridge.

I wanted to ask him about his 'jitters'; what it was that had seemed so urgent in his invitation. I wanted to find out how he was coping with his pantheon of inner demons, but we were still at a point of separation where unselfconscious conversation hadn't yet come back to us. We hadn't seen a great deal of each other this past year, and we hardly ever spoke on the phone, so at every first meeting there was inevitably some barrier-breaking to be done before we could descend to our normal level of banter. I asked him about Caius and exams. He asked me about Keele. We were in the same loop as Aunt Zinnia and the captain were in their conversations with me. Max told me that he was in the first-year hockey team and in the first reserves for fencing. I spotted a foil propped against the wall. I picked it up and gave it a swish.

'So you still fence?' I asked, unnecessarily.

'Sure.'

'Your dad still fences?'

'Sometimes.'

'I still fence too. If you have another one of these and a pair of helmets, I'll give you a workout.'

'I've got one electric and one steam,' he said, 'somewhere.' He started to rummage among a pile of discarded items in search of the other foil. 'But only one helmet.'

'Pity. Can you borrow a helmet from your dad?'

'It's OK. We'll fence barefaced,' he said. 'No high lunges, no points scored above the heart, no deep lunges.'

He recovered the missing foil and threw it my way. It was the electric one, unattached now, of course, with a modern pistol grip that I had used before but found unhelpful.

'Nothing above the nipples,' he cautioned, smiling.

'Exactly how I like it,' I said.

We cleared the unoccupied half of the room to make a piste.

'*En garde!*'

Max dropped into a low stance, bouncing on his points. I fell into the same position, knees bent low, body side-on to my opponent, left hand curled up behind, foil-arm forward. I felt uncomfortable fencing unjacketed and barefaced. Even fencing low, it was a dangerous thing to do. But here's the thing: I didn't feel uncomfortable *enough* to back away. I could perhaps have suggested that, since there was one jacket and one helmet available, then *one* of us should wear them. It would have pleased the statistician in me – halving the risk of injury – but then the match would not have been even.

We exchanged a few warm-up moves. Max was quicker than I

remembered. The warm-up in fencing is an important part of the contest. It enables each fencer to size up his opponent, to test the speed of his reflexes, and see which instinctive parry moves the other fencer makes. This information will be valuable once the bout begins. Knowing how your opponent is likely to respond to an attack enables you to feint – to change your line of attack and find a target area that the parry has exposed. We fenced carefully, keeping our points low, watching the swish and flick of the blades.

Max stepped back and gave a salute. 'Ready for a bout?'

'If you are.'

We touched blades and Max lunged immediately – an *attaque simple*. I parried and riposted and he came back with a beat attack in septime. I was concentrating on keeping my blade low, and it probably cost me an instant as I changed my parry. That was enough for Max. His blade flicked up over mine and the point touched my ribcage.

'*Touché*!'

A very quick point. I made a mental note to fence more defensively. We squared up and Max led with the same attack. I went for a *retraite* – a step backwards instead of a parry with my blade. Max followed and we fought back, pace after pace, until I was almost at the limit of the piste. It was time for a change of tactics. I tried a *seconde intention*, a move that invites a response to which I might then counter-riposte. I hoped that Max, like many young fencers, would be emboldened at this end of the piste and I could draw him into making a rash attack, a low lunge perhaps, that I could counter successfully. But he was fencing cautiously too. He stepped back from my blade and we surveyed each other, waiting for the other to make the next move. I had the disadvantage of space so I tried to recover some yards with a few fairly non-threatening moves. Max parried effectively, so then I tried an *insistence* – a *coup droit d'autorité* – where you drive an attack forward through your opponent's parry. It wasn't the defensive manoeuvre that I'd resolved to use; in fact, it was fairly reckless, and I came within a whisker of feeling Max's blade in my side. I parried hard and followed through with a flick, catching Max on his liver.

'*Touché.*'

One point each.

Why do I remember these moves, these flicks lasting an instant, when there is so much that I simply can't recall? It was the 2 March 1974, a Saturday. It was thirty-one years ago. Ask me where I was the day before, and I'd draw a blank. I was at Keele, but doing what? With whom? Yet, despite the passage of three decades, I clearly recollect the clash and thrust of our fencing blades. Max would say that I have *replayed* it, and that after a while I've stopped recalling the actual fight, and instead am remembering the *replay*. If this is true, and it probably is, then what value is there in memory at all? Max was never worried about the distinction between true memory and what he called 'remembered memory'. For his purposes, all he needed to catalogue was what was in his brain. Whether it was true or false, it was all the same to him. It was resident somewhere in his head, so he would record it.

But it disturbs me that the memory of my bout with Max in the attic room might be more imagined than real. In my memory the bout was undecided, ending on two points apiece. That's because I didn't allow his final point. We were both sweating. Max had won the third point, and we'd fought hard for the fourth, which I had taken. The assumption, I suppose, was that we'd fight a bout of five hits. In Max's memory he won the bout on the fifth point. I know this because I have read his account in The Catalogue, volume X. I read it, in his presence, as I always did, and I looked up at his impassive face, determined to challenge this recollection. But, just as I had done on so many occasions, I bit my tongue, and read on. No two people remember the same football match, as Max would have said.

What really happened during the fifth bout was that we were disturbed by the captain. He'd heard the unmistakable sound of clashing blades and had come upstairs. I turned my head as he swung open the door and Max's blade flicked my right shoulder.

'*Touché*?' he called.

'Illegal,' said the captain.

We dropped our points. I was expecting a reprimand for fencing barefaced.

'No high lunges, no points scored above the heart, no deep lunges,' said the captain. 'Not if you want to fence without helmets'.

'It would have been lower, but you put me off the stroke,' complained Max.

'Then let me referee for you,' suggested the captain. 'Best of f ... five hits.'

'We're already three–two,' Max declared.

'Two all,' I corrected.

'Then I shall referee the decider.'

'No,' said Max, impetuously tossing his foil to the captain. 'I'll referee you and Adam.'

'Are you sure?' asked the captain.

'Absolutely.'

'How about you, Adam?'

He caught my gaze. 'I don't know, sir.'

'Not sure? Why ever not?'

'I'm not ... well ... are you sure you should be fencing, sir?'

'Of course he should,' ventured Max. 'You show him, Cap'n.'

But the captain had understood my reluctance. 'Maybe Adam's right,' he said.

'Of course he isn't,' Max retorted. 'Go on. You show him.'

'Just one bout then,' I suggested.

'Very well, one bout. *En garde*!'

At fifty-one, the captain was not an elegant sight as he dropped into the stance. He kept his bearing erect, but bent his knees just slightly. Swaying like a folded spruce, he seemed rather a large target, but I knew that I should not underestimate him.

Captain Ponder had taught me to fence. He'd taught us both. When Max and I were maybe ten, or eleven, he'd bought us a set of fencing gear on one of his trips to London. 'I'm giving you boys a *sport*,' he told us as he presented us each with a parcel. We'd opened them to discover a fencing foil, an épée, a sabre, a white canvas jacket, and a wire-gauze and leather helmet. Max had giggled with glee.

The captain taught us on a makeshift outdoor piste in the back garden of the old Dupont house in Convent Gardens, in the only way that you can teach this sport – face-to-face, repeating and repeating and repeating move after move, slowly, mechanically at first, slow lunges and parries and ripostes and counter-ripostes, then again, then again, then again, then swapping roles for the same set of moves, then ever so slightly faster – until whoops, one of you makes a mistake and it's back to square one. And again. And again. It's a painstaking process, but one to which Max was very well suited, and it suited me fairly well too. Max had a love of repetition. He could understand the resonance of the constant reiteration of the same moves. Once he had memorised a move, he could duplicate it faithfully again and again. As for me, I did not share Max's endless patience; while Max would deliver an identical move time after time, my moves would vary with every repetition, a feature of our practice that caused Max constant frustration. It wasn't for a want of trying. The problem was more my lack of confidence; I was never convinced that I had the move exactly right. Perhaps the first time I'd dip my point a little too low, so the next time I'd lift it higher; and maybe that would seem like a better move to me so the next time I'd go higher still, and then Max would let out an exasperated wail. 'You're going too high!'

'I'm sorry,' I would protest.

'How is my parry supposed to work if your point is right in my face?'

'Let's try again.'

So we'd go again. And then again. There are few sports that depend quite so much on dull repetition as fencing. After years of the sport, I now understand why. In a fencing bout there are some moments when you can plan your next move, but once you *make* your move, the actions that follow happen much too fast for thought. This is why fencing makes such poor television. The sport becomes a blur of steel. The only hope that a fencer has in a contest is that lightning-fast reflexes will take over, and this is where the hours of monotonous repetition come into play. As a fencer, you find your sword arm responding on its own, in the way that it has been taught, following the pattern it has learned, like the way that your fingers will instinctively drop a hot plate before the brain is even conscious of the heat. Musicians do this too, so I've read. No pianist could sight-read a complex chord and turn it into an instant pattern of fingers on keys if the conscious brain had to work out the position of each finger for each demi-semi-quaver. No, it's all done at a much more basic level of neural activity. The chord shape triggers a conditioned response in the pianist, in just the same way that a flash of steel stimulates a response from a fencer. But somewhere, something is happening in the brain that goes even deeper. Because if reflex were *all* that there was, then there would be no contest. A good fencer can vary those reflex responses – this time a parry to the left, next time a parry to the right, next time a step backwards. How do we do this? I'm not really sure. But we do.

How useful it would be to a fencer if young Adam's skill of seeing just an instant into the future were a reality. In fencing an instant is all you need. If you could see the move before it was made, like the swing of Mrs Mukuti's panga, you could stay forever a flicker of time ahead. But Einstein and Newton have ruled against all that. There is so little time to think that fencers in practice sessions will engage in a friendly bout and then recapitulate their moves together in slow motion, calling out the names so that each can learn what the instant reflex moves were that helped them win or lose the point. Afterwards they might reflect on those moves. You lose a fencing bout when you make a mistake. Equally, you win by exploiting your opponent's mistakes.

So when the captain and I squared up to each other on Saturday 2 March 1974, on a makeshift piste in Max's bedroom, a whole lot of history took to the piste with us. I had fought the captain countless times, but rarely in a competitive bout. And years had passed. I was taller and stronger and more experienced than the last time we'd met on a piste. I'd fought as captain of my school team, and was now one of the better blades at Keele. Even so, I knew that I could not match Captain Ponder at his best. But reflexes fade over time. Muscles grow stiff, and reluctant, and the energy and physical effort expended in a five-minute bout always surprises newcomers to the sport. I believed that I could win.

We faced up and exchanged the traditional friendly warm-up moves. I could see that he was rusty, but he was taller than me, with long-reaching arms, and I'd have to get past his wavering point to score a touch.

'Get on with it,' called Max impatiently. He stood between us, just off the piste, in the position of the referee.

We saluted and faced off. The captain was waiting for me to

make the first move. He stood with a motionless blade. Then we fenced.

I shall spare you the moves. The captain took the first point, and the second. Max was ecstatic. I wasn't in any way surprised that he would favour his father over his best friend. I knew enough about Max's relationship with the captain.

I took the third point and then we both took a breather. Max was reluctant to award me the point. 'It was a little high,' he said, grudgingly.

I took the fourth point so quickly that Max barely saw it happen. The captain misread my very first feint and I scored squarely on his lower ribs.

'*Touché*,' the captain called admiringly.

So we were two all.

There are very good reasons why you should never fence without a helmet and a protective jacket. It's obvious really. Even though a foil has a blunt end, it can still do a lot of damage thrust powerfully into an eye, or a mouth, or into the throat. All these things happen. The foil has a dull edge, but a slice across the neck could still cut the flesh. It is foolish and reckless to ignore these risks. But we did.

As we squared for the final point, my attention was drawn for just an instant to the captain's eyes. Why I chose to look at his face at that second, I don't really know. But what I saw in that instant, I can hardly say. The best way I can describe it is that, just for a moment, the lights in the captain's eyes went out. He blinked, and he wobbled. Then he checked himself and gave me a bewildered look.

'Are you all right?' I asked, alarmed.

The captain nodded his head, just a little too firmly. 'No problem, old chap, just lost my balance for a tick. Shall we fence on?'

'Are you sure, sir?'

Max hadn't seen what I had seen. 'Stop backing out, Adam,' he said.

I raised my foil, but I was hesitant. I had just seen the captain black out, if only for an instant.

'Fence,' ordered Max.

The captain lunged, I tried to block the lunge with a downward parry, but he dropped low, came up under my guard and scored a hit.

It was all over, and I felt a wash of relief.

But it wasn't all over. A jubilant Max swept up my foil. 'A decider! Between the winners,' he declared. I had seen Max in this mood before, reckless, headstrong, flushed with excitement.

'I don't think your dad is up to it,' I said.

'Nonsense! He just beat *you*, didn't he?'

'I guess.'

'Look, I'm not sure if I should,' protested the captain.

'Just one touch then?' Max was insistent.

'All right. Just one touch.'

I was clearly meant to be the referee. In Max's laborious account in his catalogue, he dissects these next few seconds in several dense pages of text. For me it all happened rather too fast.

On my command they fenced. Max, in his heightened state, fought the captain down the piste and I followed. These were two fencers who knew each other's game too well to allow an easy point. The captain recovered, but not enough. Max was always a fencer who liked to move forward relentlessly and to pin his opponent at the end of the run. But the light had returned to Captain Ponder's eyes and he fought back, forcing Max to the middle, and then well into his own half. Max scored an illegal point high on the captain's torso, and I told them to fence on.

OK. This account has gone on too long and I'm pretty sure you'll already be flicking ahead to see how it ends. So this is what happened. There is a rash move in fencing known as the '*flèche*' or the 'arrow'. It is essentially a surprise attack, made when one player makes a sudden, unexpected and irreversible run at his opponent and attempts to hit him as the two fencers pass each other. A fencer cornered at the end of the piste might sometimes make this move, although it is generally more effective if used in the middle of the run. It is a risky move, for if the fencer who makes it fails to find a target then he's a sitting duck for a riposte on his back. So it is also seen as a desperate move, and slightly un-gentlemanly. One way or another, a *flèche* generally ends the bout, and in my experience the outcome is fairly random. Half the time the attacker scores the point; the other half he misses and is hit by the riposte.

Now, as far as I can remember, we hadn't discussed all the unwritten rules for barefaced fighting on that day. But had we done so, I should have expected the *flèche* to be off-limits. It's easy to be wise after the event but, all the same, I should have thought Max would have been more cautious. The speed of the move makes the eventual hit a clumsy one and, because the attacker is running forward, the force of the hit is greater than usual, raising the rare risk that a blade might bend too far, and break in half. A rare risk it may have been, but nonetheless this is what happened when Max, with a kamikaze yell, launched a *flèche* attack on his father. The captain should have stepped aside to let Max pass, and he should have tried to deflect the move. In his defence, Max may, perhaps, have slipped on the shiny floor. In his own account in The Catalogue he remembers slipping. But, more significantly, in my reconstruction of the event, the captain almost certainly suffered another blackout. He seemed to stagger, in the same way I'd seen him do just moments earlier. So, despite the full weight of Max hurtling towards him, the captain actually toppled forwards. The foil blade struck the captain right on his breastbone and Max shouted, '*Touché!*'

The impulse bent the blade and it snapped. And the short, sharp, broken end plunged right into the captain's throat.

17

ABELARD AND ELOISE

VOLUME CLII
FEBRUARY 1988

Here is what I remember of the story of Abelard [PFH(P) 47] and Eloise [PFH(P) 48]. Or Héloïse, as I think she is often called. Abelard was a philosopher in medieval France. Twelfth century, I would say, or even eleventh. I should have concentrated more in tutorials. Abelard was around forty years old when he was asked to become a tutor to Eloise; she was a mere girl of eighteen who was heading for a good, solid career in a sisterhood somewhere. Biology took over. He fell for her and she for him and they had a relationship based on good old-fashioned rumpy-pumpy. I imagine fat, old Abelard vigorously shagging Eloise during their tutorial sessions. Probably unfair. There's no evidence that he was fat, but it makes for a better picture. Anyway, the outcome of all that screwing was that Eloise got pregnant.

These days, Abelard would probably be dismissed with a strongly worded reprimand. You can't diddle your students and hope to get away without a firm rebuke. But Eloise's uncle wasn't a master of the stern letter, apparently. Instead, he sent some strong-armed men to Abelard's house and they cut off his balls. That did the trick. Needless to say, they didn't resort to anaesthesia, and I doubt if they were practised in pain management. Actually, there was more to the story than that, but I don't recall the details. I think that Abelard and Eloise had previously married in secret, and that she'd had the baby and that, afterwards, to save Abelard from losing his reputation, she went off to join a nunnery. This may have been the act that prompted her uncle to castrate poor old Abelard. Whatever the reason, the retribution was swift and painful.

Anyway, Eloise turned out to be something of a philosopher in her own right, and after the castration she swore to remain a nun all her life, which she did. Abelard survived the violent removal of his gonads, and went off to become a monk and the unfortunate couple whiled away the time by writing erotic letters to each other. Abelard didn't stay a monk though. He then became a hermit, and after that he went back to philosophy. Which is why he comes in here.

Abelard, you see, was a nominalist, a student of Roscellinus [PFH(P) to be written], who was one of the fathers of nominalism. And that's what has to be the most interesting thing about Abelard, after the sex of course, and the castration. Nominalists claim that nothing universal exists except in the mind. So if you happen to be a realist, and you probably are, you'd describe the world using adjectives and adverbs, or by grouping things together using a common label. An observer might have described Eloise as soft and pink and inviting - which is how I imagine she was.

She might have been described as a 'beautiful girl'. But as a nominalist, Abelard would have believed that these concepts, and others such as soft and pink and gently moaning, had no real existence beyond our imaginations – at least not as universals. And calling Eloise 'beautiful' would be wholly fanciful. For nominalists, beauty is always in the eye of the beholder. And for really committed nominalists, the same seems to be true of 'pink'. So a pink flower and a pink wine and the pink, enticing button of Eloise's nipple don't really share a concept that we call 'pink', except in our imaginations. Even calling Eloise a 'girl' would be lumping her into a universal class of 'girls', which is also an imaginative construct. This is where it starts to get a little sticky.

The only person I know who ever had his balls chopped off was my Great-uncle Hubert [GUH06]. He suffered from testicular cancer and they caught it in time. I knew he'd been under the knife, but I never really wondered about the nature of his operation until one day I found myself standing next to him at a urinal and he chose that moment to tell me. 'Did I tell you about my operation?' he asked me in his booming voice. 'They cut my bloody balls off!'

Anyway, Abelard was probably wrong about nominalism, although he was in pretty good company at the time. Now we include among notorious nominalists the delightfully named William of Ockham [PFH(P) to be written] and John Stuart Mill [PFH(P) 31]. Now here's a thing that has just occurred to me: where was Ockham? Not the philosopher, the town? Does it still exist? Do the good people of Ockham hold their heads up high, proud in the knowledge that one of their ancestors was a famous nominalist and believed that being poor was a jolly good thing, and that the pope was a heretic?

Personally, I've always held with the realists who accept the world as they see it, and who generally agree that 'pink' is a perfectly useful adjective and that we can happily lump things together that share this particular property and call them pink. And I reckon that modern science backs me up. But it has dawned on me in the one hundred and thirteen months that I've been scribbling this catalogue, that this whole exercise of mine is something of a tribute to nominalism. The more I write in it, the more I see what old Abelard and Roscellinus and William of Ockham were getting at. I'm weaving a thread of distinguishing narrative between all the universals of my life. The pink bougainvillea of Eastlands, the pink wallpaper of my mother's boudoir, the soft pink of raspberry ice-cream, my first daring pink shirt, the pink nipples of Elenora Twist – they don't belong together. Each deserves its own category, and its own description. Pink is a lazy shorthand to describe them all. So score one for Roscellinus, Abelard, and William of Ockham. Maybe universals really are a misleading construct; maybe they promote a parody of what life really is; maybe they prevent us from ever truly describing anything because what we really need is a different word for every possible shade and texture of pink and only then could we come close.

Elenora's nipples weren't even pink anyway.

I've described them already in volumes III, XI, XVI and LXV – and I seem to remember referencing them before as a metaphor, but I can't remember where. In volume III I described them as 'less than a centimetre in diameter, faintly textured like the skin on a scab that has almost healed, like the surface of a miniature bunch of rose grapes, brown like a cherry petal that has fallen and lost it's colour, sometimes flat against her breast and sometimes popped up like a tiny button no more than seven or eight millimetres high.' There. Not exactly a nominalist description, but certainly a nod in that direction. And no mention of the word 'pink'.

I wonder if old Abelard ever had another erection after his nads were hacked off? Do you need testosterone to get a stiffy? I don't know. I don't imagine he played away ever again. Can you imagine trying to explain to a lover why you've come to the game without a couple of key players? Then again, it could have been a cracking piece of twelfth-century birth control – which might have made him irresistible to the ladies. Who knows?

I've just opened a volume at random and discovered a passage I'd never read before – Max's recollection of the lives of Abelard and Eloise. I'd never heard of them before today, and by the sound of it, Max's recollection of their lives was a bit scant. I don't know whether to believe it all – especially the story about Abelard's castration. Quite possibly Max was confusing it with another story. Or maybe not. How reliable is memory anyway? No matter. I've copied it in here for this account. Max liked to invest his work with heavy philosophical justification. Here, because he is reminiscing about the lives of great philosophers, he is suddenly a nominalist. If you read his section on Freud, also in CLII and detailed somewhere in the appendices, you'll discover that he's searching for his id. Something in his childhood had affected his sexual awakening or some such mumbo-jumbo. Don't expect me to remember it. Max was the philosopher, not me.

In reality, Max may have suffered all sorts of damage to his id in childhood, and he may already have had a whole baggage cart of neuroses and phobias and behavioural disorders, but none of these affected Max quite like the loss of his father. You don't have to be a psychoanalyst to recognise that.

After the fencing accident, Aunt Zinnia called for an ambulance and it eventually arrived. It took the captain and Aunt Zinnia followed in a taxi, accompanied by Tutton, the blind retainer. Max and I stayed behind at The Pile. Max told me he was too stressed to leave the house. It was a very awkward time. We sat in armchairs by the telephone, waiting for a call from the hospital. I'm sitting in one of those same armchairs now. They've lasted more than thirty years, which seems pretty good to me for an armchair. In point of fact, they've lasted considerably *more* than thirty years. I've just looked them up in one of Max's appendices and it turns out that, like everything in this damned house, they're antiques. Max describes them as leather-covered Empire mahogany bergères dating from around 1810, with foliate paterae and attenuated scrolls. The arms are carved to look like dolphins and the chairs have sabre legs. They are upholstered in green leather which is much newer than the chairs themselves. Max estimates in The Catalogue that they were probably reupholstered around 1965. So now you can picture us.

Every few minutes Max would get up from his Empire mahogany armchair and pace the room, and all the time I could tell he was expecting a call to say that his father was dead. And the more he waited, the more the phone didn't ring. Max's mood turned dark. He began to descend into a circle of self-reproach. Bitter at first: 'Jesus fuck, Jesus fuck, Jesus FUCK!' He began to weep. Then angry: 'Why did we fucking do it, Adam? Why did we fucking do it?'

I didn't like the 'we' in that question. It made me nervous to think that I might end up sharing the blame.

'Hey,' I said, 'your dad was OK with it.'

'Why did I do the fucking *flèche*, man? Why did I do the *flèche*?'

'Max it was just a *move*. It was an accident.'

'It wasn't a fucking accident, man. We took a risk and we blew it. I blew it. I fucking blew it.'

Somewhere among all of this, while Max was remonstrating with himself, and with me, and with the cruelty of fate, when the anger was starting to turn to resignation, there was a knock at the door. Max shot out of his seat with a cry.

'I'll go,' I said.

Max stood quivering in the library and watched as I made my way to the front door. I don't know who I expected, but it turned out to be the police; to be accurate, a policeman and a policewoman. My heart sank. Police could only mean bad news.

'Mr Ponder?' asked the policeman rather forcefully, 'Mr Maximilian Ponder?'

'Er, no. My name is Adam Last.'

'Is Mr Ponder at home? The younger Mr Ponder?'

'Er, yes.' I let them in and Max came out. He was shaking so much that I put a hand on his shoulder to calm him.

'Mr Ponder,' said the policeman. 'We're here to question you about an assault on Captain Maximilian Ponder.'

Max blinked. 'What assault?'

'I think you know the incident I'm referring to, sir.'

'It wasn't an assault,' I found myself protesting on Max's behalf. 'It was an accident.'

'I'm sure it was, sir,' said the policewoman, 'but you understand we have to investigate incidents like this.'

'No you don't,' said Max. 'There was an accident, and my dad is in hospital.'

'It was the hospital that called us, sir. They have to call us when someone is injured in a fight or a brawl.'

'It wasn't a fight!'

'I understand you were fighting with your father and then you stabbed him through the neck with a sword.'

'A *sword*? Who the hell told you that?'

'Do you deny, sir, that you were in a fight with your father and that you stabbed him in the neck?'

Max seemed to stagger and I had to steady him. 'Is my dad all right?' he asked in a whisper.

'I really can't say, sir. But I do need to interview you about the incident.'

'You can interview me when you tell me my dad is OK.' This was no longer a whisper. There were shades of dormitory five and Taylor about him.

I looked at him anxiously. 'Take it easy, Max.'

'Sir, we can do this the easy way or we can do it the hard way.'

'Then let's do it the fucking hard way,' Max spat.

'Max, please,' I tried to intervene. 'Calm down. They're only doing their job. They need to know what happened, that's all.'

I turned to the policeman. 'He's upset.'

'My dad's dying! Of course I'm upset.'

'Why don't you come quietly and tell us all about it?' suggested the policewoman in a conciliatory tone.

'I'm not going anywhere,' declared Max.

'Can't you interview him here?' I asked.

'I think it would be better at the station, don't you?'

'I think it would be better here,' I said. 'You don't understand. Max doesn't like going outside when he's stressed.'

'We can take him in the car,' said the policewoman, failing to grasp quite what I'd meant.

'Am I under arrest?' Max asked.

'No, sir. We just need to ask you some questions. If you cooperate with us now, then you'll be able to come straight home.'

'Can Adam come with me?'

'I don't think that would be appropriate.'

'I was a witness,' I protested. 'I saw the whole thing. I was the *referee*, for god's sake!'

This seemed to puzzle the policeman. 'You were the *referee*?'

'What do you think went on here? It was a fencing match. The foil broke. It was an accident. *An accident.*'

The two cops looked at each other and the policewoman made a decision. 'Very well, sir,' she said, 'you can come with us too.'

And that is how it should have ended. We should have gone quietly to the station and answered their stupid questions, then come home and by the next day we'd probably have forgotten the whole thing.

Except that didn't happen.

Instead, Max started to back away, shaking uncontrollably. The policeman took hold of him, and Max began to panic.

The funny thing was, I knew it was coming but I also knew that I was powerless to stop it. Max's panic attacks came in different forms. Some were harmless – judders really – and he could control them with a few deep breaths and a supportive hand on his shoulder. Others were harder to control. Sometimes it would take two of us to hold him down and murmur reassuring words while he shook and swore and twisted his head violently from left to right. But even *those* fits we could control. Eventually he would blink at us and he'd be back. I once knew a guy who was prone to epileptic fits, and while I'd hate to compare Max's anxiety to epilepsy, there may have been some distant common cause because, like an epileptic, Max went somewhere when the panic started and someone else took over his flailing limbs and tortured body.

But those were the easy attacks. Max would call me a realist, I guess, because I'm lumping his anxiety seizures into neatly labelled compartments. A nominalist, I suppose, would say that every incident was unique. Which, I suppose, it was. But I am, after all, the realist, and so it was that I could recognise and classify the worst of Max's attacks. This wasn't panic, or even insolence or insubordination or fear. It was an uncontrollable frenzy. Max started shaking violently, his lips flapped loose, gibbering, his arms thrashed, his face twisted and wrenched from side to side.

'Max … Max … come back,' I grabbed him in a tight embrace. The police didn't help. Instead, they tried to grab hold of Max, and the next thing I knew they were marching Max between them.

'Let him go … please,' I pleaded. 'He's having a nervous attack.'

'Mr Ponder is simply helping us with our enquiries.'

We bustled out of the front door and onto the gravel driveway, with Max kicking and thrashing. I saw one violent kick connect with the policewoman's shin and I winced. Astonishingly the policewoman didn't let go, but there was a fierceness in her eyes as she thrust Max onto the back seat and slammed the door. I tried the door handle but it was locked.

'I thought I was coming too,' I protested.

In the back of the car Max was prostrate on the seat, screaming.

'We'll send another car for you,' said the policeman.

'He needs a lawyer.'

'Mr Ponder is not under arrest.'

'Then why are you abducting him against his will?'

The policeman gave a long sigh, and the sigh told me everything. It told me that to him I was just a hippy, a troublemaker, long-haired, unwashed, badly dressed, probably spoiled, and Max was just a hippy brat from a bourgeois family who had probably tried to murder his father, and who was having a childish tantrum in the back of the panda car. It told me that he had better things to do than to worry about how well he should treat us, and that the prospect of a preppy lawyer turning up would make his bad day even worse. But he didn't say any of this. What he said, after the sigh, was, 'I think it would be better for us all if we simply agreed that Mr Ponder freely volunteered to help us with our enquiries. Don't you?'

I was only nineteen. I didn't know how to argue for my rights with a uniformed policeman twice my age. I didn't know how to explain that Max was a highly strung individual, enormously intelligent, a Cambridge undergraduate, not a hooligan. I didn't know how to articulate his nervous condition, and even if I could, how could I explain it to a policeman who didn't *want* to understand?

'Stay right here,' the policeman said. 'Another car will come to collect you.'

And they drove off, leaving me standing alone on the gravel drive.

In the house the phone was ringing.

18

SHAKESPEARE

VOLUME XXX
DECEMBER 1977

When it comes to cataloguing the brain, here
is an interesting question. How many words
did William Shakespeare know? You can do this
yourself at home. You may think you could
find the answer by counting every word in every
one of the plays and sonnets and long poems,
but actually it still won't tell you how many
words he knew because there must have been
words that he never got round to using. The
word 'Bible', for example, doesn't appear
once, yet he must have been familiar with the
word. And what about the missing plays? Every
play has lots of words in them that don't
appear in any other play. So what were the
unique words that he used in the tragically
lost 'Cardenio' and 'Love's Labour's Won'?
We shall never know, unless someone unearths
a copy, which seems unlikely after 350-odd
years.

As it happens, I can't help you with this
because I don't have ready access to the
Complete Works, for obvious reasons. But I can
do this as a 'thought experiment', which was
first described to me by Ravi Kumar on one of
his visits to Dorset Square. Here is what
you do. You open the *Complete Works* at random

and you make a list of the first thousand words
that you come across. Then you mark on a
graph how many of those words are unique.
This will be less than one thousand because
some words will appear twice or three times
or more. So if you chose the extract that
includes, 'To be, or not to be? That is the
question', that would be ten words in total,
but only eight unique words because the words
'to' and 'be' appear twice. OK. In our thought
experiment, let us say we score up 800 unique
words in our first sample of a thousand. You
draw a bar graph with a little cross at 800
and you draw the first column up to 800. Then
you choose another 1,000 words. This time
you have to exclude all the words you found
before. Let's put the cross on the graph at
600 and draw another bar, just to the right
of the first one. Next cross comes in at, say,
450. You start to get a staircase going
downwards. By the time you've done another
ten samples, you should have established a
trend and can probably stop counting. Now
join the dots and plot the trend down until
it reaches zero. What we're doing here is
trying to find out how many 1,000-word passages
Will would have to write before he would
write one that didn't introduce a single new
word. Now you add up all the little bars you
would have had to draw if you had done this
properly, and add them to the ones you did
draw. Bingo. Add a bit of Ravi Kumar's
statistical wizardry and you'd know how many
words the Bard had in his rather extraordinary
brain. I'll wager it is a pretty large number.

So, how many words are there in my own
brain? In a few months, when I'll be close
to three years into this project, I shall do

the Shakespeare exercise on all the words
I've generated and record the result here. In
the meantime, words are one content I will
not try to catalogue. At least, not words in
English.

Although, maybe I shouldn't be so hasty.
Samuel Johnson must have had a stab at listing
every word in his brain when he compiled his
dictionary. Imagine if someone had come to
Sam with a word he'd never heard. 'What do
you mean "nadgers"?' he'd have said. 'It
doesn't exist.' 'But it does,' they'd have
protested. 'Nonsense,' he'd say, and that
would be that. In a sense, Samuel Johnson's
dictionary was a project a little like mine.
He was cataloguing the words that appeared in
his own brain.

Of course we should reflect here, just a
little, on the horribly amorphous nature of
words. What you understand by a word may be
different from what I understand.
Wittgenstein showed us that you can't even
define most words. How do you define the word
'game'? That was one of Wittgenstein's
problems. How do you frame a definition that
encompasses everything from Rugby Union to
Solitaire to British Bulldogs? You can't. So
even if I did list every word I know, it
wouldn't help because you wouldn't know my
definitions and neither would I. Incidentally,
Ludwig Wittgenstein was at school with Adolf
Hitler. Imagine that! And he went to
university in Manchester to study aeronautics
before he ended up at Trinity College.
Interesting guy.

The chap who compiled all the words for the
Oxford English Dictionary was called Murray.
I forget his first name. I do remember though

that he predicted the whole task would take three years. Do you know how far he had actually got after three years? He had got as far as the word 'ant'.

When Murray compiled the OED, he used hundreds of volunteers who trawled through old books looking for words. One of the biggest contributors was a lunatic from a local asylum.

Thinking about asylums and the word pyramid in Shakespeare reminds me of Alexander Cruden. Now he was an interesting character. Another regular inmate of lunatic asylums. I can't remember when he lived, but it was during the reign of one of the Georges. And he compiled a word-by-word list of every word in the King James Bible. The trouble is that dozens of hands wrote the Bible, so there isn't a lot to learn from that exercise. And the motley collection of bronze-age witch-doctors and shamans who wrote the random set of scrolls that Constantine the heathen Emperor of Rome decided should constitute the Christian Bible, actually wrote in a whole assortment of tribal languages. So poor old Cruden might actually have been closer to discovering how many words William Tyndale knew, because King James' translators were a lazy lot and they based most of their text on the banned translation that Tyndale delivered, for which piece of courageous scholarship and artistry he was burned at the stake.

I can't remember if Tyndale was a contemporary of Will Shakespeare, but I suspect he was a little older - by half a century or so. In the *Merry Wives of Windsor*, Will gives us the word 'fuck'. Almost. Someone is learning their Latin nouns and they confuse 'vocative' with 'focative'. 'That's a good root,' says Mistress Quickly. I miss the word 'vocative'. We hardly ever use it any more. Even better words are 'genitive' and 'ablative'. Maybe if we stop teaching Latin in schools, we could find new meanings for those words so that we could carry on using them.

But back to the point. How many conversations or encounters can I remember with, say, Connor Peterkin-Wallis? [CPW]. To date I have recorded over 400 and I know there were more. Plenty more. I shared a study with him at Eton for three years; we must have spoken ten times a day - at least - for over 200 days a year, so I make that at least 6,000 encounters. I will keep on recalling these and scribbling them into the appendices, but where does it end? Certainly it won't end with a complete catalogue of every encounter I can remember. I could use a technique like the Shakespeare word count to calculate how many CPW encounters have not yet been recorded, but I'm afraid that would fail to meet the objectives of The Catalogue. I'm not really interested in how many encounters I had with CPW, I'm interested in the detail of those encounters - what happened and where and when and what was said. The 'one-calendar-month' rule that I championed for so many months has been becoming more and more tattered. It only serves its purpose for things like Swahili nouns. I can't possibly rely on it for things like encounters with CPW. Or conversations with the captain. Or O. Or Adam.

I'm going to have to extend this. The one-

calendar-month rule is hereby rescinded.
I did think about replacing it with a two-
month rule, or a three-month rule, but the
truth is that it only works if I make it a
'very long time' rule. Damnit, Adam has
started talking about the end of the project.
I get a horrible feeling he may be planning
a party for me when the three years are up,
but I am nowhere near finished. I need at
least another two years. I need to break this
news to Adam. I feel, in a very real sense,
that when the three years are up, I won't
have got any further than 'ant'.

19

THE PROJECT

A couple of years or so into the project, Max told me that he wanted to take more time. Three years was simply not going to be long enough. We didn't really argue about it. I tried to persuade him to change his mind, but I probably knew from the start that it was futile. I argued that the definition of his project shouldn't be to catalogue *every single* memory in his brain, but to catalogue every one that he could manage within a time-span of three years. Max didn't buy that, of course. I could have forced the point by withdrawing my labour. That might have worked. I was Max's lifeline, you see. I looked after him. I had made my office in the gate-house of The Pile and this meant that I visited almost every day. I shopped for Max, took his manuscripts to the binders, took his suits to the cleaners, paid his bills, bought supplies of ink and paper and nibs, dealt with property maintenance, deflected callers. I steamed the labels off his wine bottles, repackaged his groceries into plastic containers, often cooked for him. When he was hunched over his desk scrawling away with his Sheaffer Visulated reservoir pen, time didn't seem to pass for him. He would rarely eat unless food was delivered on a tray. He would only ever wash up once every item of crockery in the kitchen was dirty and, of course, we never had a dishwasher. Dishwashers were not very 1975. His personal hygiene was OK, but only because he showered every morning. I used to cut his hair.

As the months and years passed, we developed a routine. I knew that after three years no one else could easily step into my shoes. I understood Max's rules. I would arrive at The Pile around 8 a.m., by which time Max would be up and writing. I wouldn't disturb him, but I would eventually wander into the library mid-morning with two cups of tea and four digestive biscuits and I would settle silently into one of the leather-covered Empire mahogany bergères while he wrote. Eventually, when he was ready, he would open up a conversation. 'Vegetables,' he might say. 'I'm trying to describe every bloody vegetable I can ever remember eating and it's a wretched chore. Have you eaten a Jerusalem artichoke? Don't bother. Filthy muck. Like the marrow we used to get at Kenton, only more so. Margaret Henderson. Do you remember her? Used to come to our house with her home-grown parsnips. God, they tasted awful!'

In the evenings, when I was there, I would cook dinner and we would eat together at the Rastin table and share a bottle of red wine. I'm not an adventurous cook, which is just as well. Max liked predictability in his meals. Afterwards, I would often sit in the library and keep him company while he wrote. There was no TV or radio, of course. I could read, if I wanted, as long as the book I was reading was anonymously provided with a brown paper cover.

It was generally hard to persuade Max to retire to bed. He wrote continuously, even during conversations. Eventually, I would wait for the grandfather clock to chime midnight and then I'd insist that we both turned in. On the nights when I wasn't there, god only knows if he ever went to bed at all.

The routine changed as we both grew older, but not much. My life changed, but Max's didn't. I moved out of The Pile after less than a year and bought a house in Henley. I figured that looking after Max was part of my job, and like any job you need to leave it behind and go home. I never told Max where I lived, of course. That would be polluting information. I never told Max anything at all about my life outside The Pile. I've moved house three times since then. He never knew.

In September 1982, I told Max that I would be away for two weeks. When I came back I showed up at The Pile wearing a wedding ring. I know that Max noticed it, because he paused in mid-conversation and fixed it with a look of shock. And then he carried on with his sentence as if he had noticed nothing at all.

My daughter Janie was born in October 1986. Now, unbelievably, she is nineteen. She and Max never met.

In February 2001, on a day of desperate storms I came back to The Pile with no ring. I don't know if Max noticed that at all.

It wasn't just personal things that I learned to hide from Max. There was a world out there. Sometimes little nuggets of news could escape. Sometime in the eighties Max and I were talking airily about the role of the prime minister, in general terms only, you understand, and I used the pronoun 'she'. Max nearly choked. It just shows how careful I had to be. By this stage Max had become absolutely obsessive about sealing himself off from any news of the outside world. Aunt Zinnia was a regular offender. In the early years she would visit two or three times a year. She understood the rules, yet she lapsed so often that Max begged me not to let her come again. During the Falklands War she said something like, 'we can't do that while we're still at war.' I leaped in, trying to recover the situation, 'Now, now, Zin,' I said, as if I were patronising an Alzheimer's sufferer, 'the *war* ended forty years ago.'

'Oh, sorry!' gasped Zinnia, her hand flying to her mouth, 'Yes. I meant *that* war. The German one. Not the Argenti ...' and her voice trailed off. More damage had been done than if I'd just kept quiet.

Another Sunday, a decade and a half later, Zinnia was all teary about the death of Princess Diana. 'Are you all right, Aunt Zinnia?' Max asked eventually. I knew that he knew that this was a dangerous question to ask, but he asked it anyway. 'Oh I'm so sorry, dear,' said Zinnia stubbing out tears with a hanky, 'I know you don't want to be bothered with these things, it's just ...'

'Don't, Zinnia,' I cautioned.

'Oh no ... sorry. She was just so young, that's all. And those young princes, without a mother.'

'Princes?' echoed Max, scribbling violently.

So it was that the great events of the late twentieth century and early twenty-first rolled on past, leaving Max in blissful ignorance. The strikes and recession of the late seventies, the Thatcher and Reagan years, the miners' strike, the war in the Falklands, the fall of the Berlin Wall, the collapse of communism, Tony Blair and Bill Clinton, Tony Blair and George Bush, peace in Northern Ireland, the war in the Falklands, the war in the Gulf, the war in Kosovo, the war in Afghanistan, the war in Iraq. Max missed some of the most dramatic social changes in human history. He was never aware of AIDS, or global warming, or the music of Madonna, or the famine in Ethiopia, or the rise of China, or the discovery of the wreck of the Titanic. He never watched his TV open-mouthed as airliners flew into the World Trade Centre. He never saw a compact disc, or watched a Star Wars film, or an episode of *The Simpsons*. He may have known thousands of words, but he would never know the meaning of iPod or yuppie or DVD or GM-food or hanging-chad. He still lived in a world that was caught in the 1970s, like a fly in amber. He talked about his old records and tapes. He speculated in The Catalogue about old acquaintances – would this one be a 'shop steward' by now? Would another be an 'astronaut'? Sometimes it was clear that the world he imagined outside his gates hadn't changed since he closed himself away. Harold Wilson was still prime minister. Jimmy Carter was still president. Once I used the word 'Russia' in a conversation and Max corrected me to 'USSR'. It didn't occur to him that my 'error' had been corrected by the great tide of world events.

On that clear December midnight when those of us with real lives saw out the millennium, Max was in his library writing. He knew the date, of course. He was disturbed by the sounds of explosions, and for the first time since September 1975 he drew back the curtains. There, downstream on the far riverbank was a great display of fireworks. He stood and watched for about two minutes before letting the heavy curtain fall back.

Elenora Twist was never formally dumped by Max, and for a while she behaved like a prisoner's moll bravely waiting for her man. She was more interested in conjugal visits than Max, it seemed. They used to go for it about once or twice a month in the early years, but it tailed off, and then ended abruptly in 1977. Elenora was pretty good at obeying the rules though. She would arrive and wait for Max lying naked in bed. That way, as she explained, she never had to worry about what to wear. After she stopped calling, Max never asked about her for the next twenty-eight years, and I never volunteered anything. That, if you like, is the true measure of his obsession.

20

STARS

VOLUME CXXVIII
FEBRUARY 1986

Did you know that the pope has a telescope?
Actually, he has several. No, really. Not
just a Galilean tube of lenses balanced on a
tripod on the balcony of the Vatican for the
pope to peer through, although that would be
weird enough given the church's historical
antipathy to the invention. After all, since
we have started on this diversion, let's
recall that it is only a matter of four
centuries or so since poor Giordano Bruno
was burned at the stake for daring to speculate
that there might be planets beyond our solar
system. But back to our subject. The pope's
telescopes occupy a purpose-built observatory
on a hill close to Castel Gandolfo, the pope's
summer residence. The Holy Father could
easily wander over on a summer evening to try
to spot comets. Maybe he does.

APPENDIX CLXXXVIII

Gowland, Mr M (possibly Michael) /
Caucasian / [MG]
Deputy headmaster at Kenton College between
around January 1964 and 1968.
Height: app 5'10', build: medium, features:

weathered face with a full, trimmed black beard and short, black hair, thick with a natural curl. Clothing: normally a sports jacket or blazer, brown trousers, suede shoes, light-coloured shirt and unremarkable tie. Accent: East African with possibly a faint hint of West Country – I would guess Bath or Swindon. Probable age: well, I'd put him in his late thirties in 1965, so shall we say a birth date around 1928. Demeanour: jovial and relaxed, comfortable with people. Marital status/sexual orientation: certainly unmarried when I knew him in the 1960s, and I never saw him with a girlfriend, but then he was our deputy headmaster and I don't think he would have shared his private life with prepubescent boys.

Mr M. Gowland Incident list

MG01: I am nine years old and standing in a corridor at Kenton between the fourth-form classroom and the common room; I have been to the toilet during a class. MG appears and I stand still, waiting for him to pass. I recognise him as the new deputy head who was introduced to us all at the HM's assembly after breakfast. He looks a little fearsome. As he passes, he ruffles my hair but doesn't say a word. Seconds later he is out of sight. I re-enter the classroom and receive a rap on the knuckles with a ruler from Mr Black [JBlack130] for having uncombed hair. I don't mention to him or to anyone that the real culprit was the new deputy head. C Jan 64.

MG02: I am nine years old. MG is the duty master at dinner in the junior dining room. Everyone is interested to see him. He sits at the head of our table just three places away from me and all eyes are furtively watching him to see if he will be another tyrant like MM or RP. When the vegetable marrow is served, he takes one mouthful and looks sick. 'Do we really have to eat this muck?' he whispers to the lad sitting next to him. No one else seems to hear this remark but by the next day it is widely reported. C Jan 64.

MG03: I see MG drive across the quad in his car. It is yellow, looks very dirty and is quite old. C Jan 64.

MG04: MG is on milk duty at break. Rabagliati [Rabs 307] asks him if he has to drink his milk because all the milks have curdled in the hot sun. MG tells him that everyone has to drink their milk. Then he says, 'the only way you can get away with not drinking it, is if you were to accidentally spill it on the flower bed when I was looking the other way.' Later, the flower bed is caked in lumps of old milk. C Feb 64.

MG05: MG is our new geography teacher. I don't recall many early lessons, but I remember one when he came in and the ceiling fan was broken, so we all went outside and sat on the lawn under the Eucalyptus trees. There he started to teach us about Oxbow lakes. He sent a boy to fetch a jug of water from the kitchens and we made a little river in the clay soil and then created our own little Oxbow lake and we all ended up with muddy hands. [RB388] RP came out to see what was going on and he seemed a bit huffy but MG appeased him. C 64.

MG06: MG is wearing white takkies. They are
clearly brand new. C 64.

And so on. It might interest you to know that Max lists 731
incidents with Mr Gowland. And this was just *one* teacher back in
the 1960s. Teachers at Eton get much more space, but since I never
knew any of them, I don't feel tempted to share any of his
recollections here. We are all listed in this way. He'll start with a
pen portrait, then dive into incidents. In the appendices they appear
like this:

APPENDIX CLXXXVIII

MG 634: MG throws a blackboard rubber at
Block. [Block: 179] Block ducks and it clouts
me on the face. This is in form-eight Latin
[Form8 Latin 16]. MG says, 'It must have been
meant for you, Ponder. What have you been up
to, eh?' C Sep 67.

JCowels 1255: JC comes storming across the
tennis court towards me. He thinks I cheated
with my last line call. We are on court three.
[Tennis sixteen] He is NE end. He is wearing
regulation shorts but a strictly non-
regulation T-shirt with a cannabis leaf on
it. The shirt is pale green and the cannabis
leaf is dark green, about ten inches in
diameter. He is going to jump the net but he
catches his left foot and falls and twists
his ankle. 'You bloody bummer, Ponder,' he
says, and he chucks his racket at me and it
hits me on the temple. I was just reminded of
this incident when I recorded MG 634. C Jun
71.

I've picked out a couple of extracts from The Catalogue to introduce
a tale I want to tell that sheds some light on Max's attitude to death

and also gives some suggestion of how he felt about his place in the universe. Max spends quite a lot of time on this incident in The Catalogue, which I think means that he revisited it many times in his own memory. I did think about trying to reproduce the story in full from The Catalogue, but it would take too long and you would probably lose interest. It is a story that captures Max's obsession with minutiae so, in The Catalogue, he has to include some line drawings of the Jones house (he thinks the old man may have been called Jones) and the observatory, and some painstaking descriptions of the events.

Anyway, this tale involves the deputy headmaster at Kenton. His name was Mr Gowland. I don't think I ever knew his first name although you will see that Max suspected it might have been Michael. Mr Gowland was a curious misfit at Kenton. He wasn't 'fresh out of Oxford', he was a Kenya man. He spoke with the accent. He had the weathered complexion. He was a little rough around the edges, very male, bearded, jocular, cavalier. We loved him. He was the universal scoutmaster who could pitch tents and light fires and craft delicious horror stories as we sat around the flames. He was the kind of teacher who inspired by example, a geographer and classics man who had probably picked over the ruins of Cicero's camps himself and brought the knowledge back to us first-hand. On the nights when he was duty master, he'd collect us together after evensong and regale us with tales of old Africa, of explorers and lions and gunslingers. He would hold us spellbound with stories of wartime bravery, of grisly battles, of gut-churning defeats. We waited in anticipation of Mr Gowland's stories, and he rarely disappointed us. He told us the tale of the *Titanic*, and of how we sunk the *Bismark*, and of Livingstone and Stanley, and Alexander the Great, and Douglas Bader, and Lindbergh, and Scott and Amundsen and Peary and Shackleton, of the Kon Tiki and the Wright Brothers, and of others whose names and fates are long forgotten, by me at any rate – although still today, every year or so, I'll come across an ancient tale of heroism or adventure that rings a faint bell and I'll know straight away that here again is one of Mr Gowland's stories. He had such a facility for story-telling that each tale was woven and coiled for maximum impact. And, now I come to think of it, there may have been a strong moral theme to them – although then again, maybe not. He was a cinema buff, and when he'd been to see a good film (usually a western), he'd tell us about it after evening prayers. Row upon row of impressionable boys would sit in breathless silence. 'So Dirk's feeling sore now and he lies up to lick his wounds and think things over. Sooner or later he starts to think about (dramatic pause) revenge! And the more he thinks, the thirstier he gets. So by and by he's back in the saloon, downing the old rye whisky as if it was water.'

You get the picture.

I'll spoil things now by revealing what happened to Mr Gowland because that isn't part of this story, but maybe it will help to know. He left Kenton when I was around twelve and took up the headmaster's post at Caernarvon House School – another boy's prep school out in the Rift Valley towards Nakuru. Soon afterwards, so I heard, he was removed for 'playing with the boys'. Now, I was maybe thirteen when I heard this news and had no idea what playing with the boys might involve beyond the most literal explanation. It was perhaps a decade later when it occurred to me just what his crime must have been. And to this day I'm reluctant to believe it. Mr Gowland wasn't like that. I slept in tents with the man, with a whole platoon of boys and he never ... Still. I can see how a starched governing committee of colonial wives might have misunderstood his easy rapport with the boys, his laddish outdoor ways, his risky jokes, his fondness for nights under canvas. Who am I to judge? I wasn't there. Maybe the guy was a pervert, but that wasn't the Mr Gowland Max and I knew.

Which has nothing at all to do with this story, which concerns stars. And planets.

It began on a day of blazing sunshine. At noon, when all but mad dogs and Englishmen were resting in the shade, we Kenton boys were paraded outside and assembled on the staff lawn in a semi-circle around the flagpole; Mr Gowland in command.

It was a high, flagless flagpole.

Mr Gowland grinned at us. 'Can someone tell me why we're here?' he asked.

Silence.

'There's a reward. A school trip.'

We shuffled in the heat.

'Who can tell me what day it is?'

Every hand shot up. 'It's 21st March, sir,' said one lucky boy.

'Good, good. You're on the trip. I need two more boys. Who can tell me what time it is?'

Bedlam. 'Twelve o'clock, sir!'

'Good.' That was Max added to the trip. I cast him an envious glance.

'One more boy. I need one more boy so that we fit in my car. Who can tell me why we're here,' he paused, 'On 21st March ... at twelve noon?'

One hundred and eleven dumbfounded boys stood and racked our brains in the toasting sunshine. My mind whirled. Somewhere I felt that I knew the answer.

'Look at the flagpole,' he suggested. We looked. It loomed above us, barely swaying in the still air, standing in a tiny puddle of dark shadow.

And I had it. I had it! My hand was up. 'I know sir! I know.'

'Last?'

'It's the equinox, sir. The sun is right overhead.'

He gave me the pleased smile that stays in the memory of every child who has ever earned a pleased smile from a teacher. 'Last, you're on the trip.'

He told us how the world wobbles on its axis. And how, twice a year at noon on the equator, the sun would be directly overhead. In Nairobi, we were close enough to the equator for it to make no difference, and that we could tell because the flagpole had virtually no shadow. Neither did we.

And we all looked down at the dark round shadows cast by our shamba hats on the grass and became aware for the first time that the circular puddles were tiny.

Night. We set off at night because we were astronomers. We were off to see the biggest telescope in Kenya – perhaps the biggest telescope in the world. That was what Mr Gowland told us. Then, as he drove, he explained the background. There was an old, old man, a friend it seemed, who had built a telescope in his youth and then made his name as an astronomer. The man was over one hundred years old. That much was true. And he was deaf. We were to be on our absolutely best behaviour – no pushing, no shouting, no horseplay. If we had questions, we could ask his wife who was only ninety-nine, and she would relay the question to him. Curiously, he could still hear her speak, or perhaps there was a kind of telepathy between them.

We turned into the driveway of a very ordinary colonial wooden bungalow of the kind that you might find in the thousands along the back lanes outside Nairobi, with christ-thorn hedgerows and overhanging jacaranda. In the darkness we met the bent figure of the old man. He held an ear trumpet – the only one I have ever seen. He walked us down a path to the shed where he kept the telescope. Actually, I should call it an observatory. The roof rolled back on well-oiled wheels to reveal a sky of stars. Beneath it sat a lumbering contraption that looked nothing like the sleek tube of a telescope, but telescope it was. The old man sat in front of it, turned some wheels, and squinted into an eyepiece. A noisy petrol motor started. Mr Gowland explained that this would turn the telescope at the same speed as the rotation of the Earth, so that the stars would appear to stay still.

One by one, we queued to look down the eyepiece. Venus, huge and bright. Jupiter yellow and brooding. Saturn with astonishingly clear rings and moons. Anxious to behave, we didn't hog the lens, just peering for long enough to make out the planets and count the moons. All the time the old man spoke to us in a breathy voice, telling us about the planets as if he had been there. And perhaps, in a sense, he had. 'I'd like to show you Mars,' he said, 'but he isn't up yet. Instead, I'll give you a treat.' He took us outside and directed our gaze to a featureless patch of grey in the starlit sky. 'That's where we're going to look,' he told us. Back in the shed he navigated the big machine until it was aligned. 'Now take a look.' And we did. It was a nebula, red and blue and smoking, set against a backdrop of stars invisible to the naked eye.

I find it difficult to convey the impression that this experience had on me, but here's the thing: whatever I might have felt, the impact on Max was even greater. And I suspect that it was an impression that grew with each recollection. Max knew about planets and nebulae and stars, but to actually gaze on them through the steel and glass of this great apparatus suddenly shrank the world we lived in.

After a while we all trooped into the bungalow for a cup of tea. The old woman met us, asked our names, and shook our hands. The walls of the small living room were papered with newspaper cuttings and she showed us some of them. They all told of the old man and his telescope. Many had photographs of planets, or nebulae, or the moon. Some had photographs of the old man standing by his great machine.

Then she showed us a framed document on the wall. It was a telegram from the queen, congratulating the old man on reaching one hundred years of age.

'Next year,' the old lady told us. 'I shall have one too.'

Afterwards, we drove back to school and then, instead of going straight up to our dormitories, Mr Gowland led us out onto the staff lawn and we all lay down on the grass with our heads close together and looked up at the stars. Mr Gowland pointed out some of them and told us their names.

'Look,' he said, 'that huge constellation like a big square is Orion. It has four of the brightest stars at its corners. That one is Betelgeuse, and that one is Rigel. This is looking way back in time because the light from Rigel started its journey 900 years ago and for nine centuries the light has been travelling uninterrupted through the void at an unbelievable speed until at last, now, you open your eyes and capture it and its journey is over. And there is Bellatrix. And Saiph. If you look along his belt ... there, you can see a sword. And in his sword is the great nebula of Orion – sixteen light years across – a breeding ground for new stars. And if you follow the line of Orion's belt down down, you come upon Sirius, the dog star. The brightest star in the sky.'

And so we lay on the soft grass but really we were flying up among the stars, capturing ancient light from Rigel, looking for distant planets, taking in the soft amazing sweep of the Milky Way.

There is a sort of coda to this story but it involved only Max, so I shall direct you to the passage from the autobiography section of volume CXXVIII which Max wrote in February 1986, almost

eleven years into his grand project, and nearly eighteen years after
the events he describes.

VOLUME CXXVIII
FEBRUARY 1986

Two years and eight months later, it was
another equinox - this time the December
equinox of 1968 - and I was cycling home late
from a trip. I had a cycle lamp and unlimited
energy and was freewheeling down one of the
quiet suburban lanes around Dagoretti when
I suddenly recognised where I was - by the
old wooden house - with the telescope.
I stopped my bicycle. My heart began to
flutter. There were no lights burning. All
was quiet. But when I caught the little house
in the beam of my cycle lamp I saw that all
was not well. The windows had been boarded
over with planks. The house was deserted.
I turned my lamp towards the observatory. It
was still there. My heart beat faster. I tried
the door and it swung open with a creak.
Inside, the shed was empty. The great
telescope was gone. The noisy engine was gone.
The books and tools and cameras and pictures
were all gone. It was now just an empty shed.
For a moment I thought I must be in the wrong
place. After all, one wooden bungalow is very
much like another. But then I looked up. The
roof of the observatory was open, and through
the empty gap where once the huge reflector
had scoured the universe, I could see the
stars.

21

THE PHONE CALL

We're back in March 1974. Just to recap – I want to pick up the story after the fencing match. You will remember that the captain has been 'stabbed in the throat with a sword', and Max has been arrested.

The phone call was from Aunt Zinnia, who didn't seem surprised when I answered instead of Max. 'We're on our way back,' she told me. 'The captain's going to be OK.'

'Thank god,' I said.

'Tell Max all he did was puncture Cap's windpipe. Lots of blood and all that, but not too much real damage. They've stitched him up and they're keeping him in for a couple of days for observation. Tutton and I are on our way home. The only thing is, Cap won't be able to talk for a few days. They've stitched up his throat.'

'Actually, Max isn't here.'

'Not there?'

'Er ... no. The police came round. They've taken Max away for questioning.'

There was a pause at the other end of the line. 'I see,' said Aunt Zinnia.

I knew what she meant.

'They're sending a car for me,' I said.

'Oh shit. They're not going to lock Max up or anything like that?'

'I don't know. They weren't particularly friendly.'

'I see.' There was another pause. I could hear Zinnia explaining the situation on the other end of the line, presumably to Tutton and the captain too, if he was there to hear it. 'They've gone and arrested Max,' she was saying, 'they've banged him up ... I know ... I know ... I'll ask Adam. Hang on,' She came back onto the line. 'How did he take it?'

'Not too well, I'm afraid. He had … Well, he had one of his panics.'

She explained this to whoever was with her: 'He threw a paddy.'

'Look, stay there,' she said to me. 'We'll be back in a jiffy and then we'll go and get Max.'

'OK. But I might not be here. They're sending a car for me.'

'Oh yes. Well, look, we'll be back soon.'

'Good. And the captain's really OK?'

'Right as rain. Just a sore throat,' she laughed. Then there was a pause. 'Look here,' she said. 'I'll tell you the whole story when I get home. I just don't want you to repeat any of this to Max.'

'Of course,' I promised.

'Cap was jolly lucky actually. A millimetre or so either way and it could have been a major blood vessel.'

I waited for the police car that would come and collect me, but it never came. Alone in the house, I settled back into one of the leather-covered Empire mahogany bergères. There was nothing else I could do. I seemed to spend my life waiting for Max. It was like the afternoon I had spent on the pavement in Dorset Square. Like the solitary cruise from Bukoba to Kisumu, a story I have yet to tell. I was an actor standing patiently and unseen in the wings, waiting to play my walk-on role in the Ponder family drama.

When Aunt Zinnia and Tutton arrived, I was asleep in the bergère. It was to be the first of many occasions when I would fall asleep in this chair. Tutton, tap-tapping his way with his stick, brought me a black coffee and then he disappeared into the kitchen. Aunt Zinnia perched across from me on the chaise longue. A few hours earlier, we had sat in the same places drinking champagne to toast the life of Libby the dog. Now, here we were again. Aunt Zinnia was drinking something alcoholic. 'I shan't pour you one in case the pigs really do come for you,' she said. That was her hippy heritage speaking.

'I need to tell you something about the captain,' she began. 'He isn't as well as I suggested.'

'No?'

'No.' She let out a deep sigh. 'I need you to help me keep all of this from Max.'

'Of course.' Everyone wanted to protect Max, including me.

'I think,' started Aunt Zinnia, and she paused to look into her drink. 'I think that the captain may be seriously ill. You know, more serious than I might have suggested.'

'Because of the accident?'

'No ... not just that,' said Zinnia. 'Although that did more damage than perhaps I implied on the phone.'

'Right.'

'Max must never know.'

'Of course.'

'Did you notice anything about the captain today? I mean, you know him, Adam. You've met him many times.'

'I ... well ... no. Nothing really.'

'You knew my brother, didn't you, Adam? My twin. Martin?'

'I never met him, I'm afraid.'

'No. Of course. But you see Adam, when Martin died ...'

'Yes?'

'When Martin died. Yes ... Well, he had been ill, you see. It was a terrible crash, of course, but he had this brain tumour. We had to keep it from the captain. And from Max.'

'Yes, I see.'

'But *do* you see, Adam? Do you really see?'

'Yes, Aunt Zinnia. I do see. You were worried that this might be a hereditary condition. You wanted to protect Max and the captain. You didn't want them to live their lives with this fear hanging over them. I do understand,' I said, as gently as I could.

'Max mustn't know.'

We sat for a while. Not speaking.

'They have him on some kind of breathing machine,' Zinnia said.

'The captain?'

'Yes. If he dies, Adam, then Max will think it was his fault. And it won't have been.'

'No.'

'And if he lives, then Max will find out about the tumour.'

'The captain had a plan C,' I said. I saw Zinnia looking puzzled at this information.

'A plan C?'

'A third option. He would go to Australia,' I explained. 'Then

161

Max wouldn't see him deteriorate. The first Max would know would be ... I don't know, maybe the news of a car crash, or a stroke.'

'You *knew* about this?'

'He told me,' I said.

'Then you know about Martin's tumour?'

'The captain told me.'

She thought about this. 'How long does he have?'

'He doesn't know. It could be weeks, or it could be months.'

'That's the same as Martin. It started with a stutter for him too, you know, and a limp.'

'We could still go with plan C.'

She shook her head. 'I don't think so. Not now. I can't see him being fit to travel for quite some time and by then, well, who knows ...'

'It only affects men,' I said after a while.

Zinnia blinked at me, not quite understanding.

'The cancer,' I said. 'The captain told me it wouldn't affect you.'

Zinnia nodded slowly. 'Actually, I had never really thought about that,' she said.

'Look,' I said, getting to my feet, 'I don't think I should stay.'

'No, you must.'

'But this is a family thing now.'

'You *are* family. Virtually.'

'No, Zinnia. I'm not. Not even virtually. I'll just be in the way. I should get back to Keele.'

'What about the police. I thought they wanted to talk to you?'

'You can always tell them where I am.' I thought about the dismissive way that the policeman had treated me as he bundled Max into the police car. 'They'll come for me if they want. But I wouldn't bet on it.'

Zinnia stood up. 'Well, if you must,' she said.

'Could you run me to the station?' I said. 'Then perhaps you should go to the police. They'll let Max go eventually and when they do it might be good if you were there.'

She sighed. 'You're right.'

'I need two minutes to get my things. I'll see you on the drive.'

I collected my bag and my guitar and my sheepskin coat, then I started down the six stone steps from the great front door to the driveway. On the top step I was resolved. I would leave this mess behind and retreat to my comfortable world at Keele, my unremarkable friends and the crises that never seemed to skirt the life and death issues of the Ponders.

By the second step, I was unsure. Max was my friend. My best friend. Could I leave him to the whim of random events, irate policemen, a scatty aunt and a dying father?

By the fourth step, I remembered Libby the dog. Alone among the diverse occupants of The Pile, only Adam Last could bury the dog. Max was too immature, too much a victim of his fragile disposition. The captain was too ill. Tutton was too decrepit and too blind. Zinnia was ... Well, Zinnia was Zinnia; quite incapable of digging a grave and cracking the legs of a dead Labrador.

By the bottom step, the turmoil that had swept through me like a summer dust-devil had resolved itself in quite a different way to the resolution that had seemed so secure just six steps before. This, I think, is how the great decisions in our lives are made; not through perspiration and balanced reflection, but through sudden moments of insight.

When Zinnia reappeared, I told her that I had changed my mind. I carried my bag back up to the hall. 'I'm not going yet,' I told her.
'Oh?'
'We'll go and see the captain,' I said, 'and then we'll get Max.'
'Right,' Zinnia held up the car keys. 'Let's go then.'

22

USOGA

APPENDIX CDXXIX: Diseases and Afflictions

Index of Diseases

It isn't until you sit down and start listing
all the human diseases you know, that you
start to appreciate just how much our poor
old species must have suffered over the
millennia. Every one of these grisly
infirmities must have blighted the lives of
tens of millions of people; what a thought!
A whole miserable miasma of parasites and
plagues and epidemics has afflicted us since
we came down from the trees. These are just
the ones I know and, let's face it, medicine
was never my topic of choice on *University
Challenge*. So there must be tens, hundreds,
maybe even thousands more. This will be a
depressing appendix to write.

[1] The Definitive List of all the Diseases
I Know

  1. Acne - I suffered from this when I was
fifteen. Not sure if it really qualifies as a
disease but I'll need a chapter on it anyhow.
Not infectious (as far as I know).
  2. Ague - this will be a very short chapter.
I'm not even sure if it exists or if it was

a Shakespearean invention. There was an Andrew
Aguecheek in *Twelfth Night*, wasn't there?
Let's not bother with a chapter. This is all
I know. It used to be pronounced a̲-gyu
I think. No idea if Ague was infectious or
not.

3. Allergies (various) - I need to list all
the allergies I can remember. That will
require a chapter. Not infectious.

4. Amoebic Dysentery - A short chapter,
I imagine. I know this is very nasty. Kimathi
suffered from it. [I have written about
amoebas in appendix CLXXX - Zoology]
Infectious. Caught from amoebas in human shit.

5. Anthrax - All I know about this is that
they tested it out on an island in Scotland
and now no one can live there. This will only
need a page. Infectious. Caught from animals.

6. Athlete's Foot - This is one of Adam's
afflictions. I know lots about this.
Infectious. Could be caught from Adam.

7. Bilharsia - This used to scare us when
we were kids in Nairobi. Luke Quentin [LQU
31] caught it from playing in the Kirichwa
River. Infectious. Little worms crawl through
your skin and take up residence in the liver.
Nematodes. It bleeds when you pee. I'll need
a chapter for this.

8. Black Death/Bubonic Plague - covered
pretty much in appendix CVI [Middle Ages]
and again in appendix CVIII [Stuarts] and
also in books [Pepys appendix CCLIII]. I'll
assign a chapter to this. Infectious. Rat
fleas.

9. Blackwater Fever - Nothing to write about
this. All I know is the name. I think it
might be another name for Malaria.

10. Bronchitis - Tutton used to suffer. [TUT

1122]. I think it was caused by smoking. You
could hear his cough right the way through
The Pile. Not infectious, I don't think.

11. Cancers (Detailed In A Later Section:
[cancers appendix: CDXXX].

12. Chickenpox - This needs a whole chapter.
I nearly died when I was six years old.
Ghastly. Infectious.

13. Cholera - Lots about this in [appendix
CXC]. Also see Tchaikovsky [composers
appendix DCXXVII]. I'll need a chapter.
Infectious. From dirty water.

14. Common Cold - This may require a whole
appendix volume. I've assigned appendix DCCCX
for Common Cold-related memories. Infectious.

15. Conjunctivitis - At least a chapter
needed. I lost most of my eyelashes when
I was seventeen. Infectious - I presume.

16. Cowpox - The only thing I know about
Cowpox is that (i) milkmaids used to catch
it from cows and (ii) it is similar enough to
smallpox that (iii) Edward Jenner used it to
vaccinate people against smallpox so (iv)
that's where the word vaccinate comes from
because 'vacca' is the Latin for cow. Napoleon
introduced a programme to vaccinate everyone
in France against smallpox but he used the
pus from the boils of smallpox victims.
[I think this story is also in appendix CIX.]
Infectious, from milkmaids.

17. Crabs - I'll bundle this into a chapter
on VDs. Happy to say that I'm not especially
knowledgeable on any of these. Infectious,
also from milkmaids.

Max would begin most of his appendix volumes in this way. He
would brainstorm a list over several sheets of paper. Piles of these
lists-in-progress would be heaped on his desk, and he'd add to them

every time inspiration struck. There could be a list on diseases underway and another on Latin verbs and a third on brands of chocolate bar and a fourth on popular pub names. Sometimes a dozen or more lists competed for space on the table. Only when he was satisfied that he had managed to recall enough to get started, would he take a list and sort the contents alphabetically and write his index neatly into one of the blue appendix volumes, like the list of afflictions above (which continues for fifty more entries ending up with sixty-eight: West Nile Fever; sixty-nine: Whooping Cough; and seventy: Yellow Fever).

Once Max had the index out of his system he would write a chapter or more on each subject. Cholera, for example, takes three pages; bilharsia takes eleven; leprosy, seventeen. And of course, this being Max, he would suddenly recall new additions. It could happen at any time. We might be enjoying a meal, and he would slap a hand to his forehead and cry out, 'Rift Valley Fever – how could I have forgotten?' And then he would write furiously until every memory of Rift Valley Fever had been mined out of his brain and dumped onto the page.

One appendix volume wasn't enough to exhaust the subject of disease, and so he continued into an overflow, appendix CDXXX, which also lists so much information about cancers that it too overflows into appendix CDXXXI. I no longer find it astonishing that someone who never studied medicine could carry so much information in his head about so many human afflictions. Most of what Max records is the sort of detail you or I would know, or the anecdotal stories he encountered in his childhood. Here are two more entries from the list.

36. Leprosy – Once there was a time when the word 'leprosy' triggered warm and comfortable images in my mind of Bible stories and Jesus and happy cured lepers. There was a tale, I remember, about ten lepers that he healed, and only one of them thought to come back and say thanks. There was also a joke about lepers. Did you hear about the leper who played poker? He threw in his hand. I've

never told that joke. I wouldn't be able to.
Not since Mwanza. Infectious. Just about.
I need a big chapter for this.
   43. Mumps - A horrid viral disease that
makes the glands in your neck swell, and
turns you into a vomiting, sweating, aching,
wretched invalid for about a week. A childhood
disease - one that struck me down when I was
ten. Different people suffer in different
ways. I had it particularly badly. Infectious.
Very. I need a chapter for this.

We are reassembling Max's life in fragments, like piecing together
the shards from a broken mirror. But somehow, I do feel, if we
can orient the pieces roughly within the frame, a reflection should
begin to emerge. This is another one of those pieces. It is a story
from Max's life that the psychologists will want to explore. It
happened during the long holiday of 1965, the holiday that I'd now
call 'the summer holiday' although then it was just the big, life-
enhancing void between the Trinity and Michaelmas terms. Kenton
took these things seriously of course. The school calendar, like
everything else, had been packaged up from England and dropped
into Africa. We played cricket and tennis in June, football in
October, hockey in March. We took holidays when the Bible
dictated - Christmas and Easter and Whitsun. And when the sun
shone half a world away in England, we took our long holiday.

   In the long holiday of 1965, Max and I, and Max's mother O,
took a cruise on Lake Victoria aboard a steamship, the SS *Usoga*.
If this part of the story is about anyone, then it is really about O.
She was pregnant at the time. Not huge, but visibly pregnant
nonetheless. Max and I were still ten, although Max would turn
eleven on the trip. In some senses therefore, it was a birthday treat
for him.

   Some birthday.

   I should introduce you to Max's mother. Her real name, I now
know, was Miranda, but the story goes that when she met and
married the captain, everyone thought 'Miranda Ponder' was too
alliterative, so she took to using her middle name, Ophelia. And

that, for some reason, was shortened to O. Maybe 'Ophelia' was too tinged with tragedy. So, everyone called her O. Max called her O. The captain called her O. I called her O. She introduced herself as O – a name you cannot say without sounding surprised, Oh! Or questioning, Oh? Or accusing, Oh …

O existed, it seemed, as a quiet contrast to the captain, with his loud, military bearing. Unlike my first meeting with the captain, which has somehow fixed itself in my memory, I don't have any recollection of the first time I met O. Somehow she was always there. And yet she wasn't. The adjective that always hung around her, that was even aired at her funeral, is 'distant'. It seemed to be a character trait she nourished; a faint but tangible distance. In the heat of Kenya she kept her opalescent complexion by never venturing directly into the sun, but by hiding, always, beneath a straw hat with a wide brim. She was tall and she was thin, and the mousy hair beneath her hat lent a slightly mournful look to her already long features. I remember her prominent shoulder blades, like the wings on a sedan; I remember them almost more than I remember her face.

I learned from Max that O was deaf in one ear. It meant that she had to strain just a little harder to hear you speak, and so she'd frown in concentration and lean towards you, as if eager to pick up every word, but then, in defiance of that impression, she'd turn her face away just slightly, so that her good ear could hear. It was a subtle, almost invisible mannerism, but it meant that conversation with O was always a little unsettling, her gaze forever exploring a distant horizon just out of sight, somewhere behind you but a little to the left. And truly this is how she was, as if her mind were never fully engaged, as if a wistful, lost memory had been awoken in her and her focus had been drawn elsewhere. She would draw a long, cool serpent of smoke from her Russian cigarette and let it leak seductively from the edges of her wide mouth so that it billowed beneath the brim of her hat.

O never spoke much. She thought before she spoke. She'd wait for a pause, for a prompt from the wings, and then she would unfix her gaze from the horizon, catch you with her grey eyes, and talk so softly that this time it would be your turn to lean forward.

I was too young to know, and now I can only guess, but I'd say there was a disarming sexuality about O. Perhaps we were aware of it, Max and I, prepubescent boys, as we trailed behind her through the marketplaces, watching the rolling sway of her hips. Yet she didn't present an overtly sexual image. She didn't look like a woman in search of affirmation. I don't remember bright lipstick or short skirts. She didn't wear the floral frocks and headscarves of the expats. I picture her in loose khaki jodhpurs, or long safari trousers, billowing white blouses, and always that wide straw hat; I see her sitting on the edge of a table or perching on a verandah rail, swinging her legs boyishly. She flirted endlessly with the captain, I can see that now. She teased him with a fleeting laugh and the flicker of her tongue around her lips, and a flick of her mousy hair.

O must have been around forty when we went on the cruise. Rather old to be pregnant, you might think. But then it was a Ponder thing. Rash too, you might say, to gallivant off with two ten-year-old boys on a jaunt in central Africa when carrying a child. Another Ponder thing. Besides, I can imagine the brochure for this trip. It must have looked like a luxury holiday, on board a comfortable liner, drifting silently between sunsets against a backdrop of golden beaches, civilised meals on deck, jolly camaraderie with British compatriots over canasta in the lounge; stopping off in quaint African fishing villages for drinks beneath the palms.

But let's start a little earlier. The holiday wasn't only a birthday treat, it was also partly to pick Max up after a bout of the mumps. In the Trinity Term of 1965, we had a mumps epidemic at Kenton. Epidemics were common events at boarding school. In fact, they were encouraged. We had epidemics of chickenpox, measles, German measles, whooping cough, influenza, mumps, and a whole corps of ailments that would defeat the diagnostic capabilities of the school nurse. The process generally started when a boy appeared at the sanatorium with spots or swellings or fever, but once the disease had been diagnosed, the machinery of the school would swing into action. Dormitories would be commandeered as sanatoria, and displaced boys would move to fill the unoccupied beds of those boys with the fever. Then, boys who had never suffered from the disease in question would be encouraged to visit the sick, to 'help out' alongside the most pustulant and feverish invalids, changing bedsheets, mopping up vomit, collecting dinner dishes, until they themselves succumbed.

There was a logic behind this madness. Since it was assumed that every boy would inevitably contract every disease eventually – and since most were considered to be better caught when young – what better place to suffer than at boarding school in the company of a dormitory full of other sufferers?

So Max got the mumps. You can read about it in The Catalogue in half a dozen places. It appears in his appendix of diseases, in his autobiography, and in his biography of O, and it crops up with curious regularity in places where you'd least expect it. Max was always a poor invalid; to read his accounts of the mumps you'd think he was close to death. Perhaps he was. For my part, I suffered alongside him, but a day or so ahead of him in the disease cycle, so I missed his most awful privations, being more absorbed in my own survival. In The Catalogue Max writes something to the effect that, 'Adam caught it too, but much less severely than I did'.

Well, that was forty years ago and Max is lying dead on the Rastin table, so let's not argue. Anyway, the upshot of all this was that O and the captain resolved that Max should have a holiday and naturally I had to come too.

Our cruise was to be around Lake Victoria. We sailed from the port of Kisumu at the Western end of the great railway. In a perfect world, of course, Lake Victoria would be one of the greatest holiday destinations on the planet: a huge body of fresh water, the size (so I was told, and I've never checked) of Ireland. When you're sailing you spend much of the time out of sight of land so it's an ocean really; a freshwater ocean. It heaves and groans like an ocean. Yet all around are the dark, mysterious hills and jungles of Livingstone's Africa. There's a hint of the unexplored – and the unexplorable – about the place. Straddling Uganda, Tanzania, Rwanda, Burundi and Congo, the lake is an international melting pot of African cultures and people. Around it live ancient tribes who have made their living from the beneficent lake for countless generations. Our most ancient ancestors probably sojourned here for a few millennia, feeding off the fine fish, luxuriating beneath the cool trees that overhang the bank, wading in the thousand little bays. Lake Victoria is as African as it gets. Wildlife abounds. Hippos swim languidly. Crocodiles bask menacingly. Antelope come fleetingly to the shores to drink. Great birds flock. Tiny birds trip over the water seeking flies. Insects throng and swarm and buzz incessantly.

By 1965, when our tale unfolds, the ravenous tongue of commerce had already flickered into every remote corner of Lake Victoria. Boats and ships and tugs and rafts and canoes and dhows plied the waterways from dock to dock, laden with produce. Great crates of bananas, huge bundles of cotton, boxes of tea, sacks of pulses were loaded onto the assortment of vessels from the docksides. Teams of labourers, ragged and barefoot, chanted as they sweated and heaved and swung their loads onto the decks. Tobacco wrapped in leaves. Vegetables in string bags. Crates of beer. Boxes of powdered milk. Sides of salted meat turning faintly purple. Machine parts. Oil. Coffee beans green, coffee beans red, coffee beans roasted. Fishing boats would disgorge their holds of slippery heaps of foul-smelling fish, still gasping their last in the heat as merchants squabbled and palms were spat upon and slapped.

The docks were riveting for a ten-year-old. There were beggars, holding out querulous hands for discarded coins. There were children, gaunt and round-bellied, looking on. There were the longshoremen, and the merchants who did business in raised, frenetic voices and strange middlemen who squatted on their heels beside heaps of rice and salt and yams and basketry, selling these sparse wares to the traders. Thin mongrel dogs stalked in search of scraps. Chickens, tied together by the feet, were piled in boxes. There was a smell of rotting things; unsold bananas, foetid meat.

These were the docks through which we picked our way to the Usoga, the porcelain figure of Ophelia Ponder shrouded with straw hat and cigarette smoke, Max still unnaturally pale, with his lace-up shoes and his half-frame camera and his tin of personal mementoes. Me, of course. Probably roasted brown in flip-flops, shorts and T-shirt, my uniform of choice. And our retinue of porters clutching our precious luggage; and their retinue of barefoot children; and their retinue of thin dogs.

We found the SS *Usoga*. It was not, was never, a cruise liner. Instead, it was a rusty, oily, smelly merchantman, scarcely bigger than a tug. Its engines belched and roared. It had two decks and four passenger cabins – two on either side of the upper deck.

Max and I had one cabin, O another. A young Irish couple, called the Lynams, honeymooners, had a third. The fourth was empty. We were the only passengers.

Now I should explain that being the only Europeans on board a rusting African tug cast adrift in Lake Victoria did not intimidate us in the slightest. We were British. This was our empire. We probably grumbled about the accommodation or the heat, but essentially we did the British thing. We put up with it. In fact, we bore it all quite bravely. So it was with a real sense of excitement that we stood on the deck and listened to the band as SS *Usoga* slipped away from Kisumu harbour into the shiny dark waters of Africa's largest lake.

We docked at Musoma before dawn. By daybreak the long-shoremen were already straining on the ropes that would haul their treasures up from the hold. We politely had breakfast in the dining room and were conscientiously waited upon by a uniformed waiter with a white shirt and a company tie and a red-tasselled fez. It was clear from the docks that Musoma was not a quaint fishing village. It was an African township that sprawled away from the docks in edifices of mud and concrete and rusted corrugated iron. The wharf at Musoma made Kisumu look like another world. The drains and sewers of the town, such as they were, trickled over the docksides and cascaded into the lake, so that passengers wanting to venture forth would have to navigate a stepping-stone path of broken wooden pallets in order to save them from walking through the filth. O was up for it. She was in a breezy mood as we broke away from the breakfast table. 'Let's explore,' she said.

Max, however, was in no mood for adventure, and O was in no disposition to argue. So it was Mrs Ponder and I who teetered out on the pallets to discover Musoma. She clutched my hand as if terrified she would lose me, or that one of us might slip into the grey sludge that slopped beneath our feet.

We sat in a roadside bar under a Martini umbrella and sipped Fanta through straws. O's attention was somewhere else – on the road behind me perhaps, with the Musoma rush hour of rusted vans and motor scooters, thin donkeys, cattle wagons, bicycles, and trucks that burped their black smoke into the humid air. An old man loomed close to our table, his eyes riddled with parasites. He bowed low to Mrs Ponder and unrolled an oily cloth in which there were wood carvings.

'Did you make these?' O smiled at the man, and he, responding to her smile, nodded back vigorously.

'Would you like a carving, Adam?' O asked me.

'No, thank you, Mrs Ponder.'

'Oh, but you must.' She picked up the carvings to inspect them. 'How about this?' An elephant.

'That's all right, Mrs Ponder.'

'Or this one?' A giraffe.

'Really, you don't have to buy me one. Buy one for Max.'

'Oh I *shall* buy one for Max. But let's find one for you first. Here. You choose.'

I looked at the pile of carvings and chose one quite at random. Absolutely at random. I reached into the pile and closed my fingers and I said, 'This one.'

After another day of sailing, the next destination loomed into view. Mwanza. It was 4 July 1965, the eve of Max's eleventh birthday. O was not prepared to let Max miss landfall again, despite the unpromising views of Mwanza from the deck. She gave him one of her stern looks over breakfast and sent him off in search of a suitable hat.

Whatever our experience had been of Musoma, Mwanza still came as a shock. Leprosy was rife there in 1965. As we disembarked, a lone beggar ravaged by the disease approached us. Max shrank back in horror. O delved into her bag and gave the man five shillings. Within minutes there were two more lepers, then four, then a crowd. O dispensed small coins until she had nothing more to offer. But the crowd around us had scented money. They thrust themselves forward, offering up their most mutilated body parts for examination. We hurried on into the town, joined by more lepers as we travelled. We might have guessed that all the town's lepers lurked around the docks, waiting for the rare sight of a tourist boat, but when we reached the town we learned otherwise. The lepers at the dock were simply the ones fit and whole enough to get there. For every one of them, a dozen others lay in the dust of Mwanza township. Most had lost the will to beg; they simply lay in passive acceptance of their condition and waited to die. Forty years later, this is a sight that still haunts me. I know it haunted Max. One beggar in Africa hardly makes you turn an eye. One on every corner is almost expected. But a population so ravaged and wasted by such an unforgiving disease is another matter. Although the majority of people still seemed surprisingly well, what a dread fear must have hung over them as they saw their neighbours and families struck down. And what a cruel disease. Fingers reduced to stumps. Hands reduced to roots. Skin and face and eyes riddled with wounds.

We spent nothing in Mwanza except on the beggars. O wouldn't buy us a drink – she was terrified of the leprosy – and we hurried along the streets as if speed would help us escape infection.

At one corner we passed a compound fenced off with loose corrugated iron and the smell was difficult to bear. Max clutched my arm. We stopped just for a moment. Through a broken bit of fencing, too low for O to share our perspective, Max and I could see an untidy pile of corpses. About six or seven, perhaps, maybe as many as ten. One corpse was disturbingly close to the hole in the fence. The man lay on his back with his head lolled sideways, mouth and eyes open; he seemed to stare at us as we stared back, trying in the best way that ten-year-olds could to understand the very dark meaning of death. Some of the corpses were clothed in rags, others were naked. Perhaps they had been relieved, in death, of their clothes, their last and only possessions. One naked corpse was so ravaged by the leprosy that we couldn't determine if it had once been male or female. Another seemed barely to be a human corpse at all, more a reservoir of open sores.

This was the undertaker's compound. There were half-made coffins and a man driving nails into a coffin lid.

Max started to make a gulping sound as he stood transfixed by the encounter. O leaned down to share our view and she uttered a sound like a silent scream. She tore at Max's hand and dragged us both away. We walked swiftly across the town and retreated to the safety of the *Usoga*. Max was still weeping. And at sunset we sailed.

Mwanza had a huge impact on Max. He writes about it at length in The Catalogue. Those few paragraphs I've used to tell the story of Mwanza grow into dozens of dense pages in Max's account. Max always had a better memory than I do. He seems to remember every building we passed – the garage, the primary school, the Baptist church, the place selling dried beans. As for me, I remember only the morgue.

I promised that this story would be about O, but it is, of course, another story about Max and about events that must have influenced him. Those few days, the events of Max's eleventh birthday, the bodies in the morgue, the swarm of flies, and what befell O at Bukoba, should be meat and drink to the psychoanalysts. Let them crawl over these few moments in Max's life and unpick the scars.

Back at the *Usoga* no one mentioned Mwanza, or leprosy, or bodies. It was all we could do. We sailed from the infected docksides, and the horrors of the township started to drift out of sight and into memory. Out of reach of land, we could relax. There was a long voyage ahead before we would reach our third port of call – Bukoba – and Mr Lynam, the honeymooner, used the time to teach Max and me to fish. It emerged that he had brought full sets of tackle with him so we set these up on the lower deck – rods and weights and hooks and lines – and cast off over the guard-rail into the swirling waters of the lake. Several of the ship's company had the same idea. Some of the kitchen staff and engineers and deckhands appeared with sticks and line and we all took our places democratically along the deck waiting for a bite. Every now and then, with great excitement, one of the crew would haul in a fish. It had taken some persuasion for Max to participate. He had wanted to stay in the cabin, no doubt to brood on his first brutal encounter with mortality. But in the end he joined us and landed a tiddler. He took it and showed it to O, who was suitably impressed. But she was suffering a little from the heat and the lurching of the boat and perhaps from the unfamiliar cooking. She spent most of the day in a deckchair, well shaded, reading.

On the morning of Max's eleventh birthday, as we approached Bukoba, we became aware of a curious phenomenon. We were sailing into a fog. Only it wasn't a fog. It was a swarm of lake flies. It rolled over the lake like a heavy mist, curling and swelling. When we hit the swarm, we sank into it the way that an airliner penetrates the clouds.

When we made landfall at Bukoba, the swarm was still with us.

O was unwell. She was unfit to leave the boat. The Lynams offered to take Max and me with them into the town so that O could stay behind and rest. O agreed.

I can't remember much about Bukoba. We walked around, Max, Mr Lynam, Mrs Lynam and me. Young Mrs Lynam held our hands as we crossed the roads. There were no lepers that I recall. I remember only the flies. When we got back to the *Usoga* in the middle of the afternoon the ship's master was waiting to see us. He looked grim. He took Mr Lynam aside and spoke to him. Then Mr Lynam spoke to Max, as kindly as he could. He explained that O had been taken to the local mission hospital. She had started to deliver her baby. We were to stay on the boat, which was due to leave that night. They, the Lynams, would look after us. They would cable Max's father, who would motor up and collect O once the baby was delivered.

Max didn't take the news well. In fact, he was distraught. He fled to the cabins to see if it was true. O wasn't there. He began to shake. 'I want to see her.'

'You can't,' Mrs Lynam told Max firmly.

'But I must.'

'You'll be better off here with us. She's in hospital. She's in good hands, I promise you.'

But she had reckoned without Max's tenacity; and she had reckoned without the lake flies. Half an hour later, Max had vanished from the SS *Usoga*. He slid down a mooring rope, apparently. I'm pretty vague about the details because it was, after all, four decades ago. But the shroud of lake flies was so dense that he wasn't spotted, either from the ship or from the shore. This is how he tells it. He was concealed by a swarm of flies. I can't be bothered to look this up in The Catalogue, I'm afraid, because I would have to trawl through at least half a volume of extraneous detail. But I can tell *my* side of the story and some of Max's. Something like this happened: Max, hidden by a swarm of flies, sleuthed his way through Bukoba to the hospital in search of his mother. When it became clear, just before sailing, that Max was not on board the ship, Mr Lynam and his young bride offered to go off in search of him. There was a great deal of arguing and raised voices and waving of hands because the master of the ship had to sail. He was due in

Entebbe in eight hours' time. The company would not let him delay departure. The Lynams assured him that if they were not back he should sail regardless. They would find Max and O, make their way to Entebbe and meet us there. They left in a dirty white police Land Rover that was soon swallowed by the lake flies.

They didn't make it back to the boat and, at the appointed hour, we sailed. I was now the only tourist on the cruise.

We made landfall at Entebbe at daybreak, and there was no sign of Max or the Lynams. We only stayed there for an hour before we left for Port Bell. I can't remember a single feature of Port Bell now except for the police guardroom at the dock where I sat among a crowd of arguing policemen who were trying, unsuccessfully, to get a radio phone to work. Four hours later, we were en route to Kisumu.

Somehow the majesty of the lake eluded me on the second leg of the cruise. I took no photographs. I saw crocodiles in the water. I went in to the mess room for lunch and high tea and breakfast and, as if there were no change in routine, as if the only passenger on this trip were anyone other than a ten-year-old boy, the waiter dressed for me in his suit and fez, and the cook delivered up a full fare.

At Kisumu, I packed my things and Max's. I went into O's cabin and found that her case had gone. She must have taken it with her to the hospital. I shook hands with the master and said farewell to the crew, who had become my friends, then I walked with a case in each hand down the short gangplank onto the same stinking dock from which we had boarded a lifetime ago.

On the dock I sat on my suitcase and waited. I unpacked the carving that O had bought for me. It was a figurine, a woman, willowy and lissom with a basket on her head, carved in African black wood. Something about her face reminded me of O.

Around dusk a Land Rover drove slowly onto the dock. In it was not Max, nor the Lynams. It was a gentleman from the British Embassy wearing a lightweight white suit. He greeted me warmly and told me he had come to put me on a train back to Nairobi. My parents were worried. He bustled me into the back of the Land Rover and he sat in front with the driver so that I was not able to ask him what had become of Max and O and the Lynams. When we reached Kisumu station, there was bedlam because someone had been shunted out of their sleeping compartment to make way for me. The embassy man disappeared into the mêlée to smooth things over. When he re-emerged, it was to hurry me onto the train as it was about to depart.

'What about Max?' I managed to shout as he left me on board.

'Who?' the embassy man looked puzzled.

'Max. Max Ponder. My friend.'

'Ah,' said the embassy man, and he tugged uncomfortably on his sweaty collar. 'He'll be staying here for a while, I expect. In Tanganyika, probably. His family are all here now.'

'Oh good,' I said.

'I'm sure he'll be back down soon enough,' said the embassy man, 'after the funeral.'

RULES

Max's rules for life at The Pile were never written down, and never fully articulated, but anyone who visited was subject to them anyway. It generally fell to me to explain to guests exactly what could be done, what could be said, what could be implied. It was so important to get things right. I often thought about typing up a list of rules and giving it to visitors to memorise, but I never did. Had I done so, it might have included things such as: 'Rule one: Don't wear any clothes that could *not* reasonably have been bought before June 1975.' Fashion was never one of Max's strong points, but he withdrew from the world in the 1970s when kipper ties were normal and so were long sheepskin coats, broad stripes and platform shoes. I keep a wardrobe of neutral clothes and I change into them every time I go to the house unless I am already wearing something that would pass. For me that means plain cotton trousers or jeans and a cream shirt or a simple T-shirt with no pictures or slogans, or else a grey, wool suit.

I got into trouble once, with Max, when I wore a digital watch that gave a tiny beep on the hour. It only beeped once in his presence. One tiny beep; barely audible. You probably wouldn't have noticed it. But Max did. I managed to keep him insulated entirely from mobile phones and don't think that wasn't an achievement. That would be high on the list of rules. Possibly rule two: 'Drive your car through the back entrance, park outside the stable block, and leave your phone in your car along with any other devices – cameras or music players – that might be unfamiliar to someone who withdrew from the world in 1975.'

Few people would visit anyway. We could go a whole year without a visitor, but everyone who did come would have to surrender to the rules. 'Rule three: Don't ever talk about the world outside,' I would tell them. 'Never. Even if Elvis has just died. Rule four: Don't reminisce. Just because Max lives in the past doesn't mean it's a safe place to go. Max lives in *his* past, not yours. You might remember something that he doesn't and that would be new information and all new information is pollution.' I would smile patiently and watch them take these messages on board.

'Don't use words or expressions that don't belong in 1975.' That would be rule five. 'It may be difficult. You won't even know you're doing it – but Max will spot modern idioms straight away. Be patient with him. You will meet him in a heavily shaded room. Max will sit with his back to you. He will write all the time you are there, in one of his notebooks or on one of his A4 hole-punched day log sheets. He will be recording all the pollutants associated with your visit so that they can be excised from his brain. Suppose you just happen to mention something that should not be in his brain – suppose you mention the Poll Tax riots, or the new Sainsbury's at Wycombe, or the fact that your Aunt Monica died of scurvy; all at once that will set off bushfires in his mind. He will never forget this new fact so he must record it; but it doesn't belong among the facts that he's so diligently trying to set down. He is trying to compile a complete audit of his memory from the day that his eyes first opened until the day in 1975 when he slammed shut the door of The Pile, and this new memory is an interloper.'

Of course you'll be imagining a thousand and one problems with this regime. A darkened room does not eliminate experience, you will argue. Max spent thirty years in this routine. Surely he would remember thousands of events; the events of every day? On a typical day, for example, he would manifestly remember waking, would remember the sight of his reflection while shaving, would undoubtedly remember his breakfast and the morning spent with his notebooks; he would remember, perhaps, that he mislaid a pen, that noisy aeroplanes flew past outside, that I, Adam Last, came and brought new shoes and different biscuits from last week. He would inevitably notice the incremental changes of life. He would look at me and would see me growing old and overweight and grey and losing my hair. Surely, you might contend, these daily items would become a part of his memory just as the details of everyday life are part of your memory and mine?

And, of course, you would be right. There is no way to switch off the world entirely. But routine is a good concealer of memories. Max would rise every day at the same hour to the chime of the grandfather clock, would dress in one of half a dozen familiar suits, would dine on a routine menu of conventional ingredients, would work to a set agenda; and if you do this day after day, well, the memories of one day become very much like the memories of another and soon you can't remember if the day you lost your pen was last week, or the week before, or if indeed you ever had a pen at all. Max had no Mondays, no Tuesdays, no weekends, no bank holidays, no Christmas, no Easter, no Lent. There were seasons, of course, but Max rarely ventured out of doors, and a combination of central heating and air conditioning maintained his world at a steady temperature so that behind his heavy curtains there was little to distinguish June from December. They were simply months marked by the completion of yet another volume – which showed, I suppose, that he did count the days even though he did not care to know which days those were.

Every now and then, a persistent tradesman might circumvent the locked gates, might bypass the gate-house, might somehow find their way up the drive. Knock as they might, they would never get an answer. Over the years there were incidents, of course – breaches of security. Early in Max's confinement, a pair of Jehovah's Witnesses negotiated the driveway and finding the doorbell unanswered, they tried the handle and discovered that it had been left unlocked. My fault, as it turned out. As good fortune would have it, I drove up to The Pile only minutes later and saw the open door. One of the men had already started his pitch to Max, who stood transfixed with something that may have been rage, or may have been horror, or simple confusion.

We moved the electricity meter into a box beside the gate-house, clearly marked, so that there would be no visits from meter-readers. There was no milk delivery. Post was delivered to a box at the gate-house. A sign at the gate read 'Strictly Private' and the same words marked the river bank. Once, in 1986, a rowing boat capsized on the river and the young man who had been rowing rescued his girlfriend from drowning. He hauled her out of the river through the reed-beds that normally acted as a barrier, and carried her up to the house. Finding the front door locked, he went around to the back courtyard and spotted Max through the kitchen window. Max admitted them. He told me later that he thought the girl was dead. She wasn't, as it happened, but the man was crazy with worry. He demanded to use Max's phone. Max explained that he didn't have one. The young man didn't believe him.

'You may search the place if you wish,' Max said. 'You will not find a telephone because I do not possess one and never will.'

They laid the girl on the kitchen table. Max administered the kiss of life and she spluttered back to consciousness. At this point the young man was offended that Max may have somehow *kissed* his girlfriend; but he was grateful too. He snatched up the girl's hand and tried to lift her off the table.

'If I were you,' offered Max, 'I should let her lie for a moment.' He filled the kettle and brewed some tea. By the time he had done so, the girl was sitting up, recovered.

'If you go upstairs to the far bedroom that overlooks the river, you will find a wardrobe with clothes that should fit you,' Max told them. 'Help yourself to whatever you need and then please depart.'

'We can't take your clothes,' protested the young man.

'Oh, but you must,' said Max. 'And then you must leave. You must understand that I am a recluse and I do not care to be disturbed any further.' At this Max left the two of them alone in the kitchen and shut himself in the study.

How do I know all this? Because Max recorded it, of course. I've read it, every polluting item. It took Max about four days to exhaust the incident onto paper.

Over the thirty years, Max has twice needed to see a doctor. I drove to Harley Street and found an Armenian doctor called Dr Apraham Kazerian. He was extremely compliant and agreed, not only to make a house call, but to observe all of Max's conditions as though this type of consultation was an everyday feature of his job. He never questioned Max's mental health. I found that reassuring.

The dentist was much more awkward. In 1993, Max developed an abscess that was excruciatingly painful. He fulminates on it at length in The Catalogue, as you might well imagine. I found a dentist who agreed to make a home visit, and I gave him an explanation of Max's research project. 'He is carrying out a PhD on the effects of withdrawal on human memory,' I told him. It wasn't exactly true, but it was easier to explain than the truth. The dentist airily seemed to accept this, once we had agreed an outrageous fee for his services; but when he arrived at The Pile with his equipment he was accompanied by a young dental assistant who seemed oblivious to my instructions. I tried to protest, to insist that the dentist carry out his examination unassisted, but Max was in such discomfort that he waved away my objections. 'I'll live with it,' he said. 'Let's just get the bloody tooth out.'

The extraction took about half an hour during which time the dental assistant seemed to want to talk incessantly and I spent most of the time shushing her. Then, a week later, they had to call again for some follow-up process. It took Max about a fortnight to write it all up. After that, he asked me to buy a set of dental pliers, and twice since then I've hauled teeth out of his mouth while he swore at me in agony. That, you see, is the price I pay for my job.

Did I mention that looking after Max has been my *job*? You could say it has been my career. It isn't exactly what I went to Keele to study for, but it has kept me busy enough over the years. After the captain died, Max put me in charge of the Ponder Estates. I was twenty. What did I know about running an estate? Max had been earmarked to manage the Ponder businesses after the death of his father, and in the very early days, as we planned for his great project, he airily announced that he would take over the captain's overseas interests and I was to manage the UK property portfolio. This news was delivered in Max's usual presumptive way and I didn't know if I was supposed to thank him warmly for his generosity, or to bargain with him for something better.

'Will it pay me a salary?' I asked.

'A handsome one,' he said. And that was that.

But the prospect of doing anything apart from cataloguing his brain for three years was evidently more than Max could deal with. A week or so before he began his project, when I was visiting him at The Pile to help sort out the details of his scheme, we received a visit from a city businessman, a senior and trusted employee of the captain called Michael Rattigan, who shut himself away in the study with Max for about four hours. When they emerged, it appeared that Max had signed some sort of agreement passing executive control over all the international businesses to him. 'He's honest,' Max told me. And so, I believe, he has been. I've spoken to Michael almost every month since Max went into seclusion. He is well into his seventies now, but shows little sign of slowing down, which is just as well because I really don't know what we would do without him. He sends me a quarterly report which I don't bother reading any more. But I, in turn, pass this report on to our accountant who has promised to alert me if there seems to be any concern over the running of the Ponder enterprises. There never has been. The business pays a huge salary into Max's various accounts – most of them offshore. I'm still not sure what the overseas businesses all do.

My responsibility then, turned out to be the UK properties, of which there were several. After the accountants had sold a great slew of properties to take care of death duties (which were cripplingly high in 1975), and other taxes, the captain's remaining estate included the flat in London, O's house in Devon and, of course, The Pile. In addition, there were three other apartments in the same block in Dorset Square and a row of mews cottages close to Paddington, four dairy farms in Hampshire, a hotel in Cowes, a storage warehouse in High Wycombe, two shops in Marlow, a half-share in a golf course near Winchester, a car showroom in Slough, and a beach in Cornwall that earned no revenue at all since there was no permission for building, and no opportunity to charge for its use. The beach aside, the estate earned a considerable income. It has paid me a generous salary, far more than I might ever have earned selling soap powder in Middlesbrough, and like Michael Rattigan, I've been honest. After my salary and costs, the balance has gone into growing the business and into Max's various accounts.

So there you have my career. I was handed an enviable set of properties, and I learned about the property-management business. Max never asked me – and I wouldn't have told him anyway – but I bet very effectively during the property boom of the eighties and nineties. In the spirit of the Ponders, I didn't invest in just one type of property. That would have pleased the captain, I thought. I bought a toy museum in Hampshire and a small chain of care homes that I later sold at a huge profit. I bought building land in

Milton Keynes, and riding stables in Beaconsfield. In July 1980, when Max had just completed the fifth year of The Catalogue, a property speculator drove me out to see a whole row of derelict houses and boarded-up docks and warehouses in the East End of London. The Port of London Authority had closed down all the docks in 1978 and the entire riverfront was like a bombed-out wasteland. The young developer persuaded me that *this* would be the next boom location. He was a good salesman. I wrote him out a cheque for sixty thousand pounds in return for nearly five acres of a place called Canary Wharf. I was glad I didn't have to explain it to Max. That night I lay awake, convinced that I'd become the victim of a confidence trickster. There were nearly eight miles of derelict docks in the East End. How could I have believed that *any* of it would be worth sixty thousand pounds? In my accounts at the end of the year I wrote down the investment by fifty per cent. I didn't bother trying to remarket the property. Who would buy it? Then, in 1982, just two years after my rash investment, I took a phone call from a lawyer with an American accent. A company called Olympia & York wanted to develop a ten-million square foot office complex at Canary Wharf. 'Mr Last,' the young lawyer entreated me, his voice dripping with respect, 'do we have your consent to a negotiation?'

24

TRUTH

I can't dip a biscuit into a cup of tea
without thinking of Marcel Proust. And that
in itself is a strange piece of irony, isn't
it? I haven't read all of Proust's million
and a half words (who has?), but I do know
all about the episode with the madeleine.
It's one of those things you learn when you
study philosophy. Proust's narrator (whose
name we never learn) dips a madeleine into
his tea and - hey presto - the taste of the
tea and the cake trigger a cascade of memories
that our protagonist didn't even know he
possessed. It means that we credit Proust
with inventing the concept of 'involuntary
memory' - although I am quite sure that others
had noticed the phenomenon before. These are
our 'rafiki' memories. You can't access them
simply by trying to remember. No one knows
this better than I do. These memories were at
the heart of my original 'one-calendar-month'
rule. For some reason, like the Swahili for
'friend', such memories have been sealed
away, and you never even know that they are
there. Nonetheless, Adam makes a lot of this.
He is forever telling me that half of my
memories lie hidden. He wants to persuade me

to wind up my project. Of course. This is
Adam's perpetual agenda. He believes that if
I can be convinced that my memories will never
surface without involuntary Proustian
prompts, then I can be encouraged to go
outside to experiment. Maybe today I will
walk down to the river, he thinks, and there
the smell of the willow blossom will awaken
in my mind a volume of memories that lay
waiting for this particular trigger. This,
he argues cheerfully, would be a good thing.
It would make my catalogue more complete.
The call of a moorhen, or the flash of sunlight
on the wake of water behind a passing boat,
or the scent of manure from the fields across
the water – any of these things could offer
me a ticket to a festival of unrehearsed
memory. But Adam's ruminations don't end with
a walk down to the river. He foresees an end
to my project by stealth. Today the river;
tomorrow, maybe, the gate-house. Next week
the town. And every day the new information
going in through my senses would confound any
ability I have to write it all down. Even
after all this time Adam fails to grasp the
real import of a catalogue of a human brain.
My catalogue is like an early map. Like the
Mappa Mundi. There are areas of great detail,
but boundaries too, unexplored continents.
'Here There Be Dragons.' You wouldn't write
that on a map today, but in medieval times it
was a perfectly reasonable legend. When the
scientists come to unpick my brain, they might
discover places like that. If I can't remember
something without needing a madeleine and a
cup of tea to unearth it, then let it remain
unexplored, say I.

Still, when I dunk a biscuit in my tea,

I experience a memory of Proust. The same involuntary memory that he described.

Adam has been behaving strangely. He has been in and out of the house so many times that I forget if he is here or away. He has been looking gravely at me over the top of his spectacles, and sometimes I catch him slowly shaking his head as if there are things he wants to tell me but cannot. No doubt he will try to turn our conversations around to ending the project. I despair. The captain used to have a saying: 'you don't show a fool a job half done.' I think I know what he meant.

I like madeleines. They're like little sponge scallops, zested with lemon. They used to be made, or so I've heard, by nuns in the Convent of St Magdalene. Hence the name. I haven't had one for years. A madeleine – not a nun. There's a Metro station in Paris called Madeleine. I don't think I ever went there. I wonder if it is named after the convent or the cake? And wasn't there a film called *Madeleine*? Yes, there was. I just checked and there it is – listed in appendix CLXVIII. I remember it now. It was about a Scottish woman standing trial for murder.

Apparently the town where Proust set his story now celebrates his birthday by selling millions of madeleines. People come from all over the world to try them. Perhaps they hope that dunking them into lime tea will bring back memories – but of course that isn't the way these things work, is it?

So I was a fool – according to Max – if that extract from the red volumes is to be believed. And his work was only half done, twenty-eight years in. Well, it's all over now. At any rate, it will soon be over. This will be the first time that a mobile phone will ever be used in The Pile. I've collected my telephone from my car, turned it on, and found there is an excellent signal. So when I get myself together, I will call the police. I will dial 999, and when the voice asks me the nature of my emergency, I shall tell them that a man has died from natural causes and I shall give them this address. That ought to be sufficient. I'm guessing that they'll be here within half an hour or so of the call, so I ought to clean up the house a little. Not the body – I don't intend to interfere with any of the forensic evidence – but the house is a bit of a mess.

There's no rush. That is what I must keep telling myself. Your adrenalin would be pumping too if you'd just sawed through someone's neck. Most of all, I need to calm down. I shall pour myself a very small Laphroaig from Max's indispensible and in-exhaustible supply of single-malt whiskies. Then I shall relax a bit, tidy a little, and then I'll call the police.

On that night in 1974 when the captain was admitted to hospital, when Max was arrested, on the day that we buried the dog, I found myself sitting in the Volvo alongside Aunt Zinnia on our way to Wycombe Hospital. She didn't ask what had led me to change my mind about leaving. We parked at the hospital, and made our way to the admissions ward. It was a six-bed ward, but the captain was screened off behind curtains. His neck was heavily bandaged. He appeared to be slightly sedated; but then what do I know about medication? When we arrived it took him some time to recognise us, but since he couldn't speak, and wore a face mask delivering oxygen, the disorientation seemed excusable. Zinnia made a fuss, and then we both sat down.

'Captain,' I said, 'I've been thinking about what you told me this afternoon.'

The captain furrowed his eyebrows. He seemed anxious.

'For a start,' I said, 'you need to know that Zinnia already knows.' His eyes flicked between us. 'I didn't tell her, she told *me*. She worked it all out for herself.'

The captain nodded slowly. The conversation was made easier, I realised, because he couldn't talk back.

'You spoke this afternoon about three options,' I went on, 'do you remember? Option one – 'an unfortunate accident'. Well, you seem to have had one but you're still with us. Option two – Max and I go to Australia. That isn't going to happen. Option three – *you* go to Australia. Well, I don't think that'll happen either now, will it?'

He looked confused, so I ploughed on. 'You're clearly not well enough to travel now. If we wait until you *are* fully recovered and *then* you bugger off to Australia, well, Max is going to think that you left *because* of the accident. He's going to blame himself, unless you wait for a decent interval, by which time ...'

There was a silence at this. We were talking about his death.

'I'm not sure what you're trying to suggest, Adam,' said Aunt Zinnia.

'Look, both of you have said pretty much the same thing to me. The conversation we had this afternoon, Captain – and the one we had an hour ago, Zinnia – well, you both wanted to make sure that this whole thing was kept from Max.'

'It's important, Adam,' said Zinnia. 'Max wouldn't be able to cope with this.'

'Oh, but I think he would. He's nearly twenty. He's old enough to get married, fight in a war, stand for parliament. He's certainly old, and intelligent, enough to deal with this.'

'It isn't just about *age* though,' said Zinnia. 'You remember how he was when O died?'

As it happened, I *did* remember how Max was when O died. How could I forget? This is how it was – at least from the perspective of a ten-year-old Adam Last who probably didn't know how to process death very well.

I didn't see Max until two weeks after the miscarriage that killed O. My parents had called to pay their respects, but I'd been politely advised to wait until *the time was right*. When it *seemed* right, or nearly right, I ran down the Kikuyu path and over the pipe bridge, over the muddy Kirichwa Kubwa River, and along the valley to the old Dupont house.

Strange how these memories seem so clear. More than two years had passed since I'd first encountered Max at that gate, a pale and solitary boy, small for his age and bewitched by this new continent. I'd been hesitant then. Now I was more hesitant still. What does one boy say to another who has just lost his mother? The last time

I had seen Max, we were on board the *Usoga*. Now I was frightened about what I would find.

This is what I found. I found a silent, bedridden Max. It was Aunt Zinnia who met me at the door, who took me into Max's room. Now I remember it, Max's room was heavily curtained, just like his study at The Pile would be. Max wasn't tearful, but then he wasn't anything. He barely spoke. He had withdrawn into some dark place inside himself.

And there he stayed for several months. When term began at Kenton in September 1965, Max didn't join us. I called on him at half-term, but it seemed to me that little had changed. 'He's an awful lot better, don't you think?' Aunt Zinnia said to me cheerfully. But if he was, I wasn't sure I could see it. Perhaps he was coping better. Alone in his room, Max was reading. He had the heaps of books that the captain used to buy from the old bookshop in Bazaar Street, and he was devouring them. I found him among a hill of books, and after a while of sitting silently in the half-light, he began to tell me about them. This one was an adventure story, this one a cowboy book, this one the story of a journey to the centre of the Earth, this one stories about ancient Rome.

Books became Max's escape. He went back to Kenton eventually. I'm not sure exactly when. But one day he appeared, pale and sullen, at the back of the assembly hall, and afterwards I spoke to him and he told me that the school had offered him a special regime. Other boys would go outside to play cricket and tennis and hockey, to go swimming and make dens in the long grass. But Max was to be given the private use of a room in the staff block, and there he could close himself away and escape into his books. God knows how much the captain had paid the school for this singular treatment, but Max's solitary obsession was to be indulged – for the time being at least. So this is how Max was when O died. In a manner of speaking, Max has been that way ever since.

'I do remember,' I said, 'but *that's* the point. O's death was a huge shock. It knocked Max for six. We need to make sure that the captain's death isn't such a shock. If we keep this news from Max, well, Cap will still die and Max won't be expecting it. At least if Max knows what to expect ...'

'That's not the point, though,' said Zinnia, 'Max isn't used to death. He doesn't know how to handle it.'

'Zinnia,' I said firmly, 'Max is a philosopher. Maybe this is why he chose to read philosophy. *Of course* he understands death. That's pretty much all they think about in philosophy as far as I can see. Max has seen leprous corpses piled up waiting for disposal. He has helped to fish dead and mutilated bodies out of the Nile. He understands death and he's old enough to understand this.'

The captain was gesturing at Zinnia for a pen. She found one in her bag, and a small notebook. The captain wrote, 'OK to tell Max. But *not* that he might get it too.'

Zinnia read the note. 'He's right, Adam,' she said, 'Tell him Cap is dying and we'll help him to get through it. But he doesn't need to know that this ... well, you know, is the same as what happened to Martin. And our dad.'

And so it was agreed.

And so it happened. We drove to the police station and at around 9 p.m. they let Max go home. The police had charged him with assault on a police officer and resisting arrest, but he was then interviewed by a police psychologist, and shortly after they dropped the charges and a detective merely gave him a caution. There was no suggestion, after all, that he had assaulted his father.

When Max emerged into the waiting room where Aunt Zinnia and I occupied two plastic chairs, he had shaken off the violent jitters that had affected him earlier in the day, but he looked exhausted. I had to help him back to the car. His first concern was for the captain, and we both reassured him that we had just come from the hospital, and that the captain's injuries were not serious. When we got back to The Pile, Max wanted to go straight to bed, but I told him that we needed to speak. We assembled in the study, the front room in the East Wing, the room where Max now lies lifeless on the Rastin table. This has been the room where Max has spent the waking hours of his life for over thirty years. In those days the bookshelves were almost as full as they are today, but all those fine books have been boxed up for decades and reside in a storage warehouse in High Wycombe. Today the books you can see all have a single author. You might say that every one is the product of a single brain.

I poured Max a single malt from the captain's private collection, just as I have poured one for myself today, and then I told him what the captain had told me when we were standing over the grave of Libby the dog. I told him about his father's cancer. I explained that it was inoperable. I made sure that he understood that his father was dying.

Aunt Zinnia sat nodding silently in support. I made no mention of any other Ponder being affected by the same condition.

There was a lot of talk and all of it was very measured and concerned. I don't remember enough to try recording it here, but no one got emotional and there were a lot of silent pauses.

Afterwards, Max stood up wearily and thanked me. His head was bobbing slowly. 'Let's go to bed,' he said.

25

BODIES IN THE NILE

Thinking about death is something philosophers do, apparently. Max did it a lot. When we sat around and talked at The Pile, he would often drift rather morosely onto the subject, which made me aware that he'd been pondering the great mysteries – as indeed he was quite entitled to do. But, of course, these conversations gave me a problem; I knew, or I thought I knew, the way the universe had cast its dice for Max, and I suspected that the odds of him making it to old age were not particularly attractive. So I would look for a way to change the subject. This was a manoeuvre that rarely escaped Max's attention. 'You're doing it again, Adam,' he would scold me. 'Trying to avoid the subject.'

'No, I'm not,' I would protest, 'it just bores me, that's all.'

Then Max's eyes would twinkle the way they did when he thought he had you on the run. 'Death is never boring, Adam,' he would say earnestly. 'It doesn't bore you – it frightens you.'

'It doesn't.'

'Of course it does. Death frightens everybody.'

'Well it doesn't frighten me.'

His eyes would narrow. 'You're a cold fish, Adam,' he would say.

'No I'm not. I just don't spend my life worrying about death. I don't see the point.'

'Who said I was worried about death?'

'You did. You were in your Shakespearean mode. The undiscovered country from whose bourn no traveller returns. You just quoted that, remember?'

'Ah yes. But to die, and go we know not where ...'

'That too.'

'To lie in cold corruption and to rot.'

'See what I mean.'

'This sensible warm motion to become a kneaded clod.'

'OK, OK.'

'Imagine howling, "Oh 'tis too terrible". *Measure for Measure*. Who was the chap who was condemned to death?'

I didn't answer. These questions from Max, as I've mentioned, were rhetorical. I wouldn't have known anyway.

'Oh god, I can't remember his name. Anyway, his sister Isabella had the opportunity to save him from the gallows, but first she'd have to diddle this other chap, what was it Claudio? Antonio? Can't remember. Anyway, she was a nun so getting diddled was out of the question and so she visits the brother to tell him that he has to hang to keep her virtue intact. Delicious piece of Shakespearean moral irony, don't you think?'

'At least it takes us off the subject of death.'

'Not at all. It lands us full-square in the middle of the subject like a set of false teeth in a cowpat. The only thing we can do is pick it out. Death is the only big thing we can think about but never experience. Did you ever think about that?'

'No,' I said, 'Anyway, it's bollocks.'

'No it isn't.'

'Yes it is. I can think about having sex with ...' I hesitated to make sure I picked someone Max could reference, 'Ursula Andress. I can think about having sex with Ursula Andress, but it's something I will never experience.'

'Perhaps not. But you *could* experience it. That's the point.'

'It's still bollocks. I can think about flying back in time and shooting Hitler. I can think about ... I don't know ... being some kind of superhero. But I never will be and I never could.'

This deflated him. 'OK,' he said, 'you're right. But you can never experience death. You never will.'

'Of course I will. We all will. It's the one great certainty.'

'Ah!' He raised an index finger, suggesting triumph. 'We will all *die*. Yes, yes, and yes. That is quite certain. We may well experience *dying*. Not a pleasant thought, I admit. But we won't experience death. We will never know what it is like to be dead. Because if we experience it, then we're still alive. *Cogito ergo sum*. Descartes. As usual.'

'You're discounting any possibility of life after death,' I countered. 'Descartes wouldn't have done that.'

'Indeed he wouldn't. But if there is life after death – and let's imagine for a moment that there is – then we're still not actually dead, are we? We haven't actually experienced death – we're simply experiencing a different form of life.'

'And now I think it's time to change the subject.'

Max ignored this. 'Imagine if there were an after-life,' he said, 'imagine if we really lived forever. Don't you think that is even harder to grasp intellectually than the concept of death?'

'Yes,' I said. 'Yes I do.'

'Imagine you live forever and that the rules of heaven insist that you get married, but that every million years you have to divorce and marry someone else. If that were the case then eventually the time would come when you'd have been married to every single woman who had ever lived – for a million years each!'

'Your grasp of languages would be pretty good by then,' I joked.

'They'd all have to learn English. I am not learning Serbo-Croatian for anyone. Or Chinese. Imagine how many Chinese women you'd have been married to. How many Germans. How many ancient Britons. Eventually the time would come when you'd have to start marrying the same women all over again, and then eventually, given that we're all living for eternity here, you'd have been married to every woman who had ever lived a million times, each time for a million years.'

'It doesn't bear thinking about.'

'Damn right it doesn't. And you'd be less than halfway through eternity. In fact, you'd have barely started.'

'I don't think I want to live forever,' I said. 'Not if you have to marry every woman who's ever lived. It would mean I'd have to marry Camilla Hunter.'

'Oh god! A fate worse than death.'

'Exactly. *And* I'd have to marry her mother.'

'Oh god!'

You see, we could still laugh. Even when we talked about death.

But we weren't always that light-hearted. Sometimes Max approached the subject in an altogether darker mood. One autumn evening in the late nineties, after a good bottle of Claret and a boeuf bourguignon, I was all set to leave The Pile to drive home, but Max was having none of it. He disappeared to the cellar and emerged with a fresh bottle.

'I shouldn't drink and drive,' I said. (This expression was OK. It had been common enough currency before Max went into reclusion.)

'Then stay over,' Max said. He tore off the foil and started to twist the corkscrew.

'I should get back.'

'I feel like talking.'

'Are you sure? It'll take you all night to record it.'

'Fuck it. So I'll record it. What's a few hours?'

I relented and we settled into the bergères. Max had his pen and a pile of day log pages.

'Are we going to talk about the end of the project?' I asked.

'No,' Max said. 'Or yes. It all depends on how it ends.'

'How will it end?'

'The same way everything ends.'

'And how does everything end?'

'The same way it has always done and the same way it always will. We die and we're forgotten.'

I sighed. 'Max, we're not doing death again, are we?'

Max swirled the red wine around in his glass, as if he might find inspiration within. 'OK, let's not do death,' he said. 'Let's do survival. Hmm? What do you think survives?'

'What do you mean?'

'I mean, let's imagine one of us dies. Let's imagine you die. Here. Tonight. They take you away and they drop you in a hole and they cover you with soil. Maybe they give you a headstone. Maybe you have friends and lovers who remember you, but soon enough they die too and then they join you under the Earth. Maybe there are people left who remember them, but those people don't remember *you*. So does anything of you survive? Is there any essence left on Planet Earth that is identifiably Adam Last?'

'Look, Max,' I said, 'if you want to be remembered then you need to get out more. Meet some people and give them someone to remember.'

He ignored me. Of course.

'When my grandmother was a girl,' he said, 'she used to love the music of Caruso. He was an opera singer, a tenor. Probably the most popular opera singer in history.'

'And?'

'Have you ever heard the music of Caruso?'

I shook my head. 'I don't think so.'

'Exactly. It has taken seventy years for the most popular singer in the world to be almost erased from the popular memory. Have you ever seen a film starring Rudolph Valentino? No? When he died there was mass mourning all around the world. He was the biggest star in history. Do you remember him?'

'Of course I do. Of course I remember Valentino.'

'No you don't. You remember his name and some half-baked facts about his life – but you don't remember him. How could you? I know hundreds of names of dead people. Karl Marx – revolutionary philosopher. Geoffrey Chaucer – poet. Oliver Cromwell – revolutionary. Marcus Aurelius Antoninus Augustus – Emperor of Rome. Emily Dickinson – poet. Did I ever meet any of these people? No. So can I remember them? No.'

I remained silent. Max was composing his argument and would not welcome any interruption.

'Even writing doesn't help,' he continued, 'even film. No one can tell you if William Shakespeare had bad breath or laughed like a billy goat; no one can tell us if George Washington used to scratch his bollocks in public, or if Aristotle did fishy farts. Even if we have contemporary accounts, they do little more than scratch the surface and, anyway, a pen portrait of Mark Twain will mean something different to you than it does to me. Wittgenstein showed us that. Someone could read us both a ten-page description of Martin Luther, but if he were to come through that door in three weeks' time, we wouldn't immediately recognise him and embrace him and say, "Martin, hey, how've you been?". We are forgotten and there is nothing we can ever do to change that fact.'

I nodded my agreement.

'Imagine a man so famous and so powerful and so all-reaching that he could have his likeness painted onto the moon so that from Earth all you could see was his face, and every human who would ever look at the sky from that moment on would be reminded of his existence. Even that man would be forgotten just a generation after his death once all the people who had known him had joined him in the great beyond. All his painting would ever be would be a simple picture, no different from all those anonymous faces we gaze at in portrait galleries. And eventually the day would come when even the painting would be covered over by dust from space, and no one on Earth would even know that he once existed.'

'And what good would it do him anyway?' I asked. 'Who cares if anyone remembers you? You're *dead*!'

Max liked this. 'Who cares indeed?' he mused. 'Because we don't live on. We don't sit on a cloud and watch the rest of history unfold. We occupy one of two binary states: alive, or dead. The one excludes the other.'

'Exactly. So why worry about it?'

'Exactly,' Max drummed his fingers on the desk and set about scribbling down the conversation.

I'm not quite sure why I decided to throw in a perverse alternative. 'Unless you're not,' I said.

'Unless you're not what?'

'Dead. Maybe we survive as ...' – I hunted for an expression that would not pollute Max's memory. In truth I was thinking of The Borg from *Star Trek*, but that was an example quite beyond use – ' ... as some kind of hive mind?' I offered lamely.

'Hive mind?' echoed Max scribbling this down.

'Like a single mind that shares all the memories of the ... collective.' I knew I shouldn't have started this.

'I see,' said Max. He put down his pen. 'And where would this enormous mind be located? In a huge underground bunker on Saturn perhaps? Orbiting the Earth in the Asteroid Belt?'

'Well ... no ...'

'Or, don't tell me, it's in *another dimension*?'

'Well it could be.'

Max let out a snort. 'This is what gets me about all these fairy-tale fantasies about the after-life,' he said. 'They legitimise the most ridiculous flights of fancy. And anybody can do it! Once you invent the idea of an after-life, you can just make up the rules of the universe to suit yourself. So, OK, let's imagine another dimension and conveniently locate our heaven there. Can you see Earth from your heaven? Of course you can. It wouldn't be much of a heaven otherwise. So you can sit comfortably and watch events unfold on Earth. How nice. Which bit of Earth do you see? Mauritania perhaps? The Spanish Sahara? Of course not. You see the leafy bits of England where you feel at home and you get to read obituaries in *The Times* and watch Morecambe and Wise on the telly. What physical medium are you using when you "see" Earth from heaven? It can't be visible light because otherwise we'd be able to see you back, so let's just invent something else to explain that, shall we? Some kind of new radiation that is undetectable in our dimension but dead people can use it. Do dogs go to this heaven? Are they part of this "hive mind"? Yes? No? What about chimpanzees then? They're almost human. It seems unnecessarily cruel to discriminate, don't you think? How about paedophiles? How about foetuses aborted at term? They deserve a place, don't you think? What if we don't like some of the memories we find in the "hive mind"? Can we blank them out? Go on, make up some more rules.'

'I wasn't suggesting that there was a particular definition of an after-life, just that maybe we don't know all there is to know ...'

But Max wasn't to be stopped now. 'You know what?' he said, 'I think we know enough. We may not know every last fact about the Big Bang, but we do know that when it comes down to it we are just a trumped-up bacterium that somehow clumped into a colony of cells and crawled out of the primordial slime. Anyone who thinks we're in any way different from the earthworm we cut in half with a spade is simply delusional. We don't have anything more to look forward to once the spade of destiny carves us in half any more than the worm.'

'Are you done?' I asked.

'I stopped believing in that stuff on my eleventh birthday,' Max said.

I got up and poured us both another glass of wine. Max set the whole exchange down on paper and we continued in silence.

It wasn't unique, this conversation. There were many like it. And usually, when Max was in the mood to ponder the whole death thing, it wasn't so easy to shift him off the subject. I don't think it was just his own death that obsessed him. It was O's. And the captain's. And Uncle Martin's. Maybe even Libby the dog. And the lepers. And the Tanzanian boy in the Nile.

APPENDIX CXXXVIII

AMIN01: I am sixteen years old. The captain [Cap 7176] and I are in Kampala in a street café [Kampala Café 01] drinking coffee. A tall African man in olive army uniform who looks hugely important, with a dutiful batman in tow, comes bounding up the stairs and greets Cap with a hale: 'Captain Ponder, now you are a civilian you have to get my permission to drink in my café!' All of this is said in a tone of great bonhomie, followed by booming laughter. Cap gets up straight away and greets the man like an old friend - they clap each other's shoulders and there is genial banter and so forth. Cap introduces me to the man and tells the man that I am his son. The man greets me warmly and says that one day I will be a great soldier because I am the son of a great soldier. The captain tells me that the man is a colonel and head of all the armed forces in Uganda. The colonel says, 'I outrank you now!' and they both laugh at this. Then the colonel says to me, 'I knocked your father out in the ring!' C Aug 1970.

AMIN02: We are standing on a busy street in Kampala. I see a man who is a full head taller than the rest of the crowd. He is shaking hands with people and laughing as he makes his way down the street. It is the colonel. C Aug 1970.

APPENDIX CCL

[DREAM 136] Sometime between 1970 and 72 I
dreamed this at least three times, maybe more.
It's a weird dream. We are all falling.
Everyone is falling. It's a bit like dropping
out of a plane, except that we all fall for
ever and ever and we never reach the ground.
We can fall a little faster if we dive, and
we can slow down if we hold our arms out like
a crucifix and try to fight the wind. Families
stay together by roping themselves to one
another by the ankle. I am roped to Cap and
Cap is roped to O, who is still alive.
Sometimes we see other families falling too.
Sometimes we fall past them, and sometimes
they pass us on the relentless way down. We
fall past rocks and detritus and great globes
of water and these are the things that keep
us alive. We see falling animals and trees.
We are resigned to this way of life. This is
how it has always been. We will fall for
ever.

We make friends as we fall. We talk to other
people and we share morsels of food. But in
the morning we awake to find that we have
drifted apart. Perhaps they are below us,
perhaps they are above. Perhaps they have
drifted miles over in this direction, or that
one there. There is no north or south here -
only up and down and all around.

Then, one morning, I awake to the familiar
wind in my face and I find that overnight my
ankle rope has become untied. The captain and
O are nowhere to be seen. I try to slow my
fall in case I have somehow dived below them,
but for days I cannot find them. Families pass
on their way down and I ask about my parents.

No one has seen them. Alarmed now, I dive.
But still no sign of Cap or O. I dive faster.
Soon I am a falling needle, a missile. And
that is when I come across Idi Amin in his
colonel's garb. 'I outrank you, Ponder,' he
says to me and he laughs. 'Do you know where
my father is?' I ask him. He laughs again,
only louder.

APPENDIX XIV

ZIN501: Zin and I are in the Nairobi house
[NAIH 722] when Cap telephones. Cap is in
Uganda. He is calling to tell us to meet him
at a place called [place name forgotten 1]
where he is in a camp. Adam and I are back in
Nairobi on the long holiday. This will be
our last long holiday in Africa. Adam's family
are already packing to leave for England and
the Ponders will be following soon. Cap wants
us to join him. There is work we could do.
Cap says it would be like a holiday job. You
could call it 'work experience' he says.
I say that Adam might need some convincing.
Cap laughs. I ask Zin and she shrugs and
says, 'Go for it, boyo. Whatever turns you
on.' C Dec 70

VOLUME XIX
JANUARY 1977

[UGANDA 1673] I am with Cap and Adam somewhere
up in the West Nile Province. It's north of
Murchison Falls – north of the town of Pakwach
on the Nile. Strictly speaking on the 'Albert
Nile'. [sketch] We are on a construction site
where they are building a hospital. Klass
Kleir Ponder are fitting the operating

theatres. Cap is there to sort out some of
the commercial stuff. Adam and I are there
for 'work experience' [AL 6010]. We are
surveying part of the site. We have an
instrument called a theodolite which stands
on a tripod and we do lots of measuring. One
of us squints through the theodolite and the
other one stands and holds a pole. Then we
write down some numbers and do it all again
somewhere else. We are working for a guy
called Nick Duhain [Nicholas D 01] and we
are staying in a cabin on the site.

[Long description of Nick Duhain not included here: Adam]

The site measures around 400m by 200m.
[sketch] It has been cleared from the bush
and is now a field of orange-brown mud in the
middle of which stands a half-built hospital.
I remember now that the hospital was one of
a dozen or so that were being paid for by
the Government of Sweden. Instead of building
them in areas of high population, President
Mbote allocated each one to a member of his
cabinet, so that each minister would have a
hospital built in the village of their birth.
So the hospitals were randomly dispersed –
some were in cities, but others, like this
one, were well away from population centres.
   The site is . . .

I'm copying this stuff in to help the police make sense of Max's
life so let's skip the next sixteen pages or so of description. Here's
the bit that matters:

There is a cry from a man at the river's
edge. Adam and I pay him little notice but
I remember him waving and calling and soon

afterwards a number of men from the construction site run over to the river to see what is going on. A little while later, I see Adam looking towards the river with a strange expression on his face.

'What the hell have they found?' he asks me.

All I can see is a crowd of people. They are dragging something from the water.

'Is it a crocodile?' I ask Adam.

'I think you should stay here,' he says.

'Why?'

'I think it's a body,' he says.

The bodies are a shock. The first one they pull out is scarcely a body at all – more a gory set of bones and connective tissue and skin. I watch from a distance; there is a big crowd of people now, ululating and waving as the workers from the site net the bits of floating corpse from the fast-flowing river. Adam leaves me and goes down to the river edge. He seems pretty unaffected, but I am standing there with a growing sense of shock. I can feel myself starting to shake.

The Nile flows fast here, and the rocks are like knives. The body has been filleted on the rocks. After a while Joseph joins me [JOSEPH 09]. He suggests I make my way back to the huts and tells me not to trouble myself with what is happening. What he says is, 'Bwana Max no good to look at this, no good, no good. Bwana Max you go back the huts. This no good.'

I stay because I have to stay. I know that I am witnessing something that is, in its small way, a piece of unravelling history. So I say something to Joseph and he leaves me standing alone and I make my way just a bit closer to the river.

I am slow to realise that this isn't the discovery of a single body. A second is pulled out of the river and now the men are wading into the current and the crying becomes more urgent. Then one man comes back with a head, and this causes the crowd to shrink back from the shore, and Adam [AL 6014] with a second man, a few metres to the right of the first, comes wading out of the water pulling the whole, almost undamaged, body of a male who looks so young that I know with certainty that this must have been a boy even younger than I am. Adam and the man pull the boy on to the shore and leave him lying on a sand bank alongside the first body. Then they head back to the river and I notice that Adam doesn't even look back over his shoulder. As for me, my eyes are transfixed by this second corpse. It is a human being, but it is not. Our vocabulary changes in an instant. He is a boy, he is a lad, he is a man, and then he is a body, a corpse, a cadaver. In a single moment our status changes irreversibly.
I watch the boy – the body – for any sign of movement. Maybe, I think, he is still alive. Some women start wailing and hands pull the body further up the shore.

The discoveries continue and the men at the shoreline don't manage to collect them all. I see a body floating face-down in mid-stream, way out of reach of the workers. No one tries to wade out to it, so the body just coasts by and then it is gone.

I would guess that five minutes have passed since the first discovery. People are still running down from the building site, attracted

by all the commotion. Soon the crowd is big
enough to interrupt my own view. I hesitate.
I could go forward and elbow my way in,
I could offer to help Adam, who is knee-deep
in the water helping to pull out a body, but
I am rooted in some way like a lead soldier
to a pedestal. It isn't hard to imagine what
is going on in the midst of the mêlée. I can
still see the broad sweep of the Nile, and
in among the swirl I see other bodies and
body parts, and fragments of clothing.

Some of the security men from the site office
now come down to the riverside looking
important. They are the Ascaris; in truth
they are no more important than the men who
mix the cement, but their uniforms give them
a presence and they start to bark orders at
the crowd. This has a partial effect and some
people start to drift back to work. The
Ascaris now take command and two of them wade
into the river. But one loses his footing
and I think he must have cracked his head on
a rock. Attention turns to him, and he is
hefted out onto the shore, dazed but otherwise
unharmed. The incident makes the other
Ascaris cross and they start yelling at the
workers to get back to the site and leave
this to them and then suddenly the whole scene
is in uproar. That is when Joseph emerges
from the crowd and makes his way back up to
me. 'Not good, Bwana Max,' he says, 'we must
go.' And so we do. I go back to the hut where
I must have done something but I don't
remember what. Some time later, Adam joins
me. He is wet and covered in mud and blood.
I don't feel like talking to him. I am feeling
very, very, sick. I look at Adam and I see a
flap of flesh about an inch square that has

clung to his shorts like sticky meat. I run
to the door and manage to throw up just
outside in the dirt.

Joseph comes out and waits for me to finish.
Finally he steers me back inside. 'No worry,
Bwana Max,' he says, 'I clean up. You wash.'

I do. Adam joins me and washes his face and
arms. I notice him pick the piece of flesh
off and toss it into the toilet. Then he says
he is going back down again to help. Do
I want to join him? I tell him I will come
soon. I am shaking hard.

But some time later I am drawn back to the
scene. The Ascaris are still dragging corpses
out of the river, but now there are fewer to
find. Adam is there. His expression is blank,
and I can't tell if he is affected by all
this. All along the shore there are bodies.
This time I actually brave the riverbank and
help two Ascaris to recover an arm. I even
touch the arm and it is still warm. Adam
gives me a smile. I know he is trying to send
me a message of encouragement. His smile says,
'Well done, mate, you've helped us. You'll
be glad you did.'

There is barely any smell. Cap tells me
later that this is because the bodies were
still so fresh. One Ascari tosses the arm
onto a pile and I immediately taste vomit in
my mouth but I choke it back. Ridiculously,
I feel proud of my self-control. There are
dead men all over the bank and now I feel a
sense of shame. I realise that I am crying.

We stand and watch the river for more body
parts. I am still shaking, but I'm in control.

Something is moving in the river. An Ascari
grabs my arm and pulls me away. 'Crocodile!'
he hisses. Sure enough there is the familiar

ridge of a swimming crocodile. We all retreat several feet, but the croc is swimming past us. He has an almost complete body in his mouth, and is making for the opposite shore.

Later, someone counted the corpses and we learned that there were thirty of them. Because of the bend in the stream, I think many of the bodies were washed towards the building site, but a fair number floated past. Maybe sixty bodies, we guessed. Maybe a hundred.

There are four faces that stay in my memory. The first is the boy. He has an angular face, his eyes are closed, and he has two oversized top teeth, made more prominent by the fact that he has lost his top lip. He is wearing torn black trousers and a khaki T-shirt and his feet are bare. He is very thin. His left arm has been broken and is twisted into a position that would have been impossible in life. Who is he? Does he have a name? Why is he here? Does he have a mother somewhere who is out looking for him? Does he have a brother, a father, sisters, a girlfriend? I am struck by all these thoughts at once. Did he know he was dying? Did he see the moment of his death coming up towards him? Did the hollow figure of the grim reaper stand over him as he plunged down the river towards the rocks? And where is he now? Do residual thoughts still linger in that smashed head? Did a benevolent god pluck his spirit from the waters and shepherd him off to a better place? Here, on the muddy banks of the Nile, that last proposition seems the least likely of all. Where was the benevolent god today? Not here.

A second face I remember because it is so

damaged that even the man's best friend wouldn't have recognised him, except perhaps for his eyes – both undamaged, wide open and milky.

I look at the third man for a long time. He is around twenty years old and has the kind of face you see in the markets: a wise Baganda face, open, mischievous. He looks as if he is asleep. His clothes are undamaged. He is wearing army fatigues, but then so are most of the bodies.

Then there is an old man. He is whiskered and lined. He has lost half of his jaw.

Most of the bodies, I become aware, show signs of wounds. One torso has about a dozen wounds. Someone says these are from bullets and I know that this is true.

A priest has been called. He wears a black habit and a dog collar, but he also sports a necklace of bones. Nice touch. I would describe him as being around fifty, short and stocky, maybe five foot two, very black, with a white beard and a wide smile. He chants his mumbo-jumbo for ten minutes.

A Land Rover arrives and it is Nick [Nicholas D 06]. He immediately comes over to me as if I were somehow in charge and asks me what is going on. I tell him what I have seen.

'I suggest we just leave them to it, old chap,' Nick says. 'This is none of our business.' He then speaks to one of the foremen. 'Get the chaps to dig some graves over by the car park. Let's try to get them all buried before it's dark. One grave per body. Let's not chuck them all in a pit. And get the lads to make some crosses. One cross per grave. Make it look neat.'

The foreman seems hesitant. Then he says

something to Nick in Acholi, which is a language I don't understand. Nick looks pensive. 'On second thoughts,' he says, 'don't bother with the crosses.' He gives us a rueful smile. 'And I've changed my mind about the plot by the car park. 'Dig the graves here, down by the river. One bloody big hole will do. Use the bulldozer. Let's get it done, shall we? Chop chop.'

He comes back to me. 'Whoever did this might not want us to advertise it,' he says. 'Come on, let's go and have a whisky and try to pretend we didn't see what we just saw, eh?'

We head away from the scene leaving Adam and the Ascaris there. Adam doesn't glance back. I think what a cold fish he is. I still think this. Adam is the only person I know who has a thoroughly sanguine attitude towards death – I truly believe that if I asked him to blow my head off with a shotgun, he would oblige as long as he was confident that this was my genuine wish. Then he would get on with whatever else he needed to do and the whole experience wouldn't trouble him or keep him awake at night.

26

THE ROSETTA STONE OF NEUROSCIENCE

I really don't like the way this last passage from Max's catalogue ends. I was hunting through bits of the autobiographical volumes and appendices, trying to assemble the Amin story, because I thought that these might be useful to show to the police. I also wanted to find the passage about the man who survived the incident with the bodies in the Nile, but for some reason that passage eludes me. Anyway, just for completeness, there was one chap who miraculously emerged alive from the river sometime later, and told his tale. From what I remember, he turned out to have been a Tanzanian soldier. He'd been captured by the Ugandan army in a skirmish somewhere on the border, and was in a convoy of lorries that was taking prisoners of war to a mythical camp up north. I say mythical because when they reached a bridge where the Nile gushes through a deep and narrow gorge, they were told, at gunpoint, to get out and pee over the bridge into the river below. As they peed, they were machine-gunned down. This particular soldier survived the shooting, he survived the fall, he survived the rapids, and he survived the crocodiles. The captain and Nick Duhain bundled him into the boot of a car and drove him up to the Kenyan border, and there they pointed him in the direction of some distant villages and let him set off on foot to possible safety.

Anyway, all this is by the by. The passage that gave me a start had nothing to do with Uganda, or Amin. It was that throwaway line: 'Adam is the only person I know who has a thoroughly sanguine attitude towards death – I truly believe that if I asked him to blow my head off with a shotgun, he would oblige.'

I've read and re-read this line several times. I know that Max was recording his own fallible memories and opinions and if you were to challenge him he would laugh it off and say, 'That's the way my brain is, old chap, and that's what I'm recording.'

But what if the police were to read that line?

I shall have to think very carefully about this. Thank god I didn't call the police the moment I collected my mobile phone. What if they had seen that remark before I did? And now I come to think about it, there are countless such remarks in The Catalogue. Maybe not quite so explicit – but Max always saw me as a bit of a cold fish. He uses that expression several times. There is a line, for example – god knows which volume it is hidden in – that says something like, 'I think Adam would have made an excellent assassin. He is such a cold fish.'

Isn't it strange how even your closest friend can misread you? I am not, of course, a cold fish, but I do know how to react calmly to crises, in a way that Max never could. I guess I would often overcompensate for Max's reactions, and he interpreted this as a lack of engagement; I saw it as a more even-tempered approach. Anyway. The damage is probably done.

Just as a precaution, I have torn that page out of volume XIX and I've burned it. I have also scrunched up the ash from the missing page and I've flushed it down the loo. I don't really know how diligent the forensic people will be, but it is probably best to expect the worst.

There is a rant in The Catalogue somewhere – maybe around the late 1980s – in which Max accuses me of a lot of rather unpleasant things. He accuses me of being responsible for the death of O, and also of killing the captain. It isn't hard to understand now that these were the product of Max's feverish mind. He had fits of depression sometimes, and this was written right at the heart of one such fit. I think it might be wisest to find those pages and burn them too. I don't know if I really need to – after all, history will record that I stayed on and looked after Max for another fifteen or twenty years. And I never embezzled any of his cash. And I never broke his precious rules. So, from a historical point of view at least, I am perfectly in the clear.

But you never know with the police, do you? What if they find 360 policemen and give them a volume each to read? Every reader would want to be the one who made the discovery that would prove a crime had been committed. So any copper who read that section about me would sound the alarm, and the next thing I know it could be twenty years in the nick. Not a pleasant thought, actually. Not at all. It would all have been so clean and simple if I hadn't been under clear instructions to hack off his head. That will be the thing that sets the alarm bells ringing. Even though there is a very clear reference to it in The Catalogue:

```
DAY LOG 10,610
Wednesday 21 July 2004


I have given Adam [AL21,009] very strict
instructions about what to do with me if/when
I die. We spoke last night. Me on the armchair
left, Adam right. Too dark to see each other.
  ME: I want you to promise to do something
for me.
  AL: What is it?
  ME: If this bloody tumour thing should kill
me, I want you to cut off my head and freeze
it.
  AL: Don't be so soft, Max.
  ME: Please, don't let's disagree on this.
You need to do it quickly - before, you know
. . . decay starts up.
  AL: Which is how long exactly?
  ME: How should I know? Just do it straight
away, would you.
  AL: Max, you aren't going to die.
  ME: We're all going to die, Adam.
  AL: You know what I mean. You aren't dying
yet.
  ME: In which case you don't have to worry.
Look, I just want to make sure - just in case
I do die - that my brain is preserved.'
  AL: Preserved? Why exactly?
  ME: I don't know. But someday somebody might
be able to unravel my memories. Don't you
see - mine will be the first and only brain
```

that anyone can really do that with.

AL: I see ... sort of ...

ME: So, just promise me you'll do it.

AL: Do you know what, Max, you've always said that thing to me – you know – imagine a brain on a mortuary slab? And you can never find out what's inside it? Remember that?

ME: Yes, of course I remember that, but ...

AL: Does this brain speak six languages? Can this brain decline Latin verbs? Does this brain know $E=MC^2$?

ME: For god's sake, Adam, I know I said that stuff. But you've just misunderstood the whole point of that riddle. My point is that all this stuff really is in the brain somewhere; we just don't know how to find it. Not yet. Maybe everything we remember is a little molecule of protein or maybe it's all about the way that the nerves are wired up. Who knows? But unless what goes on in the brain is some kind of supernatural magic, which it isn't, then somebody, someday is going to work out how to decode it.

AL: So that's your big idea then? You want somebody to deconstruct your brain?

ME: (probably sighing at this point) Look. I don't particularly want my brain to be deconstructed. At least, that isn't what's driving my project. You know that, Adam, better than anyone. But all the same, I do have something that I can leave behind that might just complete my work. Think about all those thousands of dead brains out there in jars of formalin on the pathology shelves of hospitals and in the anatomy departments of medical schools. There are probably thousands of frozen brains too. All those neuro-scientists need to have raw material to work with. Even Einstein's brain is out there somewhere. But we don't know how to find our way around these brains because we don't know what's in there. We don't have a map. We don't have any way to decode what's inside them. That's the difference with my brain. My brain has been catalogued. If I drop dead tomorrow then probably three-quarters of everything I know will be there in The Catalogue.

AL: Only three-quarters?

ME: Do you remember the Rosetta Stone? For centuries no one could read the weird hieroglyphs on ancient Egyptian monuments. Everyone got it into their heads that the alphabet of the pharaohs was ideographic – I think that's the right word. They thought that each little picture represented a word. Stupid, of course. But anyway, then they discovered this stone with an inscription on it in both hieroglyphs and Greek. Hey presto, they could translate it. And it turned out that the Egyptians used a normal alphabet. In no time at all they had unravelled the whole history of the pharaohs. All because of one little fragment of stone. It was a key to the code, you see. And that's what my brain could become.

AL: So you're saying your brain could be the Rosetta Stone of neuroscience?

ME: It could be. But here's another thing. You need to let the scientific world know that my brain is still intact, but don't just give it to the first researcher who comes along. You need to wait until the technology has been developed; until the techniques are in place to do it properly. Otherwise it would be like giving the Rosetta Stone to someone who wants to examine it using a sledgehammer.

AL: OK, I promise.

ME: And please god don't let the pathology people mess about with my brain. No post-mortems above the neck!

AL: Max, I really don't think you should be worrying about this stuff.

ME: Are you kidding? This is *all* I worry about these days.

AL: OK. No post-mortems on the brain.

ME: I know what they'd do. They would cut open my head to look at the tumour. 'Oooh look, a tumour', as if there were anything they could do about it by that stage. Then they'd leave me rotting in some malfunctioning fridge and by the time anyone remembered where I was, I'd be a piece of stinking meat.

AL: All right.

ME: Why would any self-respecting doctor ever want to end up doing post-mortems anyway? You spend six years of your life training to be a doctor so that you can help to make people better, and then you spend your career chopping up dead people.

AL: I guess at least those patients don't complain.

ME: Well I bloody well would. I don't want any pathologists dicking around with my brain. You need to freeze my head – freeze it properly – and keep it away from the post-mortem docs.

AL: That might not be so easy, Max . . .

ME: Yes it is.

AL: Think about it. You pop your clogs [NB: modern expression but I've heard AL use it before several times. See IDIOMS] and I chop off your head and hide it in a freezer. Then I call the morgue, or whoever you call in these situations, and they come round and find a headless body. Pretty suspicious, don't you think?

ME: It doesn't have to be. Just show them all this. Show them The Catalogue. They sure as hell won't chop all this open - this is evidence for god's sake. Give them the truth. You'll be in and out of the cop shop in thirty minutes.

AL: I wouldn't be so sure.

ME: In any case, you need to be smarter than them. You need to find somewhere to stash the brain where no one will find it.

AL: (after a long pause) I think I can do that.

ME: So that means you'll do it.

AL: Of course I'll do it.

I'll be sure to show them that bit.

27

THE FOREIGN BODY

The captain died on Monday 17 March 1975. I was in Keele. So, to that extent I was not responsible. (I've jumped back in time a bit here, but you'll be getting used to that I think.) I received the news in a telegram from Aunt Zinnia. The telegram read 'CAPT DEAD FUN MON 10 A.M. URGE COME'. It was a very Ponder telegram. Even in times of tragedy the Ponders always behaved according to form. I had to read it a few times before I worked out what 'FUN MON' meant.

I borrowed a black suit from a friend at university. I was broke, so I hitch-hiked down to Buckinghamshire for the FUN. It wasn't a good day for hitch-hiking. I missed the church service and arrived at the churchyard just as the body was being lowered into the ground. There was a large crowd there. Captain Ponder had been a well-connected man. There were chaps in army uniform, as well as a big contingent in business suits. I didn't want to make a show of arriving late, so I did the thing that they do in films when a mysterious stranger stands by a lone tree and watches the ceremony from afar. When all the prayers were done and the crowd had started to drift away, I made my way forward and found Max still staring down into the grave, his hands black with cemetery soil. What do you say? I had seen Max lose both parents. Aunt Zinnia was standing on one side, holding his arm as if Max were in danger of falling into the abyss. Elenora Twist was on the other. She looked at me with a rueful smile that I returned.

'Hello, Adam,' she said, and this alerted Max to the fact that I was there.

'Adam!' He seemed astonished to see me. 'You came!'

'Of course.'

He broke away from Zinnia and Elenora and came over to hug

me. We had been friends for twelve years, but we had rarely hugged.

'I'm so sorry, Max,' I said.

'The silly old bugger wouldn't take any treatment. Did they tell you?'

I shook my head.

'There was all this stuff they could have done, you know. Drugs. Chemotherapy. Stuff like that. But he wouldn't take it. They could have operated.'

'I suspect he didn't want to prolong the whole thing,' I said, hoping that this sounded like appropriate consolation.

'The daft old fool said "if you're going down to the city you may as well catch the early train." I said, "No you don't, you catch the last possible train", and he said "if you do that, then all you do is hang about the station and there's nowhere in the world quite so dull as a station – except for a hospital". That's what he said. Nowhere so dull as a hospital.'

Aunt Zinnia, clutching Max's arm, manoeuvred him away from the grave. We began the long, slow walk back to the real world.

'Well,' I said, trying clumsily to find something that would help ease Max's mood, 'at least he didn't suffer.'

It wasn't a good thing to say. 'Suffer?' Max said. 'Of course he bloody suffered. He had a bloody brain tumour, for god's sake.'

'No, but he would have suffered more,' I stammered, trying to recover the situation.

'You didn't see him,' Max retaliated. 'How could he have suffered more? How could anyone with an ounce of consciousness or self-awareness suffer more than by seeing their own brain evaporate slowly away, day after day? What could be worse than losing everything that makes you who you are?'

'I'm sorry, Max,' I said. I put an arm around him. We were four bowed figures from a Dickensian burial scene, hunched together in our uncomfortable black coats, trudging away from the domain of the dead.

'You know the worst thing?' said Max. 'He never really recovered from the accident. Not really. That last bout we had, Adam, in that stupid bloody fencing match – that was the last active thing he ever really did. It was like – he went into hospital this active guy who

221

could fence two good blades off the piste and he came out this old man with a stick and terminal cancer.'

'I don't think the two are connected,' said Zinnia.

'I mean, look at that day,' Max said, ignoring his aunt. 'He'd driven off to the vet, perfectly normal. He'd carried Libby into the car. He'd gone to Reading station to collect you. Probably read the *FT* while he was waiting. Probably did the crossword. He'd driven home. He'd dug a bloody great hole in the lawn for Libby and filled it in afterwards, and then he came upstairs and fought you to a standstill and then the next day he was this invalid and he never sat behind the wheel of a car again, and never held a foil again, and it was our stupid bloody fault, Adam.'

I held my breath. It wasn't worth correcting Max about who had really dug the grave, who had filled it in, or who, for good measure, had broken the legs of Libby the dog. And who indeed had stabbed the captain.

Aunt Zinnia came to the rescue. 'It was the cancer that killed him, Max,' she said, 'it had nothing to do with that silly fight.'

Max stared at us both and his eyes were very red. 'Even if you're right,' he said, 'and, heck, you probably are right, that isn't how it feels. It isn't how it *feels*, Aunt Zinnia. You want to know how it feels in *here*?' he tapped his chest. 'It feels as if we killed him. Adam and I, we killed him. We took this big, harmless bear of a man and we just pushed him over the edge and that was all it took. One little push. He was living with this tumour and it was sitting pretty dormant and he was doing all the things that he used to do; he was still working and driving and reading, and then we gave him this little push and the tumour went off into overdrive.'

We went back to The Pile and there we stood around and ate canapés and drank sherry. Max kept himself some way away from Elenora, as if having her too close might somehow dilute his grief. Elenora, for her part, gazed out of the French windows, watching the boats slide by on the river. I tried to approach Max once or twice, but he was distant. I found myself slumped in an armchair wondering what might be the politest way to take my leave.

'I've made up a bed for you in the East Wing,' said Zinnia, 'in your usual room.'

'Ah. I wasn't really intending to stay.'

'But you must. You really must.'

'I don't even have a change of clothes.'

Zinnia gave me a faint smile. 'Max needs you here,' she said.

So I stayed.

That night, at around three o'clock, I awoke to find that Elenora Twist had slipped into the bed beside me, in her underwear. 'Shhh,' she whispered urgently when she saw that I was awake. 'I need somewhere to sleep. I can't sleep with him, not tonight. It doesn't seem right.'

So we slept.

In the morning, Elenora was up before any of us. She left on an early train back to Cambridge. I stayed with Max and we spent most of the day sitting in the library on the mahogany bergères. I was still in my borrowed funeral suit. I made no mention of Elenora. Max reminisced about the captain and I let him talk.

It wasn't an easy day. Most of the time we avoided any discussion of our future plans. Max was in a difficult mood. He swung from grief and self-recrimination, to bitterness, to defiant self-assurance, and he could do all this in the context of a single short conversation. In general, it was easier to let him have his head, and just discount his wilder rantings as the product of his deep grief. But as the day wore on, I became uneasy, and at last I told Max that I had to get back. I had an exam. I was uncomfortable staying any longer.

Max was silent for a while. Silences in The Pile are measured by the soft throaty tick of the grandfather clock, every second partitioned up like a mechanical reproof for our deliberation or inaction. Eventually Max responded. 'Are you familiar with John Locke's theory of the mind?'

I was nervous of such mercurial asides. 'No,' I said.

'Then you should be,' he said. 'Let me educate you. John Locke was an empiricist, tall fellow, big, sharp nose …'

'When was this exactly?'

'Oh, I don't know. Probably about the time of Queen Anne.'

'Right.'

'Seventeen-hundredish.' Max fell silent again, his eyes focused on the middle distance. 'What was I saying?' he asked me, after a moment.

I was tempted not to remind him. 'You were talking about John Locke.'

'Ah yes. John Locke. Anyway. Empiricism is a way of understanding knowledge. Basically what it says is that all our knowledge comes from the things we have learned.'

'That seems pretty obvious, really,' I said.

'Not exactly,' Max was warming to his subject. He gave me a weak smile. 'You see, before people like John Locke came along, all we had was 'innatism'. Pretty much everyone was an innatist. Innatists thought that the mind was born preprogrammed with knowledge. So, for example, everyone would believe that, if you were English, then you were born with the English language preprogrammed into you, and that your education was a kind of unwrapping process, revealing what was already in there. Descartes was an innatist, by the way. It was all about believing that humans are built in the image of god, and the innatists said that this implied that our minds are like tiny miniature models of god's mind. But then along came Johnny Locke and his empiricist chums. They held that the mind is a 'blank slate' at birth, a *tabula rasa*. We are all born blank and then we're shaped by our experience and our memories. That was Locke's big insight. He realised that the contents of your mind make you who you are. He saw the infant mind as an empty cabinet and from the moment of birth it starts filling up. It's a bit like this library. When it was built, the shelves were empty. Now it's full of books and what makes it unique among libraries isn't the quality of the shelves, but the books that line them. No other library in the world will have exactly the same set of books, just as no two people have exactly the same set of memories. The reason one chap is a gentleman and another is a scoundrel – according to Locke – is all down to the things that found their way into the library of the mind. He thought that ninety per cent of what makes us who we are – our personality, our character, our predispositions, our beliefs – derives from the content of our memories.'

I looked at Max. A week and a day had passed since the death of the captain, and Max was still stumbling along a path somewhere between grief and the rediscovery of his wry self. I sighed. It would be easier to indulge him. 'And this is important ... why?'

'Locke thought that the stuff that happens to you in childhood has lasting consequences,' Max said. 'He believed that the association of ideas we make when we are very young becomes the foundation of the self: they form the first marks on the *tabula rasa*.'

'OK.'

'So that led to David Hume …'

'Ah …'

'But it isn't Hume we're concerned with here. It's Locke. Do you remember I told you about my little project?'

I must have looked blank, because Max responded with a hint of offence. 'We talked about it – you remember. My memory project?'

'What memory project?'

'You know. I'm going to map my memory.'

'When did we talk about it? It wasn't when I was down here, was it? You know. The day we buried Libby the dog?'

'No, no, no.' Max went silent for a moment and I began to fear that I had made a mistake in mentioning the day we buried Libby the dog. We were at Dorset House. Elenora was there. And Ravi.'

'Max, that was over a year ago!'

'No it wasn't. It was last May. Anyway, it doesn't matter. You remember the idea?'

'I remember we were messing about with some film guide and you thought it would be a good idea to try to list all the stuff in your brain.' I started to laugh but I caught myself.

Max didn't laugh. 'I'm going to do it,' he said earnestly. 'I really am going to do it – you and me, Adam. It'll be a seminal project in experimental philosophy; it will be the first project to underpin empiricism with a solid base of data.' He looked at me as if he were expecting some kind of approval. I did my best to look enthusiastic.

'Right,' I said, 'although I'm not really sure where the "you and me" bit comes into this.'

Max ignored my comment. 'I'm going to be the first person to record – in painstaking detail – *everything* in the cabinet,' he said, 'Everything in the library. This library.' And he tapped his temple with his middle finger.

'You're going to catalogue your brain?'

'Exactly.' Max slapped his thigh. 'Spot on.'

It was the most cheerful I had seen him since the fencing match. But I was suspicious of this unexpected change in his mood.

'Max,' I said, rising from the mahogany bergère, 'I have to go.'

'No, Adam, don't go. Please. I have to tell you about this project. It involves you, Adam.'

'Look, Max, I have to get back to Keele. I have to hitch-hike a hundred miles or so and it's nearly dark already. I have stuff to do. I have mock finals to prepare for. I should really be revising. The first one is tomorrow.'

'Mock finals!' said Max contemptuously, as if such a thing would never be contemplated at Cambridge.

'They may not mean much to you, but they are important to me.'

'Adam, look, I'm sorry. I didn't mean to deride your mocks.'

I tried to shrug this off. 'You mean you didn't mean to mock?'

He grinned. 'Let's toss a coin.'

'No, let's not.'

'We'll toss a coin. If you win, you go back. If you lose, then you stay here for one more day and you help me to plan my project.'

'No. If I lose, I stay here for one more *hour* and help you to plan your project – and then you give me the money for a train to get me back to Keele.'

'Done!' He started to rummage in his pockets for a coin.

'But if I win, I'm leaving now.'

'Of course.' He drew a fifty-pence piece from his pocket and placed it on his thumb. 'Heads or tails?'

'Heads.'

'Heads it is then,' he said. 'Any other outcome and you lose.'

'There is only one other outcome,' I said impatiently.

'If you say so,' and the coin was up and spinning.

I should have known, of course. You will already have guessed, but I wasn't so quick. Twelve years had passed since I last saw Max perform this trick. The previous time we had both been eight years old, perched on the edge of a tree-house in another time, another continent, another dimension it seemed. Today we occupied different bodies. There was an immeasurable gulf of history that stretched between us, long-haired student-types in our black funeral suits reclining with glasses of sherry in mahogany bergères. Here was a future I had never foreseen.

The coin rose and spun. It crested and fell. And then it vanished. Max swallowed like a frog and stuck out his tongue to show me that the coin had disappeared. 'You lose,' he crowed. Then, 'Oh god. Oh god.' He began to choke.

The original fifty-pence piece was a seven-sided coin with a diameter of thirty millimetres. I know this. Max has included this detail in The Catalogue. The diameter of the oesophagus is only around twenty millimetres but it can expand. After some choking and a certain amount of back slapping, Max seemed to be OK. The coin had clearly made its way to his stomach.

'I'll stay for a couple of hours then,' I said, reluctantly.

'Good,' said Max, still a little unsettled. 'And I'll pay for you to get a train.'

'No it's OK. I can hitch.'

'Adam, don't argue. I'll get you a ticket.'

'Thanks.'

One hour later, Max had outlined to me the whole plan for his project. He had it all sorted out. He would work in this room. He would sleep in the back bedroom that had no view from its window, apart from the courtyard. I would have a room in the attic. I would do his shopping and ward off visitors. I could even earn some money. He would find some way for the estate to pay me a salary.

Another hour later, Max was in hospital. The oesophagus, it seems, is more forgiving than the small intestine.

Aunt Zinnia drove us in the Volvo. It was the same grey hospital as the one they'd taken the captain to just over a year before. It could have been the same grey day. Max was admitted into a general ward. It was the same ward where Zinnia and I had sat on plastic chairs and broached the subject of the cancer with Captain Ponder.

When Aunt Zinnia and I left, Max was still in pain. The junior houseman who saw him in A&E had been fairly unsympathetic.

The next day, Max was no better. A different doctor told us that he was under observation. He referred to Max's problem as a 'foreign body' and told us that they would try to induce it. If that failed, then they would need to operate.

At 2:00 p.m. on Tuesday 25 March 1975 I missed my first mock final exam.

At 3:00 p.m. they cut Max open and removed the foreign body.

At around 7:00 p.m. they let us see him. He seemed suitably contrite. 'Shit, Adam, I'm sorry,' he said, 'I made you miss your exam.'

'Yes,' I said, not wanting to forgive him, but he looked so frail in his hospital bed that I went easy on him: 'I'll explain it all when I get back. I'm sure there'll be some official exemption for students who have to attend the bedside of friends who've been hospitalised for swallowing decimal coins.'

'When is your last exam?' Max asked.

'What? My last mock final?'

'No. Your last final final?'

'My final final final? I don't know off-hand,' I said. 'But I graduate on American Independence Day. The fourth of July.'

Max grinned. 'Hey! In that case we can kick off the whole memory project the next day, which will be my twenty-first birthday. How appropriate is that? I'll be twenty-one and it will be ten years to the day since O died. Saturday the 5th of July!'

Max weakly held his hand out to me, inviting me to shake it to seal my agreement to the whole enterprise.

I wanted to protest. I should have protested. I wanted no part in this undertaking. I had other plans. I had a job offer from Proctor & Gamble. I was due to start in their marketing department at a big sprawling plant in Middlesbrough sometime in August. I would be selling soap powder. I would be helping to craft strategic sales campaigns as a trainee executive and all this would be chapter one of the next stage of my life. Mentally, I had already made the move. The job paid £4,500 a year and there was a company car: a Ford Cortina. I would have my hair cut to just below my ears so that I didn't stand out, and I would buy a suit with just a slight bell-bottom to the trousers to show that once I had almost been a hippy; and I would maybe buy some fingerless driving gloves and a car radio. I would put a down-payment on a little semi – maybe somewhere select like Guisborough. I would date a girl from the personnel department. We would holiday in Majorca.

Somehow, for almost a year, I had been assembling these

components of my future and they were starting to take shape. I had even spotted a girl in Personnel when I went to Middlesbrough for my interview who, in my mind, occupied that place by my side on that beach in Majorca. This was to be my new life. I had no desire to be Max's live-in housekeeper for three years. What would my parents say? How would it look on my CV? From every angle I looked, this did not seem like a smart career move.

And this is what I shall tell the investigators when they start to unpick the story.

It all happened, I shall say, because Max swallowed the fifty-pence piece. My life and my future were bought for fifty pence. If Max hadn't swallowed the wretched foreign body, I'd have politely parried his insistent demands for my participation; and since I knew Aunt Zinnia had firmly ruled out any involvement on her part, well then, Max would have had to scale down his plans. Or he'd have done it without me. But you see, Max *had* swallowed the foreign body, and he *had* lost his father, and here I was at his bedside being offered his hand to shake. So, in another one of those miserable moments of equivocation that blight all our lives, I buried the marketing executive and the Ford Cortina and the house in Guisborough and the girl from Personnel and I shook the hand of the empiricist coin-swallower in the hospital bed; and in that moment our lives were sealed.

28

CANCER

Sometime in the autumn of 1995, I started to do some research into the cancer that killed the captain. It was something that had been on my mind for twenty years, and I was anxious to learn whether the gloomy prognosis given to me by the captain was still true, or indeed, if it had ever been true. I decided to start with the oncologist, now retired, who had treated the captain at the Royal Marsden Hospital during the last months of his illness. Aunt Zinnia reminded me of her name, Dr Ruby Ellis. She had been at the funeral, apparently, and I had a faint memory of her.

I couldn't get an address through the NHS. I tried looking through a large pile of telephone directories in the Henley library, but I had no idea where Dr Ellis might live, and Ellis is quite a common name. To compound the difficulty, most addresses at that time, in the case of married couples, were still listed according to the husband's first initial. I didn't know if Dr Ellis was married, but she might well have been. The Internet did exist in 1995, but it was still in its infancy; and if you could use it to find an address, it was still a skill that was beyond me. So I called a detective agency in London. Dramatic, I know, but within an hour I had an address in Salisbury, a telephone number, and a bill for £140.

I decided not to phone ahead. Instead, I drove to Salisbury, found the address, and rang the doorbell. Dr Ellis was a rather sprightly seventy-year-old; she wore jeans and walking boots, and a sleeveless fleece jumper. 'Are you from the council?' she demanded.

'Er, no.'

I explained my mission. I rather feared that she would refuse to help me on the grounds of patient confidentiality, but no such concern seemed to arise. She invited me into a conservatory where I was mobbed by small dogs.

'Don't mind them,' she said, settling into a garden chair, whereupon all of the dogs (on recollection perhaps there were only two) leaped up into her lap. 'Of course I remember Captain Ponder,' she said with a genuine smile. 'He wasn't the kind of man one could easily forget.'

I told her what I could about Max. Over the years I had often had to explain Max to people, and my accounts ranged from 'He's a recluse. You know, like Howard Hughes.' to the full sixty-minute story. Dr Ellis got a ten-minute version. It was probably enough.

'Has he shown any symptoms?' she asked me, after a short pause for thought.

'Not that I would recognise. What sort of thing should I be looking for?'

'Loss of balance, headaches, faulty vision, slurring of speech ...'

'No, not really. None that I've observed.'

'Well he's still quite young, isn't he?' she said.

'Forty-one.'

'Hmm. It would be best if you let someone examine him.'

'That's out of the question, I'm afraid.'

'For now maybe; but if he starts to show symptoms you'll have to seek treatment.'

'Well, we'll cross that bridge if we have to,' I said. 'For the moment I just want to know how inevitable it is that he'll develop the same condition. And if he does, what we can do about it.'

Dr Ellis gave me a long look. 'Nothing is inevitable when it comes to cancer,' she said. 'And not many cancers are really inherited. Most of the ones that we think of as inherited are more a case of an inherited predisposition.'

'Well, that's encouraging, isn't it? I mean, it sounds encouraging.'

'Well, yes,' she gave me a jolly smile, and I remember feeling that it was rather forced.

'The thing is, you really don't have to reassure me about anything,' I said. 'I just want to understand what the chances are that Max will get this cancer.'

She gave a deep sigh. 'First I should say that I haven't practised for nearly ten years.'

I nodded.

'Then I should add that Captain Ponder's astrocytoma was a

particularly rare type. I specialise in brain tumours, Mr Last, but in all my career I have only ever seen this specific cytoma twice.'

'I see.'

'Captain Ponder was one case,' she said, and then she paused. 'The other case was his brother.'

'Ahh.'

'Indeed. However, if we suppose for a moment that both Captain Ponder and his brother inherited the same unfortunate gene that led to this rather aggressive cancer, and I think we are reasonably safe in assuming this, then it is also quite safe to say that the chances of a son inheriting are probably no more than fifty per cent.'

'Right.'

'So multiply this by the chances that an individual with the defective gene will actually go on to *develop* the condition – let's be pessimistic and say that there is an eighty per cent chance of this – then the maths would tell me that fifty per cent multiplied by eighty is forty per cent. Make of that what you will.'

I contemplated this rather raw statistic. 'So Max has around a forty per cent chance of coming down with this?'

'Only if you go with our broad assumptions.'

'A figure is better than no figure – if you see what I mean.'

'I do.'

'And what should we do if Max develops symptoms?'

'Get him to hospital straight away. Don't wait to see if the symptoms recur. Here.' She pulled a pad of paper out of her pocket and wrote on it. 'Call Dr Yasir Khan at the Marsden. Tell him I told you to call.' She gave me the paper. 'The first sign of a stutter or a slur in his speech. The first time he stumbles. Or if his general coordination seems to be failing.'

'I will. Is there any treatment?'

'Surgery. If we find the tumour early enough and if it is reasonably accessible. It is a very aggressive type, so it isn't an easy one to remove completely. But yes, early surgery would probably be my first recommendation. Then some chemotherapy and radiotherapy.'

'And that would cure it?' I asked.

'Well, it might and it might not.'

'I see.'

'How is his eyesight?'

'Fine. He doesn't need glasses.'

'Good.' She gave me a smile. 'Well. Take care of him.'

'I will.'

'I shall look forward to reading all about this great brain catalogue of his.'

'I will make sure you're among the first to know when he's finished it,' I said.

'Jolly good. Though it sounds like a bit of a pointless exercise to me. I mean, you can't really catalogue your whole brain, can you?'

I made a face. 'I don't suppose you can.'

'And even if you could, then what would we do with it?'

'Exactly.'

She walked me to the door and shook my hand. 'Did you ever consider,' she asked, 'that Max might suffer from a personality disorder?'

I thought about this. 'Of course. Of course I have considered it.'

'And?'

'And I'm not sure what difference it would make. Maybe you could give me the name of a condition. A label. But then what? Then I would have a label that I could attach to him with a scientific diagnosis that might or might not be accurate. But how would that help me? How would it help *him*? He isn't a danger to anyone – not even himself. He doesn't show signs of any compulsive or repetitive behaviours. He doesn't have any serious phobias – at least none that I've observed. He has always been more comfortable indoors than out, but he isn't agoraphobic. So yes. I have wondered if Max has a personality disorder. He probably does. In fact, if you sent him off to half a dozen psychiatrists then they would probably find half a dozen different conditions. But I still can't see how it would help.'

'There are treatments for some conditions you know,' Dr Ellis said.

'Drugs you mean?'

She nodded. 'Drugs – yes. Or therapy.'

'You know ... he was always prone to extreme anxiety attacks as a teenager, but he hasn't had one since he started his project, so maybe what he's doing is the best therapy.'

'He may have APD.'

'Which stands for ...?'

'Avoidant Personality Disorder. It's a kind of social phobia.'

'And the cure would be ...?'

'Group therapy perhaps. Some cognitive therapy to help him understand his condition and to control it.'

We stood on the step and looked at each other. Dr Ellis smiled and held out a hand. 'It has been nice meeting you, Mr Last,' she said.

'It has been nice meeting you too.'

And that was that. I went back to The Pile and started watching Max for signs of a brain tumour; and that was how it was for the next nine years.

29

SYMPTOMS

The first time Max broached the subject of the cancer with me was in June 2004. I remember it clearly because this was one of the rare days when Max and I sat outside. There was a heavy wooden picnic table in the courtyard, which was not overlooked, and from which there was no view of the road, the river, or even of the garden. Every summer I would coax Max to work outside when the weather was fine, but stubbornly he would nearly always refuse.

This June day, however, he raised no objection, and we sat in the afternoon sunshine. The sun would burn his pale skin, but I knew we were unlikely to stay out for long. Let him burn, I thought.

We were drinking cold orange squash. Suddenly Max said, 'I've been thinking about my father.'

'Oh yes.'

'I've been thinking about his cancer.'

'Right.'

Max tilted his face upwards, closed his eyes, and let the sun do its work. 'My grandfather – the captain's father – died before I was born.'

'Yes.'

'I was thinking about it. He died right at the end of the war. 1945. He was born in 1895 so that would make him around fifty. The captain was twenty-two at the time. Not too different from me, eh? I was just short of twenty-one when the captain died, and he was fifty-one.'

'Well, there you go.'

'I got to thinking. Do you know, I have no idea what my grandfather died of? I know he died "after a short illness". That's what I was always told. Funny how you just accept that kind of thing when you're a kid. If someone said that to me now, I should want to know what kind of illness. Was it pneumonia? TB? Pox?'

'Well, that generation was always a little more cagey about that sort of thing,' I said, vaguely.

Max shook his head. 'Not always. O's grandfather died in the flu epidemic after the First World War. The captain's mother died of lung cancer at sixty-six. Great-aunt Hilda died of kidney failure after a stroke. Great-uncle George lost his leg in the war and died of complications following amputation. Uncle John contracted malaria in the tropics and that did for him. Great-uncle Hubert had testicular cancer and they cut off his balls, but he survived. You see these things are all part of the collective family memory, and yet my grandfather, Maximilian Ponder the First, just died after a "short illness". It doesn't make any sense.'

'I could always ask Aunt Zinnia if you wanted to know,' I suggested, knowing perfectly well what Max's response would be.

'Don't be daft.'

'In that case, it isn't worth speculating.'

'Ah, but maybe it is. Cap died of a brain tumour at fifty-one. Grandfather died of a short illness at fifty. Great-grandfather, well, he lived to see the end of the First World War, but he only lived for another year, so even if you reckon he was thirty when he fathered my granddad then he couldn't have been much more than fifty when he died – probably younger. And then there was Uncle Martin.'

'Who died in a car crash.'

'Yes. He did. But it was generally considered to be his fault and he was normally such a safe driver. He hadn't been himself for weeks before the crash. I remember thinking he was drunk. He was stumbling along like an old man the last time I saw him. I remember he had a stick! A walking stick! I had quite forgotten that, but now I remember.' Max started scribbling in his day log. 'Goddammit – how could I forget that? He had a wooden stick with a rubber foot and I assumed it was just an affectation. I was only a teenager. At that time I thought everyone over forty probably needed a walking stick. But Uncle Martin was forty-five! Why would he need a walking stick?'

'Where is this conversation headed?' I asked. 'Only I have work to do.'

Max surveyed me through narrowed eyes. 'Do you know anything about this, Adam? No. Don't answer that. It doesn't matter if you do – or if you don't. I have to work this out for myself.' He paused and his expression changed. 'I reckon they all had the same thing. I reckon there is something that kills off Ponder males around the age of fifty. And it isn't a tumour, is it? It's that thing – what was that disease in *Valley of the Dolls*? Do you remember? The guy is a nightclub singer. Tony. He has some kind of congenital condition that causes seizures and mental retardation and ends in total insanity. *Chorea sancti viti* – that's what it was. St Vitus Dance. Huntingdon's disease. Did you know that "dolls" was slang for barbiturates? Anyway. That's what I think it is. I think the Ponders have St Vitus Dance. I'm sure of it.'

'Max,' I said, rising to my feet, 'write this down.' This was what I would say to him if ever I had to impart new information. Max never liked having to do this.

'I don't want to know,' he said, waving at me crossly.

'Well I'm going to tell you anyway, so you may as well write it down.' I gave him a moment to take hold of his pen. 'You absolutely don't have Huntingdon's disease. There is no history of Huntingdon's disease in the Ponder family.'

Max scribbled this down, but curiously the news seemed to deflate him. 'Well what *do* we have then?' he demanded. 'Something is cutting the Ponders off in their prime. If it isn't Huntingdon's disease, then what is it?'

'Max. Don't worry. You're nearly fifty. You have every prospect of living to a ripe old age,' I said. 'Just promise me you won't spend the rest of your years trapped in this house. There has to be an end to this.'

'There will be,' he said, 'I keep telling you. Another few years and I shall be done.'

That was the end of the conversation.

But how strange that we even had the conversation then. I remember the balmy day, noticing all the things that I knew would upset Max – the still air, the distant hum of traffic, birdsong, bees, faraway voices on the river and the faint but distinctive chug of motor boats. I knew these would become memories for Max too, and would have to be recorded. We have a different kind of memory, for smells. Max had a way to encode and characterise smells, and that day there was a hint of cut grass and a whiff of diesel and that smell that hangs around poplar trees and willows. Max would have noted these down, I have no doubt.

Nine years had passed since my conversation with Dr Ruby Ellis, in her conservatory, with her dogs. In those nine years I had, for all practical purposes, forgotten Max's genetic heritage. For some reason I had left Salisbury that day with the confidence of the gambler who only believes in the best of outcomes.

I looked across at Max from where I stood, readying myself to leave him alone with his writing and his memories, and I saw his hand shake, just very slightly. Had I ever noticed this before? Or was this one of those tricks of association that the mind likes to play? I had been drawn into thinking about the possibility of a tumour, and now here I was making myself believe I had seen a symptom.

'Are you all right, Max?' I asked.

He looked up at me. 'Fine,' he said. 'See you later.'

30

THE STORY OF A CRAZY ENGLISHMAN

VOLUME CCCXXXIX
SEPTEMBER 2003

There was once a Victorian explorer named
Alexander Kinglake. I don't know what he
looked like, but it shouldn't be hard to
conjure up a reasonable image of a chap,
probably with an outrageous moustache and a
three-piece twill suit and quite certainly a
ridiculous hat, mounted on a camel; and if
you can picture all that, then the chap you
are picturing, give or take a few details,
would almost certainly be Alexander Kinglake.
One day Kinglake and a whole camel-train of
porters and servants set off to cross the
Sinai Desert. For days they toiled in the
heat of the blistering sun as English
explorers were wont to do until, quite by
surprise, they saw another camel-train
heading towards them. As the two camel-trains
drew closer, Kinglake was able to identify,
from clues such as the generally inappropriate
clothing, moustache, hat, and overall
deportment, that the chap on the lead camel
was another Englishman. Well gosh! Can you
imagine the awkward social problem that this
encounter was about to throw up? Here we had
two English explorers who had never been
formally introduced. What should they say?

In the end the two did the only thing that Englishmen could reasonably do in such circumstances: they rode past each other at a respectable distance and each one doffed his hat.

I have picked that story more or less at random. It already appears in The Catalogue so I am not recording it here for any particular reason except to enable me to ask a rhetorical question. What difference does it make to the future of life on this planet that I know that story – the story of Alexander Kinglake and the encounter in the desert? Imagine two futures – in one future I know the story of Alexander Kinglake, in the other I do not. Do the two futures differ in any respect? Of course not. Will the oak tree at my gate grow a single additional leaf? Will the Thames passing my garden carry a drop of water more or a drop of water less? Will my own future run a separate course because I know the story? Will I die a minute later? Will I use this information to help me avoid some dreadful social faux pas and in doing so change the course of history? No, no and a third time, no. A crazy Englishman felt obliged to observe the social mores of his time. So what? Imagine if I could simply delete that story from my memory. I would, of course, be unaware that I had ever known it. If Adam were to recount it to me, I should react with pleasure and surprise because it is, let's face it, a jolly good tale. But in terms of value, real *value*, it has none.

Actually, now you come to think of it, the same value could be placed on pretty much everything we know.

So, frankly, why do we bother? Why has

evolution saddled us with the inconvenient luggage of this memory? Why don't our brains possess a powerful censor to weigh in and assess the potential future value of every nugget of information that comes our way, then to gently discard the useless stuff into the blissful ocean of ignorance? Were *Homo sapiens* to be possessed of such a faculty, then perhaps we could have managed with a lot less brain, and that in turn would have given us smaller heads, and that by logical extension would have enabled mothers to give birth several months later extending our pitifully short neotenic gestation to a period more becoming of a mammal of our size. This, in consequence, could have reduced – over the past couple of million years – the dreadful toll of infant mortality that has afflicted our species, as well as giving parents a better night's sleep. All of this Mother Evolution could have done for us simply by ditching a lot of unnecessary cerebral storage space. But she chose not to. Which tells us that somehow, in some freakish way, there really is a value to all that rubbish we carry around in our heads. Maybe the story of Alexander Kinglake, while of no value to me, will lodge in the mind of someone who reads this account – just as it has lodged so obdurately in mine; and maybe this person will use the story to dazzling effect at a dinner party; and maybe this will help him win admiring glances from a young lady in a short dress with a burgundy lace décolletage; and ultimately the telling of the story of two Englishmen meeting in the desert might lead to a bedroom liaison that would never otherwise have happened and our protagonist will succeed in passing his genes on to the next generation.

Adam, of course, would argue that our brains already perform the censorship that I describe. He would point out that we routinely forget almost everything we ever know or learn. This is certainly true of Adam. The man spent seven years learning Latin by rote, yet today I doubt if he could conjugate a single irregular verb or correctly identify the phrasing of a simple iambic pentameter. He tells me that he has developed new skills and knowledge pertinent to his place in the 'outside world'. He tells me such things to coax and cajole me into abandoning my enterprise. I too forget things, of course. Yet the fact remains that I still carry around somewhere in my hippocampus the unmistakable picture of two chaps on camels graciously doffing pith helmets to each other. Let them search for that particular memory when they break open my brain.

31

IT'S A FUNNY THING – DEATH

I need to jump back – just one last time. Looking at Max's body, cold and stiff, I find myself reminded of a day, thirty-one years ago, and a conversation that Max and Elenora and I had about memory and death. It may help us to understand this whole cycle of events.

It was, if I remember rightly, the day after Max's twentieth birthday in July 1974. We met up in London for a one-night-only reunion at Dorset Square. Four months had passed since the day of the fencing match, the day that we buried Libby the dog. The captain was still in the early stages of his terminal illness and was back at The Pile being looked after by his cadre of professional nurses. Max was splitting his time between Cambridge and home. One night in London was all that any of us could manage to mark his birthday.

It wasn't a traditional Dorset Square weekend. The only participants were Max, Elenora and me, and I felt out of place. Max, I thought, had moved on to a deeply introspective chapter in his life, and at that time I didn't expect the chapter to include me. My own life had also taken turns that seemed set to lead me a long, long way from the curiously intense and internalised world of Max and the Ponders.

Well, not much of that turned out to be true. But it was, as it transpired, the last ever Dorset Square weekend. Eight months later, the captain would be dead, and one year later, Max would be celebrating his twenty-first birthday in the library at The Pile, carefully scribing the details of the first day of his three-year project.

When I arrived at the apartment at the pre-arranged time, there was no one home. Elenora was sitting outside on the step. Neither of us seemed surprised that Max was absent. We sat together and talked for about an hour until a taxi pulled up, and out stepped Max and Mrs Drabble, both dressed in black.

Max was apologetic. He explained that Tutton, the old family retainer, had died earlier in the week and they had just attended the cremation.

I remembered Tutton from that fateful weekend at The Pile. Blind and slightly bent, he had lurked around the house like a resident ghost. He seemed to possess just one facial expression – the garrulous look of a man who is slightly annoyed with the world and annoyed with himself, but who nonetheless soldiers on. He didn't wear the lounge suit of a butler or the rough clothes of a gardener – just twill trousers and an old blazer and a badly knotted tie. I was never quite sure what his role in the Ponder household was supposed to be. I took it as just another Ponder thing. I had rarely heard him speak. Like a practised servant, he clearly knew the value of silence. And yet, in a Ponder way, he was indisputably part of the family; one of the fixtures and fittings of the grand house, tap-tap-tapping along the corridors with his cane. No matter that he could not cook or clean or even wait tables – he could answer the telephone in the hall and admit visitors and show guests to their rooms, and perhaps, for the Ponders, this was enough.

With Max still in his funeral suit, we walked from Dorset Square to the West End. We found an Italian restaurant in Soho. Max was in a wistful mood.

'Were you very fond of him?' I asked.

'Of course,' Max said. 'Tutton wasn't an easy man to love, mind. He was an irritable old bugger most of the time. But he'd been with our family for ages – he was like part of the household.'

We did normal things that day. I remember we walked to the National Gallery and looked at paintings. We had coffee in Leicester Square. Max was very quiet.

In the evening we wound up at the apartment with a bottle of red wine and some of the captain's single-malt whisky.

'It's a funny thing, death,' said Max, as the alcohol started to take hold.

'It always makes me laugh,' said Elenora, digging Max in the ribs.

But Max wasn't in the mood for jokes. He rather coldly pushed

Elenora's hand away. 'I don't mean funny funny,' he said, 'I mean funny bloody-difficult-to-get-your-head-around funny. I mean funny shitty-tragic-fucking-complicated funny.'

'Do you remember what Nietzche said?' Elenora asked.

'What did he say?'

'If you spend too long staring into the void eventually the void starts staring back.'

'Oh, the void is staring back all right,' said Max gloomily. 'Take Tutton. Do you think he'll earn an obituary in *The Times*? No he shitting won't. The best he'll get is an announcement in the Deaths column and only then if someone feels like coughing up for one. All it will probably say is something like 'Albert Bonneville Tutton', and then, 'Born 8th October 1894 in Redruth, Cornwall, Died 28th June 1974 after a short illness in Marlow, Buckinghamshire aged 79.' And that would just about be it. A whole life, eight decades, chucked away in three lines. Is that what we are? Is that all we're worth? Three lines in the Deaths column of *The Times* that might end up being read by a couple of hundred people and only read by them because they're scouring the page looking for someone else. There you are, Albert Bonneville Tutton! That's what you're worth, mate. Apart from your name in the cast list and the details of your entrance and exit, all you get is four words – "after a short illness". Was it worth it, eh?'

Elenora slid an arm around Max, but it didn't look as if this would stop the rant.

'What should it have said?' Elenora asked, 'Go on – give us an obituary for Tutton. We'll raise a glass for him.'

'It should have said, "Here was a guy who belonged to another world and another time". It should have said, "This was Albert Bonneville Tutton who kicked and screamed his way out of a bloody birth canal in the days when Queen Victoria was still on the throne, when there were no anaesthetics or antiseptics or antibiotics or aeroplanes. He went down a tin mine when he was twelve years old." Is there anyone left alive who remembers working down a Cornish tin mine in 1906? I don't expect so. What could he have told us about those days? Do you ever see those archaeology guys out in the fields with their little trowels and brushes and their little plastic bags brushing up some piece of an old pot? How much do you think it costs for them to get that precious piece of information? A whole team of people in their wellies with their shovels and flasks of tea and hours and hours of digging and all they end up with are tiny snippets of information about the past. Oh look, this fragment of pot shows a picture of a horse – so maybe the people worshipped a kind of horse-god and maybe they used to offer up sacrifices in this very pot. And here we have a human being – a fully articulate human being with his memory intact who knows what it was like to work down a tin mine in the very early days of the twentieth century. So what do we do with all that uniquely valuable knowledge? Do we send a whole team of smart-arse archaeologists to learn everything we possibly can about his life? Do we buggery! This was a man who walked all the way to Plymouth in 1914 to sign up for the army when he was twenty. He served out nearly the whole war in the trenches. Once he was concussed by a shell that went off right by his head and he spent three days lying unconscious in a pile of mud and bodies in no man's land. When he came to, he was on a pallet of bodies being sent behind the lines for burial. A week later, he was back at the front. He survived more offensives than just about anyone in his regiment. His commanding officer was my great-grandfather, Aloysius Ponder. My great-grandfather was in his forties in 1918. He sent Tutton back on home leave that year and Tutton got engaged to a Redruth girl and I don't know anyone who even remembers her name now that Tutton is gone. Anyway, it didn't matter. With only weeks to go to the Armistice, he was back at the front and another blast got him and took his sight. He was sent home with great big bandages around his head and his girlfriend died in the flu epidemic just a few months later, before they had a chance to get married. Later that year, he had a visit from my great-grandfather. The upshot was that Tutton ended up working at The Pile and living in the gate-house. Then great-granddad died at the end of 1919. Tutton stayed on working for my grandfather, who was in his twenties at that time – about the same age as Tutton himself. And that was what he did for fifty-five years. He never learned Braille and he never had a guide dog.'

'Sad story,' said Elenora.

'Yes. Sad story. But do you want to know the saddest bit? The saddest bit is that there are only about six people alive who even *know* that story.'

'We know it now,' I offered, gamely.

'Sure,' said Elenora. 'We know it now. Let's have that drink, shall we? Let's drink to good old Tutton.'

'But in a few years' time *we'll* all be dead, and Tutton's story will have gone for ever. That's my point – don't you see? You know what we do with old buildings? We slap a preservation order on them. We say, "Look here, this building is a valuable part of our history. There are features in this building that we don't want to lose. We need people in the future to know how this window might have looked, and how that door catch worked, and the fact that the floor was made up of little wooden tiles." That's what we do. We make huge efforts to preserve every possible source of information. We make it against the law – *against the law* – to knock down old buildings or pull down old trees, or trash archaeological sites. But what do we do with the richest information we have available – the material locked away in the brains of four billion people? You know what we do? Sod all. We watch old people die in old folks' homes or on sink estates and we chuck them into a crematorium in a cheap plywood coffin and give them three lines in the local paper – if they're lucky. You know there are old guys dying out there who fought in The Boer War. There are hundreds dying every day who fought like Tutton in the trenches. There are old ladies dying who fought for emancipation when they were girls. There are people who remember *seeing* Queen Victoria. There are probably even people who can remember sitting at a great-grandfather's knee while he told them about the Battle of Waterloo. Imagine that!'

'We do know all that history though, don't we?' said Elenora.

'We *think* we do,' said Max. 'But mostly what we only know is the high-level stuff – the grand sweep of history, the sorry little love affairs of our kings and queens, who won which battle and when, who discovered Australia, who invented the Spinning Jenny. Do we even know what it was like to *use* a Spinning Jenny? Did it give you blisters on your thumbs? Did it give you backache? Did it keep on breaking, like things always do, and the little piece you needed to make it all work rolled under the sideboard and you spent thirty minutes looking for it? That's the kind of thing we want to know about the Spinning Jenny. Not just the fact that James Hargreaves had a daughter called Jenny who kicked over his spinning wheel one day, giving him the idea. Don't you see? Real history shouldn't be limited to what happened to the rich and powerful – it should be about how people lived. *Real* people. *Real* lives. What did they eat? How did they cook it? What did it taste like?'

We sat in relative silence for a while. I daresay Santana was playing in the background.

'Did you ever read Pepys' diaries?' Max asked us. We both shook our heads.

'Well, you should. You really should. Here is a guy who for a fun day out goes to a hanging. This is what I mean. History isn't just about the guy who gets hanged; it's the experience of all those people who stand on tippy-toes, trying to see what was going on. What Pepys gives us are all the details that we miss when we read history books. Like how thrilled he is when the King knows his name. Or when the Great Fire of London looks set to reach his house and he takes the precaution of burying his parmesan cheese in the garden. That was reality.'

'This isn't really about Tutton, is it?' said Elenora, after a while. 'It's about your dad.'

'No it isn't,' Max protested, but Elenora's words had suddenly brought a tear to his eye. 'Well, yes, it is about him too. When Cap dies we'll lose all *his* memories too. We'll lose all his stories, all his friendships, all his little nuggets of knowledge. We'll lose the faces he would recognise in a crowd; the jokes he heard in the officer's mess, and a million, million little facts about my mother. So when Cap dies, a big chunk of O will die all over again. We'll lose stuff about me, when I was a baby. Who can ever tell me that stuff now? Every time someone dies it's like the world loses a big chunk of information for ever. I don't mean to say that every bit of that information is especially valuable, but it's surely just as valuable as a fragment of pot from a Roman villa, or a fossil from some riverbed in China.'

'So what's the solution?' I asked.

'There isn't one. Well. For a start we should all keep a diary.'

'Should it be compulsory?' asked Elenora.

'Absolutely. Everyone should keep one. Five hundred words a day minimum.'

'And what sort of things should we write in it?'

'Everything. We shouldn't decide what matters. That decision is for whoever reads it in the future. Pepys didn't distinguish between the big stuff and the little stuff. He gives us interminable details of every battle in the war against the Dutch – which he probably thought we'd all be really interested in. But of course because we lost that war and were eventually taken over by a Dutch king, we've all conveniently forgotten the war and no one wants to be reminded of it. But then, on the same page, Pepys gives us all these other details. How he walked to Whitehall and the people he passed; the plays he enjoyed and the ones he hated; the conversations he had over dinner; his financial accounts; his vanity; the dismissive way he treats his wife. Those are things he might have felt he should leave out – but he didn't. He must have been bent over that little desk of his writing into the night. And that's what we should all be doing. We should say if we had a dodgy curry, had to run for a bus, if we bought new platform shoes, if we saw an advert on TV that made us laugh. That's what we should be recording.'

'Do you keep a diary?' Elenora asked him, with a gentle smile.

'No,' Max said. 'But I shall. I shall.'

32

AND THEN WHAT?

VOLUME CCCXLIX
JULY 2004

These are some recent news headlines. America
has, in Gerald Ford, just appointed a
president who has never been elected, even to
the position of vice-president, because (i)
Nixon just quit and (ii) the chap who was
elected to be the vice-president has also
recently quit; this job was originally
occupied by one Spiro Agnew, a man who is
distinguished by the fact that his name is an
anagram of 'grow a penis'. Aston Villa have
just won the League Cup. I forget who they
beat. Europe is troubled by a rather strange
crop of terrorists with names like 'the Baader
Meinhof' group and 'the Red Army Faction'
and 'Ordine Nuovo'. Harold Wilson is prime
minister again by a whisker, West Germany
has just won the world cup, the IRA have been
bombing pubs in Birmingham, Guildford and
London, India has exploded an atom bomb. These
are things that have been in the news
recently.

Only they haven't, have they? These are
things I remember from the news twenty-nine
years ago. I do wonder what is in the news
today. Adam believes that I have no interest
at all in events outside The Pile. But there

is a difference between not wanting to know, and having no interest.

I know that I'm on the final leg of my project. I know it now. Of course, I have always known . . . intellectually. I know, after all, that I'm fifty years old, and that the Ponders don't generally bother with a second half-century. And I know that, even if I do break the mould and live for another fifty years, Adam can't take much more. And neither, really, can I. I just haven't known this emotionally. Somehow I've spent so many years looking backwards that I've never taken the time to look forward. How will I know when my work is finished? Picasso would say that he knew when a painting was finished; it was finished when it was sold. But when will I be finished? Emotionally . . . I am only just beginning to learn the answer. Adam will often ask me this question, 'when will it all be finished?' Sometimes I tell him that the question has two answers. One answer is 'soon'. The other answer is, 'never'. Adam thinks that I'm being evasive. He thinks that I'm giving him two mutually exclusive answers to avoid telling him the truth. Only I really understand the paradox. That both answers are true.

The conversation I had sitting outdoors with Max when we talked about Huntingdon's disease took place early in June last year – that was June 2004. After that all was well. A day or so later, we even had a conversation about the end of the project. I suggested to Max that he should wind it all up on his fifty-first birthday, which was a year and a month away.

'There's only one thing that worries me,' he said, playing along with my proposal.

'And that is . . .?'

'What will happen to my brain when I finish?'

'It will go on working like every other brain on Planet Earth.'

'Except for one thing. I'll be missing the past thirty years.'

'You will.'

'God. That's scary. I won't be able to hold a conversation about anything. I won't know who was prime minister in 1990 or who was the first man on Mars, or who was secretary-general of the TUC in 2002.'

'Well I don't know that one,' I said, and Max wrote this down in his day log.

I said, 'You're scared because you used to be known as a great intellect, someone with instant command of huge amounts of knowledge. Now you'll just be known as a schmuck.'

'You're right,' he agreed. 'It isn't an appealing thought. I will have to immerse myself in all the news and current affairs of the past thirty years. It could take a year to catch up.'

I glowered at him. 'Don't think that you're going to lock yourself away in here for another year reading up on the past thirty.'

'You know what Mae West once said?'

'A hard man is good to find?'

Max laughed. 'I'd forgotten that one,' and he wrote it down.

'No you hadn't,' I corrected him. 'I've seen it in one of the appendices.'

'I know. I didn't mean I'd forgotten it. I just meant I'd forgotten about it. Which is a different thing.'

'So what did Mae West say?'

'She said, 'Keep a diary and one day it will keep you.''

'Meaning ...?'

'I guess she meant that one day you'll be able to sell the diary and live on the proceeds of all your scandalous stories. But maybe that isn't what she meant at all. Maybe she meant possess a diary and one day it will possess you.'

'I see.'

'And then there is another thing.'

'Are we off Mae West now?'

'Yes. We are back onto the things that worry me.'

'So the other thing is?'

'What will happen to my brain when I finish? What will really become of my brain? It will start becoming a different brain from day one. The day I step out of that door, I'll start to learn new things. See new things. And you know what the worst part is?'

'What is the worst part?'

'I won't be writing any of it down.'

'Of course you won't. That's the whole point!'

Max took a while to scribble all of this down. 'It will take some thinking about,' he said.

Well, they say that the calm always comes before the storm. I didn't really have any expectation that Max would wind up his project on his fifty-first birthday. Nor did I believe for one moment that he had even the slightest intention of doing so. This was a game, you see. Even Wittgenstein might have recognised the rules. Max would sense my mood on days when my patience was wearing a little thin. He would become anxious that I might choose to walk out on him, and if I did he would have to end his isolation, if only for the length of time that it would take to recruit another willing victim to fill my shoes; and that would be a wholly unpalatable idea to Max. It would introduce into his life a new personality, and the discovery of this new person and their faults and foibles, their habits, their eccentricities, the way they walked and talked and dressed, even the way that they sat down quietly and thought, would mean at least a full volume of memories. So Max had to persuade me to stay. Over the years he had exhausted his full armoury of arguments based on the scientific value of his work (I no longer believed it), the loyalty owed to him by me as a friend (no loyalty should need to stand this test), and the career that I owed to him (Ponder Estates has made me rich, but there are easier ways to earn money). He had tried calls upon my sympathy; he had ventured to forecast for me a dazzling reputation once the work was complete. 'You'll be the real hero of the story, Adam,' he had argued, 'I shall be cast as the mad villain but you – you'll have been my loyal supporter. When they make this into a film, I'll be played by Charles Laughton with a hunchback and you'll be ...' he hunted for a name, ' ... whoever the latest screen heartthrob is.'

I was tempted to say 'Brad Pitt' but I didn't. 'The guy who gets the girl?' I asked.

He hesitated. 'I don't suppose there are many girls in this screenplay.'

'Very few.'

'Well then,' he tried, cheerfully, 'we shall have to get the writers to rewrite it. When they come to make the film, we shall add a mysterious, dark lady. She could be my agent. You and she would end up in a sunset embrace.' He paused and wrote something down in his day log. 'She could be Elenora Twist,' he said.

I arched my eyebrows. It was the first time he had mentioned Elenora in several years.

'Do you think I will need an agent?' he asked.

A week after the day in the June sunshine, Max slipped on the wet floor of the bathroom after his morning shower and clouted his forehead on the sink. When I arrived at The Pile late in the morning, I found him sitting at his desk in the library with a ridiculous bandage around his head.

'Good god, Max! Whatever have you done?'

He explained about the wet floor. I unwound the bandage and examined the wound. The bleeding had stopped, but there was a lump like a bird's egg on his temple.

'Max, you need to be careful,' I said, 'you might have concussion. Have you been feeling sick at all?'

'Not in the slightest. It's nothing. Don't fuss.'

I rewound the bandage. 'This is why you need a telephone,' I told him. 'It could be an unlisted number. You wouldn't get any calls except from me. And if you ever have another emergency like this, then you can call me.'

'Don't talk nonsense,' he said. 'I haven't needed to call you in twenty-nine years.'

'Perhaps not. But you might. What if you had given yourself concussion? What then?'

'Then I'd have lain on the bathroom floor bleeding quietly until you came along.'

'And what if I had decided not to come in today? What if I was on holiday?'

'If you were on holiday then you wouldn't be answering your

phone anyway,' retorted Max, who had never conceived of a portable telephone.

'You could call the hospital.'

'Don't be bloody daft.'

But within a few weeks, Max had suffered a second fall. This time he stumbled in the kitchen while preparing coffee for the two of us. I was sitting in the library on one of the mahogany bergères when I heard the crash of plates and the thump of Max hitting the floor. I went in to find him sitting up, looking slightly dazed, amidst the debris of broken china.

'I think I lost my balance,' he said.

I helped him up. 'Has this happened before?'

'No. Not really.'

'Not *really*?'

'Well, we all lose our balance from time to time, don't we?'

'Has it happened recently?'

'No. Why? Do you think I might have a problem?'

'You might need glasses,' I told him.

'I don't need glasses.'

I made more coffees, and back in the library we settled into the armchairs.

'I think it might be an idea for you to have a check-up,' I said.

Max looked at me suspiciously. 'Why do you say that? Do you think I'm ill?'

'I think you *might* be ill.'

'With what?'

'If I knew that then I wouldn't be suggesting a check-up.'

'It's out of the question,' he said. 'I'm not having a doctor in here poking around again.'

'Max, when was the last time you had a doctor here? 1988 when you had that kidney infection.'

'1989,' he corrected me.

'OK. '89. Sixteen years ago. I think maybe you could relax the rules just a little and let me call a doctor. I could see if Dr Kazerian is still practising.'

Max looked impatient. 'For god's sake, Adam. I lost my balance. I don't think that gives any cause for concern. I'm OK.'

I looked at him sternly. 'Have you been having any headaches?'

He paused just a little too long before answering. 'No more than usual.'

'And what would be usual?'

'I've always suffered from headaches, Adam. You know that.'

'But are they more severe than usual?'

'No.'

'More frequent?'

'No.'

'Have you had any problems with your eyesight?'

'I'm telling you – I don't need glasses.'

'Everyone needs glasses eventually.'

'Well I don't. Not yet.'

Max went to bed early that night, which was not something he often did. I stayed in my bedroom in the attic; the bedroom where we had held the fencing match on the day when the whole sorry business began.

The next morning I made breakfast and took it in to Max in the library where he was already at work on a drawing, carefully inking over pencil lines with a Rotring pen. It was a map of some kind. I glanced at it before setting down the tray. It was a map of Edinburgh, rather sketchy. There was a roughly drawn hill and a castle and a long, straight road that he'd labelled 'Princes Avenue'. I didn't think to correct him. His catalogue wasn't about accuracy. It was about what was in his memory. If his memory told him that 'Princes Street' was 'Princes Avenue' then there was no point in changing it.

'I think we need to talk,' said Max, rather sullenly.

'About what?'

'All that doctor stuff.'

I pretended to look surprised. 'So you'll see a doctor then?'

'Certainly not,' he said. 'I won't see a doctor. But *you* might, if you wish.'

'And why would I want to see a doctor?'

'Because I need to know,' he said.

'What do you need to know?'

'Adam, this isn't twenty questions. Stop being so perverse. I need to know about my dad's cancer, all right?'

I relaxed. 'All right.'

'I need to know a bit more about it. Specifically, I need to know if I stand any chance of getting it too.'

'Have you had any symptoms?' I asked him.

'I don't know.'

'Tell me about them.'

'I said "I don't know". I didn't say I had symptoms.'

'No. But I know you too well, Max,' I said. 'You didn't say you *didn't* have any symptoms either. So what are these possible symptoms that you don't know about?'

Max sighed. His breakfast sat untouched on the tray. 'I do have headaches,' he admitted, after a moment.

'You told me yesterday that you didn't.'

'No, I said they weren't any more severe than usual. They're just ... different.'

'Different ... how?'

'I don't know ...' Max looked off into the near distance. 'They're more – *intense*.'

'More intense – but not more severe?'

'Not really. It's a little hard to explain. And then there's this.' Max held out his hand. It was shaking.

'How long has this been happening?'

'Only a few days. And it doesn't happen all the time.'

I let out a long sigh.

'That's why I need you to find out, Adam,' Max said. 'I need you to find out exactly what happened to the captain. And find out if I have it too.'

'Max,' I said, 'I already have found out. You might want to write this down.'

Then I told Max everything that Dr Ruby Ellis had told me and he wrote it all down. He didn't ask any questions.

'Your eggs are getting cold.'

'I know.' He was writing too fast to look up.

'I need to go,' I told him, eventually.

'Business?'

'Yes.'

I left him alone with his thoughts.

Later that day I looked up the phone number that Dr Ellis had given me. I called the Royal Marsden Hospital and asked for Dr Yasir Khan. A polite receptionist told me that he was in surgery. I told her that I was a private patient. I gave my name as Maximilian Ponder.

'Can he phone you back?' she asked.

I got the call the next morning as I was leaving my home in Henley on my way to The Pile.

'Mr Ponder?'

'Hello. You must be Dr Khan?'

'I am. What can I do for you, Mr Ponder? You should know that I was acquainted with your late father. I do hope this has nothing to do with his case?'

I outlined the situation, gave my real name, and we arranged to meet. We would not meet at the Marsden. Instead, we met at a private clinic in Harley Street where he had a consulting room.

Dr Khan turned out to be an uncommonly thin man, of Indian or Pakistani origin, expensively dressed, with greying highlights in a thick head of hair, and faintly tinted designer spectacles.

'You must have been a very young man when you knew Captain Ponder,' I said.

'Of course,' he said with a dismissive wave. 'It was a long time ago.'

I gave him my preamble about Max, the truthful version. I told him about The Catalogue, and the seclusion, and the headaches, and the falls. Dr Khan took no notes but he listened intently.

'You have to let me examine him,' he said, when I had finished.

'I don't think he will allow it.'

'Then there is nothing I can do.'

'Can you give me something for his headaches?'

He drew a pad towards him and wrote out a prescription, then passed it across his desk. 'From the information you have given me,' he said, 'I would diagnose a tumour. You do understand that Captain Ponder's condition appeared to be inheritable?'

I told him that I understood this.

'The sooner I see him, the sooner we can decide if he needs treatment,' he said. 'And the sooner we start treatment, the more likelihood we have of success.'

'I'll try to persuade him.'
'You must.'

That conversation took place on Friday 2 July 2004, three days before Max's fiftieth birthday. The following Monday, I did something that I had never done before for a birthday. I took him a cake. It was a shop-bought cake, with icing and candles, and 'Happy Fiftieth Birthday' written in blue fondant. He was cross, of course, but less than he might have been a decade or so earlier. We ate the cake in the library, where else, with Max at his desk and me on the Empire mahogany bergère. Max beamed at me as he ate, as if this were the greatest treat in his life. Perhaps it was. All the time his right hand was shaking like a sapling in high wind.

'Max,' I said to him, once I had cleared away the remnants of the cake and washed up the tea things. 'I want to give you something for your birthday.'

He looked at me suspiciously.

'I want to pay for a doctor to come and examine you.'

Max shook his head fiercely. 'Out of the question.'

'It would be my gift.'

This discomfited him slightly. 'It's a generous gesture,' he said. 'But I'm not ill.'

I tried to be gentle. 'Do you remember we spoke about the tumour that your father had?'

Max was writing feverishly. 'Adam – I'd rather you didn't continue with this.'

'Max,' I said, 'you have the same tumour.'

He stopped writing, just for a moment, and he met my eye just long enough to understand that this was true. Then he was writing again, his face bent over the paper.

'Max, did you hear what I said?'

'Yes.'

'*Do* you understand?'

He looked up. 'Of course I understand.' There was a steely expression in his eyes.

'Then you'll see a doctor?'

He finished writing a sentence and stabbed a full stop with his pen. 'No.'

I exhaled. 'Max. You have to do this.'

'How can you know?' he asked after a few moments. 'How can anyone know?'

'I spoke to a doctor.'

'But he hasn't examined me. So how can he know anything?'

I was exasperated. 'For god's sake, Max, that's exactly what I'm asking you to do. Let him come and examine you. He's very discreet – I promise you.'

'Let's change the subject.' This was a common ploy. If we were venturing close to forbidden topics, it was Max's stock response. Normally I would oblige. But today I was more stubborn.

'No, Max,' I said. 'I will not change the subject. I've been to see a doctor who understands your condition. He was part of the team that treated the captain. All he wants to do is come here and meet you.'

'And poke around,' Max said.

'Not really to poke around. He isn't going to get you to take off any clothes. I imagine he'll want to take your temperature, look in your eyes ...'

'So he'll look in my eyes,' said Max, 'and what do you suppose he might see?'

'I don't know. I'm not a doctor.'

'Maybe he'll see a bloody great tumour looking back at him.'

'Maybe he will.'

'Let's change the subject.'

'Not until you agree. I'm not going to let this drop until you agree to see Dr Khan.'

'Jesus, Adam!' Max was scribbling everything down. He was cross because I had mentioned a name and now this would have to be recorded and indexed and god knows what.

'Get me some more cake,' he snapped, 'while I write this down.'

Afterwards we sat in silence. I went upstairs for some things and when I came down and glanced into the library, there he was, pen in hand and head bowed.

'I'm off home.' I told him.

'OK.'

I stood for a moment to see if he would say anything more.

'Have you thought any more about what I said?'

His hand was flying across the page. 'No.'

'But you will think about it?'

He glanced up. 'Of course.'

'Good.' I knew then that the cause was lost, but I persisted all the same. 'Can I call the doctor?'

'Doctor Khan?' he said scathingly. 'Why don't we use his name, eh?'

'Can I call him? Please?'

'Let me think about it.' His hand wasn't shaking as he wrote. Maybe I was overreacting. I closed the door quietly and left without saying goodbye.

33

EXIT STRATEGY

APPENDIX CDXIX

The Behaviour of Women.

Is this a suitable subject for a memory catalogue? Or is it crude speculation? I wrote down this heading in another appendix and now I can't find where I wrote it. So I'll start it again.

I know that women behave differently from men. At least I think I know that they do. But is there anything empirical that I can - or I should - record? I remember Alan Turing's test for Artificial Intelligence. [APP CDLXXXVIII]. His idea was that you could put a computer in one room, and a human operator in the other. They would communicate via a typewriter keyboard and a teleprinter. The human operator would attempt a conversation with the computer. He would ask leading questions. How are you feeling today? If the moon is made of cheese then what is your favourite biscuit? But the key thing would be this: he wouldn't know if the other half of the conversation was being typed by another human being (intelligent) or by a robot (intelligence under dispute). If, after some undetermined period of time, our operator was unable to identify whether his

conversationee were a man or a machine, then
we would have created a genuine artificial
intelligence. This is what Turing argued.

So now I propose the Ponder Test: would an
experienced operator be able to distinguish,
not between a man and a computer, but between
a man and a woman? Are there any fundamental
features of the female psyche that cannot be
counterfeited or disguised? Are there any
character traits that are present in one
hundred per cent of women yet absent in one
hundred per cent of men?

I cannot conduct the Ponder Test - but I can
forecast the outcome. I cannot think of a
single behaviour that would unambiguously
allow us to separate the sexes. Even if our
operator was to threaten to drown a kitten -
well, there are women I have known who would
remain unmoved. So how can I write an appendix
entry on female behaviour if I am not even
sure that such a thing exists?

And yet, and yet, and yet . . .

I could not say that men are taller than
women, because, as we know, some women are
taller than some men. I need to employ the
language of the mathematician. I need to say
that the average man is taller than the
average woman. But if I grew up on an island
of tall women and short men, I might see
things the other way around. And, as the
statisticians would say, the average man has
fewer than two legs. And that is a nonsense.
So is my average woman fickle, temperamental,
whimsical, capricious, or is this just a
consequence of my personal experience? Is it
an affront to all women to record their
behaviour as unpredictable, or mercurial, or
fanciful? Or did my personal experience of

O, and of Zinnia, of Elenora and of Katherine, and of Mrs Drabble, and of all the girls at Cambridge, and the nurses who cared for the captain, somehow colour my perception with a palette that womankind does not deserve? And if all these adjectives are pejorative, is it equally unfair and nominalistic to classify women as sensitive, empathetic, considerate, truthful?

I went to two single-sex boys' schools. I never had sisters. I fear that my knowledge of women derives as much from literature and popular culture as it does from direct observation. I am drawn to images of Emma Woodhouse, or Madame Bovary, or Anna Karenina. I think about women and I find myself picturing a drunken Janis Joplin on stage with a whisky bottle, or Marilyn with her skirts flying, or Jackie Kennedy running off with a fat Greek millionaire. I picture Judy Garland tripping along the yellow brick road, Queen Victoria gazing sulkily from a photograph that used to hang on the wall of our lounge, Marie Curie wasting away from the cancer caused by her radium. I think of Melanie hunched over her guitar, Ophelia manically distributing flowers, Fanny Blankers-Koen storming home to win a gold medal at the London Olympics, Fanny Craddock teaching us how to pipe icing onto cakes, Fanny Hill introducing us to sex in that gorgeously pornographic eighteenth-century novel. (I used to find it endlessly amusing, by the way, that a rude word like 'fanny' could be a perfectly respectable name. But then so is 'Dick', so honours between the sexes are even.)

Well, now I've told most of the stories that should matter to the police and the press – at least, the ones that I know. The experts *should* be able to assemble a compelling case for what really happened from these accounts. They should be able to point to this incident or that and say this was why Max did this thing and why that other thing occurred. The story of the fencing match, and Taylor and the caning, and the leprous corpses at Mwanza, and the Tanzanian soldiers in the Nile; and the story of the day that Max swallowed the fifty-pence piece. There should be corroborating evidence for most of these, that will support the truth of the whole story. There will be police records following the fencing incident, hospital records of the swallowing, and witness accounts for much of the rest. That should persuade them that my version of events is true, and that will be important to me because it can look suspicious to be found in a room with a rough-wood saw and a headless corpse.

But, of course, there are so many other stories. That is the nature of life. Some stories I know, but many I don't. It would take a huge book to contain them all. And of course we know just how huge a book it would take. It would take 360 volumes and hundreds of appendices.

All Max's stories will surely be in The Catalogue somewhere, but even I have read only a small percentage of the words that Max has written. There are all the events that befell him in the years before he and I met at the gate of the Dupont house on the day when I could see into the future. There were all the adventures and encounters he had at Eton. Volumes and volumes of these Eton recollections fill the library at The Pile. I have leafed through a good many and forgotten most, but for every one that I have read, a dozen more remain unread. There were countless similar exploits at Cambridge. Then there was all that he learned of literature and language and philosophy, all of the books that he read, places he visited, plays that he saw, things that I will never know, can never hope to know. Max had travelled extensively by the time he was twenty-one. He had visited India several times. He knew Simla and Delhi (Old and New), Agra and Bombay and Jaipur. He had travelled to California and Mexico, to New York and Toronto, to Egypt, South Africa, Italy, France, Germany, Spain, Russia, and the Netherlands. He had explored East Africa, had climbed Kilimanjaro and Mount Kenya, had sailed Lake Victoria (as you know) but had also sailed around Zanzibar and Pemba and from Mombasa to the Seychelles.

However rich a life can possibly be for twenty-one years, Max had led it. He had been to operas at Glyndbourne and Verona, Shakespeare at Stratford, ballet in Moscow, musicals in London and New York, and cabaret in Berlin. He had captained a team on *University Challenge* that made it through to the semi-finals. He had visited art galleries in New York and Paris and Madrid, zoos in San Diego and London, beaches in California and Malindi, fine restaurants in at least a dozen cities, fine hotels in a dozen more.

The captain was responsible for most of this. He had sent Max hither and thither on spurious business trips, charged with 'cementing business relationships', which usually meant entertaining, good meals and fine wines. So Max had become a Renaissance man, widely read and widely travelled, urbane, articulate, entertaining. He fenced (as you know), played tennis, hockey, even some cricket. He played the piano, albeit not especially well. All of these things he did, and all are painstakingly detailed in The Catalogue.

He was less experienced, of course, in the ways of women. You might gather this from his gauche entry on female behaviour in appendix CDXIX. His first girlfriend was Katherine Dunn, the sister of a friend at Eton, whom he met at a school dance. They dated for several months. I never met her. His second girlfriend was Elenora Twist. I don't think that there is one moment that Max spent with Elenora that isn't faithfully recorded in The Catalogue. He appears to have retained every word from every conversation, every gesture, every touch, every kiss, and every intimate moment.

The first time I met Elenora, she was someone else's girlfriend. We met, of course, at a Dorset Square weekend, an early one. Elenora was there with a lumbering rugby player called Aaron Yates, one of Max's Cambridge friends. Max was on his own. Elenora didn't say much that first weekend. I remember her as a slender, boyish figure, dressed in a heavy man's pullover – probably one of Yates's. I was a little overawed by her, as any undergraduate at Keele would be overawed by any undergraduate from Cambridge, especially one of the opposite sex. I thought at once that she was cleverer than all of us. Her manner was faintly distant; not so dissimilar, now I come to think of it, to O. But she also had an *ordinary* quality about her, which might sound dismissive, but which, in fact, offered quite an alluring side. She was an ordinary girl from an ordinary family in Sutton Coldfield with no discernible accent and no particular airs or affectations. In this respect she *was* very different from O. Her father was an accountant and her mother was a nurse and her brother was a social worker in Birmingham. She had earned her place at Cambridge thanks to her ferocious intellect and raw determination.

On that first meeting, Elenora more or less ignored me. The second time, she was loosely attached to Max. This time she sought me out and befriended me. She sat alongside me on the Isfahan rug in the front room at Dorset Square and offered me a drag on a fat marijuana cigarette. Her bare knees fell apart and one knee pressed against my bare arm. She spoke to me earnestly, sometimes leaning forward to whisper in my ear. As she did so, I caught her exchanging knowing glances with Max; it felt as if her conversation with me was somehow, on some level, also a conversation between her and Max.

In The Catalogue, Max often describes Elenora as a 'free spirit'. That was the way he saw her. Perhaps it was the way he chose to see her. Max with his Eton background, with his colonial high-society roots, may well have seen any girl from an ordinary semi in Sutton Coldfield as a free spirit. When Elenora ignored the social mores, dressing inappropriately for society events, carelessly employing swear words, affecting a casual inhibition around her frequent nudity, Max saw it as libertine rebelliousness; I used to suspect that it was Elenora's way of cloaking her ignorance about the way she was *supposed* to behave.

Somewhere in The Catalogue, possibly in the day logs, there will be a detailed account of the last night that Max and Elenora spent together. It isn't a passage that I have ever sought or read. But when the psychologists come to read it, as I expect they will, they might unearth some of the reasons behind Max's continued seclusion. Those words might also help explain the last conversation he had with me in the final days of his life.

But we are getting ahead of ourselves again. We aren't ready for that yet.

Before we get there, we have the small matter of what Max called his 'exit strategy'.

The first time we discussed the exit strategy, the tumour was at a fairly early phase. That is to say, it had passed beyond the stage where we might have dismissed the symptoms as the humbling inconveniences of middle age. But it had not yet reached anything close to the physical and mental collapse that had afflicted the captain.

The captain, on that day when we sat on the damp grass in the orchard, sweating over the exertion of digging a grave for Libby the dog, had confided to me his hope that the part of his brain that controlled heartbeat would succumb to the tumour *before* the part of his brain that controlled his bowels. He was not to be that lucky. His bowels and his bladder went quite early on; balance soon followed and he ended up bedridden for the last few months of his illness. I never saw him during that period, but Max, of course, had been there throughout. The Ponders employed a bank of six agency nurses to help care for the captain as the disease progressed. The nurses, Max always said, 'were wonderful'. They are each rewarded by a chapter in The Catalogue. They looked after the captain at home, in The Pile. A hospital would have been unthinkable.

Worse than the physical deterioration that the captain experienced – as if this were not bad enough – was the mental disintegration. His eyesight went completely one day, over a period of around four hours. Soon afterwards, he began to lose parts of his memory. First he lost the recent past – what had happened that morning, or the day before. Later these missing days grew to recent weeks and months. His memory was regressing in time. One day he would awake in Kenya in the Dupont house, calling for the houseboy, Kimathi. The next day it would be the war. The captain had been sixteen when the war started. He had enlisted in 1940 and served with the Desert Rats. Afflicted with cancer in the spring of 1975, he was suddenly back with Monty in the desert.

He lost any ability to taste or recognise food. Then he lost all hearing in one ear. For a short while, he shared O's partial deafness.

Then the rest of his hearing started to fade, and what remained of his memory began to dissolve away.

'It took about two weeks,' Max told me. 'First he started forgetting words, stumbling in speech; then whole concepts were gone. Adjectives went. Then verbs. He was left with a few stuttering nouns, a few names – "bed", "drink", "dark", "pain", "Max".'

By the time his hearing had gone completely, the family were praying for the tumour to do its worst. But the captain hung on. They fed him though a drip because he could no longer take solid food. He grew thin and his skin came off in flakes and his hair dropped liked white leaves from an autumn tree. Still he survived. This great man, this soldier, this relic of an earlier age, clung onto life after all sensibility was gone. The cancer in his brain had robbed him of every scrap of dignity, every essence of life, apart from the wretched heartbeat that he had hoped it would claim, the heartbeat that kept both him, and the cancer, alive.

In the end Dr Ruby Ellis prescribed an intravenous dose of morphine that would have killed a horse. It was a therapeutic dose designed to kill the pain, but administered in the full and open knowledge that this had gone beyond pain and all that was left was the anguish of the living. The morphine did the job that the tumour had failed to do, and the captain's heart stopped.

Now Max was facing an end that looked as if it might go the same way; and he didn't like what he saw.

He called me into the library. I was in the kitchen, doing some chore. I came in and took my usual seat on the mahogany bergère.

'Do you notice anything?' Max asked.

I look at him, puzzled by the question. 'What should I notice?'

'I'm not writing any of this down.'

He was speaking the truth. His notebooks were folded away. There were no blank pages from Hawksley and Nether of Knights-bridge. His Sheaffer Visulated reservoir pen was in the drawer.

'This must be important,' I said.

'This is so important,' he said, 'that it can *never* be written down.'

I was intrigued. Max, you understand, wrote *everything* down. There was nothing that could not, should not, be recorded, itemised, and set down in black ink. To omit a single scrap would be to start the dreadful creep that Max most feared, the dreaded 'compromise of The Work'.

'Adam,' he said. 'I don't want to go the way the captain went.'

A long look went between us before I spoke.

'Then let me call a doctor,' I said. 'Call an end to this now. You've done enough. Your work is as complete as it ever needs to be. Let me get a doctor in to see you and then we shall get this wretched thing out of your brain.'

Max thought about this for what seemed like a minute. 'I don't want you to think that I haven't considered that,' he said.

'And ...'

'The tumour is too far gone.'

I was exasperated. 'Max, don't you *dare* say that it's too far gone. I put this to you last month and the month before and the month before that and you wouldn't do it then.'

'No,' Max raised a hand. 'I wouldn't do it then. And I won't do it now. The reason is the same, but now there is something else. The tumour is too far gone.'

'Max, you don't know that. You don't even know that you *have* a tumour. We're only guessing because of what happened to the captain. Maybe you have something perfectly treatable. Maybe you have diabetes.'

'Adam, you don't understand. I *do* know. Trust me. I know I have a tumour. It isn't diabetes. It isn't a head cold. It's what the captain had, and it's what Uncle Martin had, and it's what my grandfather had. And even if I didn't know what it was, well I still don't want to be cut open. You understand, don't you?'

I sighed. 'Then what is this conversation about?'

'It's about not wanting to go the way the captain went.'

I suddenly felt a little uneasy. 'So then, why aren't you writing this down?'

'Because I can't. Because if this appears in The Catalogue it could incriminate you.'

'Incriminate me? How?' This was an alarming turn to the conversation.

'Adam, don't get upset. Please understand me – I saw the captain die. I saw every stage. I know how this ... thing ... progresses. I don't want to go through that.'

'Right. And?'

'I want my brain to be preserved.'

'We've already had that conversation.'

'And have you done anything about it?'

'That depends.'

'Depends on what?'

'Depends on whether you intend to write any of this down.'

Max sighed. 'I shall n ... never write any of this down,' he said.

'What about the truth and veracity and total bloody completeness of The Catalogue?'

'Well ... it will be missing this one tiny piece. When they crack open the Rosetta Stone, they'll find it in my brain. But we shall both be long dead before that so you'll be in the clear.'

'I see.'

'So did you do anything about it?'

'Yes, Max. I did. You don't need to know any of the details, but I've done it. OK? All you need to know is that your brain will be kept preserved in a state that will last a thousand years.'

Max seemed rather pleased at this news. 'A thousand years, eh?'

'At least.'

'Good.'

'So are we done?'

'No, Adam. We're not done. Not done at all.' Max took a drink of water from a glass on his desk. 'What we need to decide is ... what we need to agree is ...'

'Is?'

'Is an exit strategy.'

'An exit strategy?'

'Exactly.'

'What sort of exit strategy did you have in mind?'

Max looked pained. 'Adam, you remember what it was like for the captain?'

'As a matter of fact, I don't. I wasn't there.'

'But you remember what I've told you about it? About all the nurses it took? How he needed cleaning up all the time? How he lost a piece of his mind every day?'

'I remember you telling me.'

'Good. Well – we can't risk that happening to me. This is *my* project. I don't want the whole thing spoiled by a stupid tumour. What if they cut open my brain in a thousand years and all they find is p ... porridge? Then the whole thirty years will have been wasted.'

'Max,' I said, 'I don't buy this. When you started this project you never mentioned *anything* about preserving your brain. You were only interested in cataloguing the contents. Where did all this big desire to freeze yourself for posterity come from? The Catalogue – that's your work. That's what you'll be remembered for. Not for some brain sitting in a freezer.'

Max sighed. 'You really need to take a long view of things sometimes,' he said wearily. 'The Catalogue is only of value if it has the owner's brain to accompany it. Otherwise what is it but another autobiography?'

'A bloody long autobiography,' I said.

'Exactly.'

I think this was the first time Max had gone so far as to imply that the real work, The Catalogue itself, might be worthless without this final sacrifice.

'So what do you suggest?'

'As soon as my memory starts to go – that's when I want you to do it.'

'Do what exactly? Chop your head off with an axe?'

'If you like,' Max said, 'although I might prefer something a little less traumatic. And also, you might miss and hit my brain.'

'Your precious brain,' I said with just a hint of sarcasm.

'It is p ... precious to me.'

'I'm sorry.' Why did I say these things? I took a deep breath. I didn't want to hurt him. But when I spoke again, even these words didn't sound conciliatory. 'In that case, here is what I shall do. I'll pop down to the chemist and buy a big bottle of arsenic and I'll leave it by your bed. Then, as soon as you feel your memory going, all you have to do is take a big swig. Job done.' Maybe I was trying to make light of it. Maybe I was in denial.

'Adam you're not taking this seriously.'

'How seriously do you want me to take it? You wanted me to come up with an idea and I've come up with two: arsenic or an axe. What more do you want?'

'I don't think you really understand how difficult this is for me.'

I found myself surrendering. 'I'm sorry, Max. I'm being an ass. Tell me your suggestion.'

'All right then ...' Max began, 'but you must promise to take this seriously.'

'I promise to listen seriously if that is what you want, but if you're going to ask *me* to end your life while you are still of sound mind, then you're wasting your time.'

'Then what am I to do?'

'I don't know. You're a grown up. Work something out.'

'And what if I'm no longer of sound mind? What then?' Max seemed to contemplate this remark. 'When the captain started to go,' he said, 'he didn't realise he was going. That was the spooky thing. When he lost a piece of his memory, he *really* lost it. I mean, it wasn't just *gone*, it was as if it had never existed. He was losing whole periods of time, but he never knew that he had lost them. That's what I'm scared of.'

'That might not be such a bad thing,' I suggested. 'It would be more scary if you *knew* you'd lost the memory. Ignorance and bliss ... you know.'

'But consider this,' said Max. 'If that *was* happening to me, then it might have already started for all I would know. Maybe I've already lost ten years. Maybe I'm sixty and I only think I'm fifty.'

'Max – what day is it?'

'Wednesday 11th August 2004 – as far as I know.'

'Spot on. You still have every one of your marbles.'

'But you could be complicit, Adam. You could be going along with it and how would I know?'

'For god's sake, Max, stop this. You know I'm not lying to you. That's a ridiculous suggestion.'

'Well, here's the thing, Adam. I know I'm still pretty much in charge of my faculties. But when they start to go, it can happen very fast. I suppose the brave thing would be to end it now. Before it starts to erode my memories. But ... you see, I'm not really the suicidal type.'

'That's exactly what your father once said to me.'

'Did he? I never knew that.'

'Don't write it down,' I said.

'I won't. But you see ... I don't know if I could do it *now*. And if I can't do it now, why should it be any easier next week, or next month? It will always be a "now" decision, won't it?'

'If you could just listen to yourself,' I said, 'you would see how crazy this all sounds. If you don't want to die, then don't die. Stay alive. Who cares about the future of your dead brain?'

'I care,' Max looked at me accusingly. 'I had hoped that you would care too.'

'Well of course I do. But I would rather have you here alive than dead in my freezer, however much theoretical good your brain might do at some theoretical point in a theoretical future.'

'So would I. But the time may come – *will* come – when that decision will go the other way. That's when I want you to do it.'

I groaned out loud. 'Suppose you tell me what exactly it is that you would like me to do?'

'OK. First, I don't want you to tell me about it. Ever. I don't want to wake up and think, "this is my final day". I don't want to know. It has to take me completely by surprise when it happens.'

'Some surprise.' I was drifting back towards sarcasm. I couldn't help myself.

Max ignored this. 'Then, I don't want poison. That might damage the brain cells.'

'*Dying* will damage the brain cells,' I said. 'Freezing will damage them too.'

'And obviously nothing that would cause trauma to the head.'

'Of course not. How about a red-hot poker up the fundament? It worked for Edward the Second.'

Max actually smiled at this. 'You could shoot me through the heart perhaps.'

'Or run you through with a rapier ...'

'Indeed – you could run me through with a rapier. But that would be messy and you might have some difficulty explaining that to the coroner.'

'So *that* would be difficult, but a headless body wouldn't?'

'Adam, you said you were going to take this seriously.'

'I'm sorry, Max, but this isn't making any sense.'

'My suggestion is a strong polythene bag.'

'You want me to suffocate you?'

'I do. That way there will be no mark on my body. You can always tell the authorities that I died naturally.' He grinned, 'And I have a clever twist coming. I want you to keep the bag here on my desk,' he tapped the desk. 'And every day – at least once a day, I want you to pick up the bag, casually ...'

'And ...?'

'And I will say, "Not today, Adam. *Umbrella.*"'

'Not today, Adam – *umbrella*?'

'It's a kind of password. We'll change it every day. Maybe tomorrow it will be "Not today, Adam – buttercup". And the next day, "not today, Adam – helicopter". You will pick up the bag, I shall say the password, and then you'll nonchalantly put the bag back down. But one day – well, one day I might look at you, puzzled. I might say "Just one moment, Adam – I've forgotten the password." I might say "Just give me some time – I need to think. What was it?" Or I might just look at you as if the whole need for a password has gone from my memory. As soon as that day comes, you have to pull the bag over my head without delay. No hesitation. You have to do it then. Right there and then.'

'I should give you *some* chance to remember it,' I protested, belatedly aware that this reply seemed to imply my consent to the scheme.

'Oh no. I won't forget the password. If I forget it – or worse, if I give you an *old* password – then that means it has started. That's the day I want to go.'

'You won't write these passwords down?'

'Of course not!'

I gave a long sigh. Part of me was impressed by the elegance of the idea. 'All right, you bugger. I'll do it.'

'Good!' Max looked triumphant. 'You have to be the one to suggest the password for each day.'

'OK.'

'So what is the password for tomorrow?'

'I don't even have the bag yet!'

'Get one. And have a spare one in your pocket. Oh – and maybe a length of rope to tie me to the chair if I struggle.'

'You're starting to talk me out of it …'
'And the password for tomorrow is …?'
I thought about it. 'Misanthrope,' I said.
Max slapped his knee. 'Misanthrope it is!'

34

HOW IT ALL ENDED

So that was it. That was Max's exit strategy. I bought some strong polythene bags from a DIY store – the kind that you might use to carry heavy gravel. I also assembled the other paraphernalia that I might need; a length of nylon rope, a leather tourniquet to hold the bag airtight around the neck, plastic cable-ties for the wrists, the rough-wood saw from the log shed, the canvas drawstring bag. I read up about the muscles in the neck – the levator scapulae, the sternothyoideus, the sternocleidomastoid. I prepared everything at the lock-up in Henley where Max's head would be frozen. I made myself a list of passwords cross-referenced against dates, and I pinned them to the wall in my attic room so that I wouldn't forget them myself. And I steeled myself for what I would have to do.

Why? You must be asking. Why would I do this? Why would I volunteer to take the life of my friend? How could I so coldly contemplate holding an airtight bag over the face of a man I had known for forty years, watching his last breath, watching him suck the unforgiving plastic into his mouth in a final, desperate hunt for air?

I dare say the police will ask this question too. And in the real world where real things happen and real rules apply, I don't suppose I would have agreed to the same undertaking. But every time I stepped off the street and re-entered the surreal universe of The Pile, I became ensnared, and all of a sudden the rules and customs of the outside world would dissolve. It was – it *is* – a curious, museum-like existence in which no visitor calls and no telephone ever rings, no newspaper is delivered, no radio or TV blares; it has been a place in which policemen hold no sway and law courts never rule. Somewhere, perhaps, in this make-believe existence of Max's I had simply mislaid my moral compass.

You need to remember that Max's project, in a sense, had been my project too. Don't misunderstand me; I don't want to take any credit for it. It wasn't my brain after all. And I have never believed that the work would attract anything *like* the level of scientific attention that Max imagined it would. I have been, for at least a quarter of a century, highly sceptical that it would have *any* value at all. But I can't escape from the fact that it was – it is – a jolly impressive body of work. Maybe it is a monumental folly, but where would the landscape of England be without our follies?

Or maybe I am just a cold fish. Maybe Max was right.

So where should we rejoin this sorry tale? Max is lying dead on the Rastin table, but Max died *today*, and today is Monday 27 June 2005. Ten months have passed since we discussed the exit strategy; ten months, you might imagine, of growing stress as we carried out the daily pantomime with the strong polythene bag and the password. But actually, after the conversation, Max collected his papers and his Sheaffer Visulated Reservoir pen and continued to write, just as if nothing had changed. And from that moment onwards, of course, we could never mention it again. And, by and large, we never did. It became a routine – one of our many routines at The Pile. I would double-check the password upstairs in my attic room; then I would write today's password and tomorrow's down on a slip of paper and put them in a pocket. Then, just as we had agreed, I would wander carelessly past Max's desk and touch the heavy bag with the tip of my finger, and Max would always notice. 'Not today, Adam, Marshmallow.' 'Not today, Adam, Aquamarine.' 'Not today, Adam, Constantinople.' Max never recorded any of this in his day logs. It was a compromise of the work, but it seemed, at last, a compromise he could live with.

The tumour progressed, but it was mercifully slow. For four pleasant months from November 2004 until early in March 2005, we both believed that the cancer had retreated. For a short time we talked about 'remission' and Max, I think, imagined that his life had been spared. We still carried out the charade with the passwords. It couldn't hurt.

Then in March, the symptoms returned. Max suffered a series of headaches that laid him up in bed for several days. I brought him aspirin and tried to persuade him to see a doctor. He wouldn't agree. It was a difficult week. I had meetings that took me to London. I would come back to The Pile to find Max in agony, begging for pain relief. I left a handful of tablets beside his bed – enough, perhaps, to kill him – he took them in ones and twos and survived the pain. He kept his day logs throughout. They told of his agonies. In one of them he wrote, 'I feel as if I am bleeding from the eyes. I feel as if a dark sea-urchin has grown inside my head and its needle-sharp, benighted spines are bursting through my skull.'

After a week in bed he rose one morning, dressed in his Savile Row suit, and came down to breakfast. 'My headache has gone,' he announced.

I must have surveyed him in disbelief.

'It's true,' he assured me, and he tapped his forehead with his middle finger.

The same week, however, he began to develop a twitch in his left arm, and a few days later he started to lose feeling in his feet.

'This is definitely it,' he told me one afternoon as we stood in the kitchen making toast. 'I used to wonder if I was imagining it. But I'm not, am I?'

'You should let me call a doctor,' I told him.

'It's t ... too late for a doctor.'

'You may need palliative care. Pain relief. Drugs.'

'I don't want them. Ask me the password.'

'OK. Tell me the password.'

'Not today, Adam – *Marsupial*.'

'Very good. Tomorrow's word is *alliteration*.'

'Alliteration,' he repeated, 'alliteration, alliteration, alliteration.'

'Don't write it down.'

'I never do.'

We dined one June evening in the library, sitting of course at the Rastin table where Max now lies dead. I had cooked a salmon in pastry with mushrooms, mint peas, and new potatoes. We opened a bottle of Claret. I talked Max into allowing me to play one of his old records on the gramophone, something we never did more than three or four times a year. Records with songs and lyrics were never permitted, but just occasionally, Beethoven was excused. That evening we played the 'Moonlight Sonata'.

We didn't speak much. It was easier that way. We left Beethoven to manage all of the emotions in the room and, as usual, he did so perfectly.

We had tinned pineapple and tinned cream. It was one of Max's favourite desserts.

After dinner Max rose and ponderously made his way back to the desk. I noticed that his limp was getting worse. He sat down heavily. 'I have a h ... headache,' he announced.

'Then don't work tonight,' I said. 'Have a break.'

I moved over to the desk and picked up his day log. It was a single sheet. On the top it read 'Friday June 17 2005. Day: 10,941'. Underneath it read, 'Breakfast: toast and marmalade.' There was no entry for lunch. Perhaps Max would update it later. Nevertheless, it was an uncharacteristically brief day log. Max's day logs would normally run to half a dozen pages or more. They would have to account for every conversation between him and me, every meal, every untoward incident. That morning a sparrow had flown into the glass window of the library with a startling bang. That should appear. That morning, at breakfast, we did indeed have toast. But we had also shared a grapefruit. It was quite unlike Max to miss out a detail like this.

'Do you want an aspirin?' I asked.

'Not yet.'

'It's a short day log,' I observed.

He looked at me and blinked. 'Is it?'

'Maybe not much has happened?'

'No. Well I d ... don't suppose it has.'

I slipped a hand into my pocket to check the password. It was an adjective today, *impetuous*. I walked around the desk and touched the folded gravel-bag.

Max looked up, and his eyes seemed just a little unsettled. 'Not today, Adam,' he said, *'pentameter'*.

My heart gave a double beat and my fingertips closed around the edge of the bag. What was Max doing? Was this a game? A test?

'A cup of coffee would be nice,' Max said. He looked at me with a steady gaze.

My fingers slowly released their grip on the bag. 'What would you do, Max,' I asked him, 'if I were to jump you now with this bag?'

He looked at me with a puzzled expression. 'I'd say, make us a coffee.'

'I'll make it,' I said.

I took the stairs two at a time. I took the incomplete day log with me and left it on my bed. I checked the password sheet on my bedroom wall. Today's password was *impetuous*. *Pentameter* had been the password three days earlier.

Downstairs I made the coffee and took it through to Max. He was sitting at the desk with a vacant expression.

'Have you seen my day log?' he asked, as I passed him his drink. 'Only it doesn't seem to be on the desk.'

'I think I must have filed it,' I said. I went to the shelves and drew down the latest log. There was an entry there for day 10,940, another for 10,939. I removed the entry for 10,938. Three days ago. The day of 'pentameter'. I slid the pages across the desk. 'Here you are.'

Max glanced at them. 'Thanks.'

I slid the logs for day 10,939 and day 10,940 out of the file and into my jacket. It would only complicate things if he were to find them.

'Would you like tomorrow's password?' I asked.

He looked up and nodded.

'Tomorrow's password is: "impetuous".'

'Impetuous, impetuous, impetuous,' he echoed, with no sense at all that he had ever encountered this password before.

I took myself quietly out of the room and left him writing, head bowed, at his desk.

I stayed at The Pile that night. The next morning I rose before Max to make him his breakfast. I took a tray up to his bedroom but found him dressed and ready to go.

'How are you feeling?' I asked.

'Fine.'

'How is the headache?'

'Headache? What headache?'

We went downstairs together.

'What day is it today?' I asked him, casually.

'Thursday,' he replied. It was Monday.

'Thursday the what?'

He paused. 'I forget,' he said.

I put a hand on his shoulder. 'What's the password, Max?' I asked him.

He looked alarmed. 'You don't normally ask this early in the m ... morning.'

'Well I am today. Today I want to ask it now and then it's out of the way.'

'OK,' he seemed to be thinking. 'Not today, Adam,' he said, '*turpentine*.'

Back upstairs I checked the chart. We had lost another five days. 'Turpentine' was over a week in the past.

Downstairs I removed the day logs back to 10,932 – Wednesday 8 June. I gave Max the blue file and a clean punched sheet and he carefully wrote Thursday 9 June 2005 Day: 10,933 on the top. I watched his pen form the words in his precise, unaffected italic hand.

I left Max that afternoon and went down to my office at the gate-house. I was there for around three hours. I made some calls, checked some emails, read some business reports, wrote a letter to a tenant. When I returned to The Pile, Max was standing in the library amidst a flurry of handwritten pages. He was staring at me aghast. As I walked into the room he shouted my name and hurled a handful of pages at me.

'What is it, Max? What's the matter?'

'Adam – you fucking fucking fucker!'

'Max – what is it with the language? What's the matter? Tell me!'

'These!' He scooped up more pages and flung them at me.

'What are they?'

'What are they? They're days, Adam. You fucker. They're days. They're days I never lived.' He sank into his chair, exhausted.

'What do you mean days you never lived?' I glanced at one of the sheets that had flown my way. It was a day log for Friday 3 June.

'What I mean ...' he rummaged for a sheet, ' ... is this.' He rose to his feet and slapped the page onto his desk. 'I never wrote this,' he said.

'Ah.'

'So who *did* write it? Did you write it?'

I shook my head, struggling to invent an explanation.

'DID YOU WRITE IT?' he demanded again.

'No,' I said. We both looked at each other.

'Then *I wrote* it?'

We stood in silence.

'Then why can't I remember it? Heh? Why can't I remember it?' Max's voice rose and his body began to shake.

'Max, please calm down.'

'My memory's going, Adam. IT'S FUCKING GOING. WHY AM I STILL HERE? KILL ME FOR GOD'S SAKE. KILL ME. KILL ME. Kill me.'

I went to him and wound my arms around him.

'Ask me the password, Adam. Ask me the bloody password.'

'OK, OK.'

He was shaking uncontrollably, like the day when we buried Libby the dog, the day of the fencing match, the day that the police marched him into a panda car.

'What's the password, Max?'

He started to cry. A sob from deep inside, a thirty-year-old well of lost emotions. 'I don't know,' he sobbed, 'I don't know the bloody password.' He pulled away and caught my gaze. 'Now you have to kill me,' he said. 'That was what we agreed. I can't remember the fucking password and you have to suffocate me. NOW.'

'Max, you *can* remember the password.'

'I can't.'

'Try, Max. You can remember.'

His shakes began to subside. I was holding him like a man might hold a weeping woman. He wept on my shoulder, drawing deep gulps of air.

'Tell me the password, Max.'

He gulped more air and shook his head.

'Tell me the password.'

He shook his head again, more violently this time.

'MAX, TELL ME THE FUCKING PASSWORD!'

My anger seemed to cow him. His breathing was slowing and I took a firm hold of his shoulders, 'Max? Tell me. Tell me the password. Tell me the password.'

'It's ...'

'It's what?'

'Not today, Adam ... *Cassandra.*'

I released my grasp. 'Well done, Max,' I said, 'You're OK.' I began to scoop up the day log pages from the floor.

'I'm OK?'

'Yes. It's Cassandra. You had me worried there for a moment.' I eased the single page on his desk from underneath his hand.

'You're sure I'm OK?'

'Max – I'm sure you're OK.' I collected up the last of the pages. 'Go upstairs and have a rest.'

'A rest? Yes, I think I will.'

'Tomorrow's password is *cappuccino.*'

'Cappuccino, cappuccino, cappuccino.' Max began to limp slowly towards the door. I watched him go through to the hall and start up the stairs.

'Cappuccino, cappuccino, cappuccino.'

I took the latest day log folder off the shelf and began to unclip another dozen pages. Then, on a whim, I snapped them back in place and put the whole folder under my arm. I stretched out my hands and shovelled up a meter or more of blue folders. I carried them out to the back and dumped them in one of the stables – a place where Max would never venture. Back in the library I wrote a note on a piece of paper and pinned it to the shelf where the missing files had been. 'DAY LOGS TEMPORARILY REMOVED FOR BINDING.' That should satisfy Max when he discovered them missing. Better an argument about missing folders than about missing memories.

Back in the library I surveyed the ranks of leather-bound copies of The Catalogue, all neatly dated on the spines. The day logs were dangerous enough; these volumes were dynamite. If Max were to lose more than a month of memories, then he would be confronted by the unexplainable presence of volume CCCLVIII, dated April 2005. I made a pile of a dozen or so of the most recent volumes and carried them out to the stables too. That should be enough,

I thought. But on reflection I made four more journeys, leaving only the volumes up to volume CCC, dated June 2000, still on the library shelves. Then I left another notice 'CATALOGUE VOLUMES TEMPORARILY REMOVED FOR REPAIRS ON BINDINGS: DUE BACK TOMORROW'.

I went into the kitchen and made myself a mug of tea. A little while later I heard Max coming down the stairs. 'Are you OK?' I called out.

He appeared at the kitchen door. 'Shouldn't I be?'

'I thought maybe you had a headache?'

His hand went up to his forehead. 'No worse than usual.' He turned to make his way to the library. 'I'll have a tea if you're making one.'

I found him back in the library screwing a new nib onto his pen. 'What's the password?' I asked him casually as I set down his tea.

'Not today, Adam ... *corridor.*'

'Do you want a biscuit with that?' I asked. 'Oh. And tomorrow's password is *cappuccino.*'

Why didn't I kill him then? I had resolved to kill him. I was ready to kill him. I wasn't afraid of the act. It would have been a kindness. I knew, even as I let him live, that I should have to do the deed eventually. So why couldn't I do it there and then? It would have offered him the dignity of death with his memories intact; and I would have kept my promise.

Yet I didn't do it.

Was I cruel to let him go on living? He had started on a cold cascade of memory loss, like a cassette tape set to rewind and erase.

But nothing truly ends, does it? Somehow, in the flick of an instant I had changed my mind, the same way I'd changed my mind descending the steps of The Pile on that March day in 1974. Something had rewired my resolve. In all the months that I had planned to take Max's life, I had imagined it to be the end of his story. The boy who had swallowed the sixpence, who had lost his mother amidst a swarm of lake flies, who had stabbed his father through the neck with a sword – he would end his life gasping for air in a builder's polythene bag with a tourniquet around his neck and cable ties around his wrists.

And yet, somehow, when Max gave me 'pentameter' instead of 'impetuous', it wasn't the time for his story to end. I saw that, and I saw it in an instant. This wasn't the end. Not truly the end. This was the start of the final scene of the final act, but the drama still had a course to run, and run it would.

We never played the password charade again. The next morning Max was somewhere in 2004, before our conversation about the exit strategy, before his fall, before we had even sat outside in the June sunshine and talked about cancer. He came down for breakfast, dressed in his Savile Row suit, complaining about aches and pains in his arms and legs and I told him he was coming down with the flu. He barely wrote that day. He sat in the kitchen for much of the time, nursing a headache and staring into the middle distance while I did chores. I left him to go to my office at the gate-house, and when I returned he was in the same kitchen chair with the same mug of coffee that he'd been holding when I left him.

A day later, and Max had lost three more years. He settled down to work in the library, grumbling about numbness and pains. I brazenly removed ten more years of leather volumes and a similar quantity of day logs. Max hardly questioned it as I carried them out. Every now and then I would nonchalantly pick up the day log sheet that always lay in front of him, and would give the appearance of reading it. Then I would replace it with a fresh, blank page. He never noticed, or remarked on this.

By nightfall he was back in the twentieth century.

Max and I had dined on salmon in pastry just ten days ago. That was day 10,941 of his great project, the day when 'impetuous' became 'pentameter'. That was day one, by my counting, of the days when his memory began to unravel like a cheap ball of wool cast down a long staircase. By day four he was back at work with a vengeance and the library was clear of books. I had removed every last volume to the stables, where they sat in piles on the concrete floor. Max's memory was unwinding so quickly by this stage that every time he looked up he would be startled by the absence of volumes on the shelves. He would forget that they were absent just moments before. 'Where's The Catalogue?' he would demand.

'Didn't I tell you?' I would innocently reply, 'They're all being copied – just as insurance, you know, in case we have a fire.'

'Ah.'

And he would work on, but his writing was a loose ramble now; fragments of sentences; unconnected words; scribbles.

I slept at The Pile every night during Max's unravelling. His appetite was fading. He would leave food untouched. I made him sweet drinks to keep his energy up, and stirred in glucose and painkillers.

On the night of day six of the unravelling I sent him upstairs early to bed, and I followed him up. Around 2 a.m. I was awoken by what sounded like a scream. I sat bolt upright and saw Max silhouetted in my doorframe.

'Max? Is that you?'

He seemed to be crying.

'Max? Are you OK? What's the matter?' I climbed out of bed, pulled on a dressing gown. Max *never* climbed the staircase to the attic floor. He hadn't been up here in thirty years. Yet here he was, shaking like a freshly caught fish.

'Let me take you downstairs,' I said. 'Come on. Let's have a cocoa.' I put my hand on his shoulder, but he seemed disinclined to move.

'You're married, aren't you?' he said. 'I know you are. Don't lie. You're married.'

I gave a sigh. Whatever conversation this was, it wasn't going to be an easy one. 'No, Max,' I said. 'I'm not married.'

'Yes you are. You are married. I've seen your ring.'

I held up my ring-less left hand. 'No, Max. I *was* married. I was married for nearly nineteen years. But now I'm not.'

This seemed to unsettle him. 'I know you m ... married her,' he said, accusingly.

'Married who?'

'Elenora.'

'Elenora?'

'Yes, Elenora. Of course. Do you think I'm stupid? Of *course* Elenora.'

'Max, why are you saying this?'

'Just tell me the truth. TELL ME THE TRUTH.'

'OK,' I said. 'Of course I'll tell you the truth. Let's go downstairs and sit in the drawing room. Then let's talk.'

'No,' Max shook his head violently, 'I want to talk here.'

'All right then, we'll talk here. But I'm sitting down.' I sat on the top step of the staircase. After a moment Max sat alongside me.

'What makes you say this?' I asked.

'Elenora told me.'

'Elenora told you we were married?' I'm sure I sounded surprised.

'No,' Max was confused. 'No, she didn't tell me you were married. She told me ... she told m ... me.'

'Told you what?'

'Told me you s ... slept together. The night my f ... father was buried.'

Max and I were sitting shoulder to shoulder on the step. It was a curious way to have a conversation. I couldn't see his face to read his expression. 'When did she tell you this?' I asked him.

'The last time I s ... saw her.'

'Did you row about it?'

'Perhaps,' he whispered.

'I see.'

'I always thought ... I always thought perhaps you had. Had s ... slept together. I went out to look for her that night ... that night after the f ... funeral; I went out to look for her and I couldn't find her. I searched nearly every room in the house except for the rooms with people in them. P ... people like you. But when I asked her where she had been, she just laughed. Just l ... laughed.'

We sat in silence and digested this. After a while I stood up and walked back to my bedroom. 'Wait there,' I said. When I came back I brought a photograph. I handed it to Max, who looked at it in bewilderment. It was the first photograph he had held or seen since his twenty-first birthday.

'Her name is Constance,' I said. 'She used to work in an estate agency in High Wycombe. She showed me around an apartment in Marlow in 1981. Afterwards we went for a drink. A week later, I phoned and asked to see the same apartment again. We were flirting on the phone. When we got to the apartment, we didn't even bother to look around. We just had sex on the carpet. I married her in September 1982.'

I reached across and took back the photograph. It was a picture of Constance as she had been, back then, so young. So very young.

'Elenora told you the truth,' I said. 'Only you chose not to hear it. Yes, we slept together. *Slept*. As in the past participle of the verb 'to sleep'. In my case I was pretty much asleep when she came into my room. All she wanted was a comfortable mattress and a blanket. I think our shoulder blades may have touched, but that was all.'

Max took the photograph from me and looked at it hard. 'Constance?' he said, after a while. His shaking had subsided.

'Yes.'

'Did you call her Connie?'

'Of course.'

'She's very pretty.' He handed me the picture. 'I think I feel like that cocoa now.'

On day eight of the unravelling, this conversation had been forgotten. Max was almost unmanageable now. He was somewhere back in the 1970s. I took breakfast up to his room and found him sitting naked on his bedside chair, shivering. He looked at me, almost astonished to see me. I'm not sure if he recognised me any more. Perhaps he thought I was Tutton – or some other household servant. Or maybe he imagined I was an elderly relative.

'Why am I in this room?' he snapped.

'Your room is being decorated,' I told him.

'Where's the captain?'

I sighed. 'The captain is out. He's at work.'

'I want him. I need to speak to him.'

'I'll send him up as soon as he gets back.'

'Make sure you do.'

'Look, Max,' I said, 'why don't you get back into bed.' I pulled back his sheets.

'I'm not well,' he said.

'I know. You have very bad flu. You should be sleeping it off.'

'All right.' Max was unexpectedly compliant. He climbed back into bed.

'Do you want some breakfast?'

'No thanks. I'm not hungry.'

'Here,' I placed the tray beside his bed. 'I'll leave it here. Have some if you're hungry.'

'Where's the captain?'

'I just told you. The captain's out. He's at work.'

'I want him. I need to speak to him.'

'I'll send him up as soon as he gets back.'

'Make sure you do.'

Downstairs, I carried all the catalogue volumes back into the library. Even if Max were to come downstairs now, he would no longer recognise them. I stowed them all away on the shelves in the right order, with volume 1 at the left corner of the highest shelf, and all 358 volumes following down the shelves in the correct order. I re-filed the day logs, the hundreds of blue ring-binders in order from the oldest to the newest, and I snapped in the loose sheets that Max had scattered around the room just a few days before. The chore took me most of the day. Just carrying volumes back from the stables took several dozen trips; each volume full of words – Max's words. They seemed heavier now than they had been when I'd hefted them out.

From time to time, I would go upstairs to check on Max. Sometimes I found him asleep. Other times he was awake and always taken aback by my appearance.

In the afternoon I picked up the folded polythene bag from Max's desk in the library and slid it into my pocket. I pulled open a drawer and retrieved the leather belt and the cable ties. The final scene of the final act was drawing to a close. Perhaps today would be the end of Max's story.

On day nine, Max was somewhere in his childhood. I helped him to get dressed in his charcoal suit with the narrow stripe and we sat in the drawing room. I made some lunch. In the afternoon we went outside into the yard. Max was confused all day. He kept asking for the captain and for O. He asked for his friend Adam. It wasn't me he wanted. It was a ten-year-old barefoot boy in Africa, a boy who could see into the future.

He couldn't walk without help. I had to lead him gingerly around. He never stopped shaking. Around mid-afternoon he stopped speaking.

*

On day ten, Max was a baby. I helped him out of bed and dressed him. I took him to the toilet. I helped him down the stairs and laid him on the sofa in the drawing room. Max, I am sure, would have liked you to know that this is a very elegant three-seater Knoll sofa with plump feather cushions of classic English design probably dating from around 1890, but more recently reupholstered in a neutral linen fabric.

When Max fell asleep, I took the polythene bag out of my pocket and unfolded it. But not yet. Not yet.

I went up to my room and I found myself packing. Just a few things. You never know. If the whole house was about to become a crime scene, I might be grateful to have taken some personal items with me. I threw some of my neutral clothes into a suitcase. I packed the photograph of Connie. I packed a snapshot I had, in a silver frame, of Max and Elenora standing on a bridge in Cambridge. Elenora is looking straight at the camera with her photograph face, but Max's gaze is off, watching something far away, behind the photographer, but to the left. In this picture he reminds me of O. On an impulse, I retrieved the wooden carving that O had bought for me so many years ago from the street hawker in Musoma. It is a gentle figurine in African black wood, a woman, still lithe, still willowy, even after all these years.

I had to leave the house – just for a while – so I left Max sleeping. He wouldn't go anywhere. He was quite immobile now.

I drove to Marlow and did some shopping. I bought bread and milk and more painkillers. I wasn't ready to go back. I drove into Reading for a business meeting with a property agent. We had lunch together sitting in the beer garden of a very pleasant pub. I wasn't Adam Last, the carer of a terminally ill recluse; I was Adam Last the property speculator. The thought of Max back in the drawing room at The Pile made me anxious but, after all, what could he do? He could lie on the sofa and get distressed, but by evening he would have forgotten it all.

I took a leisurely drive back to The Pile. I stopped my car at the gate-house to collect the post, and to check my emails. I checked again the equipment that I would need to employ; the suffocation bag, the leather tourniquet, the nylon rope, the plastic cable ties.

I laid them out and looked at them for a very long time. I had resolved that this would be the final page of the final scene. This day I would perform the very last act. I collected them all up. I thought about what I should say to Max as I did the deed. Would he even understand me any more? Probably not. Should I come at him from behind, to preserve the element of surprise? It would mean that I could avoid looking into his eyes. But that would be the act of a coward. It would be the act of a cold fish. I would tell myself that I was doing exactly what Max wanted me to do, and I would not flinch from looking into his eyes.

So this is what I shall tell the inquisitors of the Buckinghamshire constabulary. I shall look them straight in the eye and I shall spell out the last words of the final scene.

I drove up the drive to the manor house. This, I shall say, is how it was. The sun was high. I parked the car at the front where no cars should ever be parked and I climbed the six stone steps to the great front door, the steps where my resolve had so profoundly changed when I descended them thirty-two years ago.

I unlocked the front door with the heavy iron key. The house was very silent.

And that was when I found him.

The captain would have known the diagnosis. It was the very outcome that he had wished upon himself. The part of Max's brain that controlled his heartbeat had succumbed to the tumour before the part of his brain that controlled his bowels. I'm no doctor, but there was no mistaking the conclusion.

I had no need for the heavy-duty polythene bag.

I picked Max up and carried him clumsily from the drawing room into the library and laid him on the Rastin table and there he lies now. His story has ended. The police have been phoned. Around him, on three walls, properly shelved, neatly aligned, and correctly sorted, from floor to ceiling in bound volumes and notebooks and lever-arch files, are the contents of his brain.

I have left a voice message for Aunt Zinnia. She is in Madeira with a new beau. She will be sitting on a balcony sipping gin and watching the sun set over the blue Atlantic. 'Max has succumbed,' is all I said. My voice would not say more.

The clock in the hallway has begun to chime. It is a brass-dial, long-case grandfather clock, ornately carved in dark oak, and made by Thomas Dorsfield of Woking. The dial has a silvered chapter ring and an engraved silver centre. Max has recorded in The Catalogue that it was made in 1791. It was always Max's job to wind the clock, and the winding has an eight-day duration. He must have wound it on day two of his unravelling, the day I left him alone, the day that I discovered him surrounded by the crumpled pages of days he could no longer remember.

I won't rewind the clock. Let this be the last time I listen to its chimes. I shall sit patiently in the library on the mahogany bergère and I shall wait for the doorbell to ring.

POSTSCRIPTS

All characters in this book are fictional, of course, and none is based on any persons living or dead. Except:

1. Mrs Mukuti was real. That wasn't her name though. I don't remember her real name any more.

2. There really was a man bitten to death by a puff-adder; but then it has been estimated that snakebites kill 35,000 people a year in Africa, which is almost one hundred people a day, and the puff-adder is responsible for more deaths than any other snake. So this is a fairly unremarkable event.

3. The bookshop on Bazaar Street really existed, so the sikh was real too.

4. The poem 'Heraclitus' is by William (Johnson) Cory, 1823–1892.

5. The Lynams were real. They may not have been on honeymoon though. That bit is imagined.

6. Mwanza is real and so was the account of the lepers. The World Health Organisation (WHO) now provides free treatment for leprosy. Since 1990, more than fourteen million leprosy patients have been cured and the number of countries reporting leprosy cases has fallen from 122 to 3. According to the WHO, there were more than five million people living with leprosy in 1985. By 2009, this had fallen to 213,036. Nevertheless, there is still a leprosy problem in Mwanza in 2012.

7. Bukoba and the lake flies were also real.

8. The old man with the telescope was real and 'Stars' is as accurate an account of a true sequence of events as any in this book, including the coda. I think his name was Jones. But even the power of the Internet can't help me find out more. I don't think any trace is left.

9. Idi Amin was real. Of course.

10. The story of the Tanzanian soldier who survived the best attempts of the Ugandan army to kill him is also true. So too, apart from Max and Adam's involvement, is the story of the hospital site and the bodies in the Nile.

11. Melanie is real. So is Joe Cocker. They did play the Crystal Palace Bowl and it did rain.

12. Mr Gowland isn't real. The character faults are real but they belonged to another teacher altogether.

13. Captain and Mrs Ponder aren't real. But then again, there were so many people like them.

14. Wolfgang was real, although I doubt if his surname was Koch.

15. There really was a young man – of about Max's age – who impetuously swallowed a fifty-pence piece. It was the newer, smaller, version. He knows who he is.

16. The condition of Turcot's Syndrome Variant 4 is entirely an invention, based only loosely around the true and distressing condition of Turcot's Astrocytoma. No one should imagine that the symptoms and heritability that affected the Ponders are rooted in a real condition.

17. The man who compiled the *Oxford English Dictionary* was James Murray. He was forty-two when he started the project in 1879 and he was still working on the dictionary when he died thirty-six years later in 1915. The first edition of the *Oxford English Dictionary* was eventually published in 1928.

18. The Internet has allowed me to discover the fate of the SS *Usoga*. In the Kenyan newspaper, the Daily Nation, in February 2002, the editor's reply to a reader's letter appeared in the paper's Saturday magazine: 'The "whitewashed" passenger ship you saw "badly parked" alongside berth No. 2 is the SS *Usoga*, built in 1912 at Kisumu. This vessel is one of the tragedies of Kisumu port. After many years of sterling service on the lake, she became redundant with the break-up of the EA community. Eventually she was sold (given) to someone who intended to rehabilitate her. Instead she was stripped of all saleable internals and abandoned alongside the berth. She sank alongside the berth (it is not clear when but it is more than ten years ago!). Nothing has been done

by Kenya Railways (operators of the port) to refloat the casualty, and rehabilitate it.'

19. The East African Railways website reminds me that on Sundays the *Usoga* sailed clockwise from Kisumu, on Wednesdays, anti-clockwise. The overnight passage from Kisumu to Port Bell in the *Usoga* took twelve hours. After a two- to three-hour stop for cargo handling, the ship left Port Bell for the two-hour passage to Entebbe. Entebbe was a short (one-hour) stop, and from there it was an eight-and-a-half-hour passage to Bukoba in Tanzania. From Bukoba, the ship sailed overnight to Mwanza where it arrived around dawn. Leaving Mwanza at 10.30, Musoma was reached at 19.00 from where, after a two-hour stop, the final night passage brought the ship back to Kisumu at 07.00. In Max's story they went the other way around.

20. Some of the artisans identified are real, others are invented. As far as I know, for example, there never was a furniture-maker called Nicolas Rastin. Thomas Chippendale the younger, on the other hand, was real – of course.

21. It is not really possible to catalogue your own brain. DO NOT try this at home.

W&N *blog*

For exclusive short stories, poems, extracts, essays, articles, interviews, trailers, competitions and much more visit the Weidenfeld & Nicolson blog at:

www.wnblog.co.uk

Follow us on

 facebook and **twitter**

Or scan the code to access the website*